Katawasis Girls

Lindy Larsen, Volume 3

Gayle Siebert

Published by Gayle Siebert, 2021.

KATAWASIS GIRLS

First edition. October 1, 2021.

Copyright © 2021 Gayle Siebert.

ISBN: 978-1990180132

Written by Gayle Siebert.

Table of Contents

1—Hello, Katawasis Lake!

The sign says Katawasis Lake, exit 500 meters. Half a kilometer until I get my first sight of the town that will be my home for the next two years. When they told me I probably wouldn't be transferred out of Maple Creek Branch for three or four years I believed them. Looked ahead to 1987, my first full year as the branch lending officer, learning the job so I'd be promotable. I hoped to slip into the manager position when Everett got the promotion he was working toward. Instead here I am, just a few months later, about to report in as the new Assistant Manager of the Katawasis Lake Branch of Western Savings and Loan.

Maybe it's not such a bad thing to get out of Maple Creek for a while even though it means leaving my ranch, Wacasko-Wâti, just when the wine tasting room is getting real. With our new investor (my Mom), there is no worry of another loan shark disaster. With so few cattle to take care of Red and Stu can easily manage the myriad details of the expanded customer area (what we call The Bistro) and soon, the wine tasting room, without me. Good thing, because my paycheque is badly needed.

Being away will be a nice break from those sideways looks and the whispers that I was complicit in the cattle rustling that ruined so many ranchers. How could it be otherwise? I was involved with two of the guys who went to jail for it after all.

There are those who believe I was also an embezzler and framed Irene. She didn't serve time because she got a suspended sentence but she has a criminal record and lost her pension. All my fault, of course. She worked at the bank for years so she's met half the population of Maple Creek at one time or another, and she feeds the lie every time she runs into someone who will listen. She's even blaming me for the death of the rancher at the hands of the rustlers. Not that I did it, but I planned it. How else would his burned-out truck with his body inside find its way to the Badlands?

1

His ranch was miles away, after all, and in her version, he was found on Wacasko-Wâti property. At least she stopped short of claiming I eat babies.

But maybe it's better for people to think I'm a criminal genius who got away with rustling, murder and embezzlement rather than the truth: I wasn't as smart as I thought I was, in business or romance.

I'm approaching the exit and just about to leave the highway when a black dually with a logo on the door, West Coast mirrors, and clearance lights everywhere passes me at speed and cuts me off to take the exit ahead of me. I spike the brakes.

"Assmeat!" I snarl, and slow enough to allow him some distance. Being cut off is annoying at the best of times and when it's a cowboy limousine with a cowboy hat-wearing driver, it's over the top.

When I researched Katawasis Lake before agreeing to the transfer, this part of the province was described as eighty million acres of boreal forest, ancestral territory of the Woodland Cree. In fact, the name comes from the Cree word for beautiful. So, Beautiful Lake. All the advertising calls it "Beautiful Katawasis Lake". Beautiful beautiful lake. What makes it more beautiful than the hundreds of other lakes in Northern Saskatchewan? Sunsets and clouds that reflect on it, and frequent double and sometimes even reflection, rainbows.

Red is Cree and speaks a little of the language. She knew what the word meant before I told her. So did her nephew Felix. He is becoming a great winemaker and we couldn't run the winery without him. He is also an incurable flirt. When he learned where I was moving, he said I would fit right in. Why? *Because you're a Katawasis girl,* he said. The little bugger followed that with a pat on the bum. Well, he's not little, he's six feet tall, very good looking and a champion bronc rider besides. He always has a string of girls after him. I'm sure he thinks he's irresistible but he is half a dozen years younger than I am and I think of him as a nephew besides, so any romantic relationship is only in his febrile imagination. I reminded him my stint in Katawasis will be very short, no more than two years, and then I'll be back and I'll be his boss again so he'd better keep his hands to himself.

The Katawasis economy is based on commercial fishing, forestry and a plywood mill as well as increasingly, tourism. I expected to find fishermen, loggers, millworkers, and waitresses, not cowboys, here and that was part of the appeal. Now just minutes before I get sight of the town, I'm cut off by a cowboy. He had to pass me, right there? I'm driving ten clicks over the speed limit so it's not like he'd be stuck behind someone just putzing along.

He makes a left turn onto the first cross street. As it happens, it's Juniper, and I have to turn there as well. I speed up so I'm close behind him, stick my arm out the window and give him the middle finger salute. I doubt he sees it, but it makes me feel better. Then I realize given my recent experience with cowboys, I should know better. I hope there aren't traffic lights ahead where I might end up stopped right behind him. I know from the street map that the next street on my route is Katawasis Lake Road. With luck, he won't be turning.

Several blocks of old bungalows in varying stages of decay mixed with newer vinyl boxes surrounded by clutter and overgrown vegetation and an equipment rental business later, I come to a strip mall with a rustic-looking building identifying itself as Tall Tree Pub at one end, a Safeway supermarket with high, arched windows at the other, and a pizza parlor in the middle. There are other storefronts, too, and I slow to gawk. The black dually is a good distance ahead but no other cars have come from side streets to fill the gap. Where are those asshats that pull out right in front of you and then putz along when you need them?

Katawasis Lake Road is half a dozen blocks farther and Murphy's law, the dually turns there too. I breathe a sigh of relief when I come to the cul-de-sac I'm looking for and the dually continues down the road.

My destination house is at the farthest point, a stucco bungalow with a carport and a brick planter that melds into a wide brick chimney. Because it's on the circle and the lots are pie-shaped, the front yard is small and driveways serving houses on either side are just meters apart. Not much on-street parking here. Thankfully, half the carport is for my use. I back into the stall closest to the house and turn the engine off.

I haven't seen the place. When I accepted the job, my new boss' secretary called and gave me the name and phone number of a rental agent in Katawasis. The agent was kind enough to send me photos of three suites. This was the cheapest and looked as nice as the more expensive ones, so I took it. She couriered the keys to me. I hope my decision not to make the five-hour trip to search for a rental in person wasn't a mistake.

The house looks nice but I didn't rent the upstairs, just the basement suite, the entrance of which is said to be down a flight of stairs at the back of the carport. Photos don't tell you everything, such as whether it smells like an old basement. I mutter, "Okay. Let's see how bad it is." I get out of the truck and head for the gap in the hedge at the back corner of the house.

Once through the hedge, I stop and look around. *Gape around* would be more accurate. The lot slopes sharply down and there are large windows along the back of the house, both upstairs and down. Concrete steps lead down from where I'm standing to a patio for the basement suite that's partly covered by the deck serving the upstairs unit. To the right is the lake. From the Travel Saskatchewan brochure I know it's Katawasis Lake and the town is named for it.

Windows of houses on the far side of the lake reflect the sun. This means they're west-facing and the patio and all these windows face east. My suite will get the morning sun and afternoon shade. Although the front yard is just a triangular scrap of lawn and a double-wide driveway crowded by the other homes on the circle, thanks to tall hedges the wide back yard is private, but with the house is so much higher than the far end of the yard there's a panoramic view over the trees. I take a deep breath. I was worried I'd feel claustrophobic moving into town since I'm accustomed to the nearest neighbor being twenty kilometers away, but I can live with this.

I go down the stairs, unlock the door, and enter a nook festooned with hooks. It opens into the galley kitchen. So far, only a slight basement smell that'll probably disappear when I burn my first piece of toast. I deposit my keys and purse on the counter and wander through the rooms. The door on the farthest end of the cabinets next to the fridge gives access to a windowless laundry room. Next to the dryer, there's a locked door. I conclude it leads to the rest of the basement and is not for my use.

There's a window above the kitchen sink and a peninsula separates the kitchen from the combination living/dining room. There in the corner is the fireplace featured in the photos and next to it, the sliding doors that open onto the covered patio.

The furniture all looks okay but for the shock of a burgundy floral chesterfield next to an orange and brown plaid loveseat. It's a toss up which piece is the most hideous. Probably the loveseat. I'll have to get something to cover it.

The bedroom furniture is shiny thirty-year-old Formica "Three Room Special", but the mattress looks clean enough. When I bounce on the bed it squawks as if being murdered. "Good thing I've sworn off men," I mutter. I must be more tired than I thought because for some reason this strikes me as funny and I laugh out loud.

The door to a small second bedroom is next down the short hallway. Oddly, there's no bed, just a weight bench, a barbell and some weights. Across the hall is a windowless bathroom just big enough for the necessities. Bonus: the previous tenant left toilet paper. I use the toilet, then get to work hauling bags and boxes down from the truck.

I rented a furnished suite because I don't plan on being in Katawasis Lake long and I still need my furniture at home. It makes moving in simple. I only brought a couple pairs of jeans, the same number of shirts and blouses, my going-to-work clothes, bedding, TV and a few groceries. Runners, one pair of loafers and one pair of black heels completes the clothing inventory. I didn't even bring the beautiful Tony Lama boots I splurged on as a present for myself when I escaped from my abductors. As much as I love those boots, why drag them back and forth when I'll only be riding when I'm home for the occasional weekend?

With so little cargo, the truck is unloaded and the bags and boxes emptied in short order. The TV will have to sit on one of the kitchen chairs for now. "For now" may be for as long as I'm here.

A case of Wacasko-Wâti Winery wine was one of the first things I brought down from the truck. I stuck several bottles in the fridge and one in the freezer compartment before I did anything else. I pull it out and search the silverware drawer for a corkscrew. No luck. Not surprising, since the dishes provided are a mishmash of plates, bowls and assorted beer glasses. I dig the Swiss Army knife out of my pocket and use its corkscrew to wrestle the cork out of the bottle, pour a generous amount into a beer glass and put the bottle in the fridge.

I take my wine and go out to the picnic table on the patio, perch on the top with my feet on the seat and enjoy the lake view. There is greenery everywhere. This evening the lake is mirror-smooth, reflecting the orange and pink clouds. No rainbows, but even without them it earns its name.

There's the distant sound of a motor and before long a boat comes into view, raising a wake that scars the still surface of the lake. Fading sunlight makes the ripples flame-like. The boat heads to the row of houses on the far side and stops at what must be a dock. It's a peaceful, beautiful view. The difference between Katawasis Lake and the dusty beige prairie of my Wacasko-Wâti home could not be more stark.

There's a gate at the bottom end of the yard. I finish my wine, set the glass down and go to open it. It might be possible to get to the lake from here because there are no buildings or other signs of habitation, but there's a trail through the bush down a decline even sharper than the yard. I stop just a few meters in. I'm tempted to explore. There's still daylight but not enough to check out that trail. Besides, it's been a long day and I'm exhausted. I go back up to the house.

The upstairs tenants have come home while I was outside. I hear footfalls and then water gushing through the pipes as if someone flushed the toilet. Like the dorm at university, there is a downside to having someone living above. I just hope that if it's a couple, their bedroom isn't above mine. Or at least if it is, that their bed doesn't squawk.

After a shower I get into my pyjamas, set my alarm clock and crawl into bed. I fall asleep listening to the unfamiliar sounds of the tenant moving about overhead.

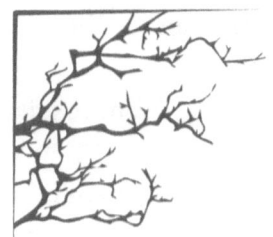

2 – On The Job

The street map of Katawasis is open on the seat beside me but it turns out I don't need it. Anyone driving into town would have a hard time missing my destination, as the branch is right on the corner of Commercial and Main, with *Western Savings & Loan* in tall red letters. I turn into the parking lot at the rear of the building, turn off the engine and sigh.

The branch is a commercial storefront with apartments above and judging by the paper-covered windows, an out-of-business retailer next door. It's no bigger than the branch I just left. How does a branch this size need an assistant manager? Isn't the point of this transfer to get management experience so I can go back home as the manager in two years? Did they only offer what seemed to be a premature promotion because they have trouble staffing these northern branches?

I get out, head for the sidewalk and fall in behind an elderly couple entering the bank. They join the queue waiting for a teller and I go to the counter at the far end. Behind the dividing half wall are three women, desks abutting one another. I wait for one of the staffers to notice me. I'm about to say something to get someone's attention when the pretty, dark-haired thirty-something woman at the near desk looks up, spots me, and gets to her feet.

"Hello," she says as she comes toward me, "can I help you?"

"Mr. Fleetwood is expecting me."

"Oh! Are you the new Assistant Manager?"

"I am," I confirm.

She comes to the counter, unlocks the latch on the gate and ushers me in, saying, "I'm Corrine."

"Lindy."

"You're a girl."

A girl? I'm not ten. And is she surprised I'm not a man? Not sure how to respond, I smile and say nothing.

She continues, "So, Lindy, Fleet's in the construction zone. Want to join him there or wait in his office?"

"I, uh, construction zone?" Just then there's a loud thump followed by a cloud of fine dust filtering down from gaps in the T-Bar ceiling, followed by voices and another thump. Only now do I notice the plastic hanging over a rough opening in the wall behind the farthest desk.

"You see why we have plastic over everything," Corrine says with a click of her tongue. "Can't cover everything, of course. I swear, there's enough plaster dust in my hair at the end of the day drywall filler runs out of it when I shower."

"Oh, the branch is expanding?"

"Yeah. There's a bunch of new stuff in the plans. Meeting room and managers' offices upstairs. Bigger lunch room and washrooms down here, plus more space for us girls. It won't be just the tellers with computers, we're all going to have them. It's going to be nice. You want to go see?"

"Sure," I agree. I feel a wave of relief. Not apartments but managers' offices upstairs. As odd as that is, it's good to know the branch is busy enough to warrant taking over more space and profitable enough to warrant spending on computers for everyone. My old branch is way down the list for computers. Maybe I haven't been shunted here just because they couldn't find anyone else dumb enough to accept the transfer.

"Right this way," Corrine says. On our way through the desks, she introduces me to the other staffers. Deena is a pretty, dark-haired, dark-eyed young woman, her green smock identifying her as a file clerk, her skin tone marking her as Indian. Mae is an attractive older woman introduced as the manager's secretary. To my great relief, she has wavy blonde hair and looks nothing like Irene.

"Are you the keeper of the keys to the stationery cupboard?" I ask her.

She cocks her head as if she hasn't heard me correctly. "Stationery cupboard?"

"You know. Where you keep the Liquid Paper, extra pens, paper clips, valuable stuff like that."

"I, er, well, no, there are no keys because it isn't locked," she tells me.

"Good to know," I say, and I feel my cheeks becoming warm. Too late I realize I'll be the prime suspect if pencils go missing. At least I don't make matters worse by asking to be shown where said cabinet is located. I consider explaining how at my last branch, Irene was the Keeper of the Stationery and anyone requesting anything had to pass a needs test, but before I can, Corrine says, "This way."

I follow her to the plastic-covered opening in the wall and behind the curtain into the construction zone. The floor is bare concrete. Two men are troweling drywall filler on walls. A crew of three is busy putting up supports for the T-bar suspended ceiling. Two women are measuring the big street-facing windows. A man in a suit is with them. He loops an arm around the younger of the two, turns her so she's standing with her back to him, and begins massaging her neck. He leans in as if to whisper something in her ear. She giggles.

"Fleet!" Corrine calls out sharply. The man in the suit releases the young woman, turns to face us and lifts his chin in acknowledgement. After saying something to the two women, he comes to join us.

"You must be Lindy," he says, and reaches out his hand.

"I am," I say as I take his hand for a quick shake. "And you must be, er, Mr. Fleetwood."

"Fleet! Please! Everyone calls me Fleet," he says, and smiles. He leans in so close I take an involuntary step back. "Welcome," he continues, and takes a step so he's crowding into my personal space again. "Corrine can show you to your desk and give you the nickel tour. I'll catch up with you as soon as I finish with the blind people." He snorts and with a tilt of his head, indicates the women measuring windows. "Blind people. Wonder how they got here. Hope they didn't drive."

"Oh, Fleet!" Corrine giggles as if it's the funniest thing she's heard in her life and gives him a pretend punch to his shoulder. From the naked adoration on her face you'd swear he's the reason the sun comes up every morning. I grin, but more because of Corrine's giggling than Fleet's Dad joke. I wonder if Mrs. Fleet has something to worry about.

Corrine continues, "I'll show Lindy around. You don't have to. And when you're done here, we can go over that invitation list."

"Sure," he replies without looking at her. He's giving me the once-over. His gaze settles on my chest and I wonder if my shirt buttons have come undone. Corrine is giving me what can only be described as a glare. I'm starting to feel uncomfortable before Fleet nods and goes back to the blind people.

Corrine turns away and heads for the doorway. I hurry to catch up and follow her back through the plastic barrier. We march single file past Mae and Deena and then along behind the tellers to the far end where there's a door marked *Manager's Office* with a solitary desk just outside of it. A plump man with heavy horn-rimmed glasses whose baby face doesn't match his shiny dome sits behind it and looks up as we approach.

"Hal," Corrine says, "this is Lindy. Lindy, Hal."

I stick out my hand and say, "How do you do?"

"How do you do," he responds automatically. I catch a whiff of cigarette smoke and when he reaches out to take my hand in a limp shake, I note the brown fingers that confirm he's a heavy smoker. He doesn't bother to stand and barely glances at me. My stepfather would have had plenty to say about that handshake. I can almost hear him saying: *If you're sitting, stand up. Make eye contact. Take his hand with just the right amount of pressure. Don't squeeze too hard and for god's sake don't let your hand hang there like a dead fish.*

"Lindy is our new assistant manager," Corrine tells him.

"Oh?"

"Hal's the Consumer Lending Officer," Corrine tells me.

"Ahh," I say, "that was part of my old job. The part I liked the least! Give me commercial credit any day."

"Yeah," Hal says. "So, I didn't know assistant managers did consumer loans."

"Depends how big, or small, the branch is I guess. My last manager had to do everything until Regional Office created a lending officer position, and I was lucky enough to get it. After that he did more admin and only looked after the bigger accounts. I did the consumer loans and smaller farm and commercial loans."

"How long were you at that, then?"

"Lending officer? Not long. Barely a year. That's why I was so surprised to be transferred here."

Hal's forehead creases in a frown. He turns away and says, "Right, then."

"Okay," I mumble, and nearly shiver at the chilly dismissal.

Corrine says, "So! Your desk is behind that wall there. The last guy left a bunch of stuff so you should be set. But if you need anything, just ask Mae to show you the *stationery cupboard.*" She gives me a look approaching a smirk.

Her expression is off-putting but I manage to keep my tone even as I reply, "Thank you."

She turns and flits off. So much for a tour. I guess one branch is pretty much like any other and I'll meet the staffers she didn't introduce me to in time. I head to the wall in question, surprised to find it's not an office, but an alcove barely big enough for the desk, which shares the space with the fax machine and photocopier. I accidentally bang the latter when I pull the chair back.

This desk would be better suited to the file clerk. How do you interview customers here? I can see why my predecessor quit, although with new offices nearly ready you'd think he could have put up with it a little longer. A short tenure isn't an option for me. I need at least two years under my belt before I qualify to be a manager, even of a branch as small as the one I left. I take a deep breath and remind myself I'm lucky to have this position. Besides, it's only temporary.

In the desk is a random supply of notepads and a handful of pens. I can't help but chuckle when I discover a red one in the mix, remembering what I went through trying to get a red pen when Irene was in charge of office supplies. Front and center on the blotter is a thick file, tattered and bristling with Post-It notes. It's labeled Katawasis Forest Products and judging by its size, they've been a customer for a long time. On top of the file is a sheet of lined paper with "1:00 Lunch with Fleet" scrawled across it in black felt pen. From that I take it he wants me to review the file so we can discuss it at lunch.

Before I dive into the file, I pull the phone book out of a drawer and find the number for setting up a new phone at my residence. It turns out to be easy since the suite is already wired for it so all they have to do is take down my information and have me pick a number from a selection of offerings. I specify I only want my initial, not my first name or my address to be in the phone book, as I read somewhere it's a wise precaution for a single woman. All I need to do now is get a phone. The helpful person at the phone company suggests the Radio Shack store at the mall.

I read through the Katawasis Forest Products file, paying particular attention to the latest financial records. I decide to take a comfort break and have just left my desk when I see Fleet returning to his office. He looks my way and smiles, but if he was going to call me into his office so we could have a little get-acquainted chat, Hal circumvents that by leaping to his feet and calling out, "Fleet! A word?"

Fleet goes into his office with Hal in hot pursuit, slamming the door shut behind him. Just then Corrine comes along, her face glowing in anticipation. She has a steno pad in her hand, as if ready to work on that invitation list. When she sees the door bang to a close, her happy countenance evaporates. She frowns and crumples into Hal's chair to wait.

Whatever Hal and Fleet are discussing is contentious. Their voices are loud but I can only make out the occasional word. As I walk through to the staff area, I notice customers looking toward Fleet's office, their attention drawn by the argument. Maybe it's a good idea to have the manager's office upstairs after all.

Finished in the ladies room, I go to the vending machines, feed in a couple of quarters, and wait while it spits out a paper cup of black coffee. Only now do I remember Corrine, and not Mae, is looking after the invitation list although it seems more like something Fleet's secretary would do. I wonder at her insistence on saving Fleet the trouble of showing me around, only to dump me at the first opportunity, and adding a snide comment at that.

And call me suspicious, but I have a sense Hal's change of demeanor when I told him I'd only been a lending officer for a short period of time is the reason for the shouting match in Fleet's office.

I think I understand the reason for the high staff turnover.

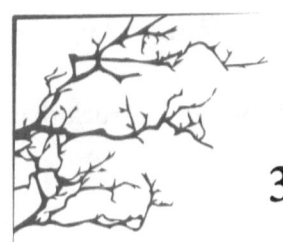

3–Lunch with Fleet

Fleet and I are walking east along Commercial Street. At the far end of the block and on the corner across the street is the Pioneer House Restaurant that's our destination. The shops lining both sides of the street appear prosperous, even one called Dolly's Dresses. I hold up for a minute for a quick window shop. Not just dresses but blouses and shoes, too. Front and center a mannequin sports a navy suit of the type a lady lawyer would wear. I spot the price tag and nearly choke.

"Unless they also sell jeans and T-shirts, Dolly's Dresses would be out of business within a month in Maple Creek," I remark.

"Don't worry, my wife keeps them in business," Fleet says. "Her and the rest of the Friends of Katawasis ladies."

"Who's that?"

"Friends of Katawasis," he replies. "It's a service club, like Rotary, but just for you gals. You should join. Good advertising for the bank. Great networking. Would look good in your personnel file."

"Oh yeah? Why wouldn't I just join Rotary? They have a park."

"You can't join Rotary. It's a men's club."

"What? That's ridiculous! It's 1987, not 1957."

"There's enough women's libbers stirring up trouble about that without you starting in on it too, Lindy. We're entitled to our own club, aren't we? Friends of Katawasis doesn't have a park but they sponsor the playground by the Public Wharf. They have fundraisers like bottle drives and running the bingo at the community center and they can always use help. I'm sure they'd approve you for membership." He smiles, but the way he says that doesn't sound like it's up for discussion.

I'm still chewing on the idea of gender-segregated clubs, fundraisers like bottle drives which I thought were for boy scouts, and whether I'm even mildly interested in joining if I have to be approved, when I notice a black dually in the angle parking. Clearance lights. West Coast mirrors. Logo on the door. It's the truck that cut me off yesterday.

I turn to Fleet, point to the truck, and ask, "You know whose truck that is?"

He looks at it, nods, and says, "Yeah. Why?"

I tell him about it cutting in front of me so I had to spike the brakes. I don't mention flipping the bird.

"Figures," Fleet says. "He's just an a-hole who thinks that truck makes him look important."

We cross the street and come to the restaurant. Fleet holds the door open and follows me inside. The woman behind the desk says, "Hi, Fleet. Two for lunch?"

"Yes. Patio. My usual table."

"Of course!" She smiles, picks up a couple of menus and says, "Right this way."

We follow her through the restaurant. Fleet greets people at every table we pass and stops to chat with a so many I wonder if we'll get to a table before it's time to go back to work. I can almost hear myself sigh when we finally make it out the door onto the patio.

The lunch hour is over for most business people so customers are leaving. The table we're headed for isn't near any others, but a couple of tables away there's a man in a cowboy hat. The moment I notice him he looks up, spots us, and acknowledges us with a lift of his chin. I expect Fleet to go and talk to him or at least say hello, but instead he abruptly turns his back and slides into a chair. I sit across from him.

Tracy rattles off the daily specials, then assures us that our waitress will be coming right along, sets the menus in front of us and leaves. The table is small and shaded both by the hedge and a large umbrella. A pleasant breeze stirs the bushes and ruffles the frill of the umbrella. I get a whiff of beef on the grill and my stomach rumbles.

"This is nice," I comment. I'd bet my lunch money the black dually belongs to the man in the cowboy hat. He may be beneath Fleet's notice but I can't help thinking he's the reason for his dark expression. In hopes it will brighten his mood, I say, "Jeez, Fleet! Are you a front man for a band on

14

weekends? It's like you're a rock star. Do you know everyone? You should run for mayor."

The frown leaves his face. He barks a laugh and as he opens his menu, says, "Funny, I've actually thought of doing that. If the bank transfers me I just might. I've been in town long enough to know I want to stay here. Job like mine, you get to know people. The right people. But since you ask, I spend my weekends on my boat. Did you see the photo of it in my office?"

"No."

"Well, take a look at it when we're back in the office. It's nice. Two staterooms and a head. That's two bedrooms and a toilet to you landlubbers. King-size bed in the master suite. Room for plenty of action."

He looks at me so intently there's no way to miss the innuendo. Still, I pretend it went over my head and respond with a noncommittal, "Oh yeah?" I turn my attention to the menu for a minute or two before asking, "What's good?"

"I always get the either the steak sandwich or the ribs," Fleet replies.

"Well, until yesterday I lived on a cattle ranch. No shortage of beef," I tell him, and continue reading the menu.

When the waitress appears with a pitcher of ice water and two glasses and sets them on the table, Fleet tells her he wants the ribs. After debating the virtues of the wines on offer by the glass, he chooses the most expensive red on the list.

I order the fresh-caught-this-morning lake Whitefish, battered and served with French fries and salad. Since Fleet's having wine, I request the house white.

I notice the man with the cowboy hat watching us, or at least when I glance his way, he's often looking back. His expression, while not unfriendly, is at best neutral. Once, I smile when we make eye contact. He holds my gaze for a heartbeat before the woman across from him says something and he turns his attention to her.

Fleet seems in no hurry to get back to work. We talk a lot about Katawasis Lake and a little about Maple Creek. I tell him about the Wacasko-Wâti ranch, the horse rescue and the winery. His expression when I tell him about our saskatoon and rhubarb wines coupled with his care in selecting the wine he's drinking tells me he's unlikely to try anything

Wacasko-Wâti has to offer. I change the subject by asking about his boat and he spews brands and horsepower and cruising speed for what seems like ten minutes. I feign interest but I'm as fascinated by boats as he is about Wacasko-Wâti and horses. When he slows down, I ask about his life before coming to Katawasis Lake. Eventually he runs out of things to brag about and we fall silent. When I look around, the cowboy hat guy and his friends are going out the gate that gives onto the side street, and Fleet and I are the only ones left on the patio.

Finally, Fleet says, "Lindy, I really wanted to talk to you about your job. Your duties. I know you haven't been a lending officer for long, and Assistant Manager comes with a lot of added responsibility. I want to make sure you're successful, so I want you to run all your loan apps by me. Even the ones you think should be turned down. Like I said, I want you to be successful and you won't be if you make too many mistakes."

"But I didn't have to do that at my last—"

"Not everyone has my management style," he says, cutting off any objections I might have. "Not many managers care as much about the success of their people as I do. This is pretty much a training position. I train them and they go on to other branches as managers. That's what you want, isn't it?"

"Yes. Of course."

"So! Are we agreed?"

What choice do I have? It's odd no one at Regional Office explained this to me when they offered me the position and I don't see how anyone could care more than Everett, my last manager. Plus it makes a lot of extra work for Fleet, micro-managing like that. But he's the boss so I say, "Agreed."

"Good," he says. "And Lindy? No one needs to know I'm doing this for you. I take no credit for it. We'll just let Regional Office think you're doing an exceptional job." He smiles, and holds his glass out to me. I raise mine and touch it to his with a clink.

"That's good of you, er, Fleet. Thank you."

"Don't mention it." After a moment he brings the conversation back to boating. "Like I said, I spend pretty much all my spare time on my boat. A lot of work to keep everything tiddly, you know. Is your husband interested in boating?"

Husband? Personnel Department must have told him the new assistant manager was single and it's not something you'd think he'd forget. I reply, "I'm not married."

"Boyfriend, then."

"No boyfriend either."

The waitress interrupts his line of questioning by coming to see if we'd like anything else. We've both had two glasses of wine and I'm feeling a buzz, so I ask for coffee.

Fleet says, "I'll have another Beaujolais. And while you're at it, bring me a Remy Martin. Neat."

Three glasses of wine and now a cognac? Talk about a liquid lunch! "I haven't seen anyone drink Remi since I left Calgary," I tell him.

"When you're promoting big wigs to get the big accounts, you have to drink something other than cheap wine. You'll learn." Then he pushes his empty wine glass away and says, "Katawasis Forest Products is a big account."

"Yeah, looks like it, going by the size of the file on my desk. What is it you want me to do with it?"

"We'll get into it tomorrow. For now, just remember we talked about it over lunch."

"Oh, okay," I agree.

We fall into an uncomfortable silence. At least I'm uncomfortable. It would help if he quit staring at me. I top up my water glass from the pitcher and take a long swallow of the ice water as I struggle to think of something to ask him about. It seems like hours before the waitress returns with Fleet's booze and my coffee.

I take a careful sip. It's too hot. I watch Fleet toss back his cognac, and say, "By the way, I don't have a phone. Do you think I could leave work a little early? I'd like to find the mall with the Radio Shack store."

"Sure thing," he agrees. "You can go now. From tomorrow on, locking up will be your responsibility so you won't have another chance to leave work early for a good long while."

"Oh, you mean every day?" This is surprising. At my previous branch the manager and I took turns.

"You're there till closing every day anyway, right?"

"Right," I agree.

"So it makes sense. But today, you can go now," he reiterates.

"Thanks, but I'll wait until you're done and walk back with you."

"I've got other things to do, Lindy, so I'm not going back just yet. You go ahead."

"Okay then." I scoop ice cubes out of my water and put them in my coffee. Now it's cool enough to drink. "So, how do I get to the mall?"

He gives me instructions. I drain my coffee, say, "Thanks for lunch. See you tomorrow," and hurry out the side gate I had seen cowboy hat's group leave by. Once on the sidewalk, I mutter under my breath, "Pompous ass."

I scan the angle parking on the far side of the street, thinking I'd like to get a closer look at the logo, but the black dually is gone.

I pat myself on the back for successfully setting up my new telephone. I'm giddy at the fact it has a built-in answering machine than can record ten messages, but it was more difficult than I expected to record a greeting that didn't make me sound like a child or let robbers know there was no one home. As if a robber is going to call to see if it's safe to burglarize a basement suite with a 13-inch Sansui combination TV/VCR even if they could get my phone number, but better safe than sorry. I'm living in the city now, and that neighborhood around the strip mall looks pretty rough. In the end I record: "Hello! You've reached the Larsens. Leave a message and one of us will call you back as soon as we finish our weight-training!" in the lowest register I can muster. I'm satisfied it sounds like I'm not only home but there's more than one of me; we use those weights in the second bedroom and we're strong so don't try anything, buster.

My first call is to Red and Stu to give them my new number and brag about the answering machine. After that, I call Mom and Reggie. I tell everyone about the construction at the branch and that I'll be moving from my glorified closet to a nice new office upstairs. I pass along what little I know about my new co-workers and that Fleet treated me to lunch and has promised a boat tour of the lake. They all think Fleet's comment about the blind people is worth at least a groan, and everything I tell them makes him sound nice. I don't mention him pressuring me to join Friends of Katawasis. Or how ridiculously easy it is to stroke his oversized ego. Or his cheap wine comment. On that, maybe I'm just too sensitive.

There's a Zeller's store in the same mall as Radio Shack and since I was there, I checked it out. I ended up buying a set of four decent wineglasses for two bucks and an avocado green bedspread marked down by seventy-five per cent because it has a faded swath across it, as if it had been in the display window too long. It nearly matches the leaves of the floral print couch, covers the hideous plaid loveseat and ends up looking okay. I've tucked in the faded section so it doesn't even show. I'm beginning to feel moved in.

I hit the sack at my usual bedtime and fall right asleep. Thumping overhead brings me wide awake. The clock on the bedside table reads 12:30. Apparently my upstairs neighbors' bedroom is in fact right above mine. I turn onto my side and pull a pillow over my head, but it's only partly effective in blocking out the rhythmic thump-thump-thump. I guess I should be grateful she's not a screamer.

But now I'm awake, and I wonder what time Fleet went back to work this afternoon. Why was he so friendly with so many people in the restaurant only to completely ignore the man in the cowboy hat?

And why was he so insistent I join Friends of Katawasis? I can take an extra long lunch on their meeting days. Whoop de do! But when he said he would let his wife know I'd be attending the next Friends of Katawasis meeting, I didn't argue. Maybe it's worth going to a few meetings to see if there are women there I can become friends with.

I think back on what Everett told me about Katawasis Lake Branch, namely that it has high staff turnover. He found out on the Q.T. that the last assistant manager left suddenly without giving notice. He didn't know the reason and concluded it was to my benefit since otherwise the position wouldn't have opened up at a time that I could be considered for it. He diplomatically didn't say I wasn't qualified for it. I know I'm not.

It's astonishing someone would just leave like that. There must have been a serious dust-up, maybe between him and Fleet, along the lines of what went on between Hal and Fleet this morning. No matter the reason, I have to work with it at least for a couple of years.

Before I accepted the transfer, I told Red what Everett said about the staff turnover and that it didn't worry me since I'm good at getting along with people. I didn't like her skeptical frown. She says I'm judgmental and that I always think my way is the right way. She's been my best friend ever since I met her the summer I followed the rodeo over a decade ago. She knows me better than anyone. I don't hold her criticism of me against her, though, proof I'm good at getting along with people.

Whatever the case may be, I got a furnished suite and I'm renting month to month, no lease. Easy to pick up and leave. Just in case.

The thumping overhead continues. I have to admire their stamina. I don't fall back asleep until it stops.

I arrive home after work to find a note taped to my door. It's an invitation to get together for coffee Saturday morning, signed: your upstairs neighbor Kristy. She dotted the "i" in her name with a little heart, put an arrow pointing up next to "neighbor", and put a big smiley face under it all. I'm surprised at how pleased I am. I wish she'd put a suggested time because I haven't yet figured out their schedule.

As I'm unlocking the door, movement in the bushes to my right draws my attention and I turn to see a small tabby cat hunkered down, half hidden under the low branches at the edge of the concrete, watching me.

I summon my best kitty-pleasing voice and say, "Hello, little one. Whose kitty are you? Want some pets? I won't hurt you." I take a step toward it. It shrinks back, then turns and melts into the undergrowth along the hedge.

I'm surprised to realize I'm disappointed. But then, animals of all sorts—horses, dogs, cats, even chickens and the odd duck—were everywhere at Wacasko-Wâti. Maybe I'm feeling homesick, but a little contact comfort from a furry creature would have been welcome. It must belong to someone in the neighborhood, maybe even Kristy, and maybe it's naughty, but I think I'll pick up some cat food tomorrow in hopes of tempting it to spend time with me.

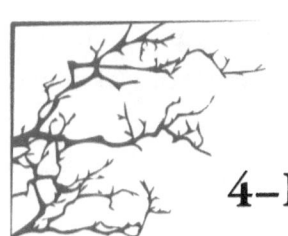

4–In trouble with Fleet

It's the last day of my first week on the job and I'm getting used to the routine. I haven't made a connection with any of the staffers, though, so I'm still very much an outsider. Deena is the most friendly, other than Fleet. He's friendly, all right. Too friendly. Always standing too close, breathing too loudly and generally giving me the heebie jeebies. I've noticed he does that to all the women and they fawn over him so it's no wonder he thinks we like it. Then again, maybe he just gets off on making people he has power over feel uncomfortable.

It would help if I was busier. There is a trickle of commercial loan apps, mostly lines of credit for small retailers, a couple of farms, but one application is for a sawmill that's large enough to need Regional Office approval.

I also have administration duties. Fleet doesn't like that side of management, especially the budget reports the Regional Comptroller requires. My second day here he made all that my responsibility. They're only due quarterly, but there are daily entries that take the better part of half an hour. He wouldn't have shuffled these tasks over to me if I hadn't mentioned doing the books for Wacasko-Wâti as well as for my mother's stores. Maybe it was less a mention and more of a boast. I wonder if I'll ever learn to keep my big mouth shut. But I'm glad of it as it's great training for that future manager position I'm hoping for and without the extra work I'd have trouble finding enough to do.

There's a loan application in the middle of my desk that wasn't there when I left yesterday. It has a note clipped to it: *customer wants answer by weekend*. It has Tuesday's date on it. Where has it been languishing these past four days? Tomorrow is Saturday so it needs to be dealt with today. I scan the form. The purpose of the loan is to purchase a tent trailer, which will be insured and the bank will be the registered lienholder. The customer has a decent credit history. It's a small amount, basic consumer credit, something that would normally be handled by the dealer or at the very least Hal should deal with it. I go to see him.

"Hey, good morning," I say as I slide into the chair in front of his desk.

He looks up from his work and after a second mumbles, "Morning."

"I think you're the guy I need to talk to about this app. Is this your note?"

He barely glances at it before responding, "Uh, no."

"Whose note is it then?"

He shrugs and says, "How should I know?"

"Okay, well, it looks like a straightforward consumer loan and in that case, it should've gone to you. I wonder why I got it."

"The girls must of gave it to you by mistake."

"I was wondering—doesn't Aspen Adventures have a floor plan with us?"

"No. And anyway, the customer wanted to finance it through us to get a lower interest rate."

"So you talked to the customer, then?"

"Of course."

"Why didn't you approve it?"

Hal pushes his glasses up and I note his face is reddening as droplets of sweat form on his brow. He looks around the branch and pushes the document back across the desk to me, avoiding eye contact as he replies, "Ask Fleet. I can't help you."

"Do you know when Fleet's coming in?"

"No."

Of course not. It's only been a week, but I've learned Fleet comes and goes at will. I make no move to take the app and say, "Maybe they want to use the new trailer this weekend. Why don't you go ahead and approve it now?"

"Take it up with Fleet."

I'm annoyed, both at Hal's answers and his tone. I take a couple of breaths to calm myself before asking, "Okay, if he has to approve it, why was it on my desk instead of his?"

He looks at me, then away. "Like I said, someone must of put it there by mistake."

"Look, Hal, why don't you just go ahead and call the customer and the dealer and tell them the loan is approved?"

"I can't do that."

"Sure you can."

"Okay, I *won't* do it. *Mister Fleetwood* has to approve it." At last he looks me in the eye and doesn't look away.

Angry words flood through my brain but fortunately don't come out my mouth. "Fine," I snap, "I'll do it." I snatch up the file and get to my feet.

Hal mutters under his breath, "You do that."

I pretend I didn't hear him and when I'm back at my desk I examine the note again, debating what to do. I think Hal is lying when he says he didn't write it, but it's a plain yellow Post-It note written in blue ballpoint pen, like anyone can get from the stationery cupboard, which turned out not to be a cupboard at all but just a section of open shelves. I haven't seen enough of Hal's writing to say it's his. But who else would even see the file? If he didn't write it and put it on my desk, he got someone else to do it. But why?

I study-read the app and find no red flags. There is no reason Hal couldn't approve it. In my previous position as consumer lending officer, same position Hal has, I approved hundreds of these routine loans without referring them to Everett. I have to refer the commercial loans to Fleet but he didn't say anything about run-of-the-mill consumer loans. I stamp the app "APPROVED", enter my initials and fax the document to the dealer.

By ten to twelve I've dictated the line of credit renewal app that needed Regional Office approval, and rather than starting on the next file this close to my lunch break, decide to check on the progress of construction upstairs. I'm in what will be my office, admiring the glamorous view of the parking lot, when I spot Fleet and a bald man near a panel van with Gregson's Floors painted on it. The bald man passes something to Fleet, then climbs into the van and drives out to the lane.

I'm puzzled at what I just saw. When I hear heavy footfalls thumping up the stairs, I leave my future office and go back out the common area to see a fifty-something man in jeans, work boots, and with a toolbelt hanging from his hips, come up the stairs.

"Hi, Calvin!"

"Hi, Lindy," he says. "Checking on your new office again? Anxious to see how it's coming along?"

"You know it. Can't get out of that broom closet soon enough. I feel like a mushroom, stuck in that dark corner next to the Xerox."

"As long as you're not being fed, er, *manure*," he says, and we share a chuckle.

"Well, let's just say I'm beginning to understand why the last guy left." As soon as it's out of my mouth, I realize saying that after his manure comment, Calvin might take it as a criticism of Fleet.

An odd expression flickers across his face but before I can explain I meant the dark corner, he shrugs and says, "So, your new office has a good-sized window. You'll get plenty of natural light. No mushrooms there."

"Yeah, it's nice. But Fleet gets the corner office with a view of Rotary Park and the lake and I get the dumpster view. I don't want to sound jealous, but I think I am."

"Rank has its privileges," Calvin says.

"I know. I still don't get why they didn't put the staff washrooms and lunch room up here and put the managers' offices and meeting room in the new part downstairs, though. It's a lot of stairs for customers to climb and I'll get my exercise running up and down to the copier and fax."

"I asked Fleet about that, too. Doesn't seem logical to me, but hey! I don't make the calls." He shrugs, pulls a pack of cigarettes out of his shirt pocket and lights one. As he blows out a cloud of smoke, he says, "Once we get you two moved up here, we'll get on with the renos in the teller area. New state-of-the-art vault, bigger vault room and new counterfittings. There's going to be one of those new automatic teller machines in its own little area just inside the new entrance, right where your desk is now. We'll do a lot of it at night but it's still going to be a big mess."

"How much longer do you think it'll take?"

"I guess we'll see," he says, and shrugs. "If we don't have to change anything, we'll finish getting the drywall filled this weekend, ready to be painted. Then carpets, and the boss will be moved up by this time next week. You too, of course."

"I don't see where Hal's office is going to be."

"He's not moving up. He gets Fleet's old office. At least one thing about this makes sense." He shakes his head, then looking past me, says, "Oh, here's Fleet now."

I turn and see Fleet just coming up the stairs. "Good morning," he says. He comes to where we're standing and before I can move out of reach, gives my shoulder a little squeeze.

I take a step away and reply, "Good morning?"

"Good afternoon, I guess." He grins and winks but at least doesn't crowd me again. Turning to Calvin, he says, "Good I caught you, Calvin. We need to talk about that carpet quote before we go any further with the order. Grab a coffee and come to my office, would you? And lose the damn cigarette."

"Sure." Calvin frowns, drops his cigarette on the floor and scrunches it out under his boot. "See you later, Lindy," as he unbuckles his tool belt and hangs it on the stepladder before following Fleet down the stairs.

The branch is closed and it's less than half an hour before quitting time. I'm shuffling things around on my desk, sorting through my in basket to make sure there's nothing that has to be dealt with before Monday, when Fleet calls my name. I look up and see him standing in the doorway. I ask, "Hi, uh, you need something?"

"We need to talk."

"Okay."

"In private," he says.

I get up and follow him into his office, closing the door behind me before perching on a chair across the desk from him, confused at his dark expression. No grin and wink?

"Lindy, I've been on the phone with Aspen Adventures. They tell me you approved a loan for one of their customers this morning."

"That's right. I wanted to talk to you about that. They don't have floor credit? I was wondering why not."

"They don't qualify for it or they would have it, Lindy," he says. "I talked to Hal. He said he told you it had to be approved by me."

"That's true."

"And we, you and I, talked about how you have to refer everything to me. Remember?"

"I remember, but I didn't think you meant consumer loans. They needed it today and no one knew if you'd be back in time—"

"No excuse!" he snaps. "I was here in plenty of time."

"But I didn't know—"

"Better for them not to get approval until Monday instead of you muddling along when you were told not to. You want me to help you learn your job or not? We're team players here, Lindy. I hope I can count on you being a team player, too." His frown is gone but his smile seems more threatening than sincere; leaning forward, his whole body is tense, reminding me of a dog about to lunge. I shrink back in my chair.

I manage to mumble, "Yes, of course."

"Good. So, going forward, anything that lands on your desk like that, my door is always open and I hope you know you can always come to me. We're a team, Lindy. Right?"

"Right," I agree.

He picks up a pen and taps the desk with it. Tap. Tap. Tap. Tap. Then he smiles, the tension leaves his body and he relaxes back into his chair. "Good," he says. "So. You like fishing by any chance?"

"Er..."

Before I can answer, he continues: "Reason I ask is because I'm taking the boat out for a little fishing in the morning and I'd like you to come along."

"Oh, that's a great offer, Fleet." I'm not a big fan of fishing, but then my experience is limited to fishing from shore. At least fishing from a boat you get a boat ride even if you don't catch fish. Still, I'm hesitant. I need time get over how awkward I feel being near him after his sharp 'muddling along' comment. I'm saved having to make an excuse thanks to the invitation to have coffee with my upstairs neighbor. "I, er, sorry, I have plans..."

"Such as?"

I wonder how it's any of his business, but answer, "My neighbors invited me for coffee. I haven't met them yet so I—"

"Fine," he snaps. "I'm sure you don't want to miss that just to go for a boat ride on a beautiful morning." The frown lines on his forehead make me think he's not used to being turned down, and doesn't like it.

"Can I take a rain cheque?"

He taps his pen a couple more times then dismisses me with a wave as he says, "Sure. See you Monday."

"Monday," I agree. I hurry out of his office to the safe haven of my desk.

Red says I have a head like a rock and claims my middle name must be Brutus. Brutus was a rope horse belonging to one of our old rodeo pals. He was good at his job but outside the arena, he had the unfortunate vice of bolting, the implication being that I charge ahead without thinking, consequences be damned. I admit I do have that tendency and it's gotten me into trouble, but I don't think what I did could be called 'muddling along' and him calling it that along with his insistence everything, even such a small consumer loan, has to be referred to him is irritating me more now that I think about it than it did when he said it. I mutter, "Assmeat," and try to push it out of my mind before smoke starts coming out of my ears.

"Who are you calling—what did you say? Assmeat?" Deena materializes beside my desk with a handful of papers to be copied. Thankfully she matched the volume of my voice when I said it and asked the question in barely more than a whisper so even Hal, just a few meters away, couldn't hear it. Did she see me coming out of Fleet's office? Does she realize that's who I was referring to?

"Oh, hi, Deena. Um, it's my best friend's favourite swear word," I explain.

"I like it," she says, and smiles as she feeds papers into the copier. "And in this place, it could describe everyone."

That comment surprises me. Maybe she feels like an outsider too, in her case possibly because she's Cree. I think I should take a coffee or lunch break when she does so I can get to know her. I have a number of Cree friends including my best friend, Red. I would at least have one connection here.

Thinking back on the day, I can't help but conclude that file being put on my desk was a trap. Although he said it must have been put there by mistake, Hal's startled expression when confronted is enough to convince me it was his doing. He didn't expect me ask him why he didn't approve it. He was probably worried I'd just toss it back to him and foil his plans but instead, I walked right into his trap. And then there was that shouting match he had with Fleet my first day, on the heels of his learning I don't have as much experience as he does.

I'll definitely be more careful in future.

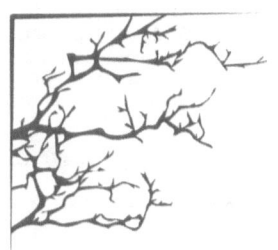

5–Meet Kristy

It's ten a.m. Saturday and I'm at my upstairs neighbor's front door. When I heard footsteps overhead earlier to confirm someone was up, I went and got a six-pack of Tim Horton's Donuts. That in hand, I fix a smile on my face and push the doorbell.

The door is pulled open by a petite, trim but busty woman about my age in one of the smallest bikinis I've ever seen. "Hello," I say. Before I have a chance to say more, she smiles and takes a few steps back.

"Come in! Come in! I'm Kristy."

I step inside and say, "Hi, Kristy. I'm Lindy. I brought these." I hold up the box of donuts.

"Nice! Do you like coffee or would you rather have tea?"

"Coffee would be great."

"I'll make a fresh pot."

"That would also be great," I agree.

She pushes the door shut behind me and says, "Come right this way. It's a nice morning so we could sit outside, if you like."

"I like," I agree. I follow her along the entry hall into the kitchen and hover around while she puts grounds and water into the coffeemaker.

"It'll be a few minutes," she says. "Meanwhile, come ahead out on the deck."

We go through the dining room and out the sliding doors onto the deck, where there's a glass-topped table with an umbrella, an open paperback turned face down, and a mug half full of coffee. She slides into the chair. I put the donuts down in the pond of shade from the umbrella and sit across from her.

"You know, I've been wondering why we were never outside at the same time so we could've met sooner," I say.

"Well, my husband and I both work shifts. He's on graveyards so he's still in bed."

"Oh no! I hope the doorbell didn't wake him."

"He can sleep through anything. I'm sure it didn't bother him. But we're going to be friends, so in future just come up on the deck and tap on the glass." She points at the doors we just came through.

"I will! And you can come down and tap on my patio door. Or the other one. And I don't mind if you ring the doorbell."

"Perfect! So, you live in Katawasis Lake long?"

"No, just moved here a week ago. You?"

"I only moved here a little while ago too. Came to town for Kyle's work. We've only been married since last fall and I thought it was too soon to move away from everyone, you know, all our friends. But you gotta work, so here we are."

"Oh, you're newlyweds. Congratulations."

"Thanks."

"So. Shiftwork. And you had no trouble getting a job so quick? What sort of work do you do?"

"I'm a waitress at Tall Trees Pub. I'm the newbie so I get the shit shifts. Lots of dinner shifts too, though, so that's why I'm not around evenings. You been in yet? To the pub, I mean?"

"Not yet."

"Well, you'll have to come in! The food's great."

"I'll make a point of it. What about your husband?"

"Kyle works security. And you?"

"I've got a plain old eight-to-five, five days a week bank job. Although we're getting set to do a trial run of Saturday openings as soon as the renovations are done, and I'll be working the odd Saturday after that."

"Wow, that would be convenient. Which bank?"

"Western Savings and Loan. Right on the corner of Main and Commercial."

"Well, that happens to be where we bank! So I'll see you often."

"For sure."

There's an awkward pause in the conversation, so I ask, "Good book?" I point to the cover of the book where a bare-chested hunk is in process of removing a busty woman's bodice, apparently on the deck of a tall ship. The crew must have been elsewhere just then.

"I guess so. It's about a pirate. What a bad bastard he is!" She giggles. "He was a lord and wouldn't have gone bad except his brother tricked his fiancé into marrying him, which I say was a good thing since she was a frigid bitch who treated him bad and wouldn't even have sex with him. But his brother cheated him out of his rightful inheritance to boot. He's on a mission to get even when he, um, piratizes a ship taking stuff to his brother's place which is rightfully his of course, and there happens to be this cute young art-restoring girl on that ship who's on her way there too. You know, because of all the valuable old paintings in the castle, which his brother cheated him out of like I said. She's just coming out of a bad break-up and has decided to quit men altogether but she's falling for him anyway. Pretty sure they're going to get it on, probably next chapter. I hope so because his big, throbbing manhood can't be denied much longer! So I should get to the juicy parts pretty quick." She giggles and I find myself chuckling right along with her. "Gotta love those bad boys! I'll give it to you when I'm done."

I'm more into Stephen King and Nelson DeMille or even Danielle Steele and I haven't read a cheesy romance novel since I was about twelve, but the offer is generous and sincere so I say, "Thanks."

"I'm pretty sure the juicy parts will end when he gets his castle back and what's the point of reading on after that? So I'll be done with it pretty quick. I do want to find out what happens with his brother and the ex-girlfriend though. Maybe he'll kill them both! It would serve them right! Ha!"

"But would the art restorer woman want to be with him if he did? Murder them, I mean?"

"No, I guess not. So I hope he kills the brother in a duel, maybe, or some sort of accident in a fight such as he falls over a cliff? And then just sends the ex-girlfriend packing." A spate of hissing comes from the kitchen. "Sounds like coffee's ready. How do you take it?"

"Black no sugar, thanks."

"I'll be right back." She gets up and heads inside.

While I'm waiting I get up and go to the rail. If I thought the view from my patio was nice, the view from up here is spectacular. From my place I can see only a small section of the lake because the back yard is enclosed by the tall hedges, but from here there's a view over the trees, a hundred and eighty degree panorama. Besides the houses on the far side of the lake that I can see from my patio, there's what looks like a large hotel, a dock with numerous boats tied up, and a crescent of sandy beach. There's a pair of binoculars on a small table next to the rail. I pick them up and train them on the hotel just as Kristy comes back with a mug in each hand.

"Here you go," she says.

I put the binoculars down and go back to the table. "Is that a hotel on the other side of the lake?" I ask.

"Yup, resort hotel. Katawasis Lake Lodge. Everyone calls it The Kat."

"It looks nice."

"It is nice. People from all over go there. Did you notice boats tied up to their dock? People with places on the lake go there by boat. They have a restaurant and a spa where you can get a glass of wine and some fancy little overpriced snacks while you have a couples massage. Me and Kyle went there for our six month anniversary."

"You have a boat? I thought that trail out the gate might lead down to the lake."

"A boat? We don't have a boat. I didn't mean *we* went by boat. We'll get one, though. Just as soon as we win a lottery. You seen our shitty old cars, right? Besides, it's worth your life to get down to the beach from here. You'd have to be a mountain goat!"

"It doesn't look all that bad. And speaking of shitty old vehicles, your husband's is the furthest thing from shitty. It's a classic."

"Yeah, and he pours a lot of money into it. Mine is definitely shitty though. Hafta add oil every time I fill gas."

"Well, if it makes you feel better, at least your car's fenders match. You must have noticed the green fender on my truck. I left Maple Creek before it got painted."

"What happened to it?"

"Slid into the ditch and hit a telephone pole during a blizzard."

"Oh. Too bad! So you have to pay the deductible."

"I cheaped out and only bought the mandatory third party liability insurance. And besides the expense, it's going to be a major inconvenience now because I can't be without it."

"Maybe they'll give you a loaner. Or, me or Kyle will drive you."

"I couldn't let you do that! To work and back for three or four days? Besides, our schedules really don't jive."

"Hmm. Well, I guess you're right."

"Um hmm. Thanks for the offer, though." I take a few tentative sips of my coffee, then say, "I guess boats are expensive."

"Kyle's been looking for a good used one but even used ones are expensive. So, it'll be a while. Unless we actually do win a lottery! How about you? Husband? Boyfriend?"

"Neither. Don't want one, either. Not that I don't want a boyfriend ever. Just not now. My history with men isn't great so I'm not anxious to start another relationship."

"What about just dating, then? No strings, just sex for the fun of it? That's what I did after my split from my husband because I didn't want to get married again. Then I met Kyle."

Recreational sex? My mind flashes back to one of my first days with Nick, when he thought I was older and more experienced than I was and suggested we have some "afternoon delight". I feel my face growing warm.

Kristy notices I'm blushing, and says, "Oh! I embarrassed you!"

"No, not really. It's just that the town I come from is so small everyone knows everyone else, and I've already, er, well, let's just say I don't want to stir up any more gossip. I tell my friends that I'm open to another relationship if the right guy comes along, but only if he has a nice truck."

"A nice truck?" Kristy chuckles and then asks, "How about a nice BMW?"

"You can't pull a horse trailer or haul hay in a car," I explain.

"Oh, we were wondering why you drive a truck instead of a car. You have a horse?"

"Actually, dozens of them. My home in Maple Creek is a ranch. Wacasko-Wâti."

"Wasaki what?"

"Wacasko-Wâti. It means rat hole in Cree, more or less. I'm only here temporarily."

"Rat hole? Why would you name your ranch rat hole?"

"That's what my ex called it. He's long gone but the name stuck. One of my partners is Cree. When we needed a name for the winery we didn't want to call it rat hole, so we went with the Cree name."

"Cool! But you're not here to stay?"

"No, just to get management experience. I'll only be here for a couple of years."

"And then you go back to your ranch? Lucky you! How did you get to keep it when you got divorced?"

"Chuck, my ex, never lived there. It belonged to my father. He left it to me."

"Oh, he's dead. I'm sorry. He must've died young."

"Too young. A plane crash. But it was more than ten years ago."

"Still sad, though," she says, and I notice her lower lip quiver a bit. I think of telling her my fiancé also died in the crash, but then my lip would probably quiver too, so I take a sip of coffee instead.

Kristy asks, "So it's a horse ranch?"

"It was a cattle ranch with a sideline of winemaking until a couple of years ago. Then we, er, got out of cattle to focus on the winery. And we still have horses. My uncle Stu, he's my other partner, is big into saving horses from being slaughtered. He haunts the auctions and brings home any that the meat buyers are bidding on. We find homes for as many as we can but we're still left with quite a few, especially the old ones or those that are too crocked to be rideable. Even those are still adoptable as companion horses. Thankfully with all the ranchland being subdivided into acreages and bought up by city folk, there's a demand for them as lawn ornaments. And I do have my own special horse, too."

"You must miss him."

"She's a *she*. Pretty palomino pinto named Chica. And yes, it's only been a week but I already miss her because I'd usually ride after supper. In winter it gets dark so early I only ride weekends so I don't think I'll miss it so much then. For now, I'll go home once a month. I'm going to get a Friday off in exchange for taking a Saturday shift at the bank."

"A long weekend every month! That's great." Kristy leans back, holding her mug in both hands, then cocks her head and says, "Say, maybe you could bring your horse here? You know there's a horse place not far from here.

They've got a big building they ride in so there's stuff going on there all year long. One of the girls I work with said she went there to watch a horse show once."

"Oh, yeah? Where is it?"

"Not even very far from here. Just past the Kat. Hey, I'm off tomorrow. We should go! If you want."

"It's a date."

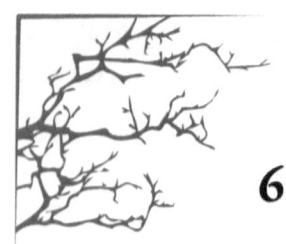

6–Windsong Stables

I downshift and slow the truck as we approach a wide driveway marked by a sign. The sign proves to be for Windsong Stables and announces they offer boarding, lessons, and are dealers for Trails West and Sundowner trailers. I turn in.

It looks promising: white plank fencing, wrought iron gates standing open to a long driveway shaded by lofty cottonwoods, their leaves stirring in the breeze.

"The song of the wind," I say.

"What?"

"The sound of the leaves rustling in the wind. Maybe that's where they got the name."

"You can hear it?"

"No, but we have a cottonwood grove at Wacasko-Wâti so I was just remembering the sound. I guess we might have named the place Windsong if we'd thought of it."

"Well, it does sound better than rat hole," she says, and giggles. "Good thing no one speaks Cree."

"No one but the Cree," I tell her. "Not even many of them."

The driveway spills out into a good-sized gravel area where there are a dozen horse trailers with for sale signs on them, and about the same number of cars and trucks angle parked at what looks like a low barn. Beyond that is a building easily twice the length and height of the nearest barn. It must be the indoor ring, with a lean-to likely housing more stalls running its length. Beside that there's a round pen and an outdoor ring where there are three riders. One circles a man in a cowboy hat. There are people watching from the fence. The driveway continues to the right of that but looks to be the lane to a sprawling ranch house at the top of the gentle rise.

"Very nice," I say as I park between a truck and car and turn off the engine. "Looks like we're in time to watch a lesson."

We exit the truck and walk to the riding ring. Three girls watching the riders glance our way as we come up to the rail and hold up near them. I say, "Hi!" They respond likewise and return their attention to the riders.

We watch as at the coach calls various instructions to the rider, and finally, tells the rider he thinks the horse is getting tired so that's enough for today. The horse slows to a walk. After a discussion with the coach that we can't hear, horse and rider head toward us, and the gate. I take this opportunity to ask the nearest girl, "Where would I find the owner?"

"K.C.? That's him there," she replies, and indicates the coach with a nod, then she and the other girls go to open the gate for the rider.

The coach follows the rider out and closes the gate behind him. The girls speak to him and one points to us. He looks our way and comes over.

I'm gobsmacked. Is he the cowboy hat guy who was at the restaurant on Monday? Can't be! Fleet would never insult someone who owns real estate and a business like this!

"Hello," he says. "Can I help you?"

"Um, yeah. My name's Lindy, and this is Kristy. They tell me you're the owner so I guess you're the guy to talk to about boarding a horse here?"

"Hi, Lindy. Kristy. I'm K.C.." He reaches out his hand for a quick shake. "So. What kind of horse?"

"Paint mare. Six years old."

His eyes narrow for a moment. Then he says, "I don't know if I'll have room. Barn's not full now but there's regular boarders who take their horses home for the summer. If I take yours and they all want to come back, I'd have to turn one of them down. Can't do that."

"Oh." Deflated, I take a deep breath.

"But they don't always all come back. Tell you what," he continues, "let's take a tour of the barns and we'll discuss it."

He leads the way to the back entrance of the smaller building. The wide sliding door is open to an alleyway with stalls on both sides. "Horses aren't in at night in the summer unless it's stormy, which is why it's empty now," he tells us.

There's a horse in the crossties with a woman tacking up. She looks up at our approach and sings out, "Good morning!"

"Hi, Beth," K.C. responds. "Go ahead and warm up. I'll be with you in a bit."

We continue to a man door, which he opens. We follow him inside. "This tack room is just for this barn. If one of these stalls opens up, you'll get one of these lockers to keep your stuff in." He opens one that doesn't have a lock on it to display a wall-mounted saddle rack with a shelf above it and hooks on the door. He asks, "So. What kind of riding do you do?"

"Um, whatever needs doing on the ranch. So I guess you'd say trail riding with a little bit of chasing cows."

"Well, now cows, but there's tons of trails out into the bush up behind the house. In fact, you can ride right down to the beach."

"That sounds nice."

"Yeah, it's a nice ride. But if you board here, part of the deal is that you take lessons once a week, in the arena. You okay with that?"

"Um, sure." Lessons? I haven't had a riding lesson in my life, although I've thought of taking Chica to a trainer over in Swift Current. Red pronounced spending money on lessons foolish since I already know how to ride. If lessons are a requirement of boarding here I won't mention it so she can't argue. I just hope they're not too expensive.

"Okay. Let's go to the big barn then. My office is there. I'll get you to fill out an application."

We stop at the gate to the indoor arena to look in and watch a couple of riders for a minute before continuing down the alleyway past the wash rack and tack-up stalls where two women are grooming horses, to his office. By now I'm positive he's the guy from the restaurant, which makes him the driver of the black dually as well, but if he recognizes me he gives no sign and I'm not about to bring it up.

We discuss fees, what board includes, and finally, how soon I need an answer. Of course there's no rush since Chica is okay where she is. He seems interested when I tell him about Wacasko-Wâti and the horse rescue. When he looks out the window facing the indoor arena and says, "Well, I see Beth is pretty well warmed up. I better get on with her lesson."

"Of course," I agree. "Any idea when you might know if you'll have an opening?"

"Depends on how soon I reach someone who's not coming back. Sorry, I can't give you a date."

"Understood. Thanks."

"Talk to you soon," he says.

We leave the office together, K.C. heading for the gate to the indoor, Kristy and me continuing down the alleyway and outside.

Kristy stops, turns to watch K.C. as he walks away and under her breath, mutters, "Damn!"

"He said he'd call the people who took their horses home for the summer to confirm that they're coming back, and he'll call you as soon as he knows," Kristy says as we're heading back to town. "I bet he'll make sure you get in. He seemed really sorry that he had to leave when he did. No wedding ring! I think he likes you."

"No wedding ring doesn't mean he's not married. And you must've noticed he was checking you out pretty good. Besides, he's a cowboy. My motto is: Big Hat Equals Big Trouble."

"Maybe in his case, good trouble! He's super good-looking. Fills out those jeans awful nice! I don't mind guys like *that* checking me out. In fact, it's a turn-on and I think Kyle might get busy as soon as we get home!" She laughs, then says, "If I wasn't married, I'd hit on him myself. And he's taller than you."

"Yeah, it's not looks or height that's the problem, it's the fact he's a cowboy. And besides, I've seen him before, and from my boss' reaction, I think there must be something sketchy about him." I tell her about him cutting me off, me flipping him the bird, and lunch at Pioneer House.

"Do you think he recognized you?"

"No, don't think so. At least he didn't act like he did."

"Isn't that truck nice, though? I bet he has other nice equipment too," she says, and gives me a sideways look. "I mean those horse trailers he has for sale."

"Yeah, I'm sure you meant horse trailers!" But I chuckle, and she joins in.

She says, "Hey, maybe he'll come into the pub! If he does, I'll phone you so you can come down and hang out with him!"

"Forget it, Kristy," I tell her. "Didn't you notice the women crawling all over that place? If he isn't married, he for sure has a girlfriend. Even if he is married, he likely has a girlfriend. Otherwise, he's gay."

"He could be between relationships, you know. And he is definitely not gay."

"Why not? Good looking, masculine men can be gay. If he's gay, I might like him better."

"Don't be crazy. All *that*? Wasted?"

"He's a cowboy," I say, as if that explains it.

"So what? They can't all be bad. Maybe he's one of the good ones."

"Maybe. And maybe pigs can fly," I say, somewhat more sharply than is called for. An over-reaction, since I really don't know anything about him. And I know so many good cowboys, I shouldn't lump them all in with the last two I dated.

I shouldn't have snapped at Kristy. To make amends, I suggest, "Think you can let Kyle sleep for another hour or so? How about lunch at your pub? It would be my treat, as a thank you for this morning. I don't know if I would've found Windsong on my own."

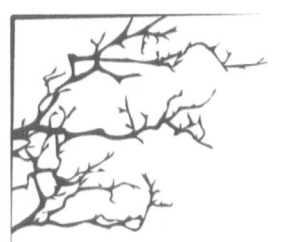

7—Ladies Lunch

My first Friends of Katawasis lunch. At Fleet's suggestion I leave the bank half an hour early and arrive at Katawasis Lake Lodge in plenty of time. From the minute you walk through the doors the place is imposing, with an arrangement of fresh flowers that has to be three feet tall and just as wide on an antique oak table in the middle of an acre of thick carpet. Twenty foot cedar ceilings rest on huge rough-hewn log pillars and beams. Groupings of loveseats and chairs are scattered here and there. A vast river rock fireplace divides the floor-to-ceiling windows offering a view of the lake. I haven't been anywhere this grand since leaving Calgary. It puts the most highbrow place in Maple Creek to shame. Logging and fishing must be a lot more lucrative than ranching.

There's a signboard indicating the Friends of Katawasis luncheon is down a wide hallway to the right. When I get to the meeting room, I see a long table set with a white cloth, pitchers of ice water, glasses and cutlery but there are no humans in sight. I debate taking a seat but decide instead to hover around and wait until someone else shows up.

I don't have long to wait. Ladies in groups of three and four start trickling in. They nod and say hello to me, but chat among themselves. At twelve sharp, two carefully made up and coiffed forty-something women arrive. One, a brunette as tall as I am, looks at me and then comes my way. Her beautifully tailored suit is definitely a Dolly's Dresses number. She's even wearing dark pantyhose despite of the fact it's a hot day, and if I tried wearing those four-inch heels I'd break an ankle. Maybe it's the Friends of Katawasis uniform, since I seem to be the only one in pants, blouse, loafers and no jacket.

"Hello," she says. "You must be Lindy."

"Yes," I agree. In this crowd, I'm underdressed, and next to her I'm also under-made up and under-coiffed. I tuck my hair behind my ears.

"I'm Meredith Fleetwood." She sticks out her hand.

"Pleased to meet you," I say, and give her hand a quick shake. As gorgeous as she is, I would never have put this woman with Fleet. No amount of skillfully-applied makeup can hide the crow's feet and furrows in her brow. She looks to be at least ten years older than he is. I hope my face doesn't register my surprise. I focus on her eyes, and smile.

"Welcome! I understand you haven't been living in our fair city for long. I hope you're settling in okay."

"Yes, I think so."

"Has Fleet invited you out on the boat yet? He gives great lake tours. The lake's big, you know, over a hundred miles long plus lots of little side bits and tons of islands. There's fishing lodges for millionaires you can only reach by boat or float plane. They come from all over the world to fish here. Betty loves it when they come into her store to buy gifts to take home to their wives. Fleet's special is what he calls his 'sunset cruise'. Sip a cocktail while you watch the sun go down and the city lights come on."

"He invited me to go fishing last Saturday, but I couldn't make it."

"Fishing? Not a tour?"

"No. Your boat sounds really nice, though. Lucky you."

"It's his boat and he's welcome to it. I have no interest in boating. Been there, done that! Five or six hours stuck out there? I go out once in a while but really, I'd rather have a root canal. So he takes other people along for company. He's such a people person."

"Umm, yeah, he sure is. But I guess he spends a lot of time on the boat. You must never see him."

"He's home enough, Lindy. Our place is lakefront. We have our own dock, so he can spend his evenings fooling around polishing things on the boat or take it out for an hour or two. No different than Betty's husband." She nods to one of the ladies chatting in a small group on the other side of the table. "He's a car guy and spends as much time in the garage polishing his cars and then cruising around the neighborhood as Fleet does on his boat. We've been married over fifteen years, Lindy. When you've been married that long you don't need a lot of together time, as long as you have quality time."

"I guess so," I agree.

"We get plenty of *quality* time," she assures me. Then she turns to the room and says, "Okay, ladies! Let's get started. Sit up here beside me, Lindy."

Everyone takes a seat at the table, with Meredith at the head and the Betty woman with the satchel of papers on her right. Meredith says, "We have a newcomer. Lindy, stand up so everyone can see you. And tell us who you are."

I dutifully get to my feet and say, "Hello. My name's Lindy Larsen." I sit back down.

"Lindy works for my husband at Western Savings and Loan," Meredith adds. "Your turn, Betty."

Betty, who had been rummaging through papers, looks up and says, "I'm Betty Hartley. I own Dolly's Dresses."

This continues around the table, although I was the only one who had to stand up. There's a restauranteur, a couple of lawyers, realtors, insurance agents and other business owners or managers. Not a single housewife, waitress or store clerk. Definitely the upper crust in Katawasis society. I guess I should be flattered to be invited. When it comes back to Meredith, she says, "And you all know me! Now, let's order lunch and get on with the meeting."

We each tell one of the waitresses hovering around behind us what we want. For this special luncheon, we are welcome to order anything from the wine list, but to avoid overloading the kitchen there's a choice of only two special lunch entrees: chicken noodle soup and roast beef sandwich on white or whole wheat, or Quiche Lorraine with chef's salad. The Caesar salad substitute is a dollar extra but I go for it anyway.

Red has often said I have the appetite of a cow hand but the meal eventually placed in front of me is what anyone would agree is barely enough to fill a hollow tooth. It does look pretty, though, what with a blue flower nestled in a bed of parsley. The one-dollar-extra Caesar salad doesn't even overflow the little bowl they put it in. The chef must think this is a fat farm. I eat slowly but it's gone before Betty finishes droning the treasurer's report. I'm thinking of eating the flower and the parsley when the waitress reaches over my shoulder and takes my plate.

The group discussion turns to who's on duty at bingo this weekend. It would go a lot faster if they'd quit getting sidetracked into discussions of who is flying off to where, what millionaire is booked in at what fishing lodge, and what so-and-so said about so-and-so.

Finally someone raises the issue of teenagers and drug addicts congregating at their project, the playground at the public wharf, and leaving a mess of condoms and odd bits of clothing—this weekend there was a pair of thong panties!—as well as syringes. Now I'm slightly interested. I think of Kyle and wonder if there is money in the budget to hire security, at least for the busiest nights. I mention it. They all turn to look at me as if I've grown another head.

"We know about security, Lindy," Meredith says, and nods indulgently.

Someone else says, "Why would we spend our money? That's what the RCMP are for." There's a chorus of agreement. I think, *Don't bitch about the problem, then,* but thankfully I still have a little wine in my glass. I use it to make sure the words don't come out of my mouth. They decide to put up more signs, as if that's going to do any good. Maybe they like having that problem to bitch about, especially if they get to talk about forgotten panties. Maybe they fantasize about being the girl who took them off.

The meeting finally over, we get our bills. I choke back a gasp. It's twice what's reasonable even though I once again showed my ignorance by ordering a glass of house white instead of something with a name. I hope I can put it on my expense account.

Betty has to leave early. I'm well on my way to escaping right behind her and nearly make it across the lobby when I'm buttonholed by Meredith. "Lindy! A couple of us are going for a glass of wine on the patio. Join us?"

"Sorry, Meredith, I'd love to but I can't! I'm already late getting back." I smile and give a little wave before bolting out the door. It doesn't matter if I'm late getting back. Fleet's already given me permission. If Meredith complains to her husband it may be a mistake running out but if I have another glass of wine on an empty stomach I'll probably be too drunk to drive.

My stomach rumbles all the way back to the bank.

I stop in at the Tall Trees Pub after work and spot Kristy as she circulates through tables taking orders and delivering drinks. I'm scanning the room deciding where to sit when she looks up and nods her head in the direction of the bar. She slides behind the bar and sets her tray with its dirty glasses on the counter just as I take a stool at the far end.

"Hi, Lindy," she says. When she's finished loading the dirty glasses into the dishwasher, she brings a little bowl of mini pretzels, sets them in front of me and leans across the bar. "What's up? Glass of wine? Beer?"

"House white would be great," I tell her, and take a handful of pretzels. "Make it a half liter."

"Oh, that kind of day, eh? Coming right up!"

When she returns, she places a glass on a coaster and pours from the carafe while asking, "So, what made this a half liter day?"

"Well, I had my first Katawasis Lake Lodge experience," I reply, and go on to give her the broad strokes of the Friends of Katawasis lunch. Or luncheon, as the refined ladies call it. "Oh, and I met Mrs. Fleet," I tell her. "Lovely lady. I'd say she's probably closer to fifty than forty, but movie star beautiful. 'Course Fleet's good looking too."

"I've noticed him at the bank. I wouldn't kick him out of bed for eating crackers. How old would you say he is? Mid-thirties?"

"I guess."

"Good for her, getting herself a boy toy."

"Is he still a boy toy when he's your husband?"

"As long as you're still playing with him, I guess he is."

"She asked if he'd invited me out for a boat tour, though, and said I should take him up on it."

"Oh yeah? She doesn't mind him cruising with a younger woman?"

"Apparently not. She seems comfortable in the relationship. When I asked if he spends so much time on the boat she hardly sees him, she said they spend plenty of time together. Actually said '*quality* time', emphasis on quality."

"Don't you get it? It was like: nudge nudge, wink wink, we fuck a lot. That's what I call quality time!" She laughs, scans the room, and says, "I'll be right back."

She goes out from behind the bar to make a tour through tables. I look around to confirm there was no one near enough to hear her say that. Thankfully there isn't. I'm not a prude and I know men talk like that, but it's a shock coming from sweet-looking little Kristy. Maybe that's why she said it.

Kristy returns with a tray of dirty glasses and tells the bartender what drinks she needs before coming back to me while she waits. "You know," she says, picking up the conversation where she left off, "she must do something really well to snag a guy what? Fifteen years younger? I wonder if he's good in bed. If they still have *quality* time after years of marriage, maybe he has a big dick and knows how to use it. You should give him a toss. You might like it, and it might be good for your career too."

I nearly choke on my wine. She notices, and gives me a wink.

"Hey, what's the name of his boat?"

"I don't know. Why?"

"Well, we could watch for it from our deck."

"Um, why would we do that? Who cares?"

"Kyle was asking," she explains. She leans a little closer and lowers her voice. "Besides, I seen a couple doing the nasty right out there in broad daylight. And lots of times there's girls suntanning in the nude. Guys showing them their, er, *equipment*. Maybe you're not the only younger woman he takes out on tours. Kyle has a camera with a big lens on it. Maybe we could get a close up of him being a naughty boy."

"I don't know that I'd want to."

"Of course you would! You could show him the photo and ask for a raise."

"I wouldn't do that."

"Never say never," she says, then straightens and takes a step to where the bartender is standing her drinks, then turns and says, "Oh, and here's a thought: next time he invites you out, ask if you can bring a friend. Me! I'd love to go."

"Okay, I guess."

"Promise?"

"Promise."

But it's a hollow promise, because I have no intention of spending any more time with Fleet than I have to, even to get a pay raise. I'll put in my two years in Katawasis Lake and then remind Regional Office that was all the time I agreed to spend here.

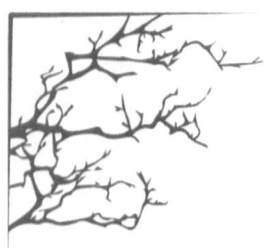

8–Easton

I've settled into a routine of work, stopping by Tall Trees on my way home, and pretty much lazing around the yard weekends. I've made a couple of forays down the bank behind my house. The slightly overgrown trail doesn't show signs of a lot of use, but it's a clear path nevertheless. The farthest I've gone so far is to a flatter spot where there's a rope swing. It's a good distance from the lake and only swings out over rocks, deadfall and bushes. My best guess would be that previous occupants had kids. It's a steep hike back up and I doubt anyone but kids would think it worthwhile.

From my farmer tan (forearms and neck brown, legs and torso fish belly white) it's obvious to anyone I'm not a sunbather, but I often visit with Kristy while she suns herself. Sometimes she's reading a romance novel, other times she's listening to her Walkman, but every nice day she's on the deck half naked.

Yes, half naked. I could call her that even if she didn't take her tiny bikini top off because her biggest article of clothing is her ballcap. So whether her top is on or off, she's half naked. She says if you got it, flaunt it. I don't qualify even if I wanted to flaunt, although I do tie my shirt tails up and put on a pair of cut-offs on hot days.

Kyle likes it or maybe he just has a chubby when he wakes up and thinks it's a shame to waste it. Even if she keeps her top on I always make sure I'm gone before he gets up. Also, I'm careful not to go upstairs when there's moaning and groaning because the last thing I want to do is catch them doing the nasty. In fairness, they're still relative newlyweds and with their conflicting work schedules, I can't blame them for taking advantage of the opportunity. I just think it would be as well if they didn't do it on the deck.

It's part of their rental agreement that they take care of the yard, but since there's only so much sitting around I can stand and my place isn't big enough to spend hours doing housework, I help out with the mowing. I said I can wait until he's up so the noise doesn't wake him, but they moved their bed to the front bedroom and told me I can mow the back, the biggest part of the job, any time. The upside to this and something I didn't expect when I offered to mow is that their bedroom is no longer above mine so I'm sleeping better.

I've just finished mowing and I'm sweeping the grass clippings off my patio when Kristy leans over the deck rail and calls down, "Hey, Lindy!"

I set the broom against the wall, go to the edge of the patio and look up. She's wearing her low cut Tall Trees t-shirt even though she usually doesn't leave for work this early. I ask, "What?"

"Wanna come to the pub with us? I gotta work but Kyle's off tonight, so he won't have to rush off and leave you sitting alone."

"Sure," I agree. "What time do you want to leave?"

"Pretty quick because I want to grab something to eat, too, and I go on at five."

I glance at my watch. Three thirty. "I have to shower. How about I meet you there?"

"Okay!" Kristy agrees. "See you there, then."

Kristy flits off and I take another few minutes to finish sweeping the patio before I go in and shower. I blow dry my hair enough that I can pull it into a ponytail, don clean jeans and t-shirt, and head out.

I arrive at the pub, park, and go inside. Kristy is at a table with a couple of men. The one with his back to me has "SECURITY" in white lettering emblazoned across his back. Kyle. Kristy is sitting across from him. She looks up and waves when she spots me. There's a third person at the table and I have a sinking feeling. Is it a set-up? If so, she could have chosen someone a little tidier. Grubby orange jacket. Shaggy hair billowing out under his ball cap. When my eyes adjust to the dim lighting I realize I've met him before.

I wend my way through the tables and take the only vacant chair, between Kyle and the other man. Last time I met the guy I didn't hate him, but his hang dog expression and chronic complaining would put a damper on any crowd. It might help if he paid more attention to personal hygiene, at least lost the scruffy Seventies beard, but then he's not much to look at to start with so it might not matter. I remind myself looks aren't important and it's a person's character that counts but I'm not sure his character would redeem him either. Kristy and Kyle are digging into their meals but he doesn't have food in front of him so there's a good chance he won't stay long. I paste a smile on my face and say, "Hi, Easton. How are ya?"

"Hi Lindy," he responds. "I've been better."

Against my better judgment, I ask, "Oh? How's that?"

"So, you know I was working in camp? They shut down for fire season and still ain't called me back. I'm behind in my rent so I need a side job. I'm starting a water taxi business. Think I'll quit logging altogether. Problem is, I ain't got a boat."

"Ahhh, well, that'll make it difficult." I look at Kyle, who saws away at his steak sandwich without glancing up. Even Kristy is uncharacteristically quiet, although she looks at me and rolls her eyes.

"Don't have to be. I got a boat lined up. It's a good deal, ain't new but in good shape. All I need is an investor. It's a sure thing and I would never stiff no one. I just need Kyle to throw in a few thou."

The reason for my friends being disengaged is obvious. It's never easy to say no. "Er, why not get bank financing?"

"I would if I could. Hey!" He sits up straighter and gives me an intense look. "You work at a bank. Kyle says you're some kinda manager there, right?"

"Right."

"You could give me a loan. For my business, eh?"

I catch movement in my peripheral vision and look at Kristy. She's shaking her head in warning, just in case I might consider it. But there's no chance I'd grant a loan to an out-of-work logger already behind in his rent. "I, er, couldn't help you out, Easton, conflict of interest, you being a friend and all, you know? Have you applied at other banks? Finance companies?"

"Yeah, of course. They're all a bunch of assholes, can't do nuthin', they're all useless. Don't even listen. Only guy who even listened said 'cause my credit ain't great there would be an extra charge, like, er, a *surcharge*. On top of all the interest? Can't go for that! There's a principle, right?"

"Right. But a surcharge? I never heard of such a thing. A bank manager told you that?"

"He said it's bank policy."

I'm puzzled. There are only three banks in Katawasis and I work at one of them. We don't have a surcharge and I can't believe the others do, either. "What bank was that, Easton?"

"I, er, I went to all of 'em. Don't remember which one it was, but I talked to the guy who does the loans. He said he had to talk to the manager, like buying a car, you know? They always gotta talk to the manager. Anyhow, the guy called me, said he'd gave my plan more thought, and met me at the Lumberman the next day. I took it as a good sign that he'd do that. Great customer service 'n' all. Then he turns out to be such a dick. Anyways, I wouldn't have to pay a surcharge if my buddy here would loan me a few bucks or at least cosign a loan for me."

"Over my dead body!" Kristy exclaims.

Easton glares at her but before he can say anything, Kyle says, "Easton, if I had money to throw around do you think I'd be driving a fifteen-year-old gas guzzler?"

"Pretty fancy goddamn gas guzzler! You could at least cosign. We could go in on it together. Partners."

"Didn't you say you have no cash to put in?"

"We both sign the loan, you put up the down payment, I do the work, and we split the profit fifty-fifty."

"You heard what my wife said."

"So, who wears the pants in your family? You pussy whipped?"

"He is," Kristy says as she gives Easton a hard look. "He likes it." She turns her attention to Kyle and says, "If you go along with his hare-brained scheme you'll never get another blow job."

"Okay, Easton," Kyle says, "you see the price I'd have to pay? Sorry, but nothing's changed since the last time you asked."

"Yeah, when you're down and out is when you find out who your real friends are. Just kick me in the teeth, why doncha?" He abruptly gets to his feet, picks up his glass and says with a scowl, "Nice knowin' you!"

He storms away, nearly bumping into Bonita, who's on her way toward us to take my order. Kyle shakes his head and takes a long swallow of beer.

When I've ordered my burger and fries, I turn to Kyle and say, "Looks like you just lost a friend."

"Good riddance," Kristy says. "But don't worry. He'll come around again the next time he needs something, all buddy-buddy like this never happened. This water taxi thing is just his latest get-rich-quick scheme."

"So he wants to start a water taxi? Like to take people out on boat rides? Isn't that a viable business?"

"In tourist season maybe. He thinks he'll get the guys from the fishing lodges, fantasizes about the big tips he'll get. Those lodges have Zodiacs they run their clients around on, free of charge. There's no way he'll be able to tap into that. So just the regular tourists, plus he wants to get set up to ferry guys who work at the mill or the log sort back and forth from the public wharf. He thinks they'd rather ride with him than spend an hour driving from town. 'Course they can ride the crummy for nothing, so I don't know why they'd want to pay him to ride on his boat. Plus everyone around here knows him well enough to doubt he's reliable. Very good chance he wouldn't show up when he's supposed to."

"Serious flaws in his business plan. But... Crummy?"

"That's what they call the company van that picks them up at Rotary Park," Kyle explains.

"Well anyhow, I guess it's time for me to get to work," Kristy says. "You two stay as long as you want but I'll move you up to the bar so the dinner crowd can have the table. I'll save this for you," she tells Kyle as she picks up her half-eaten mac and cheese, stands, and heads behind the bar. Kyle takes his plate and the beer, and we move to the bar. Bonita spots me there and brings my wine.

When we're settled, Kyle asks, "Do you believe that guy?" With a lift of his chin he indicates Easton, now at another table pleading his case to someone else. "Claims he could get bank financing if he paid a surcharge. You ever heard of that?"

"No."

"Basically a kickback."

"Sounds like it." I take a swallow of wine, then tell him, "And meeting at a pub to talk about a loan? What banker would do that? I don't believe it."

"I don't either. The whole story reeks."

"How do you know him, anyway? You haven't been in town that long, and he said he works in camp?"

"Yeah, some guys I work with know him. This is on the q.t., Lindy, poorly kept secret I guess. He's a small time drug dealer. Sells pot, mostly, although I guess he can get other stuff if you want it." He takes a swig of beer, then asks, "You want it?"

"Lord, no!"

"Have you tried it? Pot? Or Coke?"

"Pot, a few times in another life. Didn't like it. My ex liked Coke but I was too chicken to ever join in. You?"

"The same. And now I'd lose my job if I got caught." Kyle chews his last bite of steak and bread, swallows, takes a draft of beer, then says, "I would like to get a boat, though. Been looking around."

"Yeah, Kristy mentioned that."

"Maybe we can afford to get one, if I get a raise. Kristy really wants to get out on the lake, but I think she needs a better car before we buy a boat. She has to add oil every time she fills gas."

"She told me that." I nod. "And I've noticed the blue smoke that follows it everywhere."

"By the way, she said your boss has a boat and invites you out on it and you're going to take her with you."

"I, er, yeah," I agree, and take a long swallow of wine.

"What's his boat like, anyway?"

"I've only seen the photo of it in his office. It's white and has a sort of cabin-looking part with windows, and a sort of tent thing up on the roof."

"Command bridge. What's the name of it?"

"Jeez, Kyle, what's with you and Kristy and wanting to know the name of the friggin' boat? You want to watch for it when you're scanning the lake with your binoculars? You can see it without knowing the name."

"Sure, but there's other boats like that, so how would I know it was his? How come you don't know the name?"

"Because I don't give a shit what it's called. Why do you?" My potty mouth is getting bad. I blame it on spending so much time with Kristy. "I like seeing them out on the lake, too, but who cares who owns them? It's not like you're going to wave and yell hello."

"I don't give a shit either, I'm interested, that's all. I like going down to the public wharf to look at the boats. There's some real dandies. Plus the float planes come and go from there." He leans back and drains his mug of beer before continuing, "Kristy is booked for the afternoon shift tomorrow. If it's nice, do you want to come with me? There's an ice cream parlor. We can get a cone and wander around. If we see him down there maybe he takes us out on the water."

"Now you want to go on his boat, too? Tell you what. Next time he invites me, I'll ask if I can bring the two of you along. But for tomorrow, he doesn't keep the boat at the public wharf." Besides, I don't say so but it feels creepy, strolling down the wharf licking an ice cream cone with Kyle while his wife—my only Katawasis Lake friend—is working? Too much like a date.

"No? Sounds like a big boat to take out of the water and only launch it when he wants to use it."

"They have their own dock."

"He's got a boat like that *and* they've got a place on the water? Jesus! I didn't know banks paid so good. Maybe I should apply there! What's the house like?"

"I don't know. I haven't been there."

"Hmm," he murmurs, and takes a long swallow of beer.

Bonita brings my burger. Thankfully Kyle doesn't renew his invitation to go with him to the public wharf.

Later, I leave Kyle at the bar and get home just as sunlight is fading. I make myself a cup of chamomile tea and go outside to watch the sunset on the lake, taking my usual perch on the picnic table with my feet on the seat. Such a fabulous, peaceful view. I think I'll miss this place when my stint here is over.

It's nearly dark and my tea is gone; I climb down off the table and when I start toward the door, I see something on the patio just below my bedroom window. Has Kitty brought me a mouse? I check it out and discover it's a clump of grass clippings. I swept here. How did I miss that? In a hurry to leave, I guess.

I go inside, get into my jammies, and put the video I rented yesterday in the VCR. As I'm salivating over Tom Cruise in Risky Business, I think about Kyle's comment when he learned Fleet's place is waterfront. Call me obtuse, but when Meredith mentioned they have their own wharf it didn't dawn on me that a house on the water would be expensive. I should have known, because my mother and stepfather lived on Lake Bonavista in Calgary and their house was appraised in the high six figures when they divorced. But then, the house was huge and Calgary with its oil money is a different market. Out here, maybe waterfront isn't such a big deal. Maybe the house is nothing special, just one of those places that used to be someone's summer cottage.

One way to find out. I check my phone book for an address, but there isn't a single Fleetwood listed. No matter, I'm not about to go skulking around their place tonight anyway and I can get his address from bank records.

Until Kyle mentioned it, it didn't occur to me that the manager of a small branch who has a stay-at-home wife, a new Cadillac and an expensive boat might be living beyond his means. The suit Meredith was wearing at the Friends lunch was like the one in Dolly's Dresses' window and would pay my rent for a month. Fleet has been on the job years longer than I have and is way up the pay scale, so it makes sense he would be better off financially. But that much?

Easton's comment about a lender adding a surcharge makes me wonder. Could Fleet be the guy who met him at the Lumberman? Are meetings like that the reason Fleet is away from the office so much? I'm intrigued. Seeing Fleet's house might add to the body of evidence, or lay my suspicions to rest. At the very least I can report back to Kyle.

Or, could it be Hal? Did he talk to Fleet about it during one of their closed door meetings, and did Fleet ream him out for turning it down? It's definitely like Hal to refer everything to Fleet, nothing odd there, but surely he'd call the customer back and have him come into the branch to sign the documents. It couldn't be Hal. Unless he's in on it.

I ask myself, in on what? Is my imagination running away with me? I know nothing about Hal's lifestyle other than he wears the same suit, which wouldn't have been nice even fifty pounds ago, every day and he drives a rattletrap Cherokee. He doesn't seem to be living beyond his means. But who knows about his wife and kids? Seeing his house would be a starting point. I check the phone book for his address, find it, and write it on the cover. There. Two places to check out.

I can almost hear Red saying *You are the most suspicious person I have ever knew, always lettin' yer imagination go wild. Ain't you learnt nuthin' from the last time you went skulkin' around where you had no business bein'? Don't go stickin' yer beak in where it don't belong.*

I know it's nonsensical, but once my suspicions are aroused they're like a hatch of golden garden spiders. I would gladly leave Fleet well enough alone. Hal too, for that matter. But I can't. Not until I lay those suspicions to rest.

I've been right before, after all.

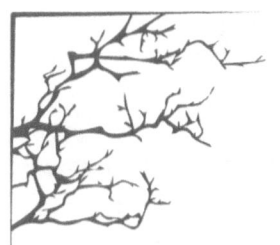

9–Fleeting Invite

Monday morning I'm at the communal computer terminal behind the tellers' stations. I've pulled up Fleet's account and glanced over it, noting a healthy but reasonable balance. I'm writing his address on my hand when Deena materializes beside me. Deena is the file clerk. She's friendly and helpful, if a little too silent on her feet. Startled, I quickly hit the page up key in hopes she didn't notice whose account I was looking at. How does she always manage to creep up on me like that? I paste a smile on my face, hide my hand in my pants pocket, and say, "Hi, Deena. Did you have a good weekend?"

"Hi," she replies. I'm getting to know her since I noticed she always ate her lunch alone and started joining her. "Yeah. Me and my cousin took horses up Katawasis Creek. Camped out overnight."

"Oh, you've got horses?"

"My cousin does."

"Well, that sounds nice. I have horses back home."

"You do? We have extra horses. You should come out and ride with us sometime."

"Thanks! I'd like that."

"You do anything fun on the weekend?"

"Oh, yeah, if you call mowing the lawn and watching a Tom Cruise video fun. You bring your lunch today?"

"Yeah."

"I was thinking of going down to the beach to eat my lunch. Come with me?"

"Sure!"

"Okay! Come by my desk when you're ready to go."

At noon she's at my desk, brown bag in hand. I grab my lunch and purse out of my bottom desk drawer; we leave the branch and go across the street to Rotary Park. It's a pleasant walk down to the lake. We find a vacant bench where we have a view of the beach and the Friends of Katawasis-sponsored playground, and eat as we peoplewatch.

The playground looks nice, clean and freshly painted, so I guess the Friends of Katawasis ladies are on top of maintenance. It's busy with moms and their offspring. The beach and path along it has a mix of seniors, tourists, and office workers strolling or picnicking. Three young men are throwing a frisbee on the lawn and a couple of spandex-clad women jog by on the pavement.

Away from the other staffers Deena seems more relaxed, and when I ask how she likes her job, she says, "It's okay, and I'm lucky to have it. But I'd rather be a teller. I'm hoping they'll need another one when the Saturday morning openings start."

"Don't get your hopes up, Deena. There's talk that new automatic teller machine will mean we don't have to add another human teller. But you could go on record as being interested the next time a teller position opens up. I'd vouch for you and I'm sure Fleet or Hal or Corrine would too."

"You? Sure. Thanks. But the rest? I doubt it," she says quietly. Then she draws a deep breath and shrugs. "You know the only reason I got the job at all is to be the token Indian. Thanks to my uncle."

"Your uncle?"

"You know my last name is Bright Bird, right? Darius Bright Bird is my uncle. Katawasis Lake Cree First Nation owns Katawasis Forest Products and he's on the Band Council."

"Hmmm." I pull the Ziplock bag of Pirate cookies out of my brown bag and offer her one. "I didn't know that, but surely that's not the only reason you were hired. Wouldn't you qualify for the job anyway?"

"Thanks," she says, as she takes a cookie. "You think they'd willingly hire someone from the Rez?"

I shrug and shake my head, remembering how townspeople treat my friends from the Nekaneet Reserve near Wacasko-Wâti, even Felix, despite his being a rodeo star. The way clerks hover around Red when we shop. I lived in a white bread world and until I moved to Wacasko-Wâti I knew people mocked Indian names and how Indians spoke, but I didn't realize how racist it was. Maybe I needed a reminder of how different it is to live in a brown skin.

"So," Deena continues, "The mayor met with Chief and Council to complain most of the people working at KFP are from the Rez. My uncle said they told him the whole point of starting businesses on the Rez was to provide employment for our people and pointed out how few of our people work in town. What do you know, people from the Rez started getting jobs in town after that. I got hired by the bank. I've applied for half a dozen jobs and this is the first time I even got a phone call."

"Was this the first one you, er, met the prerequisites for?"

"No. I've got my Grade Twelve and I also took a business course at North Saskatchewan College and instead they hired Julie right out of high school. I've applied for jobs three or four times before."

"Really?"

"I guess the others didn't last long. There's a lot of turnover."

"So I've heard. I wouldn't have this job otherwise."

"But you're, um, you were already a lending officer."

"Yeah, but only for a short time. My last manager, Everett, he's, well, let me just say he's not like Fleet. He's more... I don't know, *friendly* isn't the right word. At least not friendly the way Fleet is. You know. He never gave me a neck rub. But we're friends. He's the reason I was promoted to lending officer, so you know he's on my side. When R. O. offered me this job, he said I wasn't ready for it, but he vouched for me anyway. They needed someone in a hurry and here I am. I guess that's why Fleet has to go over everything. Every. Little. Thing! *Pfft!*" I hear the irritation in my voice. Deena gives me a quizzical look, so I smile and continue in a more even tone: "Everett said he heard my predecessor just walked out, no resignation letter, no notice even. We figured there must've been some sort of dust-up. You were here then. Do you know what happened?"

"I was here, but an argument? If there was one, I didn't see or hear anything."

"No? Hmm. So, what was he like?"

"Jerry? Nice. Young, maybe twenty-five? Single. Always chatted with me when I was at the copier. Talked about baseball a lot, especially liked to brag about his brother who's some kind of baseball player. He had a baseball signed by a guy he said was famous in a plastic cube on his desk. I thought it was a joke because it's signed by a cartoon character. But he was real proud of it so I went along. Used to pick it up and toss it around, like juggling but with one thing? Whenever we talked. Like I said, he was nice. A little flirty. But nice."

"And he just up and left?"

"Yeah. One morning, his office was cleaned out and he was gone. We had a staff pow wow and Fleet told us Jerry had an offer he couldn't refuse and was going to another bank. I was disappointed he never said goodbye." She sighs and clicks her tongue. "I miss him. You know what the rest of the people in that place are like." She gives me a sideways glance, looks at her watch and stands. "I guess we should head back."

I get to my feet and say, "We've got a little time. Let's take the long way back."

"Okay, sure," Deena agrees.

We set off on the path along the lake shore and turn at the first path leading back to Main Street, three blocks past Western Savings. I glance to my left, checking for traffic before stepping into the crosswalk, and I see a dark-haired man in a black shirt coming out of the Toronto-Dominion Bank a block farther on and across the street. He looks familiar. Kyle? I must be mistaken. Kristy said they bank at Western and never mentioned having another account.

Deena and I cross the street and I hold up on the sidewalk, waiting for him to come this way. If it is Kyle, I'll tease him about checking out my bank's competition. But he turns and walks away, disappearing around the corner.

"Someone you know?" Deena asks.

"I guess not," I reply. But I'm not so sure about that. There was bold white lettering on the back of his shirt.

If no one ever sits with Deena, they aren't climbing over each other to join to me either. Not that they're rude or give me the cold shoulder or anything, but a smile and a hello is all I've come to expect. Deena is used to being an outsider in any group of Caucasians but I couldn't be any whiter, being blue-eyed and blonde-haired thanks to my Norwegian roots. Maybe it's the boss/employee divide and my logical buddies are the managers. In other words, Fleet and possibly Hal.

Hal is at best cool toward me. He probably thought he was in line for the assistant manager position, which would be a reasonable expectation and which of course he didn't get because, well, here I am. Personnel Department in Regional Office made the decision so it's not my fault, but I get why he's resentful. It does seem odd, though. Why wouldn't they promote him and put someone like me in his position? He works so closely with Fleet, you'd think Fleet would've recommended it. I can't understand what's holding him back.

So. Fleet. I can't figure him out. Am I being a bonehead, rejecting his overtures? Am I reading too much into how he always crowds me? His habit of giving me a neck rub every time he comes into my cubicle? He does that to everyone. It's just his way. Maybe at some point I'll get used to it. Maybe spending more time with him is the way to get over my fight or flight response when he comes near me.

I'm back at my desk working on the renewal of the operating credit for Strubb's Brake and Muffler. Just as I get up to copy their financial reports, Fleet comes in and sidles up beside me. I take a step away. He takes another step closer, grins, and puts his hand on my shoulder to give it the usual squeeze.

"Caught you," he says.

"Um, hi," I say. I really do feel caught.

He's still cupping my shoulder when he says, "I was looking for you half an hour ago. Where were you?"

"I, er, was at lunch."

"You weren't in the lunch room."

"I went down to the beach." I'm cornered. I get an adrenalin rush and my heart beats faster. My hands feel sweaty. He looks pleased, as if he knows he's making me uncomfortable and enjoys it. I take a deep breath and tell myself to relax.

He tugs my shoulder as if to bring me closer and says, "That sounds nice. You could've invited me."

"I didn't take you for a brown bagger."

"You're right, I'm not. But my boat's tied up at the wharf. We could have our lunch on it. Plenty of room. Food in the fridge. Nice big bed. A real home away from home. We could make an afternoon of it."

Big bed? Make an afternoon of it? Now I'm really uncomfortable. There's no way to miss his meaning, but I pretend it went over my head.

He leans in so close he's almost whispering in my ear and his breath tickles my neck. I take another step back but bump up against the stand with the fax machine on it. I can't retreat farther. "I usually eat lunch with Deena, but you're welcome to join us," I tell him.

He straightens and takes half a step away. "About that, Lindy. Spending time with Deena. You want to be careful. People notice. It's not doing your career any good."

"What do you mean?"

"You know what I mean. There's our people, and there's *those* people. Stick with our people."

There's a bolus of heat forming in the pit of my stomach. I tell myself to breathe and remain calm even though I have a mental image of my fist connecting with his kisser. I hold the little packet of documents between us as a barrier in hopes it prevents him from moving even closer, and change the subject by asking, "Why were you looking for me?"

"Uh, yeah, I wanted to invite you out on the boat. Meredith's instructions. She said tour, not fishing. So how about it? After work today? Nice sunset cruise?"

What a stroke of luck! Now I can reconnoiter his place without skulking around. But this is Meredith's idea? Really? "That sounds nice."

"By the way, Meredith said to tell you how sorry she is they didn't have enough votes to admit you into their club."

"I'm sorry about that too. I know it's not Meredith's fault. She's always nice and friendly when she comes into the branch. Besides. She said maybe next year." I hope my sigh of regret isn't overdoing it.

He takes it at face value. "Maybe I can pull some strings. Make it so you don't have to wait that long. But wear something nicer next time you're invited to one of their luncheons, eh? Upgrade your wardrobe," he suggests. "Nice short skirt. Low cut blouse. High heeled shoes. I'd like to see you dressed like that around here, too."

"I, er, well, um, sure," I agree. "Soon as I win a lottery!"

"Come on, Lindy, you make good money. For a girl."

"Sure. But I have, er, lots of expenses. You ever hear about the rancher that won the Irish Sweepstakes? When they asked him what he would do with the money, he said he'd just keep ranching until it was all gone."

He doesn't laugh, but at least he appears amused. "Oh yeah. Your ranch. Not profitable, I take it?"

"You could say that. Not yet, anyway. Big capital expenditure because of the expansion, you know." Was mentioning ranch finances a mistake? He's looking at me as if I'm a steer and he's calculating whether I'm at market weight. I say, "About tonight, I'll bring ciders or something. What does Meredith like to drink?"

"Meredith? She won't be there. She's got Friends stuff going on, as usual. You don't need to bring anything. We'll have the boat all to ourselves."

Not an idea I savor. "Well, I, er, that is, I told my friend you invited me out on your boat and she really, really wants to come along. Would that be okay?"

"I suppose."

"Could we do it Sunday, then? Because she works most afternoons but she's usually off Sundays."

"Sure. We can do both tonight and Sunday. Timely, too. I want to talk to you about something."

"Oh? What?"

"Not here, Lindy. We'll talk about it later."

He's nothing if not tenacious and I've run out of excuses. I was just thinking maybe I should get to know him better, but I'd rather do that some way other than one on one where there's no escape. But if I keep turning him down, how long before he gets annoyed? Would he be spiteful enough to give me a bad performance review? Tank my chances for my one-year pay raise? Maybe even get me busted down to lending officer? Damn him straight to hell! Wacasko-Wâti finances are so bad right now I can't take a chance and thanks to my big mouth, he knows it.

"Tonight sounds lovely," I say, and hope my smile looks genuine. "Um, so, what time should I be at your place?"

"Oh, you don't have to go all the way out there. I'll pick you up at the public wharf. My boat's already there, like I said."

"Okay."

As he turns to walk away he says, "Public wharf. I'll meet you at the playground beside the jungle gym at seven." He whistles tunelessly as he strolls behind the tellers, heading for the construction zone.

So I not only won't see where he lives, but I'll have to spend alone time with him on his boat besides.

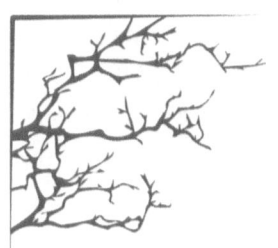

10—Lake Tour

We're only halfway through the parking lot when I spot three men at the jungle gym in the Friends of Katawasis playground. They look our way and I recognize Fleet as one of them. There's a discussion we're too far away to hear, then the other men turn and hurry away. Fleet stands hands on hips as we approach, his forehead creased in a frown, his eyes narrowed. Pretty much the reception I expected.

I greet him with a cheery tone and a big smile as if I'm excited about the boat ride. "Hi Fleet! We're a little early. Hope it's okay. This is Kyle. Kyle, Fleet."

"Good meeting you," Kyle says. He switches the six pack of Corona to his left hand and reaches out his right.

Fleet takes his hand for a quick shake and responds, "Yeah. Same."

"You said my friend could come, but like I told you, she usually works evenings. Kyle is her husband, and he is *crazy* about boats, so I didn't think you'd mind if he came with us. He brought the beer. I brought the lime," I say, and smile as I show him the Ziplock bag of lime slices.

"Yeah, no, I don't mind," Fleet says. "Let's get going, then. My boat's on the last finger."

We follow him along the paved walkway and down the gangway to the wharf. There are fingers going off on both sides of the main wharf, all with boats of varying sizes crowded together. His boat is at the end. He releases the ropes from the cleats, then climbs aboard. He takes my arm as I step unsteadily from the bobbing wharf to the bobbing deck, then goes to the steering wheel, turns the key, and the engines chortle to life.

If Fleet was so concerned about how I'd get aboard that he took my arm to steady me, Kyle is on his own. For a heartbeat I wonder if Fleet's going to drive away and leave him standing there, but Kyle hops from the wharf to the boat deck as if he's done it all his life. Fleet hits the gas and we roar away.

"Wow, this boat's a beauty! Stern drive. Twin Mercs?" Kyle asks.

"Twin Volvos."

I expect Fleet to start in telling Kyle all about those motors and every other detail about the thing as he did when he bragged to me about his boat, but he says nothing more.

"Sweet," Kyle says. He opens a beer and holds it out to Fleet. "You want a lime?"

Fleet shakes his head and says, "No time for beer tonight. This is going to be a quick trip."

"Oh no!" I say. "I thought we were going to see the sunset from the middle of the lake. And you said you wanted to talk to me."

"That was the plan, but something came up," Fleet says. His nostrils flare and he gives me a quick side eye. I swear, if he was a horse, his ears would be flattened and his teeth bared. I know what the "something" is: Kyle.

"That's disappointing," I say, "but since that beer's open, I'll drink it. Fleet's too busy, Kyle, but you might as well join me." I take the beer out of Kyle's hand, root a lime slice out of the baggie and push it into the bottle, then go to sit on one of the upholstered built-in benches along the back.

Kyle gets his Corona opened and limed, then takes the stool nearest Fleet and tries to engage him in boat talk, asking its top speed, how often he uses it, how much it costs to run, details like that. Fleet remains uncharacteristically terse.

We travel along not far from shore past waterfront houses of varying sizes, most with docks. "Lindy tells me you're lucky enough to live on the water, Fleet," Kyle says. "Is one of these places yours?"

"No," Fleet says.

"Are we going to see your place?" I ask.

"No. Time to head back."

I've barely finished my beer and we're already turning back? Kyle quits trying to engage Fleet in friendly conversation and spends the remaining time exploring the boat. He's got more jam than I do, that's for sure, because when he's snooping in the galley, looks up to the captain's seat and sees Fleet glaring at him, he just grins and says, "Real nice."

"Come back up," Fleet growls. "We're nearing the dock."

Not even eight o'clock and Kyle and I are on the public wharf watching his boat heading east.

"So it's called *The Fleetship,*" I tell Kyle. "You catch that?"

"I did."

"It was good of you to call in sick on such short notice so you could come with me. I'm probably just being paranoid. It's probably perfectly safe for me to spend an evening on a boat ride with him."

"The way he reacted when he saw me with you, I wouldn't be so sure."

We walk along the path to the parking lot and get into Kyle's car. He starts the engine. It chortles noisily. He revs it a couple of times as he always does, and says, "I guess she's not gonna stall."

"Come on, Kyle, it runs like a top thanks to you tinkering on it," I say. "You just like the sound."

"You got me. Love a big block V8, except at the gas pump." He grins, revs the engine again, puts it in gear and backs out, then turns to me and asks, "Wanna stop in at the pub?"

"Might as well, since we've got this unexpected extra time," I agree. "Kyle, I'm sorry Fleet was such an ass. He was glaring at you the whole time, and when you went to see the rest of the boat he was watching you like a hawk. As if you were going to steal something. And the way he told you to get back up on deck? Rude! You miss pay for a full shift just to be given the bum's rush."

"I guess he only likes the ladies checking out that bedroom," he says with a chuckle. "Don't worry about it. The only thing I'm sorry about is that I left him four beers."

At work the next morning, I'm apprehensive about seeing Fleet after the aborted lake tour. I decide to be super cheerful, thank him for the nice boat ride, and tell him how impressed we both were with his boat. I've mentally rehearsed my story enough I think I can sell it.

I needn't have worried. He goes straight to his office without saying anything or even looking at me.

Although I planned to check out Fleet's house one of these evenings, I've put that on a back burner in favour of doing it on the weekend. He agreed to take Kristy and me for a lake tour and maybe we'll start from his place then. If that invitation is still open, that is.

I'm sure I'll never get an invite to Hal's place for any reason though, so on my lunch hour I take a drive by. The address is a Sixties raised bungalow on a corner lot. There is what must be his wife's car, a rust-pocked grey sedan, in the driveway. Like Meredith, Hal's wife doesn't work outside the home but I don't see anything that wouldn't be possible on a single income.

Everything looks shabby, with shrubs overgrown and crumbling planters inundated with weeds, paint on the trim boards peeling, driveway concrete spalling. The utility trailer in the gravel area at the side of the driveway is overflowing with yard waste well on its way to compost and has a flat tire and weeds growing up through the tongue. It's not going anywhere anytime soon, but it does explain the trailer hitch on Hal's Jeep.

I pull into the lane behind the house. Through a gap in the hedge I see a girl of three or four in a sandbox. A large woman in cut-offs and an oversized T-shirt is on the stoop outside the back door. She looks my way, frowns, and puts her hands on her hips. She can't see me and it's unlikely she would think there's anything odd about a truck in the back lane unless I hang around too long, so I drive on to the end of the lane and out onto the street. I take the added precaution of going an extra block over before turning back toward downtown.

Once back at the bank, I take some papers for cover and go to the communal computer terminal to check Hal's account balance. It's on par with my own. If he's getting kickbacks, he's obviously not spending it on his house and must have the cash in a sock under his mattress.

The week passes and except for one neck massage I have little interaction with Fleet. He's made no mention of Kyle. No mention of another boat ride. Too bad, because for a change I wouldn't have to make up an excuse. I'm getting a long week-end and I'm going home.

Construction on the new offices has gone more slowly than anticipated owing to another change: the meeting room wall had to be moved back and wiring had to be reconfigured to accommodate the new location of the copier and fax machines. I guess Fleet didn't want to have to climb stairs every time he had to use either of those, but it means now support staff will have to do just that and they use them more than he does. Rank has its privilege, Calvin reminded me.

Also, and I only know this from Calvin because Fleet doesn't confer with me on these things, the order for the carpet was pulled from the first store and a new deal was made with another store, which meant delivery took longer than expected. But everything's finally ready for the cleaning crew. They're due to come in this weekend. That's why it's a long weekend for me even though Saturday openings haven't started yet. Movers are coming to shift my desk and everything over the weekend and the I.T. guy will be in to get our computers set up Monday, so I'd just be in the way.

The I.T. guy says before long everyone will be connected through something called the World Wide Web. It's everywhere already but here in the backwoods of northern Saskatchewan, still a few years off. We'll be set up to use it when it gets here, he says. Probably still a few years off in Maple Creek, too, but I can't stop thinking of ways a computer could be useful at Wacasko-Wâti.

The ranch has been pulling at me strongly, so this unexpected long weekend is a gift. I'm leaving tonight right after work.

It's not just the ranch I miss, but the family, too: with my adopted uncle Stu, their two foster kids, plus any of Red's cousins that happen to show up around meal time, we're one big extended family. So I often end up at the Tall Trees Pub, drinking too much wine and eating too much pub grub. I throw in a Caesar salad a couple of times a week to compensate for all the French fries but I have noticed the waistband on my jeans is getting a little snug.

No Tall Trees Pub today, though. It would have been nice to take off an hour or so early, but as is usual for a Friday, Fleet hasn't come back after lunch so I can't beg him to lock up just this once, and there's no use asking Hal. I'm stuck here until five. At last even Mae is out the door; I set the alarm, lock the door and head for my truck.

Once home, I change out of my office clothes, stuff a handful of granola bars in my purse, and I'm about to run out the door when the phone rings. For a second I consider ignoring it. I've already told Kristy I'll be away for the weekend and got her to promise to feed Kitty and make sure she has water. Red knows I'm coming home tonight. Who else would be calling me?

Telemarketer, probably. Astonishing how often they manage to call right at supper time. Then I hear the start of the message: "Hello, Lindy? It's K.C...." I dump my purse on the counter and pick up the phone.

"K.C.! Hello."

"Oh, you're there."

"Sorry, it took me, er, I was..."

"It's okay. I just wanted to tell you, turns out one of my regulars isn't coming back this fall, so if you're still interested, you can bring your mare any time."

"Oh, that's great! And you know what? The timing couldn't be better. I'm going home this weekend, so I can bring her on Monday."

"Sure, Monday's good. Any idea what time?"

"Well, um, let's see... Probably around two or three."

"That's good. Gives the horse a chance to see everything in the daylight. Get settled in. I'll see you then."

"See you." The line goes dead.

"Awesome!" I announce to the empty suite. I realize it's a good thing Mae was late leaving today or I would have missed his call, gone to Wacasko-Wâti and come back without my horse. Sometimes things work out for the best.

K.C. sure has a nice voice...

Where did that thought come from? I remind myself I'm not interested in romantic entanglements. Not that there's been any indication he's inclined to entangle. But in case that changes, to harden my resolve I mutter: "Big Hat Equals Big Trouble", pick up my purse and keys, lock my door, and head for home with a song in my heart.

With no upstairs tenants to make noise and the fact I didn't roll in until nearly midnight, you wouldn't think I'd wake up at two a.m., but I do. It takes me a second to realize where I am. It's so quiet I can't get back to sleep so I get up and get a loaf of bread out of the freezer to make toast. No margarine in the fridge so I put peanut butter on it and I eat it while standing on the porch looking around the moonlit yard. There's a pond of light in front of the barn. A shadow slinks along the barn wall and in through the door. Barn cat on the hunt. In the distance, a cow moos. The night time sights and sounds of Wacasko-Wâti. It even smells like home. I breathe deep and feel contentment settle over me. I go back to bed.

I wake up four hours later, pull on my jeans and head out to the corrals where there are half a dozen horses looking at me as if wondering what good I am, since I have no hay. These are the horses Stu and the boys are working with to get them ready for adoption. I watch for a few minutes, savoring the horse manure smells and the sounds of their occasional soft blows and tail swishes. A couple come to the fence to say hello and I stroke their necks. My own horse is out in the pasture. I'll hold off going to see her until I check in with Red and the others.

I go up to Red and Stu's trailer, tap on the door, and step inside. Red is at the stove getting breakfast ready. Stu is at the table with a mug of coffee. We greet each other and Red says, "Git a coffee, Lindy! Grub'll be a few minutes."

"Can I help with something?"

"Nope, all I'm doin' here is sausages 'n' pancakes 'n' that's a one-woman operation. Okay?"

"Okay? Pancakes and sausages is great." I get a mug off the rack and fill it before going to sit next to Stu. "How's the work coming along?" I ask. "No more ancient Indian burials?"

"Nuthin' major, thank christ! Another one of them shut-downs 'n' we'd be lucky to finish building next year at this time," Stu replies. He blows out a long breath and shrugs. "Payroll's my biggest problem really. Me 'n' Red're doin' okay with it fer now but we're gonna need help pretty quick, what with you not bein' able to be home as much as you thought you'd be to take care of it. You know we had to hire a couple guys to help with the rhubarb 'n' of course the new saskatoon bushes ain't established yet so they need daily waterin' 'n' so on. But the rest is more'n me 'n' the kids can look after on our own now that Felix is away rodeoin' so much."

"Felix is gonna be sorry he missed you," Red says. She brings a platter of sausages and another of pancakes and sets them on the table before getting herself a mug of coffee and joining us. "Eat 'em while they're hot! 'N' as far as

71

hirin' more hands, it's a temporary bump. Summer's a busy time, is all. We're sure gonna need yer paycheque this month, Lindy. Sorry."

"Knew that going in," I assure her, and help myself to a stack of pancakes and three sausages. As I butter my cakes and pour syrup over them, I say, "I'll do payroll while I'm here. You have everyone's hours?"

"Not yet but you'll have 'em by the end of the day," Stu replies. "Far as construction, that's been goin' good. The big boss contractor's been around lots plus his project manager seems to be on top of things. I just have to ride herd on 'em now 'n' then so's they keep the old part decent so's not to scare off customers while all that's goin' on. Plus they ain't here as often as I wisht. Like today, they ain't comin'. Don't no one work Saturdays no more? Can you imagine a cowboy tellin' the boss he ain't gonna work 'cause it's Saturday? He'd be lookin' fer another outfit before sundown."

"Them was the good ol' days, Stu," Red says. "Hadda hire a couple new inside people, Lindy. I told you 'bout that? We're open later these days fer the after-work crowd."

"Yeah, you mentioned that on top of the tour buses the road crew's keeping the Bistro busy. Speaking of the road crew, from what I saw driving in last night, they haven't made as much progress as I expected. Do you know how much longer they're going to be at it?"

"No idea. They're behind schedule, is all I heard. We're so busy now what with the boys workin' over at Rockin' R so much, dunno how we'd've managed if we hadn't lost our herd," Stu says. "'Member I told you I was talkin' to some guys at the wine festival? They hire seasonal workers, guys that come up from Mexico. Actually have little cottages fer 'em if you can believe it. Maybe we could make a bunkhouse out of a couple stalls in the barn."

"We can't we get enough people from the Rez?"

"It's a small reserve," Stu replies. "Problem is, so few of 'em's cowboys anymore. We got enough trouble findin' them that want to work in the berry or rhubarb patch, men or women."

"We even got trouble gittin' gals fer the store," Red says. "Seems like no one wants to work bad enough they'll commute from town. A forty-five minute drive is all, same as you done when you worked in town. Since you left we ended up hirin' a fella fer the Bistro. Turns out better'n I expected. What with Stu so busy doin' everything else he's never around to do the heavy liftin' 'n' he's a big guy. Real strong. He's a great waiter 'n' even helps out makin' pies when it ain't busy out front."

"Sounds like a keeper." I mop up the syrup on my plate with the last forkful of pancake, then say, "So, what I haven't told you yet is that just before I left home last night, I got a call that a stall has opened up for Chica at that stable near me. So I'll be taking her back with me."

"Oh, that's good news," Red says. "They got an indoor arena so you can ride all winter, eh? Must be some fancy place."

"Pretty nice," I agree. "I hope when the summer rush is over, you guys can get away for a couple of days and come up for a visit. I'll show you around. The lake is gorgeous! There's a big resort pretty close by where you can have a couples massage while you sip wine and eat fancy little snacks. I'll book one for you."

"What? Me 'n' him git naked 'n' have someone rub us all over? Pfft! I don't think so!" Red exclaims.

"I thought that would be your reaction," I say, and laugh. "We could go there for supper but after that lunch deal I told you about, I think maybe a drink on the patio so you can say you've been there, and then to Tall Trees Pub for some real food. But for this weekend, what's going on around here?"

"The usual," Red replies.

"Speakin' of which, I gotta go git the chickens on the barbeque," Stu says. "Store opens at nine 'n' you never know when someone's gonna come in early 'n' want one." He takes his plate to deposit it on the counter above the dishwasher and returns to the table with the coffee carafe to top up our mugs. He picks his mug up and heads to the door with it, calling, "See you down there," over his shoulder.

When the door closes behind Stu, I turn to Red and say, "Red, I have a couple of problems I want to bounce off you."

"Bounce ahead," she says.

"One I already mentioned to you when we talked on the phone. The damn branch manager and his neck rubs. Everyone in town treats him like he's some kind of god, but he gives me the willies. Don't know why."

"Well, go with yer gut, I say. 'N' I don't know what you do about them neck rubs but if he goes too far, like crosses the line, you have no choice. Until then, you suck it up. You won't have to put up with it forever."

"That's pretty much what I figured, too. If I say anything, he can make my life hell."

"If it ain't the branch manager, it's the cook in the diner or the captain on the fish boat or the ranch foreman. That's men fer you. Men who have power over you, anyhow. Always been that way. Always will."

"I hope you don't mean *this* ranch foreman!?!"

"*Hell* no! I'd kill him! You know that!"

"And he knows it," I agree with a chuckle. "He doesn't have it in him, anyway."

"No, he doesn't. I meant just in general. What's the other thing?"

I tell her about seeing Kyle coming out of a competitor bank. "When I told Kristy where I work, she said that's where they bank too, no mention of another account. What if he's hiding it from her? Do I confront him, as if it's any of my business where he keeps his money? Should I tell her and hurt her feelings, and also maybe cause a big problem between them? Besides, I could be wrong, and then I'd just be stirring up shit for nothing."

Red clicks her tongue, then chews her lower lip while she considers it. "Yer right, yer in a pickle. In yer boots, I guess I wouldn't bring it up with neither of them. Not until the time is right."

"The time hasn't been right so far and it's been weeks. When will the time ever be right?"

"Maybe never." She reaches across the table and gives my forearm a rub. "I know I ain't much help."

"You are, though. If you don't think I owe it to my friend to tell her, then I'll leave it like that and feel better about saying nothing."

I'm in the store loading a fresh batch of cinnamon buns into the display case when my old boss, Everett, comes in, followed by his wife and daughter.

"Hey, guys! What a nice surprise! What are you doing in this neck of the woods?" They live in Swift Current, an hour and a half away. Definitely not in our neck of the woods.

"Hi, Lindy," Everett says. "Stu was in the bank a couple days ago and mentioned you'd be home this weekend so I thought we'd swing by and say hello."

"Well, that's great! I'll take a break and join you. Can I get something for you?" I take their orders, get their cinnamon buns on plates and hand them over, explain drinks are self-serve and give them their mugs, with a glass for their daughter's pop. Then I go back into the kitchen and tell Red I'm taking a break. I get myself a coffee and join Everett and his family.

We chat for a bit about what they've been doing since I left: Their daughter, Heather, will be going into Grade Nine in the fall. They're thinking of getting a dog. Emmaline entered three button dahlias in the flower show and won second place overall. Just comfortable conversation about ordinary life.

I tell them as much as I know about Katawasis Lake and how prosperous the town is owing to tourism, logging and the mill. "You wouldn't believe it, Emmaline, there's a store right in the high rent district on Commercial Street that sells hundred dollar jeans and a blazer will set you back three hundred bucks."

"We'll have to go up for a weekend," Emmaline says, and gives me a wink.

"Maybe on a Sunday," Everett says. "That store's closed Sundays, right?"

"Do you think it would be all right if I went to see the horses?" Heather asks.

"Sure. I think my nephews are around somewhere. Tell them I sent you. Don't go into the corral unless one of them goes with you."

"I'll go with her and leave you two to talk," Emmaline says. "Nice to see you, Lindy."

"You too," I respond.

The two of them get up and head out the door.

"That sounds ominous," I say. "You'd almost think you set this up so we could have a private chat."

"I did," Everett admits. "I heard something through the grapevine about Katawasis Lake Branch."

"What?"

"Well, not *heard*. I should've said I saw something. So, I was in Regional Office for a meeting. I'm being transferred."

"Well, that's great! Back to Swift Current, like you wanted?"

"No, Regional Office. I never told you this, but I've been talking to them about this for a while. Since before your promotion even. Ever since I agreed to come to Maple Creek, in fact. And it's not official yet so you can't say anything to anyone, but you're looking at the new conventional credit supervisor."

"Wow! That's a big deal, Everett, and don't worry, I won't breathe a word of it until I see the notice," I promise, and smile although my spirits take a nosedive. Him being transferred out of Maple Creek now, before I'm qualified for the manager's job, throws a monkey wrench into my hopes for the future.

"Anyhow, I happened to see the file for Katawasis Lake Branch on a desk while I was there. No details, but it was flagged for something. There's something they're taking a hard look at. Obviously I couldn't ask questions. So I wanted to ask you about it in case it's something for you to be concerned about. Any idea?"

"Hmm." Should I tell him about Fleet's unconventional management style? How I have to refer everything to him? My budding suspicions? Not without proof. I decide to act dumb. At the moment it doesn't feel like an act.

"Have you seen anything unusual?"

I shake my head. "No. Not really."

"Well, it could just be about the high staff turnover. Or more likely, there were too many irregularities in the last branch review and they're going to schedule another one sooner than usual. Once I'm in R. O. I'll be able to find out more. Meanwhile, keep your eyes open."

"Thanks. I will." His transfer means someone else will be posted to Maple Creek Branch and it's unlikely that person would be transferred out again in under five years. Will I be stuck in Katawasis longer than two years? But it's not about me. It's a great promotion for Everett. I paste a smile on my face and say, "Congratulations on the promotion. You deserve it."

"Thanks. Not everyone's happy about moving to Calgary though. Especially Heather."

"I suppose not. Hard on kids, having to change schools. Leave their friends."

He makes a *tsk* sound and nods.

"More coffee?"

"No thanks, Lindy. I'll go find my better half now. We're going to go to Fort Walsh and then head home. What do I owe you?"

"It's on the house."

"Oh, that's real nice, Lindy. Thanks." He gets to his feet and naturally, I stand up too. "Good to see you," he says.

"You too. I miss my old branch and I'm glad you came."

"Let's keep in touch," he says. He tucks a five dollar bill in the tip jar on the pastry display case, then turns and heads out the door.

I go back to work, ruminating about our conversation as I measure and dump ingredients for the next batch of pie crust into the big mixer. Regional Office flagged Katawasis Lake Branch for something? Doubtful it's the poor office morale, although they might wonder about the staff turnover. Everett is right, it's likely irregularities such as loans not meeting the required down payment or something else equally nit picky.

"Ain't you already done that?" Red says, breaking into my thoughts as I dump the container of flour into the mixer bowl.

I look at the contents of the bowl and realize I added flour twice. Now I have to dump it and start over. Get your head in the game, Lindy, I tell myself.

There's no way I'll be able to guess the reason for Regional Office taking a particular interest in Katawasis Branch. But I already have niggling suspicions and Everett's news adds fuel to them. I'll keep my eyes open, all right.

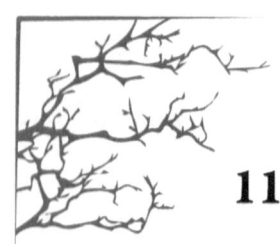

11 – Light in the Bushes

Moving Chica up to Katawasis Lake means instead of having most of Monday at home I'm leaving Wacasko-Wâti early. I have my tack and my horse loaded into the trailer, say goodbye to everyone, and pull out of the yard by nine.

At 2:30 I turn up Windsong's driveway. Chica is bobbling around in the trailer and lets out a loud whinny. When I pull into the parking lot, horses in their paddocks watch and some whinny back. I shift into neutral and set the parking brake just as K.C. materializes out of the near barn and comes to my window to greet me.

"Hey, Lindy," he says. "Any problems on the trip up?"

"Nope, all good. I think Chica will be happy to get out of the trailer, though."

"Well, go ahead and unload her here. You can move your rig and park your trailer up with the others once she's settled in."

"Great, thanks." I get out of the truck and go to open the trailer window. Chica promptly sticks her head out and gawks around. "Get back," I tell her. I have to tell her a couple of times before she complies so I can reach in to release her from the trailer tie and hook the lead rope onto her halter. Then I go around to the back, open the door, and unclip the bum chain. I tell her to back, and she carefully steps out. I catch the lead rope and turn to K.C.

"Nice horse," he says.

"Thanks. I bought her as a weanling. Couldn't afford her otherwise." I know how much a well-bred, halter-quality horse like Chica is worth and I don't want him to think I'm made of money in case Windsong has perks available at an added fee. Like à la carte items in a restaurant maybe. If my twelve-year-old truck with mis-matched fenders isn't enough of a clue. "Where to?"

K.C. leaves me to settle in after showing me my locker, stall (in the big barn!) and paddock. I stay with Chica until it's nearly dark, leading her around so she can have a look at everything, through the barns and paddocks, even the indoor ring. I want to give her a chance to settle in before I ride her.

At the end of the work day other boarders start showing up and I introduce myself and Chica to half a dozen of them. Women from their late teens to pushing sixty, they all have quality horses. Why am I surprised? This town is prosperous enough to have Katawasis Lake Lodge and Dolly's Dresses, after all.

Everyone seems interested in showing and they all ask me if I am. I'm not ready for that! But they tell me when they go to shows, they all stable together and Windsong has a big banner they put up to hang their ribbons on. They say even if I don't enter I should come to provide moral support.

I have found my tribe. It's a good feeling. I can't thank Kristy enough. I might never have known about this place if not for her. It just shows you how a simple decision can change the course of your life, in this case, renting the suite in the same house as Kristy and Kyle.

I'm tired, have a headache and need a shower but more importantly, I'm ravenous. Since I haven't bought groceries in weeks and there isn't so much as an egg or a loaf of bread at home, I head into the pub. Kristy greets me as I take my favourite stool at the end of the bar.

"Hey, Lindy," she says as she comes to put a bowl of pretzels in front of me. "It's long past Happy Hour but I'll give you these anyway."

"Thanks!"

"I expected you home earlier. You in for dinner?"

"Yeah. Haven't eaten all day."

"What can I get you?"

"Mac and cheese, I think. And a glass of house—"

"I know, house anything white that isn't chardonnay. Coming right up." She goes to put my food order in, then comes back with my wine.

I take a sip, then ask, "How was your weekend?"

"The usual," she replies. Then she shakes her head and adds, "That's a lie. We went to Al and Karen's place Sunday afternoon for a barbeque. They're Kyle's friends, really. So of course the guys did nothing all afternoon but talk about football and boats and of course cars, and there me and Karen sat, bored to death. Least I was. I got nothing to talk to her about and she feels the same way about me."

"Seems like guys think all the wives should be best friends."

"Yeah, they do, don't they? Karen and me got nothing in common. She's trying to get pregnant so once she told me all about her menstrual cycle troubles, which I couldn't give a *shit* about, we just listened to the guys and drank the wine. I got a little tipsy. Like I said, we got nothing in common. I feel like she thinks I'm beneath her because she works in a lawyer's office and I'm a lowly waitress. Plus, when I tried to tell her about the book I'm reading, you know, to make conversation, she rolled her eyes. And to make it worse, when me and Kyle were in the car on the way home he said I got sloppy drunk and embarrassed him and I told him to fuck off and he could sleep in the other room. We haven't made up yet. Maybe we won't this time."

"Oh no! I'm sorry, Kristy. But he loves you. One little thing like this won't be the end."

"Pfft!"

I reach across the bar and give her forearm a rub. "It'll be okay. Wait and see. And we can talk about this, er, I don't know. Meet me for lunch tomorrow?"

She nods.

I wrack my brain for something to change the subject. I come up with: "What are you reading that made her roll her eyes, anyway?"

"It's called, um, 'Cowgirl and the Single Dad'. I'm nearly done. I'll give it to you in a few days."

"Thanks," I tell her. I hope my eyes didn't roll. If they did, she didn't notice as she was looking toward the door.

"Oh, jeez! Easton just came in! I do *not* want to talk to him! Sorry, but I gotta get busy." She scoots out from behind the bar, says, "Hey, Easton," as she crosses his path, and scurries to the raised area at the far end of the room.

Worse luck, Easton spots me and makes a beeline for the bar.

"Hi Lindy," he says as he slides onto the stool next to me. I'm surprised to note his clean jeans and Ralph Lauren polo shirt, plus it appears he's trimmed his beard. Thankfully he still has the mass of greasy hair or I might not have recognized him without his faded floater jacket. Despite his new, clean look, he brings a miasma of cigarette and marijuana stench with him.

"Hi Easton. How are you?" It's out of my mouth before I realize I've said it. It's a mistake to ask because he always takes the question at face value and asking is letting me in for a list of grievances.

To my surprise, he says, "I'm good! How are you?"

"Great," I reply, and let out a long breath. I point to the clunky gold band on his wrist and ask, "You come into some money?"

"Yeah. Rolex. It's waterproof and you never have to wind it. Beauty, eh"

"Beauty," I agree.

He says, "So. Did you hear I got my boat?"

"No! Good for you! Got any customers lined up yet?"

"Yeah, I got some good connections now. One major customer already. He's going to need me for a few hours every day. *Every day*, Lindy. When the gyppo calls me to go back, I can tell them to f—, er, go to hell."

"You'll give up logging? That's taking a chance, isn't it? What if the tour business doesn't pan out?"

"I can always go back. They always need fallers. Besides, this ain't a tour I'm talkin' about, it's a delivery service. One of the guys I'm hooked up with, he delivers The Regina Leader Post and the Katawasis Free Press. I mean, he drops off bundles for the paperboys, not that he delivers them himself. And now I'll be dropping off bundles at a couple of fishing camps. There's other deliveries, too, like to waterfront houses."

"Deliveries of what to waterfront houses?"

"Anything. Whatever they want delivered." He leans closer and drops his voice to a near whisper. "The Lumberman sells booze out the back door. All hush hush, ain't legal of course. They only sell to a few guys they trust and I'm one of them. Keep it under your hat."

"Of course. And good for you, Easton!" I'm genuinely pleased for him. The liquor delivery thing is illegal but at worst he might get a fine. Maybe this is a turning point in his life. "So you got your bank financing, then?"

"Yeah. 'Member I told you about meeting that guy at the Lumberman?"

I nod.

"Well, he got back in touch with me. Said he thought about my business plan some more and decided to give me the loan. No surcharge but the interest is pretty steep. I can live with it."

"Good luck!"

"Don't need luck when you got a good plan." He looks around, raps his knuckles on the bar and tells me, "I gotta go talk to them guys. Drum up some more business, you know?"

"Sure," I reply. He goes off and joins a group of men in the big corner booth. When Kristy comes back she goes around behind the bar, gives the bartender her order, and comes to talk to me while she waits.

"I thought you'd be stuck with him for hours," she says. "He's over there buying a round for the whole table. Must of got his welfare cheque."

"No, he's in the money. Got that boat he was talking about. He's cleaned up and got himself a Rolex, for crying out loud."

"Really? I hope he doesn't get a nice truck or you'll want to jump his bones."

"Pfft!" I hiss.

She giggles.

The cook calls out, "Order Up!" and Kristy scoots off to get my mac and cheese. It looks like way too much to eat. That's what I love about this place. I manage to eat every last mac, polish off my wine, and after reminding Kristy about lunch tomorrow, head home.

I'm greeted by Kitty, waiting by her empty dish. Did Kristy forget to feed her? I unlock the door and go in, leaving the door standing open. When I come back with a scoop of kibble, Kitty is on the doorsill with her little white paws almost inside. This is promising. But when I take a careful step toward her, she runs off.

I go out on the patio and fill the kitty dish with kibble, then take a moment to enjoy the view of the lake. There's a boat pulling up to that house on the other side. I think it's the same boat going to the same house I noticed on my first evening here and I wonder about the people who live there. What takes them away every day, to come home at this hour every night? Shiftwork?

Dark clouds are building at the east end of the lake and there's the scent of rain in the air. Clouds often form there in the evening, but the rain never comes this far. Tonight the clouds are roiling and seem to be moving this way so maybe that's about to change. I hope so. The lawn could use a good soaker. Hopefully it'll rain for a day or two. I haven't seen the rainbows the lake is famous for. Maybe tomorrow will be the day.

Kitty is busy chowing down. I hunch down and talk to her for a minute, holding out my hand for her to sniff, but when I try to touch her, she shrinks back. I'd really like to catch her because I noticed a poster about feral cats in the window at Chevron. There's a group of volunteers on a mission to reduce the number of unwanted strays. They catch strays and release them after they're spayed and vaccinated, a good thing because one intact female cat can result in hundreds of offspring in a short period of time. They suffer from injuries and disease. I've try to explain to Kitty that her life would be better with me, but she's a hard sell. I apologize for being so presumptuous and go back inside.

I unpack my suitcase, take the cosmetics bag to the bathroom and brush my teeth. Then I get the aspirin bottle, shake a couple into my hand, and take a couple of sips of water straight from the tap to wash them down. When I open the medicine cabinet to put the aspirin bottle away, I stop. Something is wrong. Things are out of place. The space where I always put the aspirins has my pack of cough candies on it. How is that possible? I must have moved things around when I packed to go away for the weekend, and just don't remember doing it. I put the cough candies back where they belong, the aspirins on the shelf where they always go, and close the door. I turn on the shower, strip and climb in.

When I'm toweling off, thunder rumbles in the distance. I wrap a towel around my head, slip into my robe, and spend half an hour or so on the recliner reading while I wait for my hair to dry. When it's at least not dripping wet, I get a dry towel and spread it on my pillow, get into my jammies, and I'm settling into bed when the first rain drops begin pattering on the window.

I come awake while it's still dark. I look at the clock radio and see it's 3:10. What woke me? The wind has risen and the venetian blind is tapping against the window. Tap. Tap. Tap. I get up, close the window and go through the dark house to the kitchen for a glass of water. As I fill the glass I glance out the window. There's a light, just a couple of quick flashes, in the bushes at the far end of the lawn. Is someone down there with a flashlight? I watch for several minutes but see nothing more.

I've only been down the trail as far as the rope swing and that was challenging enough in daylight. It got steeper from there. No one would be down there in the dark and rain. I must have imagined it. The sky is illuminated by a flash of lightning, followed in seconds by a loud thunderclap and the scent of ozone. I take my drink, go to the bathroom, and get back to bed.

The rain ends sometime before my alarm sounds. As I'm leaving for work, I take a minute to check to see if there are rainbows but see nothing other than grey, overcast sky. There's more rain coming.

I'm turning away when I stop in my tracks. The grass is still wet, glistening with remnants of rain, but the sun is already warm enough to raise clouds of mist. In a straight line leading from the patio to the gate at the far end of the yard, the wet grass has been flattened as if someone walked across the it. The trail ends right where I'm standing. Whoever it was either went up the steps to Kristy and Kyle's place, or across the patio, in which case they would have passed within feet of my bedroom window.

A shudder passes through me and my heart pounds. I take a few calming breaths, telling myself it's nothing. But it's not nothing. Only someone up to no good would be skulking around in the middle of the night. I remember getting up to close the window and now I wonder if I locked it. I go to it, lay my palms on it, and give it a shove. It's alarming how easily I'm able to slide it. I go back inside and lock all the windows. When I come back out I pull the door shut and jiggle the knob to confirm it's locked.

Maybe Kyle went down to the gate. Kyle works security. Once, after too many glasses of wine, I teased him by saying rent-a-cops work for whoever pays them, just glorified prostitutes. He said he's a permanent employee, so he's a purchase and not a rental so I can't really accuse him of being a prostitute. Then I called him a Mountie Wannabe, which surprisingly, he didn't find amusing. I told him it was a compliment because Wacasko-Wâti has friendly cops who come in for coffee all the time, and he reminds me of them. He really does, and I'm not sure why, exactly. Maybe it's his bearing or the way he always seems to be watching everything or his military-style haircut, but it's easy to imagine him in a uniform. Did he see that light and go to check it out? I'll probably see him at the pub later tonight and I'll ask him.

For the first time, I'm nervous about living alone. I can't believe I've been going to bed, and even to work, leaving the windows not just unlocked, but open. Thank heavens Kyle and Kristy live upstairs, over-active libidos notwithstanding. Once the sun was warm enough to dry the lawn so the blades of grass straightened, I would never have known anyone had been out here.

Maybe I'd be better off.

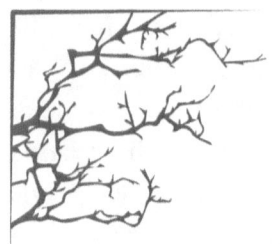

12 – To the Beach

We walked from the branch to the Pioneer House for lunch. As soon as we left the office Kristy told me she and Kyle had made up. If I thought this might be the time to tell her about my sighting of Kyle at another bank, it's off the table now.

We're nearly finished eating when she seems to think I need to know more about the current state of her marriage. "We had great make-up sex," she says.

"Um, good," I reply.

"He's got this new idea. A new position he likes. I'm on my back and he—"

"Too much information, Kristy," I interject.

"Yeah, sorry. I guess that's kinda rubbing your nose in it."

I shrug and assure her, "I'm just happy you guys made up."

"Yeah, we're all good until the next time. Honest, he can be such a stick-in-the-mud."

"He's a good guy, Kristy. A decent man who loves you. And handsome, too."

"Don't forget a good lay. Or is that too much information too?" she asks as she grins coquettishly, stabs her last shrimp and pushes it around in the alfredo sauce.

"I could've figured that out on my own, at least if all it takes is stamina." She gives me a quizzical look. "I live downstairs from you, remember?"

"Oh, you mean..."

I nod.

"Cool!"

"It's better since you moved your bed to the front room," I tell her. She doesn't look embarrassed. With her exhibitionist tendencies, she probably likes me knowing when they're doing the nasty. I change the subject: "Hey, have you ever seen anyone coming through our yard? Like cutting through to get to the gate at the end?"

"No. Why would anyone do that?"

"That's what I can't figure out." I tell her about the light and the trail of flattened grass. "I thought maybe you went to see who was down there."

"Well, I don't know anything about any flashlight in the bushes and if I had seen it you must be nuts if you think I would go out, even if it wasn't raining."

"I meant Kyle, really. Did he say anything?"

"No."

"Can you ask him, though? Just to be sure?"

"Sure. If you want me to."

"I want you to." The waitress comes by asking if we want anything else and I say, "Just the bill, please. Sorry, Kristy, I forgot how slow the service is here. I'm already late."

"You leave. I'll get the bill. You can pay me back when you come to the pub tonight."

"Thanks! See you later." I get up and leave. I glance back just before going out and see a man that had been eyeballing Kristy all through lunch is now hovering over her so I guess those come-on looks she'd been giving him in return are paying off. I wonder if she and Kyle can stay together, no matter how many new positions they come up with.

After I spend a couple of hours at Windsong, I stop by the pub on my way home to repay Kristy for my lunch and ask if she had spoken to Kyle about the tracks through the grass.

"Yeah, and he said it was likely raccoons," she says.

"I've never seen racoons in our yard," I respond.

"Well, you wouldn't, would you? They come around at night. Kyle says you're attracting them by having food out for that stray cat."

"Oh. Maybe. But what about the flash of light?"

"He thinks you imagined it. Or maybe it was someone on a boat scanning the shore with a spotlight. He said to tell you it's nothing to worry about."

I'm not satisfied but don't want to argue. I'll talk to Kyle about it myself because I think I can sell it better than Kristy did, but tonight I'm too late, since Kyle has been here and gone. Kristy has more thoughts on the subject, though.

"You know, about someone coming into our yard... You know what I think?" she asks as she clears the empty Caesar salad bowl from in front of me.

"What? And don't say racoons."

"Okay, I won't. Here's what I think: you've been reading so many romance novels you're fantasizing about the pirate prince coming up from his ship on the lake to ravish you! You need a man!" She gives the bar a wipe with her cloth.

"You always think everything's about sex, Kristy."

"Everything always *is* about sex. I wonder how you don't know that by now. Hey! How about the guy in the blue ball cap over by the fireplace? Wanna meet him? He's a fishing guide. He might have a nice truck. Want me to go ask?" She giggles. "Ya know, if you say it a certain way, that sounds *deliciously* dirty. *'Hey, big guy! You got a nice truck?'* See what I mean?"

She's threatened to introduce me to pretty well every guy in the pub at one time or another, even hauled a few over to meet me. I don't even turn my head to see who she's talking about this time. "Thanks, but no thanks. I'm heading out." I put a twenty on the bar and leave.

Kristy doesn't believe I'm serious about taking a break from boyfriends or that I don't want what she calls a friend with benefits (although my resolve is weakening in regard to the latter). She doesn't believe there's anything to the light in the bushes or the path in the wet grass. I'll wait and talk to Kyle about it. The last two, anyway.

But first, some detective work.

Saturday morning, I'm up early. I fry an egg and put it on a toasted hamburger bun with a couple strips of bacon and a slice of cheddar. As always happens when I make this bunwich I take a trip down memory lane to my first morning with Nick, when he bought me one of these from the Cantina at the Calgary Stampede. It's taken years but now instead of grief, the memory is a blessing.

I take my bunwich and a mug of coffee out to the picnic table. It's barely seven but I hear the neighbor's lawnmower chortle to life. I like to mow later in the day because the grass is too tough when it's wet like this, but looking at the bank of dark clouds in the east and the spirited northeasterly wind it looks like another storm is on the way and later it might be raining again. In that case there's always tomorrow and if it's raining, it just means I ride Chica in the indoor ring. Indoor ring! How awesome is that?

Soon, the scent of the neighbor's fresh cut grass fills the breeze. I draw deep of the pleasant primal smell, think about my wonderful horse at a place where I can ride rain or shine surrounded by people I have something in common with, and feel glad to be alive.

Kyle won't be up for hours and I have to go to Windsong for my first lesson right after lunch, so I'll explore the no man's land beyond the gate on my own this morning. What do I hope to find? If nothing else, a bit of beach or at least a nice picnic spot, in which case I won't bother Kyle with questions about the light and so on. But if there are signs of human traffic, maybe we should do something about it. What, exactly, I don't know. Maybe Kristy and Kyle don't care if people can come up from the bush and go through our yard since their windows are out of reach, but it gives me the heebie jeebies thinking someone could be looking in my windows while I sleep. I can make sure to close the blinds, but I'd rather they weren't out there at all. Maybe the fix is as simple as putting a lock on the gate.

I go back inside, deposit my mug in the sink and get my Nikes from the boot tray by the door. Once they're laced up, I set off across the lawn and through the gate into the bush.

It's five degrees cooler in the shade as I start down the trail. I wish I'd worn a jacket or at least a long-sleeved shirt. The ground is a little slippery and a lot rocky. I'm being careful, studying my surroundings as I go. There are deer tracks but no human footprints, not unexpected after that rain.

But neither are there scraps of clothing snagged on branches or a carelessly discarded cigarette pack or a Tim Horton's paper cup. I was an idiot if I really thought there would be.

When I get to the flat spot that is the take-off point for riding the rope swing I hold up and scan the bush, listening to birdsong and the rustlings of small animals. Somewhere nearby a raven squawks. I scan the canopy but can't see it. Then with a clattering of wings and several more loud squawks, it lifts off from above me. Now I spot the seemingly haphazard knot of branches that is its nest.

The Cree believe ravens are tricksters, but also paradoxically symbolize both death and fertility. I'm not spiritual so I don't believe any of it, but given a choice between death and fertility, I'd chose the latter. Maybe it's a good thing I've sworn off men. I'll stay on the birth control pills though, just in case.

From here, there's a sharp decline in the path. I grab branches and half walk, half slide down to where the path flattens again. It's fairly easy going after that. In minutes I'm standing on a narrow, sandy shingle with water lapping at my feet. Ridges of rock jut out into the lake on both sides, so you'd have to wade to get farther along the shore in either direction. Sheltered and private it's a prime picnic spot, even if the hike back up won't be fun.

At the edge of the vegetation there are logs partly buried in the sand. One closest to where the sand stops and the vegetation begins is propped up on another, making it an ideal height to sit on. I go and park my keister on it, regretting not having brought a travel mug of coffee with me to enjoy and let myself become one with my surroundings.

But since I don't have coffee there's no reason to stay. I get up to start back but have only taken a couple of steps when I spot something behind the log, almost hidden by the dogwood. Cigarette butts? I go for a closer look and find dozens of them, as if someone sat just about where I did and used that patch of sand as an ashtray. I pick one up. Its logo is half burned off but still complete enough to identify the brand: Sportsman.

Someone was definitely here, on this beach, and often. Evidence! I select a couple of the more recent-looking ones then realize I can't put them in my pocket because they'll be smashed. I carefully close them in my hand and start the trek back up the bank.

A gust of wind heavy enough to make even the biggest aspens rock is followed by a loud boom of thunder. Rain starts pelting down. This is not a safe place in a storm even if you don't mind getting wet. I quicken my steps but rainwater is running off my head and down my face by the time I reach the steep section under the rope swing. From this side, it looks vertical and muddy rivulets run down it. I'm going to need both hands on branches to climb so I need to do something with the butts. I carefully slip them into my jeans pocket, grab branches, and climb.

Near the top, my feet slip and I'm on my knees in the mud. I crawl the last couple of feet. Once on flat ground, I get to my feet and start off at a jog. I'm flat out running when I reach the gate and cross the lawn to the shelter of my covered patio.

Once in my suite, I ditch my wet shoes and socks and peel off my t-shirt and muddy jeans, leaving everything in a heap on the entryway floor. I trot through to the bathroom to towel off as much as possible, wrap my hair in the towel, then go to my room and don dry clothes. I take the clothes hamper to the laundry room and empty it into the washer, then get my wet clothes from the entryway and add them. The towel off my head completes the careless mix of colours that would make Red shake her head. I set the water temp to cold wash and cold rinse in hopes it's enough to stop the dye from the turquoise shirt from running, dump in detergent and start the machine.

There's half a carafe of coffee on the warmer, still hot. It both looks and smells like shoe polish but it'll do until the fresh pot is ready. I fill a mug before pouring the rest down the drain, then dump water and fresh grounds into the coffeemaker and push the on button.

The message light on my phone is flashing. It's Devon, the barn manager, saying the barn is closed until further notice because some of the cottonwoods blew down on the driveway and she doesn't know how long it will take to clear them. She'll call when the driveway is open again. So, no lesson. I wonder if my disappointment is because I won't be able to ride, or because I won't have Mister K. C. Garland to myself for forty-five minutes. My god, where did that come from?

Mug of coffee sludge in hand, I get comfortable on the recliner with "Taming The Cowboy", Kristy's latest hand-me down paperback. She's switched from romance on the high seas to romance on the bald open prairie, with titles like "Ranch Romance" or "Summer Boyfriend (Romance at the Double K)" or "Rodeo Romance". I'm pretty sure "Taming The Cowboy" will be like the others, mindless escapism. Still, I admire the cover photo of the bare chested guy with the big silver buckle on his belt more than I need to.

By the time the fresh pot of coffee is ready it's raining so hard the gutters are overflowing; water pounding on the concrete sounds like Niagara Falls, and a glance out the window shows the hedges whipping around in the wind. And there pressed up against the glass huddles a very bedraggled Kitty. I get kibble and go to the door, hoping to entice her inside. She's reluctant but I'm able to get close enough to grab her by the scruff and pull her inside, quickly closing the door.

"Congratulations, Kitty! You've been adopted!"

She's not impressed and promptly skitters off and starts yowling. It's surprising a creature so small can produce such volume. But she begins reconnaissance, a good sign. I'll probably eventually have to haul her out from behind the couch or under the bed but for now, she's dry and safe. I put her food in the laundry room and decide I'll put off venturing out to get litter and a box for it until after lunch. She likely won't come out to find it until tonight anyway.

At least I don't have to feel guilty about drinking coffee and reading instead of mowing the lawn. I put a pot of chili on to simmer while I read. I have a cornbread mix and I'll get that in the oven to go with it. Having the oven on will take the damp chill off my suite too. And with a nice spread like that to offer, I'll invite Kyle and Kristy down for an early supper and show them the cigarette butts then.

The cigarette butts!

Too late I remember they're in my jeans pocket. I bolt into the laundry room, punch the control knob to stop the washer, open the lid and paw through the wet mass to pull out the jeans. Which pocket? Which pocket? I stick my hand inside the front right pocket and carefully turn it inside out. The filters survived. The rest is a mess.

"Shit!" I exclaim, and put the remains of the butts on a Kleenex. "Detective Lindy, you're fired."

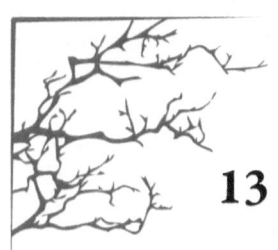

13 – Neighbors Fighting

The nearby Safeway supermarket has a few pet supplies. I select a litter tray and a box of litter, plus a cardboard scratching board, a couple of furry mouse toys, kibble and some tinned cat food. As I leave the store with my purchases, I pass a table set up under the front canopy where a couple of ladies are handing out brochures, hoping for donations. Normally I ignore these grifters, but when I notice the brochure has a photo of a cat that looks like my kitty, I stop. Like the poster I saw a Chevron, the charity is called CatNap.

"Hello," I say. "You chose a lousy day to be doing this!"

"That's for sure. Don't think we'll be staying much longer."

"What is CatNap?" I ask.

The younger of the two women says, "It's short for Cats Need Assistance and Protection. We rescue feral cats. We call it CatNapping them."

"How do you do, er, how do you, um, CatNap them?"

"In live traps. Volunteers trap feral cats, or what you might call strays. We have them spayed or neutered, vaccinated, and if they need other vetting like broken teeth pulled, we get that done. Then we release them back where we found them."

"So, that helps them?"

"Yes. No more fighting, if they're toms. No more endless cycle of litters, for females. And they're protected against disease. Plus, if we catch the babies and they're not crazy wild, they go to SPCA for adoption."

"Well then, I guess I just CatNapped a stray cat. She's been hanging around for weeks, and I was finally able to grab her and pull her inside this morning."

"She's tame enough you can touch her?"

"Well, it took her a while to trust me and now I think she might be sorry she did. She's hiding under my bed at the moment. I hope she'll eventually get used to the idea."

"She will. Give her time."

The older woman says, "Sounds like you'd be a great CatNapper! We're always looking for volunteers. Would you be interested?"

"Maybe," I agree. "Right now I have company coming so I have to get home. But I'll think about it." I wave the brochure before tucking it in one of my grocery bags, drop one of the new gold-coloured dollar coins everyone is calling a Loonie in the donation jar, and hurry out through the bucketing down rain to my truck.

I've just filled the litter box and left the laundry room when the door bell rings. Before I get there, I hear the door open and Kristy calling out, "Hello! We're here!" She and Kyle materialize in my kitchen.

"Hey, something sure smells good," Kyle says. He spots the cornbread on the counter, puts a six pack of Corona down next to it and goes to the stove to have a look in the chili pot. "Mmmm! Thought you were like my wife and couldn't cook."

"I'm a pretty good cook," Kristy contradicts, "and like Joni Mitchell, I'm sittin' on my groceries."

Kyle fixes her with a disapproving frown. I shake my head but can't help grinning. I tell him, "Hold off making a judgment until you taste it. The cornbread should be okay, though, being as it's from a mix."

"Kyle thought Corona would be better than wine, since you said you were making chili," Kristy says. "When we drink this, there's another six pack in our fridge."

"That's great. Thank you! Thought I saw your car at Tall Trees but I couldn't believe you'd go out in this weather." I keep three bottles out and put the others in the fridge. I hand him a bottle opener.

"Well, you went out. How come?" Kyle asks.

"I finally was able to grab Kitty," I reply, "so I needed a litter box. For when she finally comes out from under my bed."

When we've each got a beer, we perch on stools at the peninsula. "Have you guys got candles by any chance?" I ask. "I didn't think to get some when I was out. I heard from Windsong their driveway's blocked by trees that blew down. On the radio they say there's trees down all over the place and we might have power outages."

"Nope," Kristy says. "The power hardly ever goes out so I never even thought of getting candles. I guess if we end up in the dark, we'll just go to bed."

"All well and good for you but how does it help me?"

"Did I say me and Kyle or did I say *we*?" She laughs. And laughs. "You should see your face! I sure know how to get you going, don't I? You didn't really think I was suggesting a threesome? You must realize that if I wanted a threesome, it wouldn't be with another girl."

"Don't I have any say in this?" Kyle asks with a leer. No frown for Kristy now.

"No," Kristy responds.

I let a few minutes of Kristy's Tales from the Tall Trees Pub pass and then tell them, "Oh, by the way, I went down to the beach this morning."

"What beach? Where?" Kristy asks.

"Here. Right out our back gate."

"Why'd you do that?" Kyle asks. His dark eyebrows drawn together in a frown make me wonder if I did something wrong.

I continue, "I wanted to see if there was anything there. You know, because you guys didn't believe me when I told you I saw something."

"Oh yeah," Kristy says, "you still think someone was in the bushes and then came up and went through our yard."

"I told you, there's nothing to worry about," Kyle says. "You'll make yourself crazy worrying about it."

I feel like telling him I'll worry if I want to, but I just say, "Yeah, but I found proof."

Kyle swivels his stool to face me more directly. "Proof?"

"Yes." I get up and go into the laundry room to retrieve the remains of the cigarette butts on Kleenex, bring them back and spread the whole business neatly on the counter in front of them.

"Cigarette butts," Kyle states as he pokes at it. "Or used to be."

"Well, I got caught in the rain and fell in the mud, then forgot they were in my pocket before I washed my clothes. But they were pristine when I put them in there."

"Okay, so... How far down the trail did you find them?"

"Not on the trail. Right down at the beach."

"I wouldn't call that evidence," he says with snort. "Bound to be plenty of butts on the beach. People on boats flick 'em in the water and they float to shore."

"Sure, but this isn't just a couple of butts washing up. There are dozens of them, all stuck in the sand in an area about the size of a plate behind a log. They didn't float there. I think someone was waiting there, and not just once. Come with me tomorrow and I'll show you."

"Like I am going to join you in your beach clean-up," Kyle says. He sniffs loudly and slowly shakes his head.

I don't accept that, and press him: "How about it, Kyle?"

"Okay, I guess. But not if it's still raining and blowing to beat hell."

"Of course!" I grin. Tomorrow. Vindication.

Later, after we've eaten the surprisingly good chili, the first six pack and half the second is gone and we've run out of things to talk about, we say our goodbyes. The Pattersons go back upstairs and I go into the laundry room. I'm transferring the clothes from the washer to the dryer when I hear angry voices. There are several loud thumps as if doors are being slammed. This sounds serious. Would Kyle hurt Kristy? Should I do something?

But whatever the argument is about, it's quickly over and quiet is restored. I expect the next thumps I hear will be of the rhythmic variety coming from their bedroom.

But another fight on the heels of the one she told me they had last weekend? Kyle often kind of scolds her about her risqué comments but I've never heard a truly angry word between them. What could this be about? I didn't see anything different about them while they were here. Kyle didn't say much, but then he never does. They seemed fine when they left. What could have set them off just minutes later? Surely he couldn't have dredged up that groceries comment.

I'll see them tomorrow when we go down to the beach and maybe there'll be some clue to what was going on. In any event, it's none of my business. I put it out of my mind.

Still no sign of Kitty. I get my flashlight and look under the bed. The beam dims but before the batteries die completely, I see her eyes glowing. She stares. I try to coax her out but she doesn't move a muscle. At least she's quit yowling.

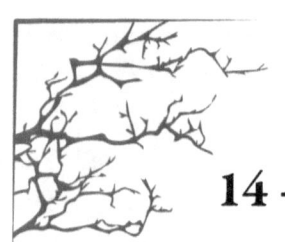

14 – First Riding Lesson

Sunday it's still raining but the wind has calmed. All quiet upstairs, so I won't bother them. We definitely won't be hiking down to the lake unless the weather improves, but I can spend the morning at Windsong and be home by lunch in case it does. Devon hasn't called yet, but I decide to go even if it means I have to walk in from the road and climb over the fallen trees.

I arrive at the driveway but as soon as I turn in I can see downed trees near the parking lot still blocking the way. I back out and park as far off the roadway as possible without winding up in the ditch, get out, lock the door and start walking.

There's the sound of a chainsaw and I see a man in an Aussie Outback oilskin and a cowboy hat on the far side of the windfall. When I get close I recognize K.C., lopping branches off the main trunk. The branch he's working on drops, he lets the saw idle, looks up and spots me. He calls out, "Good morning, Lindy."

"Good morning. What a mess, eh? Shame to lose these trees."

"That's the worst of it."

"What a storm! But I was looking forward to my lesson yesterday. Sorry I missed it."

"Yeah." He pulls off a glove and wipes his hand over his face. "Don't worry. You can make it up sometime this week."

"Good. Thanks."

When I started out this morning I knew there would be trees across the driveway, but the mess before me bears no resemblance to the picture I had in my mind. So many branches! And the main trunk is at least half a meter in diameter, propped up off the ground by the root ball on one end and branches all along the length of it. How am I going to climb over this?

As if reading my mind, K.C. says, "Maybe you should come back this afternoon."

"Um, no, other plans," I tell him. It's not exactly true. It's more like tentative plans. Weather dependent. I'm hoping the rain will clear so Kyle and I can go down to the beach. Otherwise, it'll mean putting it off until next weekend.

"Well, you'll have to go around that end," he says, with a wave at the end of the tree that's a good three meters into the pasture. "It's real boggy out there."

Great. A bog, and me in my only pair of runners. My rubber barn boots are in the tack compartment of my trailer. When I was unpacking my horse stuff I figured I wouldn't need them at least until winter or if I did, I'd need them at the barn. I didn't think I'd need them to get *to* the barn.

Should I do the sensible thing and go home to wait for the all clear call? The rain might pass by then so Kyle might agree to go down to the beach and I'll miss out on riding altogether. Country girl like me, defeated by a little mud? I only think about it for half a minute before heading along the fallen trees and over the smashed planks of the fence.

Although I skirt the worst of the mud, it sucks at my feet and I haven't gone far before I'm in it up to my ankles. I step cautiously, making sure that when I lift my foot, my shoe doesn't stay behind, or worse, lose my balance and can't get my foot out in time to avoid going face first into the mud. My feet completely disappear in the muck and I feel cold water on my ankles. This was a really dumb decision. Too late to turn back now.

K.C. is watching, not smiling exactly, but definitely looking amused. Couldn't he have gone back to work? Of course not. If ever there was a time to say 'what are *you* looking at', this is it. My face starts to feel warm. But I can't let on that I'm bothered, so when I'm back on the driveway, I smile as if everything's great, wave at the mess of leaves and branches, and say, "Good luck." I trot away, my shoes squelching with every step.

He calls after me, "I'll have enough cleared to drive through pretty quick and you can move your truck into the lot."

"Good, thanks," I yell. I hear the chainsaw start up again.

With the driveway blocked and the sane boarders waiting for the all clear phone call, there's no one around other than Devon, who lives in the apartment above the office. The big door at the far end of the alleyway is open and she's leading a horse out. As I go along the side of the building heading for my trailer, we come face to face.

"Hi, Lindy," she says. "Has K.C. got the driveway cleared already?"

"Not yet," I respond. It's embarrassing to admit I came to Windsong and plowed through the mud when any person with a brain would wait for the all-clear. Definitely a Brutus move—charge ahead, consequences be damned. My muddy runners are in plain view so I might as well own it. "I walked up. Had to go through the mud to get around it."

"Aren't you gung ho," she says. I can't tell from her flat tone or expression if she thinks it's a good thing.

"Gung ho, or stupid," I reply. "When I moved in here, I left my barn boots in my trailer instead of taking them home."

She says, "Isn't that always the way."

"The horses were in overnight?" I ask.

"Yeah. They get stupid in stormy weather, so we always bring them in. Which means a lot of stalls to clean. I hope K.C. gets the driveway open PDQ so the working students can come. Otherwise I'll be doing them all myself."

"He said he figured he'd have it passable pretty soon."

The horse tugs at the lead rope. "I hope so. Your horse is already turned out," she says, and carries on leading the horse down the lane between the rows of paddocks while I go up to where the boarders' trailers are parked. I fish the keys out of my pocket, unlock the door and open the tack compartment to get my boots. I turn them upside down and give them a shake to dislodge any spiders that may have taken up residence, trade them for my runners, then go to bring Chica in.

Half an hour later, I have my Tony Lamas on over my soaking wet socks. Chica is in the crossties, feet picked, groomed and saddled, and I'm just about to switch her halter for her bridle when K.C. comes into the barn.

"You all done out there?" I ask as he stops at Chica's head.

"Enough to drive through, anyway. I thought since you're here now and I have time, we could do your make-up lesson," K.C. says, smiling as he gives Chica's forehead a rub. "If you're up for it."

"Oh, that's great! I am definitely up for it."

"Okay. Just let me grab a coffee and I'll meet you in the ring." He turns and walks away.

As I watch him go I experience a warm flutter in my solar plexus. I put it down to apprehension at my first riding lesson rather than the fact that even in the bulky oilskin coat he would give the guy on the cover of "Taming The Cowboy" a run for his money in a Hot Guy contest. "Big hat, Lindy," I mutter. "Remember. Big hat."

I lead Chica out into the arena, mount, and nudge her forward into a walk around the perimeter. I've walked around the ring a number of times, then cross the ring diagonally and circle in the opposite direction. I glance up at the big schoolhouse clock above the gate and note I've been at this for ten minutes and K.C. still isn't here. Where did he have to go to get that coffee, anyway? Then I realize that coffee in hand, he's standing watching me from the window in his office. He has his phone to his ear and lifts his mug to acknowledge me. In a minute, he's in the ring.

"Sorry. That call lasted longer than I expected," he says.

"It's okay."

"So. Tell me about this horse and what your plans with her are."

We chat about her breeding, I tell him I had the help of my cowboy uncle and nephews when I started her at age three, and haven't done much with her outside of riding around the ranch since then. I mention that the other ladies at Windsong were talking about showing, and maybe I'll give it a try. Ranch riding sounds like it might be for me. He says, "Okay, for starters, your walk. It should be a strong, purposeful march. Don't let her just dink along. Even at walk she should be in front of your leg. It should always be purposeful and forward. Let's see her move out."

In front of my leg? What's that? Seems like at least half of her is in front of my leg. I don't ask for an explanation because I think I should be able to figure it out. I give Chica a nudge with my heel and she breaks to a jog. I tug her back to a walk and try again. It's three tries later that K.C. says, "Okay, there's your walk. Now go on a circle around me and up to trot."

I set off and after he watches me go around once, he says, "You know that's a jog, right? Push on. I want to see her trot."

So I do. It's not a comfortable gait and I'm wishing he would let me stop. Instead, he says, "You can go rising. You know what that is?"

"Yes. I thought it was English."

"Yeah, western riders do it too. Just give it a try."

I've always instinctively done it, I just didn't think it would be okay, being as I'm not riding English. But I know how to do it, so away I go. He says, "Check your diagonal."

"Diagonal?"

"Stop for a minute and we'll talk about it.

I halt near K.C. and he says, "At trot the horse's legs move in diagonal pairs. Rising on the correct diagonal means you rise when your horse's outside front leg (and inside hind leg) are moving forward."

"Okay, but why? Thought we didn't trot in western."

"You'll see it in ranch riding. Even if you have no plans to show, it's a good thing to do in your warm up. It communicates rhythm to your horse and helps her develop the relaxation that follows with moving rhythmically. This is new to her. We want her to stretch along her top line. Help her relax and soften."

He sends me out on the rail to go rising trot around the perimeter. I think I'm getting the hang of it when he says, "Check your diagonal. And sit up straight. Think about your seat bones. Is your weight equal on both of them? Your shoulders should be parallel to Chica's. Shift yourself farther right because you're sitting off to the left. Drop your weight into your stirrups." This isn't all at once, of course, it's just now and then as I go around.

After a bit, Chica starts blowing and lowering her head. Thank God he finally says, "Now, prepare to stop. No pulling, just a little pressure on the reins. Squeeze your shoulder blades together, stop rising and stop your back from following the motion."

Chica seems to understand and promptly breaks to walk. I think I must be huffing and puffing harder than she is. I'm sure my face is turning red, and we're only halfway through the lesson.

K.C. says, "I know it's hard work. But you need to be a rider, not a passenger. You're not a backpack on a hiker."

I don't know how to respond to that or even if I should, so I say nothing. Besides, at the moment I don't have the breath for words. Too soon, we start again. The lesson goes on with more trot and near constant reminders to check my diagonal.

At last he either thinks the trot is perfect or he's realized the impossibility of getting me to do what he asks, and he tells me to lope. I may not have known about diagonals but at least I know about leads. I start off on the correct one.

"Push on, Lindy. She's on the forehand and four-beating. We want some energy. Let's get her to engage that big engine in the rear so she's not pulling herself along with her front legs. We want a consistently rhythmic, energetic lope."

Four beating? Something else I'm blissfully unaware of. I thought Chica's nice slow lope was perfect and K.C. doesn't like it. Not wishing to prove my ignorance I don't ask for an explanation, but take a cue from his telling me to "push on". I push Chica on. I think she's as confused as I am. I've always wanted her to lope nice and slow, and now I want her to go faster?

Seems like pushing on was the answer and I think I've got it, but still K.C. has plenty to say. "Much better. Think three beats. Ta-da-dum, ta-da-dum. Grab the horn and pull yourself down into the saddle. Roll those hips. Don't lean. Chin up! Don't look down. Keep your seat under you. Keep your jeans pockets on the saddle and roll those hips!" And more in that vein.

He says, "We'll take a walk break, then try the other lead."

We don't lope right lead more than a couple of minutes when he says, "I think that's enough for Chica today," K.C. says at last. "You can practice in your rides this week. Always warm up in that nice, long ground-covering trot, and make sure you don't practice a four-beat lope. If you feel her four-beating, either push her on or do a down transition and ask for lope again. We'll see how it looks next Saturday. And we'll work on better transitions then too."

Enough for Chica? It's enough for me. I've never felt this exhausted after riding less than an hour. Before I realize what I'm doing, I pull her to a stop then glance his way for the frown I expect him to have. I'm not disappointed.

"That was terrible, Lindy!"

"Sorry."

"Well, do it again. Around me."

So back to lope on a circle around K.C. We do three lope-trot-walks before he says, "Okay. Better."

"Thank you," I tell him. I don't know if I'm really thankful. At the moment I think I'm feeling resentful. I didn't expect him to shower me with compliments, but Uncle Stu always said I was a natural born rider so I didn't expect Mister K.C. Garland to be so nitpicky either. Then I realize that's what lessons are for. Still, I can't help being disheartened. I didn't know I was such a bad rider. I had no idea I knew so little or needed lessons so badly.

"This is a good horse, Lindy," he says as he comes close and gives her a scratch on her shoulder. "You've done a good job getting her to where she is. Being so pretty doesn't hurt neither. And you and her are a good partnership. I'd say you've got potential to do real good in ranch riding. She's six, you said?"

"Yes. She was a late foal, so she just turned six."

"You're off to a good start," he says.

A good start? It sure doesn't feel like it, after all the things he picked at.

He glances at his watch and says, "Well, I'm running behind schedule so I gotta go. See you."

"See you."

He gives me a look I suppose is intended to be encouraging. I notice his smile is slightly asymmetrical. It's not a detractor; it actually makes his smile more appealing. I think maybe his eyes are hazel. I hope he's happily married or in a committed relationship or at the very least, never becomes attracted to me, because I'm attracted to him despite his big hat.

He leaves and in minutes, I hear his truck engine roar to life. Yes, it's a nice truck.

Damn cowboys.

I've put Chica back in her paddock, my tack in my locker, changed my Tony Lamas for gum boots and I'm heading out the door when I realize I left my runners at my horse trailer. I make a U-turn and go out to my trailer to retrieve them. I'm coming back through the barn, muddy shoes in hand, when I see a man come out of the tack room and head for the alleyway door. There are a couple of men boarding horses here but he's not one of them.

There's something familiar about him, though. I hear a door slam and then a vehicle engine chortles to life just as Devon comes out of the tack room.

"Lindy!" she exclaims. A flicker of annoyance crosses her face, but in an instant she smiles and says, "You startled me! I thought you left."

"I forgot my shoes," I explain, and hold them up.

"Oh. Well, you'll be glad to know the driveway's passable. You won't have to go through the field to get back to your truck."

"Yeah, K.C. said. Hey, who was that guy? I think I know him."

"Oh, him? I, um, don't know his name. Just someone looking for K.C. See you." She dismisses me with a wave of her hand, turns and hurries away.

"See you," I reply. Why did she seem flustered when I asked about that guy? And what was it about him that was familiar? I ponder that as I walk out to the road and get in my truck. Half way home it comes to me. That mass of shaggy dark hair sticking out around his cap and over the collar of his jacket. Easton. Why would he be looking for K.C.? Maybe he wants to get him in on the delivery business. Or maybe it's his other occupation. Or maybe it wasn't K.C. he wanted to see, but Devon.

Does it matter? Not to me. Devon or K.C., they can smoke dope or snort coke all day if they want to for all I care.

Then I think about my lesson and K.C.'s touch as he adjusted my lower leg on Chica's side and then my hands on the reins. His asymmetrical grin as he looked up at me and said, "Like so."

I wish well-built, handsome men in cowboy hats weren't so damned attractive.

15—How Not to Succeed

I'm settling into my new office very nicely. I'm grateful for the stairs, because trotting up and down a dozen times a day is great cardio. Now all I need is a way to build core strength. I need to get fit so I can be a rider instead of a passenger.

One drawback to being up here is that it's so private Fleet feels free to come up behind me and give me a neck rub anytime, and for longer than before. He even nuzzles my hair. I'm sick and tired of sucking it up as Red suggested and I'd like to tell him to quit. I just don't know how. He's my boss and maybe he thinks it's a nice thing to do. It's creepy and makes me uncomfortable, but it must not be sexual as there hasn't been another mention of the big bed on the boat. Or an invitation for a boat ride, for that matter. Maybe he's just a naturally touchy-feely guy.

Another downside is that I spend too much time gazing out the window. I usually only do it when I'm lost in thought and it's not always about K.C. or my horse or Wacasko-Wâti. In fact, most of the time I'm puzzling about work and I don't even notice what I'm seeing. It's not like a view of the parking lot, dumpster and back alley is spellbinding.

Overall, having my own window isn't as great as I hoped. I can't even have it open because Fleet claims to be allergic to cigarette smoke so it's forbidden in the branch. I'm happy about that, but it means smokers have to go outside for their nicotine fixes. They congregate under my window on their smoke breaks and the smoke wafts into my office.

This morning, though, movement by the dumpster brings me out of my reverie and I sit up for a better look. It's Hal, and he's not out there for a smoke break. He has something in his hand. He looks around, then lifts the dumpster lid a few inches and slides what he's holding into it before turning and scurrying back toward the building. He looks up and sees me in the window. I smile and raise my hand in a wave. He ignores me.

Now that's odd. Not him ignoring me, that's normal. It's the fact he took something out to the dumpster. What? I could ask him, but he would say *garbage, what do you think?* or more likely, *how's it any of your business?* The custodians empty the waste baskets every night. Why did Hal need to discard one small item that would easily fit in his waste basket? It can only be something he doesn't want anyone to know about. Call me suspicious, but I have to see what it is. I'll check it out on my lunch break.

I get deep into the branch quarterly report and before I know it, it's nearly one o'clock. I go down to the lunchroom and find Deena at a table by herself, as usual. I sit across from her.

"You're late," she says.

"Yeah. Got in a muddle over the R. O. report and lost track of time. Soon as I eat, I'm going for a walk. Coming?" I ask.

"Sorry, can't. I was here at twelve so my lunch break is over."

"Totally my fault. We'll catch up tomorrow."

"For sure," she agrees. She gets up and leaves the lunch room, turning to give me a little wave just as she walks out the door.

I finish my lunch, toss my empty bag in the garbage, and go through the branch to the staff door, which opens out into the parking lot. I stop at the dumpster and push the lid up, holding it open enough to peer in. There on top of the black plastic garbage bags is a file folder. The bin is nearly empty so it's too far down for me to reach but I can see enough of it to notice the tab where there would usually be a file label is blank. Some of the pages inside are pink, marking them as loan applications that go to Regional Office.

If my curiosity was piqued before, it's firing on all eight cylinders now. No consumer loans have to be approved by Regional Office, so what is Hal doing with a folder full of R. O. applications? And why the need to sneak out and toss them in the dumpster? I really need to climb in there and fish them out. I'm looking around for something to stand on so I can do that, when I see Fleet's new Cadillac turn up the back alley.

Fleet needs to know about this. But I suspect he already does. I drop the lid and I'm almost at the sidewalk when Fleet drives into the lot and parks in his assigned spot. There's another man in the passenger seat. I don't recognize him but don't stick around for an introduction, just give them a wave and hurry on.

After work when everyone else has gone, I'll figure out how to get into the dumpster. Maybe I'll get Deena to help. When I get back to the office, I make a point of seeking her out. She's at the file cabinets putting customer files away.

"Hey, Deena," I say. "Since we didn't connect at lunch, how about going for a glass of wine after work?" I'm speaking louder than I need to so Corrine and Mae can hear me. It won't be long before my continued fraternizing with one of "those people" is reported up the chain of command. If he hasn't figured it out from the fact I still haven't showed up in a short skirt and low-cut blouse, Fleet should know by now I don't like being told what to do, at least outside of work tasks.

"Oh, I'd love to, Lindy!"

"Okay, good. I have to lock up, you know. So I'll meet you at the back door."

I'm at my desk planning my dumpster dive. If Hal can take out his own trash, I can too. Since I'm the person who locks up, I'll wait until everyone but Deena's gone to take my waste basket out and dump it. Then I'll turn it over and stand on it to climb in. Deena can hand it back to me so I can get out again and also stand watch, as if we're up to something illegal. It's not illegal, of course, but definitely clandestine.

From the lane, there's the growl of a large truck engine and the hiss of airbrakes. I look out and see the blue NorSask Waste Management truck turn into the lot. What's this? They only come when someone phones to tell them the bin is full and it's a long ways from that. I get up and stand by the window to watch as with practiced ease, the operator slides the forks into the slots on the dumpster. Then with more hissing, growling and clanking, the dumpster is lifted over the cab and its contents topple into the back.

I should feel relieved that I don't have to worry about how to get in and out of the dumpster, but instead, I feel cheated. "Damn! Damn! Damn!" I mutter.

"Damn what?"

I turn to see that Fleet has come into my office.

"I, er, just remembered I wanted to, um, return a movie to Blockbuster after work and I forgot it at home." Coming up with believable lies on short notice is a talent I've honed over a lifetime, or at least since I was a teenager. I probably shouldn't be as proud of it as I am.

"Oh. So nothing you saw when you were looking out the window, then? Nothing you want to tell me? Like nothing work-related?"

"Um, no."

"Well, just a head's up. Regional Office is doing a surprise review. The first guy got here just before lunch so we went out for a sandwich."

"Oh, so that's who I saw with you."

"Yeah. Another guy's coming, though. He'll be here bright and early tomorrow."

"They're double-teaming us? Must want to get it done in a hurry. But didn't they do a review just before I got here?"

"Yeah, they did. So I can only conclude this review must be because of you. Maybe you should go over your files and make sure everything's tiddly. I don't know where he's going to start but he admitted he's interest in your stuff."

"Why my stuff?"

"I don't know. Because of all the delinquencies in your loans?"

"What?" I'm astonished and sink to my chair. "No! You've approved everything. They're all good loans otherwise you would have told me, right?"

"Well, you know me and paperwork." He comes around my desk and stands behind me, puts his hands on my shoulders and begins the neck massage. "You're so tight in here, Lindy. So tense! Don't worry. Whatever it is, I can fix it for you. We're one big happy family here."

He gives a few more rubs. No hair nuzzling this time, and he's digging his thumbs in so hard it's painful. I squirm my shoulders in hopes he'll quit but he starts pressing harder. Pushing his thumbs in so hard I flinch. I lean forward to get away but he holds me in place and digs in harder.

"Fleet! That hurts!"

"Have to get these knots to release. You've got such knots." His thumbs press and press and press. I try to get up but he's holding me firmly in my chair. "You wouldn't be so tense if you were more of a team player, Lindy. Can you be a team player, Lindy?"

"Yes, of course!"

"We'll talk some more." Only now does he take his hands off me, turn and leave.

I lean forward, put my elbows on my desk and cover my face with my hands. No nice touchy feely Fleet today! That was a threat. And it's related to what I saw Hal tossing in the dumpster.

But what did he mean by delinquencies in loans I've approved? I've passed everything on to him as instructed. He keeps the lists to himself but even with his aversion to administrative duties you'd think he'd be interested in slow paying or delinquent loans and warn me if any were falling behind so I could call the borrower, find out the reason and possibly restructure.

I know he keeps the monthly status reports in his office. I'm the one who makes them and I've reported every slow paying account. Does he change them before they're sent off? That's crazy. But I can't convince myself that he wouldn't. With how often he's away, I have plenty of opportunity to go in his office, find them, and see. It's risky, since I never know how long he'll be away. I ask myself, if he caught me snooping what's the worst he could do? Fire me? Right now with Wacasko-Wâti expenses as they are, losing my job would be disastrous. But as long as the inspectors are here I doubt Fleet will leave the office, so for this week at least, it's off.

Meanwhile, should I report that brutal neck rub? I should, but how? To whom? The inspectors? Would anything come back on him? He would just say he was being nice, acknowledge that touching is not okay, promise to do better, certainly never meant to hurt me, and I'd end up shuffled off to another branch still farther from Maple Creek. Or I'm left here and it's an even more toxic work environment.

Everett would know what to do. I call Maple Creek Branch, only to be told he's no longer there, having left for Regional Office. I start to dial R. O. when I look up to see Corrine, the matriarch of our big happy family, at the photocopier. As the machine spits out copies, she watches me through narrowed eyes. Can she hear what I'm saying over the noise of the Xerox? Did she hear me ask for Everett and if so, does she know who he is? Is she wondering why I'm calling my old boss? I smile and give her a little wave as I put the handset back on its cradle. She doesn't return my smile but acknowledges me with a lift of her chin.

Call me paranoid, but I'm beginning to think I'm the only one in this place who is not a member of the big happy family. Well, Deena isn't either so there's two of us. If I'm going to ask Everett what I should do about what I now realize was an assault, I'd best do it away from the office or at least with my door closed. While I'm at it, I should tell him about Hal throwing paperwork in the dumpster, because I think the two are connected. He did say I should keep my eyes open. So I'll put off calling Everett until I know more.

There's always a chance I'll come to my senses by the time the inspectors leave. But I doubt it.

Deena and I head for Tall Trees after work and walk into the dark, smoky room together. The place is filling up with the after work crowd; there are a couple of guys at the bar, one right where I usually sit, so we go to the raised area at the far end and find a booth there. This is Bonita's section and she's taking our drink orders when Kristy spots me and comes over.

"Hey, Lindy. Haven't seen you in here so early since you brought Chica to Windsong."

"Yeah, I decided she could have a day off. I want you to meet my friend Deena. Deena, Kristy."

"Oh, this is Deena from work?"

"Right."

"Nice to meet you, Deena."

"You, too. Lindy talks about you a lot."

"All good things?"

"All good," Deena agrees.

"So, Kristy, I've been wanting you two to meet. Since the Katawasis ladies wouldn't let me join their club, I figured we could start our own. "

"Sure thing, Lindy. What is it, a club of three?"

"Yeah, just us three. Unless someone else wants to join. Friends of Katawasis and Rotary are both gender biased. Maybe we should be more progressive and let guys join too?"

Without a moment's hesitation, Kristy exclaims, "I vote no! To hell with men! They can do stuff for us, but our meetings are going to be private!" She blows out a sharp breath then looks around. Our faces must be registering our surprise at her outburst because she adds, "We are going to have meetings, aren't we?"

"Sure," I agree. "We'll just have to figure out what to meet about. If gabbing and drinking wine isn't enough."

"We could talk about books. Like book club," Kristy suggests. "And go clubbing! That new club out by the highway, Nashville North. Been there?"

"I haven't been anywhere," Deena says.

"Kristy, what about Kyle?" I ask. "Would he let you go to a place like that without him?"

"He's my husband, not my jailer." Kristy frowns uncharacteristically. I bite my lower lip, sorry that they seem to be going through a rough patch so early in their marriage.

"I don't know about going to a place like that, though," Deena says. "It's a long way for me to go home. I'd have to leave early."

"You could get Easton to take you home on his boat."

"Easton?"

"He's a guy we know who just got a boat. He's doing lake tours, plus deliveries."

"I heard about him. He been making booze deliveries to the Rez," Deena says. "If he's your friend, you better warn him it's a dry Rez and there's people who really don't like it."

"Oh yeah? Well, I don't know how reliable he is, either. It was a dumb suggestion. I've got a couch. You can stay overnight at my place."

A man in a ball cap at a table in her section waves an empty pitcher and calls out, "Hey, Kristy! You still workin' here or what?"

"Guess I'd better hop to it."

"Let's schedule our first meeting. Not here, since we're always here. Definitely not at the Kat. Ideas, anyone?"

"Dunno. Whatever you decide," Kristy says.

"Okay, then. You let me know what evening next week that you're not working, Kristy. And in the meantime, we all have to think of where to meet and what would be a good name for our club."

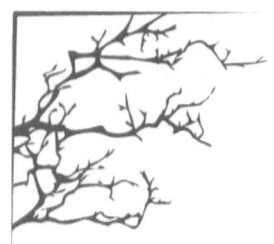

16–The Body

It's Saturday and I had my second riding lesson as scheduled this morning. I rode four times since my first lesson, practicing what I learned, so I was hopeful K.C. would be impressed. If he was, he didn't show it. I told him I would like Chica to go like the other ladies' horses do, with her head lower, and asked him to show me how to get her to do that. He spent five minutes explaining that as long as I'm riding her with an inverted back I'd have to pull her head down which is totally wrong and that she will naturally lower her head when she's softer through the back and working off her hind end. He pointed out we had the start of it in our last lesson, and it's a process. She has to develop the muscles to lift her back and it'll take time.

If I left my first lesson astonished at how much I didn't know, I left my second feeling the same way. At least this time he didn't compare me to a backpack so I suppose that's progress.

I didn't hang around after my lesson but hurred home because Kyle agreed to go down to the beach with me right after lunch. I'm having a coffee and dunking a Cheez Whiz fold-over in it when I see Kyle and Kristy coming across the patio headed for my door. I go and open it.

"Ready to go, Lindy?" Kyle asks.

"Just about. You coming along after all, Kristy?"

"Yup, changed my mind about staying home when I got on the bathroom scale this morning. I've gained five pounds. I need the exercise."

"Yeah, it happens. My jeans were getting a little tight before I started riding again."

"Riding is exercise? Doesn't the horse do all the work?"

"I might have thought that before I started taking lessons, but now I get a workout every time," I tell her. "K.C. said I need to start being a rider and not just a passenger. He said I'm like the backpack on a hiker. I told you that, remember?"

"Oh yeah, and I still think he had a lot of nerve saying that!" Kristy says, and giggles.

"Ready to go?" Kyle asks.

"I am," I respond, and stuff the rest of the sandwich in my mouth.

We head across the lawn and out the gate. I lead the way to the clear area at the trailhead. It's easier going today than the first time I went because now everything is dry. To my surprise, Kristy doesn't complain, doesn't hold us up, and seems glad she decided to come along.

This time the raven I encountered on my first trip isn't near his nest, or at least if he is, I don't spot him. But when we near the beach, half a dozen of them fly up. It's unusual to see so many together and I conclude they must be the parents with their juveniles.

"Damn crows," Kyle exclaims. "You know they eat windshield wipers?"

"Really? Well, there's no windshield wipers down here," I point out. "Besides, those are ravens."

"Ravens, crows, same damn thing. Wish I brought my .22 pistol."

"You have a gun?" I ask.

"Well, I had one. Don't have it now. Gave it up when they started making noise about everyone having to register them," he explains. "So. Where's all these cigarette butts?"

"Well, um, it looks different now. There's a lot more logs," I tell them.

"Probably from the storm," Kyle says.

"I don't even know if the one I sat on is still where it was," I say, and search the bank for the dogwood bush. When I spot it, I climb over the newly-deposited logs and look for the cigarette butt dump. Nothing. I straighten up.

"What is it?" Kyle asks.

"It was right here! Now there's nothing. I wasn't making it up, Kyle."

He comes and stands next to me, shrugs, and says, "Yup. Nothing to see here. I guess the waves that carried the logs up washed them away."

"But the sand isn't wet."

"It dried."

I'm perplexed. The sand here runs through my fingers when I scoop it up, while the sand just on the beach side of the log is damp and hard enough that walking on it barely leaves footprints.

My thoughts are cut off by Kristy's screams. She has her back to us and is on the other side of the beach near where a couple of logs are bobbing up against the rocky escarpment.

Kyle reaches her before I do. "Oh my god!" he exclaims. He encircles Kristy with his arms and lifts her away. "It's okay. It's okay," he murmurs into her hair.

"What?" I ask as I come up beside Kyle. "What is it?" He jerks his head toward the escarpment. There, partly floating between the logs and the rocks, is a man's body. His face is in shreds and there are dark holes where his eyes should be. A scruffy mass of hair haloes his head. His left arm bobs in the gentle waves and something on his wrist catches a sunbeam. I recognize the watch.

"Oh, god! I think it's Easton," I cry.

Kristy starts sobbing. I might cry too if I didn't have such a tangle of thoughts racing through my brain.

Kristy's sobs turn to shrieks. Kyle tightens his embrace and half carries, half walks her away, using his body to shield her view of the mutilated corpse.

I stand immobile, thinking *this can't be real*, and staring at the bobbing body, the eyeless, half-eaten face, and know it *is* real. I don't want to look but can't tear my gaze away. His hand has some kind of glove on it. Then I realize it's not a glove but loose skin sloughing off. Or being pulled off. Now I know what attracted the ravens. Without warning the coffee-soaked Cheez Whiz sandwich comes rocketing up. I bend over a fraction of a second before it cascades out onto the sand.

"You okay, Lindy?" Kyle asks. "Maybe go sit on a log for a minute."

I nod as I wipe my mouth on my arm and turn away from the corpse. I don't make it to a log, though; instead I crumple to the sand, pull my knees up to rest my forehead on them, and close my eyes.

"We have to call the police," Kyle says at last. "You girls go home and call 911. I'll stay with the, er, with him. Go with Lindy, honey." Kyle holds Kristy away and comes to take my hand to help me up.

Together Kristy and I head across the sand and onto the trail. The climb back up seems to take forever. If I'm out of shape, Kristy really struggles. We want to hurry but have to stop a couple of times to catch our breath.

I tell myself there's no urgency. He's already dead, after all.

The rest of the afternoon is like a scene from a movie and passes in a blur of police cruisers plugging up the cul-de-sac, endless streams of people coming and going on the stairs and over my patio. There's a Global TV news crew with their cameras set up on the road as close as the police will allow.

When the first cops come, I escort them through the gate as far as the trailhead and leave them to find their own way from there. Kyle comes back up and joins us shortly after. Detectives arrive. The older one introduces himself as Detective Allard and his partner as Detective Malone. We're taken aside to give our statements. When we're finally released, we huddle together in my living room, drink coffee and compare notes.

We all had to explain how and when we found the body, how we know who it is, everything we know about Easton and when we last saw him. Kyle and Kristy say they told them about Easton hitting them up for a loan and that although Kyle hadn't seen him since that night, Kristy and I both saw him the night he told me he got his boat. I remember Deena said some people on the Rez were taking a dim view of him delivering liquor there, and I told the cops that, as well as confirming I saw him at the pub when Kristy did. But I also saw him after that, because he was at Windsong on Sunday. I explained the barn manager told me he'd come looking for K.C., but I don't know what about. I only saw him leaving so no, I didn't speak to him then.

We aren't alone for long when the detectives are back and have more questions. This time, they come into my living room and speak to all of us at once. Detective Allard looks at me and asks, "So, what did you do after you saw the deceased on Sunday?"

"It rained all afternoon or Kyle and I would've gone down to the beach. I went and got groceries instead."

"Why did you and Kyle want to go down to the beach?"

"Well, really, it was only me that *wanted* to go down."

Detective Allard and his partner exchange a look that says *'it's been a long day.'* He says, "Okay. Why did *you* want to go down?"

"I went down before and found a bunch of cigarette butts, like someone spent quite a bit of time there. Kyle didn't believe me. I wanted him to go with me so I could show him."

"Why did you care about the cigarette butts? Or that someone might have been spending time there?"

"I wouldn't, if I thought they got there from the lake. But I think someone has been going through our yard to get to that spot, and often. I think that's the only reason that trail isn't completely overgrown, and they go through our yard because it's the closest to the trail. You could get to it from the yards on both sides of this one, but the brush is a lot more dense. So if you have to go through a yard anyway, it might as well be this one."

I tell him about the light I saw and the tracks through the wet grass. "It made me nervous. I don't want to think about what they're up to, and they're passing within feet of my bedroom. Usually my window is open. I'm creeped out that someone could've been watching me sleep. Kyle said he didn't think I had anything to worry about, or actually, he thought I was imagining things. I hoped to find something to prove to him that I'm not just a hysterical woman whose imagination runs away with her. I found a bunch of cigarette butts in one spot in the sand, as if someone spent time there or went there often. I had some of the cigarette butts, but forgot they were in my pocket and washed the jeans. And when we went today, the butts were all gone."

"You still have them, though? The butts?"

"What's left of them. You want them?"

"Yeah."

I go to the laundry room, fish the Kleenex with the butts in it out of the wastebasket and give it to Detective Allard, who after a quick look, puts it in a little evidence bag. I can't help feeling smug and give Kyle an 'I told you so' look.

"What do you think is the cause of death? Was he murdered there or somewhere else and just floated ashore with the logs?" I ask.

Detective Allard studies me for a heartbeat before replying, "It's early in the investigation, Ms. Larsen. We don't know he was murdered. We'll have to wait for the medical examiner to do his autopsy." He hands me his card. "If you think of anything else, anyone you might have seen on your street that seemed out of place, anything, call me."

"Well, there is something else I was wondering about," I say.

"What's that?"

"His skin, the skin on his hand, is coming off. How long was he dead, do you think, in order for that to happen?"

"Like I said, we're only at the very beginning of the investigation, Ms. Larsen, and that's another question for the M.E." He gives me a look that tells me it's the end of the discussion. Or, none of my business. Or he's anxious to get home to his wife/girlfriend/bottle of rye. Can't say I blame him.

His partner gives us his card, and says, "Your yard will be behind yellow tape, as a security zone. Ms. Larsen, you'll have to come behind the tape to access your suite, but you, Mr. and Mrs. Patterson, use your front door for now, okay?"

We all nod and mumble agreement before he continues, "The area past that gate and of course the beach itself is a crime scene. There's going to be more people coming and going, and we'll have a cruiser in front of your house to make sure no one that isn't supposed to go in sneaks past. And I'll ask you all to stay away until they release the scene."

"I don't think I'll ever go there again," Kristy says, and utters a quiet sob.

"These things happen," Detective Allard tells her. "It looks like a nice little spot. Don't let this ruin it for you."

Kristy snuffles. Kyle pulls her closer.

"One more thing. We'll need you to come in to the detachment so we can get your fingerprints."

"Our fingerprints? Why?" Kristy asks.

"Elimination fingerprints. If you're right and someone's been going through your yard, they would have to touch the gate. I assume you've touched that gate too?"

"I never touched the gate," Kristy says.

"Okay, Lindy and Kyle, you come and get printed."

Kyle and I nod agreement and finally they're all gone. I bust out a family size bottle of Wacasko-Wâti rhubarb wine and although Kyle is a beer guy, pour a glass for each of us. And we don't stop with one glass.

"I guess maybe you were right when you, er, you know, I mean what you said about someone coming around here, Lindy," Kyle says. "Cops seem to be interested, anyway."

"All I can say is that I'm glad I don't live alone. I mean, I do live alone, but I have you and Kristy right upstairs."

"Yeah, scream and I'll send Kyle right down," Kristy offers. "Just don't do it on the nights he's at work." Her lip quivers and she looks as if she's going to start crying again.

"Tell you what, Lindy," Kyle says, "we can unlock the door that leads to the basement. So, if you're scared, you can just run up. Even if I'm not home you can escape. I don't think you'll ever need to but it might make you feel better just knowing you can."

"That's a great idea," I agree. "It's locked from your side, though. Do you have the key?"

"No, but I'll get it from the landlord."

"Thank you," I say, and I feel a rush of gratitude. "You guys are the best."

It's nearing midnight when Kyle and Kristy go home. I fix myself a cup of chamomile tea and take it along with Taming The Cowboy to bed with me, thinking that as long and as difficult as the day has been, I'm still too keyed up to sleep.

I must have dozed off, because I suddenly awake with a start. I look up and see Kitty has jumped up on the foot of my bed. That's a first, and maybe that's what woke me. I roll over, put the book on the nightstand, turn off the lamp and squeeze my eyes shut in hopes of falling back to sleep.

Then I realize that if someone comes into my suite, having the escape route through the laundry room might do no good at all. I'll have to pass him to get to the laundry room and he might block the way. What could I do about that? I stabbed someone once so I think I could do it again. Should I keep a knife in the bedside table? Not a good choice because it's violent and messy and too up-close. It would mean the guy grabbed me and then who knows? He might be able to get the knife away and use it on me.

I could buy a baseball bat, a cheap one, maybe Zellers has them. I'd have to make my first swing a good one and what if I missed? Or if he put an arm up to deflect the blow, grabbed the bat and got it away from me?

Maybe wasp spray or bear spray. Things that can be used from a distance. Bear spray seems the best choice. I wonder where they sell it.

If it happens at night (which seems most likely) when Kyle's at work, getting upstairs might not save me. Kristy might be asleep and she wouldn't be much help, little thing that she is. I might just be leading the bad guy to her. We'd have to escape out the front door before he had a chance to cut us off.

Then I wonder if Easton caught up with K.C. after missing him at Windsong. Did Devon know where K.C. went and tell Easton where to find him? Does it take a week for a body to start sloughing its skin enough that the ravens could pull it off? Did he die last Sunday and was K.C. the last person to see him alive? I don't like to consider what that would mean.

I'll never think of ravens the same way again.

17—Home Security Upgrade

The discovery of the body is all anyone can talk about and everyone has an opinion on whether he was murdered on the beach, or murdered somewhere else and dumped in the lake to be washed ashore, or drowned accidentally.

I don't mention I was one of those who found him. His name hasn't been reported yet. Deena will surely ask me about it when she learns who it is, but until then, for once I keep my big yap shut. No one questions my need to leave the bank for an hour. I go to the cop shop and get fingerprinted.

Speculation Easton was murdered makes me even more nervous, if that's possible. Johnson's Hardware has a good-sized ad in the Yellow Pages claiming they carry everything for the outdoorsman, so I stop in there after work. They have bear spray. I get two cans.

On Tuesday, the branch inspectors leave without saying anything other than the usual polite hello and goodbye. I had a private meeting with them, but it was brief and nothing was said about delinquent loans. Mostly they seemed interested in me, how I was settling in, things I might like to change. It was my chance to complain about how cliquey the place is in general or how inappropriately touchy-feely Fleet is, but I just told them I've made friends in town and I'm settling in fine. Are they comparing notes, gathering evidence, getting ready to fire me? Or is it safe to quit worrying about it? Red says worrying about the future ruins the present and solves nothing but I'm a worrier, so I worry. It's my nature, like being suspicious. Maybe the two go together.

Thursday after work, I'm unlocking my door when something rubs against my leg. Kitty?

"Hey! How did you get out?" I ask her. In typical cat fashion she ignores me and rubs against me again, this time in the opposite direction. A chill passes over me. The only way she could be out is if someone was in my place and let her out. Maybe Kristy, wanting to borrow something? She'll have left a note. I take a deep breath and open the door. Kitty runs in to her food dish in the laundry room. I search, but there is no note from Kristy.

I was planning to ride, but I'm unable to convince myself it was Kristy who was in my suite, so I'm spooked. I decide to give Chica a day off and go to Tall Trees as soon as I've changed into jeans. I take my usual seat at the short end of the bar. Hedly, the bartender, spots me and asks, "Glass of house Pinot Grigio, Lindy?"

"You know it!" I reply. "Make it a nine ouncer."

He nods, fills a glass and brings it, a coaster, and a dish of pretzels.

"Thanks," I say.

"You bet," he says, and goes to serve someone at the opposite end of the bar.

I spot Kristy across the room, on her way back with a tray of dirty glasses. She looks up and smiles as we make eye contact. She comes behind the bar, sets the dirty glasses in the dish pit, and tells Hedly what drinks she needs before coming to stand across from me.

"How are ya?" she asks.

"Good thanks. You?"

"Well I sure wish everyone would quit talking about...you know."

"Me too," I admit. "I wonder if they've gotten in touch with his family yet. They still haven't released his name, so maybe not."

"I don't even know if he had a girlfriend. Or whatever."

"Yeah. He always just talked about, er..." I was going to say I never heard him talk about anyone but himself and how badly treated he was. Such a persecution complex! Turns out maybe he was right. I take a long drink of wine, then ask, "Hey, Kristy, did you go into my suite today? Like maybe to borrow a cup of sugar or something?"

"No, of course not, Lindy," she replies. "I wouldn't go in your place when you weren't there! Without you knowing about it! Jeez, Lindy!"

"Sorry, Kristy, didn't mean it as an insult. It's just that someone was in there. Must've been Kyle, then."

"Why would he go into your place? What makes you think someone was in there, anyway?"

"Well, Kitty was outside when I got home."

"Kitty?" She frowns and cocks her head. "Don't you let her out?"

"No. I've been trying to socialize her. I've been keeping her in so she can learn to be a pet. And somehow, she got out today."

Kristy's eyes widen. A chill passes over me.

"I'll call Kyle right now and ask him if it was him," Kristy says.

"No, don't. He'll be here pretty quick anyway."

She frowns and presses her lips together. "It would be an asshole thing for him to do, Lindy. Just the latest in a string of asshole things."

I take a deep breath. Hedly calls out, "Your drinks, Kristy!"

"I'll be right back," she tells me, and hurries off, leaving me to wonder how the wheels fell off what seemed like a loving marriage just a couple of months ago.

When next Kristy stops for a quick chat between serving duties, I say, "You know, Kristy, I've thought about it. I don't think we should ask Kyle if he was in my suite. It probably wasn't him, but if it was, then maybe it's better if we just let him think I didn't notice anything."

"Okay, but why?"

"I don't know. I don't think it's the first time someone was in my place. When I went to Wacasko-Wâti a few weeks ago, someone moved things in my medicine cabinet. I thought I just remembered wrong, but now I think otherwise. I have no idea why anyone would do it. But until I know more, let's just keep it between us."

"Sure. If you're sure. Aren't you spooked, though? Even more than before?"

"Yeah. I thought about locking the door in the laundry room again, but that would tip my hand. If it is Kyle, that is. And I'll figure out some way of making sure there's no possibility anyone can get in anywhere else."

"How?"

"Don't know, exactly." I look up and see Kyle coming in the door. I smile and give a little wave, then tell Kristy, "He's here. Mum's the word, right?"

"Right."

"I know we decided not to allow men in our club, but let's make it totally secret. Nothing we discuss goes farther than us Katawasis girls."

When I get home, I take advantage of what's left of daylight to go out the garden gate and into the bush. Since I went to live on the ranch, at Uncle Stu's insistence I always have my Swiss Army knife in my jeans pocket. He says you never know when you'll come across something that needs cutting. He was right. It saved Felix and me from some very nasty people a couple of years ago, although that wasn't what he had in mind. I pull it out, open it, and cut several suitable branches. I strip off the side branches and leaves and once back inside, cut them to the right length to lay in the tracks of all the windows. They won't slide open now.

Then I use the knife's much smaller scalpel-like blade to cut a tiny notch in the frame of the door between the laundry room and the rest of the basement. It's nothing more than a sliver, really, just enough to slip one of my hairs into it, and drape the other end over the doorknob. Now no one can come through a window unless they're willing to break it, and if anyone comes through the laundry room door, I'll know about it.

The problem now is the entrance door. It opens in and of course I can't put a hair across it when I'm on the other side. Since I think the most likely suspect is Kyle, this is probably all I need anyway.

I like Kyle. I really hope I'm wrong.

Fleet remains in the office every day until Friday, when he leaves for a lunch at one. I watch the parking lot to make sure he hasn't just walked down to the Pioneer House, and see him get in his car and drive away. When he hasn't returned by three o'clock, it's safe to assume he won't be coming back. I take a tour through downstairs, confirm Hal is deep in conversation with a customer and Corrine has headphones in her ears transcribing dictation, then go back upstairs and into Fleet's office. There's nothing but a few customer files on his desk. He'd likely keep record files in the drawers.

The left hand file drawer contains no files, just a bottle of Chivas and a couple of glasses. This is a surprise. I wonder if that's the real reason for his frequent closed door meetings with Hal. I slide the drawer shut and swivel to the right-hand drawer. It's locked.

I'm poking through the shallow drawer above the knee hole in search of the key when I see Corrine coming this way. Damn! You'd almost think she was checking up on me. No use slamming the drawer shut and pretending I'm not doing anything because that would be suspicious. As if sitting in the boss' chair isn't suspicious on its own.

We make eye contact. She hesitates for a heartbeat, then tosses the papers she carries onto the Xerox and comes into Fleet's office, her reddening face twisted in anger. "What are you doing?" she demands. "You have no right to be in here!"

"Of course I do!" I've heard it said the best defence is a good strong offence, so I match my tone to hers. "He was working on the Caledonia Glass app and I need the numbers for the weekly report. I guess the app is in the drawer, and it's locked. I'm looking for the key. Do you know where he keeps it?"

She snorts derisively, then says, "No, I don't. And I wouldn't tell you if I did. You'll have to wait and get it from him."

"Sure thing, but what if he doesn't get back in time?" Fingers crossed he doesn't by some miracle actually come back or I'm busted.

"Then it'll just have to wait until Monday, won't it?"

"The report has to go in the clearing today." In fact, the report is already in the bag for the courier. If she thinks I'm lying she might check, but I doubt she's that smart.

That's not fair. Corrine isn't stupid, it's just that she doesn't have my suspicious nature. But the bag is sealed and she'd have to be certain I'm lying and determined to catch me in the lie to have it unsealed this close to pick-up time.

Maybe I give her credit for being smarter than she is, because the fact the bag is always sealed by this time of the day and there's no way my report isn't already in it doesn't occur to her. She believes the lie and comes back with, "That's your problem. You should've finished your report before he left."

Forcing myself to keep calm, I lean my elbows on the desk, tent my hands, smile and say, "You know, Corrine, maybe you should rethink your attitude. Employee appraisal reports have sections for both the manager *and* the assistant manager to fill out, remember?"

"If you put anything bad on mine, I'll have plenty to say about you," she warns. "You know, if the Christmas party fund went missing someone would say they saw you snooping through the drawer where it's kept. You're a real snoop, aren't you, *Ms.* Larsen? Poking around the dumpster. Stalking Hal's house. You're lucky his wife didn't call the cops. I had you pegged from your first day. You hadn't even been here five minutes when you asked Mae about keys. And now this. Believe me, Fleet's going to have plenty to say." Unchastened, she turns away.

I have an overwhelming urge to yell *tattletale!* at her retreating back, but I remind myself I'm not ten.

Suddenly, Corrine turns back and says, "You'll stick to doing your job and mind your own business if you know what's good for you."

"What the hell does that mean?" I demand.

"Keep at it and you'll find out," she says, then hurries away.

"Drama queen," I mutter, but I'm unsettled by her intense glare and the vitriol in her voice as much as her warning. Surely an innocent question about keys asked as an ice-breaker doesn't warrant a threat like that.

As for today's blunder, I wonder if Fleet will believe I was looking for an application. He doesn't pay attention to the reports so I probably don't have to worry. But Corrine might be a problem. Of course I haven't snooped through her desk, but all she has to do is to make the allegation. How do I prove I didn't? Dishonesty is the surest way to get fired.

And what's that about stalking Hal? I take a deep breath and think back. When I drove down the lane, I was at least fifty feet from where his wife stood, with the fence and ragged hedge between us. How could she see me well enough to give a description that Hal would recognize me from? Then I realize that even if his wife doesn't know enough about vehicles to identify my truck as a Chevy, a white truck with a green fender would be enough. I really have to get that painted.

I'm busted, but Corrine is gone and not likely to come back, so I keep searching Fleet's drawer. There's nothing but the usual odds and ends:

paperclips, dozens of pens, a few coins, his Rotary pin, scratch pads and a mangled pack of Juicy Fruit, but no key. I shut the drawer. I'm about to give up when I see the spiral-bound calendar pad on his desktop next to his phone, open at today's date. There's an entry at two o'clock: just initials and a phone number. I use his scratch pad and pen to jot both down, and leaf back. There are numerous entries but only three with initials instead of names. I add those to my list, glance at my watch and decide one month back is far enough. I return the calendar to today's date and note in hand, return to my office.

I'm wondering how to find out who the phone numbers belong to when my phone rings. I answer it, and hear an unfamiliar male voice.

"Am I speaking with Lindy Larsen?"

My immediate assumption is that it's either a customer or another detective with more questions about Easton. I reply, "Yes?"

"Ms. Larsen, my name is Jim Spears, Regional Office Audit. I've been chatting with your friend Everett. He suggested you might be able to help me with something."

As strange as this seems, I agree, "Sure thing."

"Good," he says. "We have a lot to talk about then. Have you got a few minutes for a private conversation or would it be better if I called you at home?"

"At home? Um, no. I'm in my office. I can just close the door. How can I help you?"

"Well, I'm the guy who deals with internal fraud."

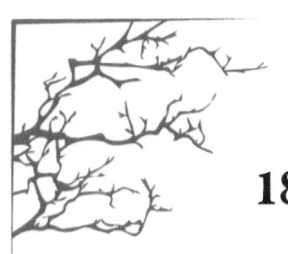

18—New Everything

I'm at the cashier desk at Dolly's Dresses, where the clerk is ringing in my purchases.

"Oh!" I exclaim. "Look how gorgeous!" I pull a gawdy necklace from the rack on the counter, a garish clunky thing I wouldn't be caught dead wearing that has a price tag of half a day's pay. I hold it up to one of the blouses she just rang in.

"It's a Nicolina DiAngelica and it's perfect with that blouse," the clerk says, and gives the rack a half turn so another side of it faces me. "There's a matching bracelet."

"Oh, great! I'll take one of those, too," I say as I pluck it off the rack and hand it to her.

She adds the two new items, hits the total button on the register, then says, "That'll be nine forty-nine fifty, please. Cash or credit?"

"I'll give you a cheque," I tell her. I've got my cheque book out and I'm filling in the amount. "You have a stamp for the payee?"

"We do," she says, and gets the stamp and its pad out from under the cash register. She gives me a big smile as I hand her the cheque. "I'm going to need to see some i.d."

I dig my driver's license out of my wallet and give it to her. "I haven't been in town long so I haven't got my new address on the license yet," I tell her, "but I work at Western Savings just down the street."

"I guess that's why we haven't seen you in here before. Welcome to Katawasis Lake," she says. She writes my license number and place of employment on the back of the cheque and stashes it in the cash drawer. As she hands me my bag of clothes she tells me, "We'll be having a sale soon. New fall items are arriving so we'll be clearing out older stock. A lot of things aren't seasonal, like pants and blouses, a lot of our suits and so on, but they'll be on sale with everything else."

"I look forward to it," I assure her. I leave the store and walk the half block back to the branch. Instead of going to the parking lot to put the bag in my nice new truck, I parade through the office with it. Within fifteen minutes, Deena comes in.

"Did I see you with a Dolly's Dresses bag?" she asks. "More new clothes?"

"Um, yeah."

"Can I see?"

"No, Deena. Some of us have work to do. So if you don't mind?" My tone is sharp and I've said it loudly enough that anyone on this floor could hear. I give her a wink.

"Oh. I'm sorry," Deena says, and leaves.

Minutes later, Fleet comes into my office. No neck rub this time. He stands just inside the doorway and says, "You were a little short with Deena just now."

The best I hoped for was that one of his groupies would be at the fax or Xerox. Deena planned it so when anyone headed upstairs with papers in their hand, she would follow. That was as close as we could get to making sure someone was around to hear and report back to Fleet. But this is much better. Fleet himself heard the exchange, and more surprisingly, came to talk about it.

"I know. I'm sorry. But *those people* are so presumptuous. The old story, give 'em an inch and they take a mile."

He tilts his head as he studies me, possibly wondering if I really could have become such a bitch overnight. I'm first to break eye contact because I feel my face getting warm. A second or two longer and I might tell him it was a joke because she's my friend. In other words, I'd ruin it. And there's too much at stake for me to fold up that easily. At last he shrugs, points at my Dolly's Dresses bag and says, "More new clothes?"

"Yeah, well, I took your advice to heart."

"I thought you might have. I've noticed your, shall we say, *upgraded* wardrobe?"

"I hope you approve."

"I do. In fact, I was thinking you should come with me when I get Doug McClelland out for drinks."

"Doug McClelland?"

"He's the C.E.O. of NorSask Waste Management. I know him from Rotary. We're friendly, but I've never been able to convince him to move his accounts over to us. Still working on it. Be nice to him and maybe he'll finally do it."

"I'd be glad to do what I can," I say, and try to imitate Corrine's swooning adoration so he'll think I've turned into a solid team player, yet another female unable to resist his charms. It must seem authentic because judging by how he puffs up, he buys it.

"Good. I'll set something up." He gives me a wink and turns to leave.

"Oh, Fleet!" I call after him.

He turns to face me and I continue: "I, er, don't know if you remember… I mean, of course you remember, but you offered to take me on a lake tour on your boat and I couldn't shake Kyle off that one time but I was wondering if I could still take you up on it? No Kyle this time, I won't tell him—"

"Sure," he agrees, "I'll get back to you after I've checked my calendar."

"Thank you!" I hope I look and sound like I'm grateful.

As he walks away, I blow out a *hmpff* breath. Check his calendar, my ass. He's playing hard to get, like a teenage girl.

I wonder what he'll do when that cheque I wrote an hour ago hits our branch and gets flagged N.S.F. The plan is for him to order a credit report, discover the staggering sums of phony credit card debt and the big fake loan for the new truck Regional Office set up, check out my drained bank account, and conclude that with financial problems about to get real I'll be receptive to joining or at least assisting him in whatever fraud operation he's running. They're sure he's up to something, but can't figure out what. Enter Lindy Larsen. Thanks a whole bunch, Everett! Well, I get to keep the truck no matter how things turn out. It's a real upgrade, even has leather bucket seats and air conditioning. I do need to thank Everett for negotiating that on my behalf.

I wonder about NorSask. It's the only waste management outfit in the area so it's possible they have a contract with the Rez. With her uncle Darius on the Tribal Council, Deena might be able to find out more, both about the company and Mr. McClelland. It would be a bonus if he knows of some reason McClelland doesn't want to move his company's business to his friend's bank. On the Q.T. of course.

Our only chance of keeping everyone in the loop is our meetings. I talk to Kristy in my nearly nightly visits to the pub, but since we've agreed Kyle has to be kept out of the monkey business I'm embroiled in, never when he's there. Besides, we're nervous Deena and me meeting there on a regular basis might be noticed. I can't be obnoxious to her at work and all buddy-buddy at Tall Trees. Deena can't be seen coming to my place for the same reason. As unlikely as it is that anyone who knows us would see us and report to Fleet, the devil is in the details as they say.

K.C. is fine with us using the lounge overlooking the indoor ring at Windsong. Deena can get there without going through town and if anyone from the branch did spot her, no worries, she goes there on horse business for her cousin. We have a meeting planned for Sunday morning. We can't talk at work so it'll have to wait until then. I rub my face and realize my forehead is sweaty. Being a mole is tricky business. And exhausting.

At last this day—this week—is coming to an end. The branch is closed. Two hours until I can lock up and go home. Even though I have tasks I should attend to, I can't focus on work. I watch the minutes slowly ticking by.

My intercom buzzes and I punch the button. "Yes?"

"Lindy, there's a guy here who wanted to talk to Fleet," Mae says, "but he's gone for the day. I wouldn't have let him in but he was so insistent and he asked for Fleet by name... It's only a few minutes after three so I thought... If he's a friend of Fleet's I...um..."

"It's okay."

"Okay? Will you see him?"

"Send him up," I tell her, and think about how to ream her out, in a nice way. She should never unlock the door for anyone, no matter how insistent they are. She's been working here long enough to know that. I mutter, "Just walk away, Mae. It's that easy."

I go to stand near the stairwell and greet the blonde, good-looking, twenty-something man who comes up. I thought he must be an important customer, like the CEO of a company Fleet might be promoting, but he looks too young. I wonder what I've let myself in for.

"Hello," I say, and stick out my hand for a quick shake. "I'm Lindy. Fleet's not here just now but I'm the assistant manager."

"Ken," he responds. He doesn't return my smile.

"Right this way," I say, and lead him into my office.

"Take a seat." When he sits and I'm settled across the desk from him, I ask, "So, Ken, what can I do for you? Is there a problem with your account?"

"Account? No. I don't bank here. I don't even live here. I came to Katawasis Lake to find my brother."

"Your brother?"

"Yeah. Jerry."

"Jerry?"

"Yeah, you must know him. He worked here."

"Oh. Jerry! I got this job after he quit, so I never met him. Sorry. I don't know how I can help you."

"Can't you at least tell me where he went?"

"Sorry, I can't. Not that I don't want to, but all I know is that he left suddenly and didn't give notice."

"Why would he do that? Leave like that?"

"I, er, I thought he had a better offer at another bank. There must've been, um, time constraints. A reason he had to be at the new job right away."

"Still..." Ken scratches he head, then blows out a long breath and asks, "What bank was that?"

I bite my lip as I try to remember what Deena said about it. I'm sure she didn't say what bank. "You know, Ken, I was never told. But that was a few months ago. Haven't you had any contact with him since then?"

"No, nothing."

"What about your parents? Have they..."

"They're gone. It's just Jerry and me. And it's not like him to... Well, we don't phone a lot but we keep in touch, mostly by mail, usually a letter a week. He likes writing. Wants to be the next Ray Fitzgerald. You know, the sportswriter for the Boston Globe?"

I shake my head.

"I guess you don't follow baseball. Anyway, when I hadn't heard anything for a while I called, but his phone number isn't in service anymore. I sent him a birthday card. Always put a few baseball cards in with it, you know, signed by some of the team, a little birthday present. Who knows? Those might be worth something some day, right? Anyway, I wasn't really worried until the card I sent came back marked *moved, no forwarding address.* I thought he moved and just hadn't changed anything yet, so I called here and that's when I was told he didn't work here anymore. No one would tell me more than that. So that's why I came. It's harder to brush someone off when they're standing right in front of you. You, the bank that is, must have a record of where he went."

"I'm sorry, Ken, I can check the personnel files but they're in a locked drawer in the manager's office. It's too bad you didn't get here before he left. I can ask him when he's back at work Monday, though."

"Not until Monday? The team is in Calgary so I took a day off. Drove all day to get here and I have to be back on Monday."

"The team?"

"I play for the Vancouver Canadians. Blue Jays' farm team."

"Oh. That's cool," I tell him, and really mean it. I wrack my brain trying to remember if Deena said anything else that might help, and conclude she didn't. "Sorry, that's the best I can do. Other than...hmm..." I check my watch. There might still be someone in Regional Office. "I'll make a call."

I phone Regional Office Personnel Department and leave a message for the manager. I wonder if all managers sneak out early Fridays. I look at Ken and say, "Well, you heard. I doubt he'll call back until Monday. How can I contact you?"

"I'll have to phone you," he says. He chews his lip as he slowly shakes his head. "I really thought... Well, thanks for trying." He takes my card from the little plastic bin on my desk.

"Here," I say, taking another card and writing my home phone number on the back. "This is my home number. I doubt I'll hear anything today but next week, if you can't reach me here, you can phone me at home."

"Thanks, Lindy." He smiles for the first time since he came in, and takes the card. He gets up and leaves.

I puzzle over what just happened. Deena was the one who told me Jerry was just gone one day and staff was told he had a better offer. She wouldn't necessarily know more than that, but Fleet surely would. I'll ask him on Monday.

Then I wonder about Ken. What if there's animosity between the brothers and Jerry doesn't want to be found? But that doesn't make sense.

Not if Ken is his only family, the brother Jerry bragged about. He might not have thought to contact the post office to have them forward his mail but there is no valid reason for him not to contact his brother in all this time.

A chill passes over me and I shiver. Red would say a goose walked on my grave.

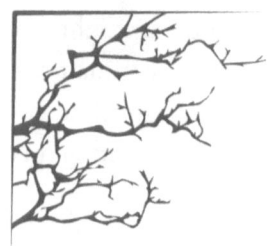

19—K.C.

There's no return call from the Personnel Department manager. I go home, change into riding clothes and head for Windsong.

With no lesson today, I have a short ride, just half an hour or so of stretching and bending and lots of transitions. I'm putting the last of my tack away when K.C. comes into the tack room.

"Hi, Lindy," he says. "I saw a little bit of your ride. Looking good."

"Thank you."

"Where are you off to now? I mean, have you got plans for tonight?"

I stop in the process of closing the padlock on my locker and study his face. "I, er, I'm starving. Haven't had supper yet. I'm going to Tall Trees. You met my friend Kristy. She works there so I get what she calls the 'frequent flyer' discount."

"Nice," he says.

I rattle on: "It's not that big a deal. Usually just means she puts a little extra in the half liter. But I love their Caesar salad." I click the padlock shut, then ask, "Want to join me?" Sometimes really stupid things come out of my mouth. If I thought I was getting smarter about men, I still have a long way to go. I feel my face getting warm and brace for a stream of excuses.

Instead he smiles and says, "I'd love to."

Kristy is going to have a field day with this.

As expected, Kristy is giddy at seeing K.C. join me at the bar. She insists we move to a table, which just happens to be in a corner screened from the rest of the bar by one of the main supporting columns and the only potted plant in the place. In other words, the most private table at Tall Trees. Coincidence? I think not.

There's an upside to having this secluded table. It's a little less smokey and a lot more quiet, so conversation is easy. K.C. and I have a lot to talk about, probably because he was a rancher and horse breeder until about five years ago when he had to sell his property to pay out his wife's share in the divorce. That was when he sold all but a few of his horses and came to Katawasis Lake to manage Windsong. It turns out Windsong is owned by Katawasis Lake Lodge. There are plans for a big residential development, a casino and a hotel.

"They own all the land from the road down to the lake," he tells me. "There's a few houses they rent out. I live in one of them. Part of my salary package."

"Oh yeah? I can see those houses from my place. I've often noticed a boat going from the Kat to one of them. I guess if they're all owned by the same people, it makes sense. Probably just taking someone back and forth."

"Owned, yes, but they've got long-term leases on them," K.C. tells me. "That's actually a problem for their big development plans. Some folks aren't giving their leases up, and they don't expire for another twenty years. Personally I hope they never sell out. It would mean the end of Windsong. But as for a boat going back and forth? More likely it's delivering some*thing* rather than some*one*."

"Oh. Deliveries. To you?"

"No. I'm not in one of the waterfront houses. My cabin is in the bush behind the big house you see from the barn."

"Do you like it there, though?" I ask. We've finished our meals and I've polished off my half liter of house white. I glance at my watch, surprised that it's after midnight. I stifle a yawn.

"I do." He notices me checking the time and says, "I guess we should call it a night."

"Yeah. Long day. Crazy day."

"Crazy? How?"

"A story for another day," I say. "Ready?"

"I am if you are."

"Yeah, past my bed time." We both get up and go to the cashier station at the far end of the bar. Kristy spots us there and comes to give us the bill, with her usual cute Kristy with a heart signature.

"I got this," K.C. says.

"Oh, thanks, but I didn't suggest you join me so I could stick you with the bill. Let me at least pay for mine."

"Nope. Absolutely not. Don't take her money, Kristy," he insists, and hands her a credit card.

"You got it," Kristy agrees, and gives me a wink.

Bill paid, we walk together to my truck, close but not hand-holding close. "Nice truck," he says. "Come into some money?"

Obviously I can't tell him the truth, so I just say, "Well, I work at a bank. I get the employee rate on loans. Plus it's not brand new. Has five thousand miles on it."

"Better than brand new. I have to say, it suits you better than the one with the odd-colored fender."

"I always meant to get that painted. Ended up trading it before I got around to it."

"Well, there's quite a few of these around. Your old truck was one of a kind. Maybe you ought to be careful who you flip off when you're driving. What with all the road rage these days."

Oh my God! He saw that. And he knows it was me.

"I'm sorry I cut you off," he continues. "No excuse, but I was distracted and the exit snuck up on me. I should've dropped back behind you. It was a poor decision."

My face must be reflecting my befuddlement because he laughs, cups my shoulders and pulls me into a hug. His body is solid and warm; as he strokes my back I take in his scent. He smells a little of horse, a little of aftershave, and a lot of man. "I had a nice time tonight, Lindy," he whispers in my ear. "Thank you." He gives my back a last stroke, then straightens and stands back.

"Um, no, thank *you*." I take a deep breath and for a second, visualize grabbing him and pulling him back for a kiss. Just for a second, though, because if that's what he wanted, he would have initiated it. Besides, I don't want to start something I might not have the will to stop. So we just stand there looking at each other until finally I come to my senses, turn and unlock the door. He pulls it open. I climb in and start the engine.

He asks, "See you tomorrow?"

"Tomorrow," I agree. He pushes the door shut. I give him a smile and a little wave as I drive away.

I'm still fantasizing about his asymmetrical smile, deep melodious voice, biceps straining his shirt sleeves, and the feel of his body pressed against mine when I get home. So much so, I have to remind myself to check the hair on the laundry room door. It's still there.

I go to my bedroom and I'm getting into my pyjamas when I notice the underwear drawer of the dresser isn't completely closed. I reach out to push it shut, then stop. Why isn't it closed? It's sticky and you have to push it the last couple of inches, but I always do. Maybe I didn't give it that last push this morning. But why didn't I notice it when I was here to change into jeans after work?

I feel the squeezing of my insides I recognize as a surge of adrenalin, the fight or flight response, and take a few deep breaths while wondering what to do. I decide the best thing would be to see if everything inside is as I left it. I pull the drawer open. It's neat and tidy: bras on the right and panties on the left as usual. It must be that earlier today I just didn't notice the drawer wasn't fully shut.

Then I realize there's a frill of black lace on the top panty. The three lacey black bikini panties I bought in a pack are always on the bottom of the pile. The lace is itchy. I only wear them when there's a likelihood of someone seeing them, which means they're not in the daily granny panty rotation. Since I brought them with me to Katawasis, I have to admit I'm a little wishy-washy on my no boyfriend decision. But they should all be at the bottom of the pile.

In case I somehow messed them up when I was putting things away, I root through the panties in search of the other two bikinis.

I find only one.

That makes two pairs of bikinis when there should be three. No way I could mess this up.

I hurry out to the kitchen and locate Detective Allard's card under the telephone, then realize it's too late to call now. I'll do it first thing in the morning.

Although it's unlikely whoever was in here tonight will come back when I'm home, I dig empty tin cans and a pickle jar out of the garbage and stack them on the inside of the entrance door. Now the door can't be opened without it making a racket. Then with a blanket and pillow, bear spray and Taming The Cowboy, I head for the couch.

It's likely to be another sleepless night.

"So, whoever it was somehow got in through the door. No forced entry," Detective Allard says. "Is this the only way in?"

I'm so relieved that he's taking me seriously I could almost kiss him, even though he's at least thirty years older than I am and going by his breath, a heavy smoker. It definitely wouldn't be anything other than a gesture of gratitude. "Yeah, unless you count the windows and patio door. But the sticks in the tracks make them secure. Oh, and there's a door into the rest of the basement and the upstairs suite. Whoever was in here would have to go through their place to use that door."

"And you don't think it's him? Your upstairs neighbor, I mean?"

"No, it wasn't him."

"You'd be surprised. Stalkers are often someone you know. The pimply cashier at the gas station might believe he has a relationship with you because you smile at him when you pay for your gas. Or it could be an ex-boyfriend. A flirty co-worker you ignore. The guy who lives upstairs that fantasizes about you, but can't do anything about it because he's married to your friend."

"Well, my ex-boyfriends are, er, not around here." I nearly told him my two most recent boyfriends are in jail. Not a good thing to have on your resumé. "There's only two men at work. One flirts with everyone and the other completely ignores me. I mean completely. And it's definitely not Kyle. I'll show you." I lead him into the laundry room and show him the hair on the doorknob.

"Simple but effective," he says. "If anyone comes through that door you'll know it, but they won't know that you know. Where'd you get the idea?"

"I read a lot of crime and spy novels," I tell him. Since he can't have missed Taming The Cowboy laying open on the coffee table I doubt he believes me, so I add, "You know. Nelson DeMille. Joseph Wambaugh. John LeCarré. Robert Ludlow."

"Sure," he says, his tone leaving me with the idea he only half buys it.

I follow him out of the laundry room to the door. He asks, "So you think this would be the third time he's been in? No idea how he's gaining access?"

"No idea. Unless he has a key, but that could only be the landlord or the rental agent and I've never met either of them." I explain how I rented the suite through the rental agent, sight unseen. "How does someone who doesn't have a key get in? It's not that easy to pick a lock. From what I've read it takes training. And practice."

"Yeah. If it's not one of those people, or a previous tenant who didn't turn in their key, it's someone with some skills. Easier to just stick something in. You know a door can be opened with a credit card? You should ask your landlord to install a deadbolt. A lot harder to cheat."

"Okay. Thank you. I'll let the leasing agent know," I say, and nod. "Say, Detective, any news about, er, you know, Easton? Do you know if he was murdered?"

"Lindy, you know I can't comment on an ongoing investigation." He pulls the door open and steps out. "The Evidence Recovery team will be here as soon as they can mobilize. Meantime, stay out of your bedroom. In fact, don't touch anything anywhere if you can avoid it. If the guy had enough time in here, he might have, er, been everywhere."

"I'll see if I can hang with my neighbors."

"Good. I'll be in touch," he promises, and heads for the stairs.

I close the door and even though I'm inside and not going anywhere, lock it.

No riding lesson today.

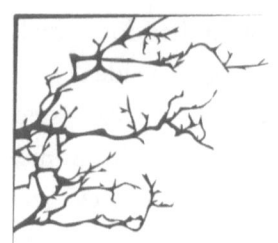

20—Roommates

Kristy says, "Well, so much for giving the forensics guys a thrill. They're both girls!"

Ever since I told Kristy why Detective Allard was at my place and why I needed to hang out with her and Kyle, she had been keeping a close eye on the street, waiting for the evidence recovery team to show up. When the van appeared in the driveway, she came out on the deck and draped herself over the rail, affording anyone coming down the stairs to my door a fine view of her overflowing bikini top. I draped my t-shirted self over the rail and told them to go ahead on in, then returned to the chair under the umbrella.

"So what's the story, Lindy?" Kyle asks. He's only been up for a few minutes. I wonder if the dark expression on his face is because he's only on his first coffee, or because I'm here and his chubby will go to waste. "Someone was in your place and stole a pair of panties?"

"That's right. As you know, it's not the first time I thought someone was in there but as far as I know, this is the first time he took anything. And panties, for chrissakes."

"Clean ones?" Kristy asks.

I frown. "Yeah, clean ones. You don't think he'd root through the dirty clothes hamper, do you?"

"Maybe. In fact, I bet that's what he done the other times he was there. If you didn't leave a pair on the floor, that is."

I'd like to deny leaving clothes on the floor, especially panties, and I'm a pretty good liar, but I let the comment pass. "Why would he..."

"Guys like that want panties that you've worn. You know, so they can smell the klitty litter on them. Gives them a woody." She giggles. "Maybe they wear them on their face while they jack off!"

That visual gives me a chuckle. I'm about to say that if worn correctly, the crotch would cover his nose and mouth and he'd be able to look out the leg holes at, say, a Playboy centerfold, but change my mind when Kyle snarls, "Jesus, Kristy!"

I have to add something to Kristy's story, though. Katawasis girls solidarity, and all. I say, "So now I need to check my clothes hamper to make sure there isn't more underwear missing. What did I do to deserve this?"

"Nothing other than just being a gorgeous girl," Kristy says.

"Well, thank you, I guess. Anyway, they were clean panties."

"Have you got any idea who it might be?" Kyle asks. "That creep you work with, maybe?"

"Which one?" I ask, then I chuckle when I visualize sexless Hal choking his monkey, man boobs and lardy ass jiggling, lacy black panties with just enough cloth to cover his nose and mouth. "I don't think it's Fleet's style, and I doubt Hal has enough testosterone to get a stiffy, even if he had juicy panties on his face." *There you go, Kyle, how do you like that? Going to snarl at me?*

A frown flickers across his face but his tone is matter-of-fact when he says, "You'd be surprised. His kind are the worst." He takes a long swallow of his beer, burps, then sets the bottle on the table with a thump. "Hafta make a beer run."

"Pick up some burger patties and buns while you're out, and we'll barbeque," Kristy says.

"I've got frozen patties. Should be okay for me to go back inside and get them out of the freezer if I don't touch anything," I tell them. "All you need to get is buns, Kyle."

"Why don't you go?" Kyle asks, lifting his chin to indicate he's talking to Kristy. "I'm only going to the off sales at the pub."

"Yeah, and there's a Safeway store right there. Why should I go anywhere when you're already going out?"

"Why didn't you shop this week so we'd be set for the weekend?"

"Doesn't matter why, fact is I didn't. Why didn't you? I work too, if you haven't noticed."

Kyle snorts and says, "Fine." He gets up and goes into the house. A few minutes later, there's the V-8 growl of his car as he revs the engine a couple of times, then drives away.

I'm astonished at the tone of their exchange and that Kyle didn't give Kristy a goodbye kiss or even so much as stroke her shoulder or pat her head as he walked behind her chair. It's a big change from how they were not that long ago when they couldn't keep their hands off each other.

I look at Kristy, who's leaning back in her chair, head thrown back and eyes closed. "Why is he so grouchy? You two on the outs again, Kristy?" I ask.

"That's an understatement," she replies, and straightens. "I'll be right back." She goes into the house and comes back a few minutes later wearing t-shirt and shorts, a cold cider in each hand. She puts one on the table in front of me, and takes the chair across from me.

"So, what's going on, Kristy?"

"It's not what's going on. It's what *isn't* going on," she says. "He figures because his buddy is trying to get his wife pregnant, we should have a kid, too. I told him from the start I don't want kids. He says he thought I'd change my mind. Well, I haven't. And he won't put on a condom, I guess hoping I'll either give in or get so horny I forget or something. But neither of those things are going to happen and he's not getting laid until I have my next period so I can start back on the pill, even though they make me fat. Besides that, he's pissy about everything. Doesn't matter what I do or say, it so-called embarrasses him. Never bothered him before, though. You heard him snarl at me just now. And it's endless bitching. Why can't you be more like Karen? Karen this, Karen that! I finally told him to go fuck Karen, then. And I said maybe he could get her pregnant since it seems like Al can't."

"Oh, Kristy!"

"He's an asshole. Am I right?"

"Well—"

"I know, it takes two to fight." She lets out a long sigh and concludes, "I don't think we were ever in love. Just in lust. It's only ever been about sex. We don't have anything to talk about beyond *what's for lunch* and *pass the salt.*" She clicks her tongue and takes a deep breath. "You know, Lindy, I've been thinking of leaving him. So far everything's always smoothed over before I actually do anything about it, though. One time, I was at the door into your laundry room but it was the middle of the night, and, well, you know. I didn't want to wake you up and I'd have to crawl into bed with you and I didn't think you'd want that so I figured I'd have to bring my own blanket and pillow and when I went back up to get it, Kyle apologized and I changed my mind. Anyway, I was wondering—could I move in with you?"

The shock of being asked must register on my face because she adds, "Before you say no, keep in mind it would only be until I found another place."

How long I could stand having a roommate? Would that much togetherness end up with me not liking Kristy anymore? Then I remember the fight they had after leaving my place that time. The banging around and thumping that went on. It seemed pretty violent, although Kristy never said he'd hurt her. Maybe it would escalate, though. I can't say no.

"You absolutely are welcome to move in with me," I tell her, and reach across the table to give her forearm and rub. "Doesn't matter what time. If you have to get away, come any time. Until we move your bed down my couch is pretty comfortable, or you can sleep with me. I've shared a bed with a girlfriend before. As long as you don't snore or want the right-hand side, I'm okay with it."

"I mean, what if I didn't wait until we had a fight to leave?"

"It's up to you, Kristy. Whatever is right for you."

"I knew I could count on you, Lindy." She straightens, takes a deep breath, and smiles. "Okay! Go get your hamburger patties, and I'll get the ketchup and stuff ready. I hope he's back soon. I'm starving!" She jumps to her feet and heads to the patio doors. She turns and looks back. "Oh, do you have a tomato? How about an onion? As the asshole pointed out, I haven't bought groceries for a while."

"Tomato yes, onion, no."

"Well, he'll just have to do without it, then," she says, and disappears inside. I think she's humming. If she's really as unemotional as she seems about splitting up with Kyle, I guess it's the right thing to do. I hope Kyle is as calm about it as she is.

It is certainly going to be a interesting evening.

It turns out it's me, not Kristy, who moves. Well, Kyle and me. We switch places. We have a tense but mostly civil discussion about how it makes sense since the upper suite is bigger and more suitable for two people, being the entire upper floor, compared to the basement suite being little more than half the floor area. Plus it means we don't have to move a bed.

Kristy and I will split the rent of the more expensive suite so there's a financial benefit for me as half the rent upstairs is less than full rent downstairs. Kristy says she was paying half the rent before anyway so it's no big deal for her. I think that's odd since they're married and not just roommates, but keep my opinion to myself. Who knows what works for couples?

We'll split the phone, gas and electric company bills as well. I notify the few people that have my number, and leave my phone downstairs. Kyle will let me know in the unlikely event I get a message. It means I don't have to change my phone number or the address on my cheques or bank records and I won't even notify SaskPower. It's about as simple as a move can be. Also easy enough to change back should they make up, although I don't voice that thought. I pack up my belongings and hump everything up the stairs. Kyle will move his things downstairs while Kristy and I are at Windsong this morning. All very civilized.

I ride while Kristy stands at the gate and watches while socializing with anyone who happens to cross her path, including K.C. of course. I notice them standing together, apparently sharing something amusing, as he's smiling and she giggles. That's friendly, lovable Kristy for you.

I've finished my ride and have Chica in the crossties to untack. I hand Kristy a brush and we're one on either side, giving Chica a quick brushing before I put her out in her paddock when K.C. comes along.

"Ladies," he says, "is your meeting still going ahead?"

"It is," I reply.

"Good enough. Come find me after, please Lindy?"

"Sure. Oh, there's Deena now." I point to the open doorway at the parking lot end of the alleyway where Deena has just made an appearance. I wave and Kristy goes to meet her.

Once she's out of earshot, I ask. "Something wrong, K.C.?"

"No, it's just... Oh damn, Lindy! I wanted to ask if you'll go out for supper with me. I just didn't want to ask in front of Kristy, in case, you know—"

"Yes! I mean, I'd love that."

"Okay!" he grins. "Today?"

"Well, I... Thing is, K.C., um..." I was planning on unpacking and getting everything put away later but the idea of having supper with K.C. is way more appealing. I can get at anything I need to get ready for work tomorrow without unpacking. "Yes!"

"Yes? Great! I'll pick you up at six?"

Our meeting likely won't last long. I glance at my watch, decide I'll have time to get home and shower by then, so I agree and give him my new phone number along with directions to my place.

"See you at six," he says,.

"Six it is," I agree. K.C. grins, then turns and strides away. Kristy, Deena and I head upstairs into the lounge.

The lounge is the full width of the building and has windows offering a view of the arena all the way along. There's a scattering of pub tables with stools, two couches with armchairs around low tables, and a counter with a sink, microwave, coffee maker and a Coca-Cola vending machine against the back wall. A few people are in chairs or standing to look down on activities in the ring. We each get our favourite pop from the machine, then settle at one of the pub tables.

"I have news," Kristy tells Deena. "Actually, me and Lindy have news. I kicked my husband out and now me and her are roomies."

"Oh! I'm sorry, Kristy," Deena says.

"You know what? Don't be sorry! I feel like a weight is off my shoulders."

I study Kristy's face but see no sign that the statement is anything but the truth. I have to concede she made the right decision. When she's finished explaining to Deena how we switched things around, I tell Deena about the panty thief. And then about the visit I had from Jerry's brother. "Did Jerry ever talk about his brother, Deena?" I ask.

"Yeah, quite a lot, actually. Lots of stories about crazy things they did growing up."

"Did you have a sense that they liked each other? Or was there some, er, animosity between them, do you think?"

"No, not at all. He was real proud of him, talked all the time about him playing for some team in Vancouver. It's not the big league, he said, but his brother would likely go from there to the Toronto Blue Jays."

"Yeah, the Vancouver Canadians. It's impressive," I say. "Well, if you think of anything, let me know. I suppose I understand why Fleet wouldn't give out any information over the phone. Still, it's too bad because it sounds like they've lost contact with each other. His brother is worried."

"So who's Jerry?" Kristy asks.

"He's the guy I replaced. Well, not that I really replaced him. I didn't get the job until he was already gone."

"So, this Jerry guy had your job before you and he's missing? Another mystery," Kristy says. "Just like Easton."

"You mean you think he's dead? Jerry, I mean?" Deena asks.

"Naw," Kristy replies, "I just meant it's a mystery."

"There's something else I wanted to ask you about, Deena. Fleet wants me to have lunch with him and some guy named McClelland. CEO of NorSask Waste. I was wondering if your uncle Darius knows him? Do you know if NorSask has a contract with the Tribal Council for their garbage pickup maybe?"

"No, I'm sure they don't," Deena says. "The Rez has its own trucks and guys to pick up garbage and we have our own incinerator, a big one, near the mill. I'll talk to Darius, though. He knows a lot of people so he might know him."

"I was hoping he might have said something that would explain why NorSask doesn't already deal with our bank, being as Fleet and McClelland are such good buddies. And we have the account for Katawasis Forest Products so you'd think your uncle would recommend Western Savings."

"Even if Darius doesn't know that McClelland guy, if the tribe has business dealings with Fleet, he might tell us something about him," Kristy points out. "Maybe there's money changing hands under the table."

"Excellent point, Kristy. Not just another pretty face, are you? He has to be financing his champagne tastes somehow," I say. "Well, he makes good money but I don't think it's enough to cover that big boat of his, the new Caddy and a waterfront property. Not to mention Meredith's clothes."

"I hate to say it, but money could be going the other way, too," Deena says. "Uncle Darius lives pretty high on the hog. I haven't seen Meredith's clothes, but Darius dresses really well. He says he has to look good because he's our representative to the National Assembly of First Nations. And Fleet has more suits than all my uncles combined. Did you know... Oh, you weren't there when he came into the lunchroom and wanted all us girls feel his tie. Said it's silk and cost eighty dollars. Imagine."

"Eighty bucks for a tie? That doesn't seem possible," Kristy says.

"Have you ever been in Gold's Menswear?" I ask.

"No. Have you?"

"No, but if it's anything like Dolly's Dresses, it's possible they have eighty dollar silk ties."

"I'll check it out," Kristy says. "I'll tell them I'm shopping for my husband."

"Why would you do that?" Deena asks.

"It's the start of our file on good ol' Fleet, Deena," I say. "I think it's a good idea, Kristy. But rather than saying you're shopping for your husband, tell the salesman your friend works at the bank and wants to get Fleet a gift for, um, as a thank you or something. If he's a regular there, maybe you can sweet talk the salesman into telling you about him."

"Leave it with me," she says, and giggles.

"Perfect! Meanwhile, we should figure out what to call ourselves. I haven't thought of anything. In my mind I call us the Katawasis Girls."

"What's wrong with that?" Deena asks.

"Well, I don't like women being called girls, but Katawasis Women doesn't sound right."

"I like it!" Kristy exclaims. "How about you, Deena? Okay with you?"

Deena says, "Why not? It's better than Friends of Katawasis, if you ask me. And you know Katawasis means beautiful?"

"That's us! Beautiful! So, it's settled," Kristy declares, "we're the Katawasis Girls. Now all we need is a, hmm, a purpose."

"Yeah, we need a mission statement," I say. "How about being crime solvers? Detectives?"

"Sure, at least until we locate Jerry," Deena says.

"And figure out about Fleet," I remind her. "Also, we need to help Detective Allard catch the panty stealer and maybe Easton's killer while we're at it."

"His death wasn't an accident?" Kristy asks.

"I asked Detective Allard if he was murdered and he didn't say no. So that's a yes, in my book. And there's also the mystery of who's been on our beach and what they're doing there and why they come through our yard."

"We'll be the beautiful girl detectives," Kristy says, and giggles. "This will be fun."

I wonder how much fun we're actually going to have. We could be getting on the wrong side of people who aren't very nice.

"Okay, Katawasis Girls," I say, and pull my Swiss Army knife out of my pocket to show them. "I want both of you to get one of these and keep it on you at all times. And I mean accessible, in your pocket, not in the bottom of your purse. And we'll each have two cans of bear spray: one for at home, and one in our vehicle."

Kristy laughs outright at this. "I'm okay with the bear spray, Lindy, but a knife in my pocket? There's no pockets in women's clothes, you know! Unless you're in jeans, of course. I can wear jeans to work, but does the bank allow you guys to wear jeans?"

"No."

"So where are we supposed to keep these little doo-dads, other than in our purse?"

"Well, we all wear bras," Deena says. "I guess a little knife like that wouldn't be too uncomfortable stuck in there."

"Let's give it a try," I suggest, and scan the room to make sure no one's watching before I pull my shirttail out of my jeans, lift it, and slip the knife into my bra. I try a couple of spots before positioning it vertically under my arm next to the underwire. "That works. It's secure and I barely feel it." I pull it back out and hand it to Kristy. "Here. Give it a try," I suggest, and explain where I placed it.

Kristy gets it set in place and agrees it's no problem there, then hands it to Deena, who does likewise.

"Okay," Deena says, "It's fine I guess. But do you really think we have to? I mean, you think there's a need?"

"Well, er..." I'm on the verge of telling them it saved my life once, but decide against it because they'd want details. I don't want to relive the experience enough to tell them about it. Also, I don't want to spook them. "No, not really. But it'll be like our secret trademark thing. We don't have a membership pin like Rotary or Friends of Katawasis, but we have a secret knife in our bra. Just make sure you don't get a big one."

"It's cute," Kristy decides. "Imagine some guy copping a feel and coming up with that! Make sure that if you want things to go that far, you wear something with pockets so you can put the Swiss thingie elsewhere during the date," Kristy says, and giggles. "On the other hand, it might be a turn-on."

Trust Kristy to come up with that! Deena laughs but my chuckle is forced. We could be poking a very big, very grouchy bear. I hope we never stop laughing about our secret knives.

K.C. and I have a nice supper at El Sombrero, a Mexican restaurant that I didn't even know existed even though it's on Main Street only a dozen or so blocks past the branch. Of course until the day I saw Kyle coming out of the Toronto-Dominion, I'd never gone farther than the branch.

It turns out K.C. acquired an appreciation for Mexican food when he was showing horses in the southern U.S. He orders a platter of various items so I can try different things and see what I like. The Chicken Mole Chimichangas are to die for and the salsa macha[1] for dipping the warm, house-made tortillas is beyond wonderful. The servings are big enough to satisfy even my cowhand appetite. I think I'm going to be an El Sombrero regular.

The date goes very well. As before, we have plenty to talk about, and at the end K.C. walks me to my door. He's very chivalrous. And for a cowboy, surprisingly restrained. He must not be good at reading body language

---

1. https://www.bonappetit.com/recipe/salsa-macha

because if he made the slightest move I'd be all over him. Maybe that's what he's afraid of.

I didn't need to worry about the whereabouts of my Swiss Army Knife.

Fleet is already in his office when I arrive at eight Monday. This is a first. I wonder what he's got going on that brought him in so early.

I settle into my desk, checking the day's calendar and the files I'm working on before I go in to tap on his doorframe. When he looks up, I ask, "Got a minute?"

"For you, Lindy, I've always got a minute. What's up?"

I take a chair across the desk from him. "I had a visit from Ken Christiansen on Friday," I begin.

"Who?"

"Ken Christiansen. He says his brother Jerry worked here. Had my job before me, in fact."

"Oh yeah? What did he want?"

"He wanted to know where Jerry went after leaving here."

Fleet frowns, leans back in his chair and scans the office as if the answer might be written on the wall behind me before saying, "I think he phoned and asked before, and I told him I don't know. All I know was that he had a better offer, and he left. Asshole didn't even give us the two weeks' notice he owed us."

"But it's surprising he didn't tell you where this better offer was from. Where he was going. Didn't you ask?"

Fleet's face twists in a frown; he snaps, "He didn't have the courtesy of telling me. He told Hal instead. He was no good at his job. I was about to fire him anyway so it saved me the trouble. I was glad to be rid of him." He breathes out a long breath before continuing more evenly: "I tried to spare his brother's feelings before but if he shows up again, I'll tell him that. He's making a damn nuisance of himself."

"Okay. I, um don't think he's coming back..."

"Good. Anything else?"

"No, that's all," I say, and get to my feet.

"Sit for a minute," Fleet demands. "I have something else I want to talk to you about."

I drop back down into the chair and ask, "Oh? What?"

He opens a drawer and produces an envelope, opens it, and pulls out my cheque to Dolly's. He pushes it across the desk toward me. "What's this about, Lindy? You know better than to write a rubber cheque."

Well, finally! I was beginning to think he was never going to ask me about it. "I, er, um, that is, yeah, Fleet! You know, I thought I'd get paid before that got through their bank and, um..." I hang my head and try to look embarrassed, worried, humiliated, or whatever's appropriate for someone caught doing something really stupid.

He studies me through narrowed eyes, then puts the cheque back in the envelope. "Don't worry, it won't bounce. I'll hang onto it until payday."

"Thank you," I say quietly as I look up under my lashes. Hopefully that's a coquettish look.

"Of course now you've got those big payments on your truck every month. Went a little hog wild, did you?"

Oh, good! He got a credit report too! "Well, my old truck..."

"Never mind. We can't have the A.M. driving around in a heap like that anyway. I'd rather you got yourself a nice car but—"

"I need a truck to haul my horse trailer."

"I see. But the point I was coming to is that you might have ongoing, um, *money problems.* So I think the best thing would be to increase the overdraft protection on your account so you don't have to worry. How does an O.D. limit of ten thousand sound?"

"That would be great, Fleet!"

"Okay. I'll get it set up right away. And again, don't worry about this cheque to Dolly's."

"Thank you!"

"One other thing. No more snooping through my desk. All right?"

Just when I thought he either didn't care about it or Corrine didn't rat me out. "I, er—"

"Whatever," he snaps, cutting me off. "My desk—in fact my office—is off limits."

"Sorry," I mutter.

"All right."

Just then I hear my phone ringing so I get up, give Fleet a little wave and hurry back to my office, close the door behind me, and answer it.

I'm expecting a call from Personnel Department in Regional Office, but it's Jim Spears. I'm surprised, since I'm supposed to check in with him from my home phone. "Jim! Hello! What's up?"

"You called Personnel Department and left a message that you wanted information about a past employee?"

"I did. Why?"

"You should've called me."

"Well, it's, er, unrelated to what we're working on. His brother was here wanting to know where Jerry went when he left here. Fleet doesn't know. I'd like to help the guy and I thought a forwarding address might be in his R. O. Personnel file. You know, for his T4."

"I see. So it's nothing to do with what we're interested in?"

"No."

"Okay. Hmm. I doubt Personnel will tell you anything."

"I was hoping I could persuade them."

"Doubtful, but they'll give me the information. I'll check into it for you, Lindy. Of course they need an address to send his income tax docs to, like you say. So I'll have something for you by our regular check-in time Wednesday."

"Great."

"By the way, those initials and phone numbers you gave me? I ran them and got names. Any of these ring a bell? B.B.'s comes back to someone known to police, a call girl, Brandy Beliveau. Craig Jellinik is C.J., nothing on him. E.N. is also known to police. Easton Nunes."

Easton Nunes! "Oh my god, Jim! Easton Nunes is dead!" I explain how Easton was seeking financing for his new water taxi business and said he met a banker or at least a lender at a pub. "Not just any pub, one that's way out in the industrial area. He gets the money, buys the boat, and then he turns up dead under suspicious circumstances."

"And his initials and phone number were in Fleet's day timer," Jim says. "You have to wonder if Fleet was the mysterious lender. Find out if there's an account in his name. If there is, it could be that surcharge you mentioned. If not, he could be a loan shark. Who only identifies the people they have appointments with by their initials? And you say he's away from the office a lot."

"True. But as far as Easton's murder, what loan shark kills people who owe them money? It would mean they'd never collect. Besides, Easton was dealing drugs so wouldn't it be more likely related to that? He was just getting started using his boat to deliver product to fishing lodges. Maybe he was moving in on someone else's territory. And also, he may have run afoul of someone on the Rez because of delivering both liquor and dope there."

"You're probably right. But for god's sake be careful, Lindy. In fact, why don't you stand down for the time being."

"But a couple more things. That big cheque I wrote? Fleet finally called me on it. His solution is to increase my overdraft protection to ten thousand."

"Ten *thousand*?"

"Yup. Nearly half a year's salary. He's given me enough rope to hang myself. I think we just hooked the fish."

"Sounds like it."

"There's just one more thing. I just got reamed out for a, er, an incident. Corrine caught me going through Fleet's desk and of course anything Corrine knows, Fleet will know within minutes. He just told me his office is off limits. He keeps the bottom drawer locked."

"Could just be personnel files. Sensitive stuff."

"Could be. But I wonder if Jerry's file is in there. Maybe other stuff too, something related to the names you just gave me. I need to check it out."

"Don't do it unless there is zero chance you'll be caught," Jim says. "I'm not kidding, Lindy. I hate to say it or even think it, but if he met with someone who's since turned up dead—"

"I'll be very careful. Talk to you Wednesday." I give him my new phone number, and we say goodbye.

I had no time to think about my discussion with Fleet before my phone conversation with Jim, but now I sit back and stare blankly out my window, digesting both Jim's news and Fleet's hostile reaction to me asking about Jerry. That really touched a nerve. He claims Jerry only told Hal he was leaving, but did they have an argument, maybe after hours when everyone else had left the branch? Something that could have ended with Jerry walking out?

Then I realize Jerry must've had an account here and there should be information in our system. No need to wait for an opportunity to get into Fleet's locked drawer to look for that. I boot up my computer and spend time scrolling through the records, finding nothing. In case it's my brain not engaging with my eye due to having had only one cup of coffee this morning, I ask the computer to search for it, and still come up with nothing. I remember our I.T. guy explaining that computers are smart but they can't think like a person does. If I spelled something wrong in my search or if the name was input incorrectly, a person could look at anything close and find what I'm looking for. Computers don't do that. There are a couple of Christiansen accounts but nothing with initials J or G. I try Christianson and Christansen. Still nothing and I can't think of any other way of spelling or misspelling it. It's possible Jerry moved his account with him, which would be logical, and the bank has no reason to keep a record of where it went.

Hopefully Jim can find something in the personnel records that explains it, but as it happens, when Ken calls later in the day I still have no news for him. I let him know I expect to hear something from Regional Office Wednesday. He tells me he'll call me Thursday. If I haven't found out more by then, he's going to report his brother as missing.

I'm at Windsong Monday night having a make-up lesson for the one I missed because of the drama over the weekend. I must be doing better because K.C. doesn't pick at me much, other than frequent reminders to check my diagonal. I finally figured out that if it feels right to me, I'm on the wrong one. I make a note to myself to always check it before he notices.

If I thought he and I would interact differently because of our one sort of and one actual date, I was only partly right. He treats me pretty much the same as always, but with slightly more touching. I mean, he put his hand on my thigh and gave it what I'd like to think was an affectionate rub when he came up beside the horse to give me a little snippet of theory. Baby steps.

We spend a little time walking in a circle with me focusing on what Chica's body is doing. Is she dropping a shoulder? What about her bend? He says her body arch should be around my left leg when I ask for left lead canter. I should see the corner of her left eye. It's interesting, I guess, but I'm not really sure why it matters.

"Okay," K.C. explains, "performance horsemanship is all about body position, athleticism, and being in a correct frame so she can do whatever comes next. You're her coach, you need to help her gain the muscle memory she needs to be balanced and correct. Now let's try it."

The exercise is to lope on the circle, then go to the middle of the circle and stop. I then push Chica away from my left leg toward the outside of the circle and when I can see the corner of her left eye, ask for lope on the left lead. Repeat, but this time, push her off my right leg and ask for right lope. She's not at the level where she can go straight from a standstill to lope or lope to halt so there are a couple of walk and trot steps in between, but K.C. seems satisfied and says she'll get there. We end the lesson with a nice long and low trot stretch. I decide to go for a walk around the yard to cool her out. He walks beside me to open the gate and let me out of the arena. I'm hoping he'll come around again when I'm back and getting Chica put away, but I see his truck heading down the driveway when I'm still up at the back paddocks.

I wonder if one date was enough for him. Did I talk about Wacasko-Wâti too much? Did he hate the way I eat? I don't think I was smacking my lips and I definitely don't chew with my mouth open. Did I let my cowhand appetite get the better of me and behave in a totally unladylike manner by eating more than my share of that platter? Maybe he decided I'm not his type after all. Maybe he's a boob man and I have little to offer in that department. But surely he noticed that before asking me out. Maybe I should've worn something more feminine or opened another button on my shirt. Then I tell myself if he doesn't want another date, it's his loss. I don't want a boyfriend anyway. I just wish I didn't have to keep telling myself that.

It's nearly nine when I swing into Tall Trees, possibly smelling of horse and definitely hungry enough to eat one. I take my usual seat at the end of the bar. As soon as Kristy spots me, she fills a half liter carafe of house white and brings it and a glass to put in front of me.

"I guess I must look like I need a half liter," I say.

"You'll drink it but if you don't, I'll put a lid on it and you can take it home," she says. "Just don't tell nobody. Did you see the news?"

"No. What news?"

She points up at the TV and says, "Katawasis was on Global National six o'clock news. Maybe they'll run it again later."

"Katawasis made the national news? Why?"

"Because they found a body in the lake. Some fisherman snagged it."

A feeling of dread washes over me. I tell myself it isn't necessarily Jerry but I can't quite make myself believe it. "Did they give a name?"

"No, they just said it had been in the water a long time. I guess that's their way of saying it's rotted so bad they can't tell who it is. So, you want a menu or..."

My face must be reflecting the clenching I'm feeling in my guts.

"What is it?" Kristy asks.

"I talked to Ken today. He says he's going to report Jerry as missing."

Now Kristy takes a deep breath and I imagine she's feeling the same trepidation I am.

"I wondered if it could be him," she says quietly. "I was hoping it wasn't and that you'd found out where he went."

"No. I guess there's still a chance. But I'm not holding out hope."

How can I get into that locked bottom drawer in Fleet's desk? I need luck and time. If I can't find the key, I don't know how to pick locks, so I'm defeated. Likewise if Corrine is breathing down my neck. Since I'm the person who locks the door after everyone else has gone, I can stay inside, claiming to work late. It's my best chance to find the key. Tonight's the night. I hope Fleet doesn't keep the key with him.

I hear thumping, then shouts. I go to the top of the stairs to see what the commotion is all about and there is Fleet at the bottom, sprawled across the bottom step, propped up with his back against the wall. I hurry down and I'm just about to crouch beside him when Corrine comes scurrying around the corner and pushes me out of the way kneel next to him. I have to back up a couple of steps to avoid being on my butt next to him.

"Fleet! What happened?" she shrieks.

"What does it look like, for chrissakes? You think I just decided to sit here? I fell." He squirms in an effort to get up, and utters a long groan. "Shit! My ankle! I think I broke it."

"Call an ambulance!" Corrine shrieks. "Someone call an ambulance!"

Fleet is wheeled to the ambulance. A sobbing Corrine scurries along beside the gurney and assures him, "I'll follow in my car!"

I'm sure it's a great comfort that his office wife will be with him until his actual wife can get there and take over the hand-holding. Or maybe they share the duties, one on each hand. I walk away shaking my head, telling myself not to smile.

It's not that I find Fleet's accident and obvious pain humorous. Despite the many times I've sent telepathic messages to him suggesting he fall on his head I wouldn't really have wished him harm, but didn't I say I needed time and luck? I just got both, in spades.

Once in my office, I keep an eye on the parking lot until I see Corrine drive away. Fleet didn't send her up to lock his desk and she'll be out of the branch for at least a couple of hours. The only other person who might come into Fleet's office is Hal, and since he grumbles about having to climb the stairs when Fleet calls him up for his daily command performance, there's virtually no chance of him interrupting me.

I go into Fleet's office, sit in his chair, and try the drawer. It opens. I thumb through the files. My excitement fades. If I was hoping for something that screamed "FRAUD", I was an idiot. There are personnel folders, maybe entertaining but no more than that. A quick look through the few customer files tells me nothing. I pull his expense account file and look back to when I started here. The worst I can find is that he did, indeed, charge our lunch with those pricey drinks to his expense account. Apparently I was the new manager of Dolly's Dresses that day. There may be other lunches he shouldn't have expensed, but it would take some work to prove it.

Jerry would've had a personnel file like everyone else, but there's no trace of it. Maybe it went in the dumpster and I'm too late. Disappointed, I'm about to give up when I realize there's something in the open space between the rack of files and the back of the drawer that the files in the hangar marked XYZ brush on when I slide them. I push the files apart to see what it is. If I hadn't moved the file labelled Year End 1981 I would never have noticed it.

Often in movies or TV shows, someone asks, "what are you looking for?" and the answer is, "I'll know when I find it."

I just found it.

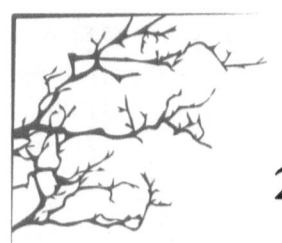

21—Breakthrough

Wednesday morning, I get a phone call from Fleet telling me I'm going to be in charge for the next short while. He explains that although he didn't break any bones, he has a bad ankle sprain, can't weight bear on that leg, and the stairs would be killer for him to go up and down hobbling on one foot and crutches.

"I'd likely fall again and maybe break my neck," he complains. "It's worse at home, we've got stairs everywhere and Meredith is no help. I'm going to spend a week on the boat. I'm using sick days so I don't have to use my vacation days. Might as well take advantage, right?"

"Right," I agree.

"I gave Corrine my keys so she's going to go lock up my office. Did she tell you she's taking some of her vacation days, since I won't be there to need her for anything?"

"No."

"Okay, well, she should be there to do that soon. Give her a few sick days so she'll still have a good whack of vacation days coming to her."

"Will do."

"And since you can't reach me by phone, I want you to put everything on hold until I'm back. Except the stuff you normally look after yourself, I mean. And you can sign the R. O. reports, the ones you prepare and I usually sign off on. It's okay to send them in with just your signature, for now."

"Okay. You won't be gone that long, though, will you?"

"No. Maybe a week. Look for me a week from today."

"Don't worry about a thing, Fleet," I tell him, hoping my voice is dripping with sympathy and concern. "I'll miss you, but it's important that you just rest that leg and get well."

When I'm off the phone, I feel a little guilty for the lie about missing him and hope I didn't oversell it. Still, it's all I can do not to bust out in song. Having Fleet and possibly Corrine gone for a week is as good as a vacation.

No Windsong after work tonight because I'm hanging around home waiting for Jim's scheduled Wednesday call. I'm enjoying a glass of wine on the deck, watching the sky turn pink as the sun sets and boats going back and forth on the lake, wondering if one of them is the *Fleetship*. I wish Kyle had left his binoculars up here. Next time I see him, I'll tell him it's all right for him to come up, at least when Kristy is at work in case that's awkward, and by the way could you leave your binoculars?

The phone rings and I dash inside to answer it. But it's not Jim, it's K.C.

"Hi, Lindy," he says. "You didn't come to ride tonight?"

"No, I'm waiting for an important phone call. A work thing. I thought he'd've called before now. What's up?"

"Nothing, really. I just..." His thoughts apparently trail off and we lapse into an uncomfortable silence.

"Hey," I say after a few heartbeats, "what are you doing right now? Want to come over? It's nice on the deck and I have a beer in the fridge." Yeah, I'm a glutton for punishment. Why do I open myself up for disappointment like that?

"I'll be right there," he says.

Well, knock me over with a feather! I rush into the bathroom to brush my teeth so my breath doesn't reek of garlic from the Tall Trees Caesar salad I had for supper, and then pull off my t-shirt, give my pits a swipe with a washcloth, and don one of my nice new Dolly's Dresses blouses. I leave the top two buttons open, check my look in the mirror and open a third. The doorbell rings while I'm still tucking my blouse into my cut-offs. It can't be K.C. already.

But it is. I open the door and there he is, six pack of Labatt's Blue in hand. "Hey! How'd you get here so fast?"

"Well, I, er... I guess I might as well admit it. I went to Tall Trees thinking you'd be there. Kristy let me use the house phone to call you. Hope it's okay."

"Of course." *Thank you, Kristy!* "Come on in."

He follows me inside, hands me the beer and says, "Put these in the fridge?"

"Sure, but you didn't have to bring anything. I told you I have beer."

"You said you have *a* beer," he says. "I'm hoping for more than one."

Is the shy cowboy coming out of his shell? But he looks so serious I'm not sure how to take that comment. "Figure of speech, but okay," I say. We go into the kitchen. I hand him a beer and I'm just sticking the rest in the fridge when the phone rings.

"That's probably Jim now," I say. "Go ahead on out and I'll join you in a bit. This won't take long."

I go to the phone and pick up the handset. "Hello?"

"Hi Lindy. It's Jim."

"Hi Jim."

"Sorry I'm so late calling."

"It's all right. Did you find anything?"

"Yeah. Dunno what it means, but there's no forwarding address in his R. O. file either. The T4 sent to his Katawasis address is in there, returned marked *not at this address.*"

"Well, damn!" I chew my bottom lip, wondering what else to do. "What's the address? Maybe I can go ask the neighbors if they know where he went."

"Sure. Got something to write with?"

"Yeah," I say, and get a pen and scratch pad from the junk drawer under the phone. "Shoot."

"Downstairs, 2208 Katawasis Lake Close."

I gasp, loudly enough that Jim asks, "What is it? Something wrong?"

"That's my address," I tell him. "Or it was, before I moved upstairs."

"So you were living in the same suite he lived in?"

"It would seem so."

He's quiet for a moment and I can almost hear the wheels in his head grinding as mine are. Finally, he asks, "How likely is that?"

"Well, it's an amazing coincidence if nothing else. But then, there weren't many furnished suites to choose from. I know it was the nicest of the three or four they sent me photos of when I was looking, and it was the least expensive. I thought it must have a chronic sewer backup problem or something in order for it to be so cheap, but it's actually very nice. I think I have to go and have a chat with the rental agent to see if Jerry left a forwarding address for his damage deposit refund. I planned to do that anyway, but I won't put it off any longer. I'll go tomorrow. Meanwhile, Fleet's away this week." I explain how he fell down the stairs, not all the way but the last three or four steps, and is taking time off to heal his sprained ankle.

"That surprises me, I mean, that he would take time off," Jim says. "Looks like he seldom even had a vacation since he took over that branch a decade ago. A real workaholic."

"Well, he doesn't work hard or put much time in, so I guess his job isn't too taxing. But here's something interesting. Since he neglected to lock his desk before the ambulance hauled him away I was able to get into that drawer. He's got a baseball in a plastic cube. The certificate of authentication says it's signed by Yogi Berra. I think it's the one that Deena said Jerry always kept on his desk. She thought it was a joke, like signed by a cartoon character. She was probably thinking of Yogi Bear cartoons."

"Definitely something Jerry had?"

"Yeah, and not something you'd come across every day. According to Deena, he was real proud of it."

"Not something he would leave behind."

"Not likely. And it's no more likely that he would take off without letting the brother he was so proud of know where he was going. What I don't get is why Fleet would keep that ball."

"Might be a collector's item. Maybe worth something. Or maybe he thinks Jerry will want it back so he's saving it for him."

"Whatever, there's only one reason for it to be stashed away in the back of a locked file drawer. He doesn't want anyone to know he has it."

"No. You're right."

"I don't like the thoughts I'm thinking about Mister Arnold Fleetwood right now."

"Me neither. I told you to be careful. That goes double triple now. I'm going to clear my schedule so I can come to Katawasis. Until then, stand down."

"But I haven't found out how or even if Fleet is embezzling..."

"Leave it for the time being, at least until we locate Jerry. I mean it, Lindy. Okay?"

"I will," I agree. "But not until after I talk to the rental agent. I don't see how there could be a connection there, and even if there is one, Fleet's out on his boat and can't be reached by phone this week. That should be safe enough. Okay?"

"Okay. So it sounds like it's safe for me to call you at work until Fleet's back in the office. I'll let you know if I find out anything else, and when I can be there. Over and out."

"Over and out," I respond, and we hang up. I blow out a long breath, wondering how it could be a coincidence that I was living in the same suite Jerry vacated. I turn to go out to join K.C. on the deck and find him standing in the doorway watching me.

He exhales loudly and says, "I guess we should talk."

I'm not sure what I'm feeling. I told him to go out onto the deck and I'd join him there; instead, he hovers in the doorway eavesdropping. Is it bad manners or is there another motive? Does he have something going on with Fleet? Is there some nefarious reason they don't want it known that they're connected and acted as if they didn't like each other that day at the restaurant? If Jim thinks I have to be careful because Fleet might be dangerous, do I also have to be wary of K.C.? Is his lukewarm interest in me a ploy to get near enough to me to find out if I'm a danger to them? If so, what he just overheard would do it. I hesitate to go near him and certainly don't want to spend time with him.

As if sensing my trepidation he says, "Please. I have to explain something to you."

"Explain away."

"Can we sit?" he asks, and nods his head in the direction of the patio table.

"Maybe. It depends on what you want to talk about."

"It's about Fleet. I heard what you were talking about. It sounds like you, er, don't like him. That's why I have some explaining to do."

I'm at the ReMax Realty office waiting for the rentals manager to graciously bestow five minutes of her time upon me. I can't believe she's so busy on a Thursday morning that she has to keep me cooling my heels in the waiting area this long.

A young couple comes out of a back office, followed by a pert, fifty-something woman wearing a blazer with the ReMax Realty logo embroidered on it. She promises to let them know as soon as a rental in their price range becomes available. I'm not annoyed with her anymore. The couple passes without a glance at me as they head for the door. The lady at the front desk says something to the agent and they both look my way.

I stand as she comes toward me, reaches out her hand and says, "Hi, I'm Elaine. Can I help you?"

I give her hand a quick shake and say, "I hope so. I'm not looking for a rental, though. I already rent from you. I moved in a little while ago, and on the weekend I was moving some furniture around and I found something I think belongs to the last tenants. I think they'd like to have it, so I want to contact them but I don't know who they are or where they went. I thought maybe you had forwarding information. Like maybe you needed it to send them their damage deposit refund."

"Oh, hmm. What was the address?"

I rattle it off. She says, "I'll get the file. Come and wait in my office."

I follow her and she points me to her office while she goes to a bank of file cabinets nearby. I squeeze into the space between her desk and the wall and sit in the first chair. After some clanging and banging of file drawers she comes in, file in hand, to sit behind the desk.

"Here we are," she says, and puts the file down in front of her. She opens it and leafs through. After a moment, she looks up at me and says, "You must be Lindy Larsen."

I'd much prefer remaining anonymous but for my story to hold water, I have to admit who I am. I was prepared for this. "That's me."

"You and I didn't meet when you rented the suite. Now I remember. We couriered the keys to you."

"That's right. Thanks for doing that, by the way."

"You're welcome. So, how are you finding things?"

"I like it." I think about asking for a better door lock but decide not to muddy the waters by explaining about the panty thief or the switch in occupants. Kyle is on his own.

"Good. So, it's a *him*, not a *they*. I should have remembered him from the address. We didn't refund the damage deposit because he left without giving notice and didn't bother to take his furniture. We were going to have to pay more than the deposit to have someone haul it all away but then the owners suggested we rent it as a furnished suite and save the money."

"Makes sense." That explains the weight bench, thrift store dishes and crap furniture. "So I guess if you didn't have to spend to have things hauled away, you still owe him a refund."

"No. His last cheque bounced," she says, and points to the cheque clearly stamped NSF. Colour rises in her cheeks. I have a sense there was never any intention of returning his deposit. If not for unpaid rent, in a typical landlord con they would've found some other reason to keep it. She concentrates on the file, flips papers, then shakes her head and shrugs. "Nothing here about where he went. What is it you want to return to him? Something valuable?"

"I think so. It's a ring, like a school ring. Pretty nice, gold with a red stone in it and some sort of crest. I found it when I, um, moved the dresser. Like it must've fallen down behind it and if he missed it, he never thought to look there."

"Well, leave it with me," she says, and smiles. "I'm sure he'll contact us about his damage deposit, so I'll be able to get it back to him."

"You must still have post-dated cheques on file. If you give me his name and the bank the cheques are drawn on, I'll get the ring to the bank. You know, to put in their safe."

Her smile evaporates. She thinks for a moment, then says, "I guess it's okay to tell you. His first name is Jerry. Last name, pronounced just like Christianson but spelled differently." She spells it out: "K-r-i-s-t-j-a-n-s-e-n.

And the cheque is drawn on Western Savings and Loan. Actually, Western Savings owns the house."

"The bank owns the house?"

"Yeah. A foreclosure. I was surprised Mr. Kristjansen left. I don't have anything else as nice for the price," she says. "His loss is your gain. But I remember now. You didn't sign a lease. You're lucky the bank let you off without it."

"Yeah. Lucky." I lean as far over her desk as I can without it being too obvious that I'm reading the contents of the file. There are lease documents for both suites. As Elaine flips the pages I spot one with a familiar signature. She turns the page before I can make out the entire date, but I see enough.

Elaine looks up and frowns when she realizes I'm able to read even though the papers are upside down. Maybe it also dawns on her she's already told me more than she should have. She abruptly closes the file. "Anything else?"

"Well, er, no, that's it, thanks."

We both get up and leave Elaine's office together. She escorts me as far as the waiting area. I thank her for her time and escape.

I'm sickened to my core.

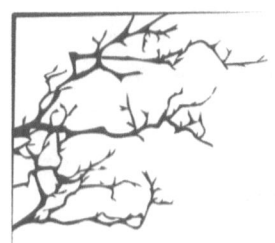

22—Meet Jim

The man sitting across the desk from me is ex-RCMP, tall, and handsome despite some acne scarring on his cheeks. I suspect that under that Saskatchewan Roughriders ballcap, his blond hair is thinning. He's wearing jeans and a bomber jacket rather than a banker's suit because he's pretending to be a Saskatchewanite here in the guise of talking to me about a line of credit for a business he wants to start. In fact, he flew in from Regional Office this morning.

"You don't look anything like I pictured you from our telephone conversations," I tell him. "I thought with your credentials and that you retired from the RCMP you'd be a lot older. But I did expect the cop haircut."

"Yeah, I guess I should let it grow out a little."

"No, it's perfect. Once a cop, always a cop, at least in how you think. You never lose the cop brain," I say, and give him a smile. "So, what made you suspicious something was going on here?"

"Well, we started paying attention when branch profits tanked a few years ago. We thought it was because of the downturn in the economy. Since the renos were already budgeted for, Real Estate Department decided to go ahead on them anyway, thinking Katawasis Lake would soon recover. But with the cost overruns on the reno and the fact business hasn't come back and in fact is falling behind—well... Is it a manager problem? Is he incompetent? Not doing enough promotion? Or just flat out unlikeable?"

I click my tongue and shrug. "I was with him at a restaurant once. My first day here, actually. He knew half the people in the place, on a first name basis with everyone, everyone seemed friendly toward him," I say. Then I remember K.C. and amend that to, "Almost everyone."

"From his expense account it would seem he's getting clients out for lunch or golf or drinks often. Is it the local economy?"

"I don't think so," I tell him. "The mills are going strong. Katawasis Lake isn't just a mill town, either. Those jobs aren't seasonal and the forestry and fishing companies are doing well. I'd even say they're depression proof."

"So what do you think is going on?"

"All I can think is that Fleet has a bunch of tricks up his sleeve."

"Tricks?"

"For starters, and this is a small thing in the overall scheme of things, I think it would be pretty easy to nail him for padding his expense account." I explain about that expensive lunch on my first day at work and how it turned up on his expense report. "I would bet if we looked into it, we'd find a lot of the charges are bogus."

"That only has a small effect on the branch bottom line, though," he points out.

"True, but it's something he can be terminated for with no worry about a wrongful dismissal lawsuit. If it comes to that."

"I see. Something to keep in mind."

"As for the big picture, I don't know exactly, but here's what I'm thinking: Kickbacks. What he calls a surcharge. Not on every loan, but a lot of them, especially the ones where he can convince the borrower they don't qualify. That their loans are too high risk. So when funds are disbursed, he's first in line with his hand out. The borrower ends up with less than what they're going to have to pay back because a percentage goes to Fleet. The mechanics of that, I haven't figured out yet. And I realize it's astonishing no one has blown the whistle on him."

"Well, there'll be names and contact info on file. I'll talk to the borrowers," Jim offers. "Unlike you, I can dig into those files and Fleet will have to suck up his objections."

"Yes. But I have a niggling suspicion Jerry found out about it. He didn't go along with it, and that's why he's missing. I'm still hoping he's just buggered off somewhere but it's looking less and less likely."

"You think Jerry's been murdered?"

"That's what haunts my thoughts. But surely you don't kill someone for what could only be a couple thousand bucks here and there."

"People have killed for less. And if you're right, his operation could be a lot bigger than that."

"I was wondering about that too, especially after what K.C. told me. I'll let him give you the details of his experience with Fleet, but the broad strokes are that it's more than just surcharges on loans. For big accounts like KFP—Katawasis Forest Products—maybe they give him a kickback up front and then pay him again and again, every time their loan comes up for renewal. They can't go elsewhere because they don't really qualify for the limits he gives them, and they lean on it pretty heavily so no other bank will give them enough to pay our loan out. I suspect he cooks the applications in order to get R. O. approval, in which case we might be sitting on a heap of loans that are about to go bad. There may be some fake accounts he's already using to make payments to keep them current. And in the case of KFP, which is the branch's biggest account, it's possible he shares the bucks with their finance guy. Just an added layer of risk prevention for him there. Not a hundred per cent sure of that yet, but we might be able to prove it."

"We?"

"My friend, Deena Bright Bird. She's a clerk here. I told you about her. She was friendly with Jerry and she's the one who told me about the baseball. Her uncle, Darius Bright Bird, is the KFP finance guy. Fleet might have a similar arrangement with other companies, too. And once he got enough of his own money, he started loaning that out at loan shark rates. That's the reason every application has to be 'approved' by him, so he can cherry pick the ones he wants in his own portfolio. As for collections, he has people. Maybe some of the guys identified in his calendar only by initials, other than the call girl of course, and his appointments are to meet with them so they can hand over the cash. And one of them was Easton Nunes."

"That's the guy whose name you recognized?"

"Yeah. I think he gave him a loan to buy a boat, then set him up to make what he called deliveries. Easton was a small time drug dealer plus he also did legitimate deliveries, which was good cover for making his collection runs. Kind of a sketchy character, though. I think he started skimming right from the get go, enough to buy himself a Rolex, and that's why he wound up floating in the lake."

"You think Fleet killed him, too? You think he's killed two people?"

"More likely got someone to do it for him. Although you never really know what someone's capable of, do you? It's possible he took him out on his boat, hit him over the head and dumped him overboard."

I bring Jim up to speed on how the two people I thought were my friends and I discovered Easton's body. "Detective Allard hasn't told me anything, not even the cause of death, other than what everyone else knows: that it's suspicious but appears to have been targeted and there's no threat to the general public. He hasn't gotten back to me about the guy I call the panty stealer, either. I'm not sure the two are connected because I don't know why Fleet would want to snoop through my things, but someone's been in my place at least three times. Couldn't figure out how he was getting in because there was never forced entry. Now that I know the bank owns the house, it makes sense Fleet would have keys. Maybe he has Jerry's keys, too. Easy access anytime. If the guy hadn't stolen a pair of panties, I'd never have known. I don't see Fleet stealing panties, though."

"Maybe he's got people for that, too," Jim says.

That seems like it must be a joke, but he looks serious, so I ask, "What possible reason would he have to snoop on me?"

"Maybe it's just as simple as that he doesn't trust you."

"Well, I wasn't, as he put it, a team player. I think I've got him on my side now, though."

"He might think you're a plant, to get the goods on him. Guys with something to hide are paranoid and there was some suggestion your promotion was, um, premature, considering your short tenure at the bank. He could have thought that, too."

"I'm sure everyone thinks I didn't deserve the promotion. I'd bet money that Hal figured he was in line for the job. I've always thought it would've made more sense to promote Hal to A.M. and give me his position. Not that I would've moved here for that. But you get my point."

"Hal will never move up to lending officer if his performance appraisals don't improve," Jim opines.

"Oh. Well, Fleet is the one responsible for those and I wouldn't take Fleet's opinion at face value. He might be using it as leverage to keep Hal in line."

"So he's just another toady who has to do what Fleet wants?"

"I think so. Fleet probably throws him a bone once in a while to make sure he remains a loyal member of he Fleet Admiration Society."

Jim chuckles at that, then says, "There's one other thing holding Hal back. He's on record that he won't move."

"What? I thought you had to be mobile in Saskatchewan in order to even get a lending officer position. Definitely if you're being groomed for management."

"That's right. He agreed to it, and moved here from Regina to take this position. Since then he's had a change of heart. Says he won't move now that his kids are in school."

"But they're so young. That's crazy! They won't be out of school for years. It's not the end of the world for kids to change schools."

"Yeah. My ex would agree with him on that point, though. But for Hal, if he doesn't get a promotion to management here, he's stuck as a consumer loans officer. He'll never get another raise except for cost of living increases."

"No wonder he hates me."

"So anyway, about the snooping in your house, Fleet might hope to get something on you. Either something to hold over you or something to prove you're a plant. Correspondence? Notes? Maybe something on your answering machine?"

"Oh! I guess he could play the messages on my phone! I didn't even think of that. If he happened to go in between the time you left that message and I erased it, he's heard at least one message from you."

"Yeah. That's unfortunate. But this guy you mentioned, the one who has first hand knowledge about Fleet's creative financing..."

"K.C. Garland. He's the guy that's meeting us for lunch," I tell him. "Like I said, I'll let him confirm the details."

"Right. What about your roommate—Kristy?—what has she got to say for herself?"

"I haven't confronted her yet."

"You're going to have to. She may have a reasonable explanation."

"What possible excuse is there for lying about when you moved in? Never a mention of knowing Jerry? The only thing I can think of is that she was in on it with Fleet from the very beginning. I feel so betrayed I don't even want to see her."

"Since you're living together, that's going to be a problem."

"Don't I know it. And her husband. If he's Fleet's muscle or works for him in some other capacity, convenient that he works nights and somehow never gets a day shift, isn't it? And he sure didn't want me going down to the beach. I think it's a hand-off zone for something. A boat, like maybe a zodiac, could easily run up on the beach and Kyle could meet it there. I know someone waited there, someone who smokes Sportsman cigarettes. Kyle smokes but not that brand so I'm still putting pieces together. But I'm sure he knows about it because I told him about a bunch of butts I found in one spot there. I think he went and picked them all up so that when we went together so I could show him, they were gone. That's why we were on the beach the day we found Easton's body. Kyle said waves from the storm washed them away, but I don't think the water ever got that high."

Jim closes his eyes and rubs his face with both hands, then looks at me and says, "I think maybe we ought to get you out of there until we find out for sure your, er, *friends* aren't involved. I'm meeting with Allard after our lunch with K.C., but after that we'll see about getting a monthly rate from a motel somewhere. Okay?"

I breathe a sigh of relief. "Okay." Until just now I didn't realize how uneasy I've felt on learning Kristy and Kyle had been in the house since last December when Kristy claimed they had only moved in shortly before I did. They must have known Jerry. They could be involved in his disappearance.

Then I realize Kristy agreed to do some detective work. "You know, Jim, maybe it's better if I just carry on as if I never saw her signature on that lease. Kristy offered to go to Gold's Menswear and see if any of the clerks will tell her about Fleet's shopping habits. If he's spending big bucks at a high-end store, it bolsters our suspicions that he's living beyond his means. So I need to keep to business as usual until she reports back on that."

Jim draws a couple of quick breaths and breathes out loudly. "I don't like the idea of leaving you in there, in case Fleet's behind—what? A murder and a disappearance? Maybe two murders? This is way more than a bank fraud investigation. I'm going to touch base with some of my old RCMP buddies and I'll contact your Detective Allard as well. I don't think finding out Fleetwood's been buying expensive clothes is that important."

"How else can we prove he's living beyond his means? He's covering his tracks so carefully R. O. hasn't been able to figure out what he's doing. If he's paying cash for everything, there won't be bank or credit card records to prove there's more money going out than what's coming in. Also, it could be a test for Kristy."

"She could just make something up. Say they wouldn't talk to her or whatever."

"I suppose. But it's just a little longer. And I'm really hoping I'm wrong about her. This might do it."

"I'll think about it," he agrees. He looks at his watch and says, "I guess it's time we left. Where is this place we're meeting?"

I give him directions to the diner K.C. suggested, on the highway north of town. "I'll leave here about ten minutes after you do."

Now who's paranoid?

I pull into the diner's parking lot and drive around to park behind it, out of sight from the highway per Jim's suggestion. There's a vacant spot next to K.C.'s truck but in an abundance of caution, I don't park next to it, choosing instead a spot practically in the bushes at the far end.

A cowbell over the door jangles as I walk in. K.C. is in a booth at the back, watching for me. He waves. Jim has obviously already figured out who he is and is sitting across from him. Great detective skills, or the fact K.C. is the only one in the place wearing a cowboy hat? I want to say it's the skills but have to admit it's likely the hat.

They both have coffee. Menus lie unopened on the table.

"Hi," K.C. says, and gives my knee an affectionate squeeze as I slide in beside him. "We've been talking while we waited for you."

"Well, you're the one with the information," I say.

"Sure, but..."

He's interrupted by the waitress. "Hi, there," she says to me, "coffee? Or are we ready to order?"

"Haven't looked at the menu yet," I tell her, "but yes to the coffee."

"You got it, hon," she says. "I'll be right back with a mug."

"We should order," Jim suggests. "I think we all have work to do this afternoon."

"Oh? What are you planning?" I ask.

"As I told you, Detective Allard agreed to meet with me. Besides that, I need to call Ed Ferguson at Regional Office. He's the Real Estate Department Supervisor. Find out why that house you live in isn't listed for sale. We're not in the rentals business. And the more I think about it, you and your predecessor wind up living in it? How does that happen? I wonder..."

"You're wondering if that rental agent is also a member of the Fleet Admiration Society?" I interrupt.

"Yeah. It crossed my mind."

"Seeing spiders everywhere?" I ask.

"I have that cop brain as you pointed out, so it's par for the course. What excuse do you have?"

I smile and shrug. "Just naturally suspicious."

"If Everett wasn't exaggerating, seems like you've got a cop's brain too. At least your suspicions panned out once before."

The waitress returns with my coffee and wants to take our orders but I still haven't looked at the menu. I open it now, tell the others to go ahead and order while I peruse it. I'm not even really seeing the menu as my mind is on what Jim just said. Finally I tell the waitress I'll have what K.C. ordered, and carefully sip my coffee. When the waitress flits away, I look at Jim and ask, "What, exactly, did Everett tell you?"

"Er, um," Jim stammers, "he said something about a murder, bank fraud and rustlers. That you got evidence that took them down."

"Murder? Rustlers?" K.C. asks.

"It was a couple years ago. You might have heard about it," I tell him. "I'll explain another time. For right now, I'd really like you, Jim, to answer one question: was I, in fact, a plant?"

Jim fiddles with his napkin-wrapped bundle of cutlery as if choosing his words carefully, then looks me in the eye and says, "Full disclosure? We wanted inside information and didn't know who to tap. It had to be someone working closely with Fleet. Someone who knew the workings. We thought about Jerry and Hal, but Jerry disappeared and Hal, um, didn't impress.

None of the secretaries did, either, not for what we needed, anyway. And how to be sure whomever we chose wasn't in on it? It had to be someone from outside and Everett said if anyone could find out what was going on, it was you. Jerry's abrupt departure created an open position we could reasonably say you were qualified for. So here you are."

"You already knew Jerry's T4 was returned when I asked you about it. Right?"

"Um, well, yeah. We tried to find him, but couldn't." He clicks his tongue and adds, "Don't be mad. We had no idea you were living in the same suite. No one put that together. There was some forehead slapping when they pulled your personnel file, believe me. You're good at your job and you *are* qualified, even if you're a little green."

Now the reason for Everett coming to Wacasko-Wâti and making sure his wife and daughter left us alone for a private conversation that day is obvious. He is my handler and he was just checking in. I don't know if I'm mad or not. Maybe just betrayed. A feeling I've had a lot lately. "A heads up would've been nice," I say. "We can talk about this later. Right now, I'll let K.C. tell you what he knows." I sink back into the upholstery and hope it's not obvious I'm fuming.

"Well, I uh," K.C. starts, "I only know Fleet slightly. I went to the bank to get a line of credit for my horse trailer dealership and of course I was referred to him. In his opinion, I was a bad credit risk. Cleaned out by my divorce, no residence stability, starting a new business. Later his flunky called and said that Mr. Fleetwood had decided to approve my loan after all. More than I asked for, and they'd give me a preferred interest rate but there would be a surcharge, to be paid in cash at the first of every month. I told him he should tell Mister Fleetwood to put it where the sun don't shine. Apparently no one's ever said that before because he seemed offended. I would've thought he'd be used to it. Ha!" He chuckles. "Anyhow, I went to your competition and they were happy to set me up with flooring credit for the dealership as well as a line of credit for the whole business, stable and all."

"Not such a bad credit risk after all, I guess?" Jim says.

"Well, we started off small and built it up."

"Sensible," Jim opines.

"Didn't stop that asshole from having his flunky calling and harassing me, though. There are things involving my trailer dealership he could tell the Better Business Bureau about, he said. He even threatened to tell the cops I, er, have an unhealthy interest in my young female students. If I moved my accounts over to Western, none of that would happen. Course he won't say anything face to face. We're both in Rotary and he pretends like he doesn't know me. He finally quit calling me and sent his muscle to Windsong instead. Not that long ago, actually. I wasn't there when he came and you would've thought that would be the end of it, but the asshole came back later and cornered me."

Fleet's muscle? Could that be Easton, and was that why I saw him at Windsong? I feel a chill. "What was that guy's name?" I ask.

"Um, kind of an unusual one. I didn't pay much attention but Devon wrote it down. Evan? Ethan? Something like that."

"Easton?"

"That's it."

I draw a quick breath. So K.C. could be the last person to see Easton alive. On top of that, could the things Fleet threatened K.C. with be true?

The waitress brings our meals, sets them in front of us and asks if she can bring anything else. We all mutter something like 'that's it for now' and she leaves.

"So if K.C.'s not a customer at our bank, how did you find him?" Jim asks me. He picks up his burger with both hands and manages to get an impressive amount of it in his mouth.

"I'm a customer of his," I reply. "I board my horse at his stable. So it wasn't super sleuthing or anything like that. Just plain dumb luck." I look at my food and realize K.C. and I are having probably the only Mexican-inspired item on the menu, chicken quesadillas. He picks up one of the stuffed tortilla triangles on his plate and dips it in the sour cream and salsa before taking a bite. I do likewise with mine.

When K.C. swallows his first bite, he says, "I'd say I was the lucky one."

"Oh, yeah?" Jim asks.

"Yeah. You ever see a beautiful girl and wonder if she could be single, then see her with the biggest shithead in town? That's what happened. I was at a restaurant. She came in with Fleet. Didn't seem much like a business lunch, the rate they were putting away the booze. I thought if she's with him, well, you know. The company you keep. Then she shows up at my barn. I almost didn't let her bring her horse. Especially after I saw her truck." He explains how I flipped him off my first day in town. Now it seems quite funny.

"With a rocky start like that, I'm surprised you're together," Jim says.

"That's a relatively new development," I mutter, and glower at K.C. I feel my face growing warm.

He grins at me and continues, "I thought, here's this beautiful girl, landed in my lap almost, I should at least give her the benefit of the doubt. And then I saw her horse and that was it for me." There's a twinkle in his eye as he faces me and winks.

I give him a jab with my elbow.

"Ow!" he exclaims. As if it hurt!

"Must be some horse," Jim comments, and grins.

"She's a beauty," K.C. agrees. He chuckles and continues: "Seriously, though, I wanted to find out what her connection to Fleet was before things got more, um, interesting. I knew from her application for board that she worked at the bank, but I needed to know if she was in on his scam or didn't even know about it. Plus, it wouldn't be the first time a secretary had an affair with the boss. When I overheard her on the phone, the things she was saying about Fleet, I, um..."

"*That* was it," I finish his sentence for him.

"And the rest is history," Jim says, and puts the last bite of burger in his mouth, glances at his watch and says, "Sorry, folks, I gotta run. I'll see you back at the branch later, Lindy. We'll talk about your living arrangements then." He takes a last French fry and gets to his feet. "Put this on your expense account, Lindy."

As we watch him walk away, K.C. says, "So. Rustlers?"

"I, er, it's a long story. No time for it now. I have to get back to work."

"Me, too. Farrier's coming this afternoon."

"You're still going to hold Chica for me, right?"

"Right. But I'd like to know more about those rustlers."

"Here's the Reader's Digest version: I had a relationship with two of them. They're both in jail. It's the reason I swore off men in general and cowboys in particular. And yet, here I am."

Yeah, here I am. Hooked up with another cowboy, this one possibly even worse than the last two.

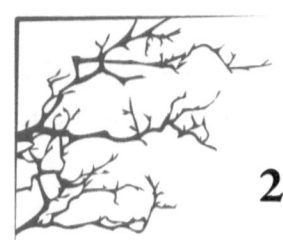

23—Fleetship Down

As I head back to work my thoughts are in a stew over K.C.'s revelation that he met with Easton. As I near the branch, I'm passed by a speeding RCMP cruiser, sirens blaring, lights flashing. It slows enough to make the turn into Rotary Park. In seconds, another cruiser and a fire truck with lights and sirens approach from the other direction and also turn into the park. Something serious must be happening there. I pull into my assigned slot in the bank parking lot and go inside.

A crowd of customers is forming at the window facing the park, their attention drawn by the police presence and the cloud of black smoke off in the distance. I go upstairs and into Fleet's office. From this vantage point I make out a boat on fire. Little fires on floating debris surround it. It must have exploded. Other boats are gathering, likely to rescue anyone who might be in the water. The police boat approaches at speed but there's nothing anyone can do other than watch it burn itself out. I hope no one was hurt but it seems impossible anyone could have escaped.

I return to my desk and I'm working through the files R. O. approved, especially interested in the two-page single-spaced suggestions for restructuring for Korsky's Furniture, organizing my thoughts ahead of a meeting with their owner. This is Mr. Janzen's file. He's the R. O. supervisor I shadowed when I was first promoted to lending officer. He always gives reasons for the solutions he suggests, so it's a great learning opportunity. I'm leaning back in my chair to stretch when Kristy, in a very short white skirt and equally skimpy tank top, appears in my doorway.

"Knock, knock!" she says. "Got a minute?"

"Of course. Come on in. Have a seat and tell me what brings you downtown today."

"Well, remember my Katawasis Girls' task was to check out Gold's Menswear?"

"Oh, yeah. You did that today?"

"Yup. And man, you should see all the eighty dollar ties! Blew my mind! And a hundred dollar belt! Just a plain black thing. I was almost afraid to touch anything."

"The men's equivalent of Dolly's Dresses," I conclude. "Did the clerk tell you anything?"

"Of course!" She giggles. Her earrings remind me of the chandelier in my mother's dining room. I can almost hear them tinkle as she shakes her head. All in all, it looks like she chose her best floozie outfit for the occasion. "You think I don't know how to get a man to talk?"

"I mean, without going to bed with him."

"Well, that does make it a little harder," she agrees. "But you should've seen them. Even the old guy with the tape measure around his neck. They crowded in so close when they were showing me stuff that I couldn't keep my boobs from bumping up against one or the other. When I slid along the young guy's arm, I think he got a stiffy. You would of thought they never seen boobs before."

"Well, not like yours, except in Playboy. So, did you accomplish anything other than giving a couple of clerks some cheap thrills? Which by the way, I think you probably enjoyed as much as they did?"

"Yeah, I did! I knew this Katawasis Girls thing was going to be fun!" She giggles and says, "Anyhow, they know Fleet and had a couple suggestions." She pulls a plastic Gold's Menswear bag from her oversized purse.

"You bought something?" I ask.

"Nothing big. Some ties. And these." She roots through the bag and pulls out a plastic-wrapped packet. "Did you know he wears boxers? Lookit this! Hearts all over them! It's like a joke but they called to me. I told the guys I was gonna put them away for Valentine's day."

"But Kristy, the expense!"

"Obviously I didn't spend *my* money. And they said he can exchange anything if he wants to and I can come back anytime, even if I'm not looking for anything in particular. You know, just to check out the new stock. They'll be getting in lots of new robes and slippers pretty soon. Gloves and scarfs too. Great for Christmas shopping."

"Kristy! Focus! How did you buy that stuff if not with your own money?"

"Well, here's the thing. Maybe I was a little naughty." She giggles and squirms. Her earrings tinkle. "Remember we talked about how I would pretend to be shopping for a present from the staff? Well, I thought—and here's what might be naughty, but I think he has it coming—what if I pretended to be his girlfriend instead? I didn't plan it that way, it just came to me when I was there. I figured they'll probably think he's a real player, which is the downside because they'll admire him for it, but maybe it'll get back to his wife. Whatever happens in that case, he deserves it for all the trouble he makes for you."

"Um, well..." I have to admit I'm impressed. "It's a good plan, Kristy. A great plan. But again, how did you get away without paying?"

"I just put it all on Fleet's account! You see? I couldn't have done that if I wasn't his girlfriend. In fact, I'm surprised they let me do it at all."

"Wow! Really? I'm surprised, too. But did you find out anything that actually helps us?"

"Um, well, maybe. Maybe not. Anyhow it's something I didn't expect. They say Fleet never pays for anything. He just puts it on his account. Which is when I thought they might let me put something on his account if I talked sweet enough. Which they did. I can get a man to do more than just tell me stuff!"

"He puts it on his account? That's not really a surprise."

"No? Well, here's what's surprising: his sugar daddy comes in every month, and pays."

"Sugar daddy? You can't be serious! Did they give you a name?"

"Um, no. They didn't call him that, of course, but they did sort of chuckle about him. Like they know his dirty secret and wanted me to know they knew. Like a jab, like maybe his girlfriend would give him trouble if she found out about a boyfriend. Whoever this guy is, apparently he doesn't buy his clothes there. And he's what they called 'husky'. But he always has a bundle of cash, no cheque or credit card, and the clerks figure with all that money he could let them get him into something 'nicer for a man his size.'" She holds up both hands to make air quotation marks. "He must be an asshole to deal with, 'cause they said he's not like Fleet and they all think Fleet's nice. So. Does that sound like anyone you know?"

"Hmm. A big guy who doesn't dress well, has money and is obnoxious? Not much to go on and I have no idea."

"I sure don't. Let's both think about it. We should have a Katawasis Girls meeting."

"Yeah. Let's see when we can arrange it. With your work schedule..."

"I'm on this afternoon, just a four hour shift so I'm off at six. Are you sure we couldn't meet at our place?"

"I guess it's probably okay. I'll see what Deena has going on."

"Okay! I need to get a move on if I'm going to get to work on time. Besides, I want to go see what's going on over at the park. Must be a fire. All that smoke!"

"There's a boat on fire out on the lake. You can see it from the window in Fleet's office."

"Oh yeah? Well, I'm going to go over for a closer look. I'll see you later."

"Yeah, see you later," I respond, and give her a smile.

She stands and flits out the door.

Other than being a surprisingly good actress/spy, I conclude that what you see is not what you get with Kristy. Her dumb act is just that, an act. I am going to ask her about her moving date, now half-ways confident she will have an explanation. This gives my spirits a lift.

But Fleet is more of an enigma than ever. Who is the money man? Does this mean Fleet isn't embezzling from the bank to finance his lifestyle, but has a generous boyfriend? Could his unexplained absences be trysts with his lover?

I need to talk to Jim. And we definitely need a meeting of the Katawasis Girls.

I expected Jim back in the office, but he doesn't show. He doesn't even call until a few minutes before five.

"Much to discuss, Lindy. Some significant developments. I'm sorry it's so late. I was thinking maybe we could talk over dinner, if K.C. doesn't mind."

"For the record, K.C. has nothing to say about it. But, um, actually I have plans. Just staying home but I've invited Deena for supper and Kristy will be there too. You could join us, though."

After a moment's hesitation, he agrees. "Sure, I guess. As long as we have a chance to talk privately at some point."

"You're going to want to hear what Kristy has to say," I tell him, "then you can decide if you really need privacy."

"Now I'm intrigued."

"Okay. I was just going to pick up KFC, so don't expect much."

"I'll pick up the chicken, and see you in a bit."

Although it's another fabulous evening and we'd all rather be out on the deck enjoying the view, we are gathered around the kitchen table. We can't risk being overheard. By whom? Maybe the neighbors, because although we can't see through the hedge, we've heard them talking so we know they can hear us. And then there's Kyle, who definitely could overhear everything even if he's not outside, just by opening a window. I may have eliminated him as the beach smoker but I don't trust him yet. So here we sit, munching KFC, the already cold KFC fries, and coleslaw bitter enough to have been made days ago. Jim also came armed with a dozen beer, and of course a bottle of Wacasko-Wâti rhubarb wine is open on the table.

"The wine's good," Jim says. "Didn't know how it would be, not being made from grapes, but I like it."

"Thanks," I say. My opinion of him climbs a few notches.

"Where'd you say that winery of yours is? Near Maple Creek? I'm going to have to swing by there the next time I'm at that branch."

"I hope you never have to go to that branch, Jim! But come ahead on the Labour Day Weekend. We're going to have pony rides. Well, big ponies of the horse type. Bring your kids."

"My ex has the boys that weekend but I'll see if I can pry them away. Switch weekends or something."

"Okay! So, meeting called to order!" I say. "First, if Jim and Kristy don't mind, because I haven't heard from you yet, Deena please bring us up to date on the KFP angle."

"I, um, I'm sorry, Lindy, I have nothing to report. Uncle Darius wouldn't discuss Band business so he didn't tell me anything. He more or less just patted me on the head as if I'm a child. I guess I am still a child as far as he's concerned."

"It's okay, Deena. It was a stretch, thinking he'd tell you anything anyway. If he's got something cooking with Fleet he's not going to say anything to give himself away. And he's also not going to badmouth him or pass along gossip from the NorSask CEO. And I doubt the CEO would tell Darius why he doesn't bank at Western anyway. We'd have to get Darius to ask him about it, and from the sound of it, Darius isn't going to go along with that."

"Maybe I should go and interview him," Kristy says. "Does he like white girls?"

"I don't know," Deena admits.

"You're so tanned you barely look like a white girl," I point out, "but what excuse would you possibly have to meet with him, Kristy?" I ask.

"None, I guess. But maybe we could have a party at Deena's, or something?"

"Okay, let's put that on a back burner, though. Kristy, tell everyone what you told me this afternoon."

She giggles and embellishes the story a bit, but otherwise gets the information across.

"So, you think he's not, er..." Jim begins, and looks around.

"Don't worry, Jim," I tell him, "we're sworn to secrecy. Nothing we discuss leaves this room. Or at least, we don't talk about it to anyone else."

"Yeah. We're the Katawasis Girl Detectives," Kristy tells him, and slides her chair a little closer to his. She was looking at him with great interest from the moment he came in but since his comment that made it plain he's not married she's really warming to him. I wonder if he's going to need that motel room he booked.

"Katawasis Girl..."

"You'll think we're a bunch of ten-year-olds, but it's our club," I explain. "We invented it when I was denied the privilege of joining the Friends of Katawasis, a hoity-toity Rotary wannabe ladies group Fleet's wife is president of."

"Okay," he says, and shrugs. "I guess I should've told you my news first, because it pretty much means all the detective work you've done wasn't necessary. But then of course I would've missed out on Kristy's very entertaining story." The two of them lock eyes for longer than necessary before he continues: "This is going to be on the news once next of kin are notified anyway. The boat that exploded? They towed what's left of it to the marine ways and pulled it out of the water. It's still too hot to board but they've seen two skulls. Since the boat is the Fleetship and the guys at the ways know it belongs to Fleet, it's likely one is Fleet's. No idea yet who the other person is."

We all gasp and I say, "Fleet's boat?!? Oh my god!" I take a long drink of wine, then close my eyes as I process this. Fleet's boat. Two bodies. What is the likelihood they weren't lovers? Slim to none. I've wondered about him and Corrine from my first day here. And now he's got a boyfriend, too? We don't know who or where the boyfriend is, but Corrine booked a week off the same day Fleet told me he was going out on his boat. Coincidence? I doubt it. I say, "I think the second person might be Corrine."

"Who's Corrine?" Kristy asks.

"I call her his office wife," I reply. "She took a week's vacation out of the blue the day Fleet announced he'd be 'recuperating' on his boat for a week. Fleet told me to give her some sick days so as not to use up the holidays she had coming. Hope I'm wrong, but I'd bet money her vacation was going to be with him, on his boat."

"Could be his wife," Jim suggests. "They haven't been able to locate her."

"She doesn't like going out on the boat," I tell them. "But if she went this time, they have a young daughter. She'd likely be with them. So there should be three bodies."

"They might find a third once it cools enough that they can go over it," Jim says

"Well, whoever it is, they were definitely knocking boots or she wouldn't be on the boat with him for a week," Kristy says.

"Could've been a day trip," I point out.

"If it's Corrine, how unimaginative," Kristy continues as if I haven't spoken. "The boss and the secretary! But he's got a mistress plus a boyfriend and was making moves on Lindy, too? Horny bastard!" She giggles and then says, "Oops! Not funny. This is where Kyle would say, *Jesus, Kristy*."

"It's okay, Kristy," Jim says, "I was thinking it, too, except I didn't know he was, um, bothering Lindy."

"He bothers everyone. Not just me," I tell him, "although I've never seen him give Hal a neck rub."

"So, about that," Kristy says, "if he's AC/DC, why didn't he ever give Hal a neck rub?"

"You haven't met Hal," Deena says.

"Hal isn't much to look at, it's true, but I don't think it's about sex," I opine. "I think it's more a control thing. I mean, sometimes it was just friendly or he thought it was sexy, but it could also be about control. There was one neck rub I was recently on the receiving end of that left bruises."

"I shouldn't say it, but if one of those skulls is his, I'm starting to feel less sorry," Jim says.

I top up everyone's glass and we all retreat into our own thoughts. I spear another forkful of fries, stuff them in my mouth and after a few chews, wash them down with wine. As unappetizing as they are, if no one else wants any more, I'll polish them off. My cowhand appetite isn't deterred by greasy limp fries.

"So," Jim says after a bit, "I've got tons of work to do if Lindy's right about the possibility of fake accounts, but I can do most of that from my office at R. O. My work here is almost done. I've let Detective Allard know we're halting our fraud investigation."

"What if there's someone at the branch who can pick up the reins and carry on, though?" I ask.

"Who would that be? There's no one other than you who would be in a position to do it."

"Hal, maybe?"

"Hal? Doubt he's got the smarts. But tell you what. Business as usual. Any accounts Fleet's been propping up by making payments from fake accounts will soon go into arrears and we can deal with them then. If the branch performance improves, that means the problem ended with Fleet. If not, we'll take another run at it. Okay?"

"You're the boss," I agree.

"Are we done, then?" Deena asks. "Meeting over? If so, I'll take off."

"Yes, go ahead. I'll see you tomorrow."

Deena stands, says goodbye to everyone, and leaves.

Jim and Kristy give no indication they're going anywhere. She giggles and says, "You don't have to hurry away tonight, do you?"

"Um, no."

"When are you going back home?"

"Not till Friday. I still have a few things to do in town."

"Aww! Do you have to leave so soon? Maybe you could take a couple vacation days and stay the weekend."

"Maybe I could, at that," he agrees.

"Oh, damn!" I exclaim, "I forgot to get cream. For coffee in the morning. I'm going to run out and get some."

Kristy seldom drinks coffee and knows I don't take cream in mine. Besides, she's never up before I leave. But if she heard what I said it didn't compute. And I'm pretty sure neither of them notices me leaving.

24—Detectives at Large

The news the Western Savings and Loan bank manager was one of the victims of yesterday's boat explosion is all over radio and TV news this morning. I call a staff meeting. We cluster around the table in the staff room, some sitting, some standing, while I stand at the end wall to face them. From their expressions you'd think they lost a loved one.

"As sad as we all are at this awful thing and how we've come to love Fleet, to Regional Office he's just another manager. They'll assign an interim manager to serve until a permanent manager is appointed," I tell them, hoping my voice makes me sound like I'm as miserable as they look.

"Won't they promote you to manager, Lindy?" Mae asks.

"Heavens, no!" I reply. "If I'd been here longer they probably wouldn't need an interim manager, but as I'm sure you all know, I'm a rookie. I'm not even qualified for the interim position let alone the permanent one. There are plenty of people more qualified. They've got seventy-some branches in our region to choose from, remember, and they could even tap someone in another region. As soon as I find out who it's going to be, I'll let you know. Meanwhile, it's business as usual. If you have any questions, my door is always open, and Hal is always close at hand and happy to help, too."

Hal has squeezed his ample frame into the space between the fridge and the bank of storage shelves as if in the hope no one would notice him there. Maybe he just wanted to be as far from me as possible. Besides Deena and me, he might be the only staffer who isn't grieving. I give him a look I hope is oozing sincerity, wondering if the ego-stroking won him over. Judging by his scowl, it didn't. Maybe he knows no one would ever ask him for help. At least no one laughed when I suggested it.

One of the tellers asks, "What do we tell people who ask about him?"

"You just say we're all saddened. If they ask if he had kids, you comment on his young daughter. Then ask what you can do for them today. Okay everyone?"

There's a chorus of agreement, and I close the meeting with: "So, back to work, business as usual, then."

I have a couple of things I was working on yesterday to finish up, so it's definitely business as usual for me. As everyone files out of the room, I say, "Deena? Come up when you have a minute, please. I have a job for you."

Deena appears within minutes, and asks, "What's up?"

"Come in and close the door."

She does, and takes a chair across from me.

"Remember when we were talking about it at my place yesterday, Jim seemed to think the whole issue with Fleet ended with his death? Like us Katawasis Girls could stand down?"

"Yeah...?"

"Well, my first thought was that at least you and I can go back to being friends at work."

"I thought so, too."

"Then I thought about it some more and decided that for the time being, we should carry on as if I was firmly on Fleet's side, which means you're still someone I'm too good to associate with."

"Okay..."

"Jim only really cares about fraud. That's his job, after all, and he thinks his case is solved. I'm not so sure about that, but even if I'm wrong, Katawasis Girls doesn't end with the bank fraud. We're like, um, detectives at large and we still have the Jerry and Easton mysteries. We know Jerry is connected to this place. His disappearance may not have anything to do with Fleet, but we can't rule it out. Thanks to K.C. we know Easton was connected to Fleet. And what if whoever killed Easton and, um, *disappeared* Jerry, is also responsible for the boat exploding?"

"Oh!" She cocks her head and chews her lip, then asks, "You don't think Fleet was behind Easton and Jerry?"

"Maybe not. And if Fleet's not responsible, the perpetrator is still here."

"Still here?"

"Yeah. Still here. And still a danger."

Jim doesn't make an appearance until nearly noon. For a second I don't realize it's him now that he's in a suit and tie and isn't wearing a ballcap. If I worried the staffer who sent him up to my office yesterday when he was pretending to be a prospective customer might recognize him, I'm not worried now. Good lord! He was easy to look at in his jeans, a sort of blond Rob Lowe, but dressed like this he's downright breathtaking! He might be ten years older than she is, but I can't blame Kristy for being attracted to him. He comes into my office with a mug of coffee in one hand and a napkin-wrapped donut in the other. "Good morning," he says.

At least if I'm drooling it can be put down to the sight of the donut. "Good morning. So. Coffee and a donut. Breakfast or lunch?" His rental car was still in front of our house when I left this morning so I think it could be the former.

"Call it brunch. I stopped by Tim Horton's and picked up a couple boxes of these," he says, lifting his donut. "They're in the lunchroom. You could say I'm sucking up to the staff. Would've brought one up for you but I thought you'd rather choose for yourself."

"Oh, thanks. I'll go down in a bit," I tell him. From his expression and general body language, I think he had a pretty good night even though I doubt he got much sleep. I return his smile and say, "You might as well use Fleet's office. We had a meeting this morning so everyone's expecting interim managers. First one might as well be you."

"So we're on the same page. Not that I know more about lending or the management side of banking. You'll still have all that on your plate, but I'm more senior than you so I'll be a sort of figurehead holding down the fort until a permanent manager gets here. I've already been in touch with R. O. and they agree, so I'll be here for longer than I thought. By the way, I owe you girls for a long distance call I made from your house."

"You can pay us in donuts," I suggest.

He grins and nods, then continues: "I have more phone calls to make and I'm going to go over some of the files. Is Fleet's desk locked?"

"I, er, yeah. Corrine locked it before she left and if there's another key somewhere, I haven't found it."

An expression of mock surprise crosses his face. "Some Katawasis Girl Detective you are, defeated by a simple lock," he chuckles, and leaves my office, heading for Fleet's. In a moment, he calls, "Yup! Locked!"

Rather than shouting back, I go to the door of Fleet's—now Jim's—office to tell him I'll call a locksmith and find him in the chair, bent over, fussing with something. There's a little leather case like a manicure set containing what look like crochet hooks open on the desk to. In a moment, he pops upright, puts his tools down, and pulls the drawer open. "Eureka!" he exclaims.

"You gotta teach me to do that," I say.

"It just takes practice," he replies. "If you want to be detectives, all you Katawasis Girls should have the skills. These desk locks are simple. You don't even need these tools. Could've unlocked it with a couple of paperclips." He might be poking fun but I can't tell, as he turns and leans over the bottom desk drawer and thumbs through files. "What's Corrine's last name?"

"Um, Bennett. Corrine Bennett."

"Here we are," he says. He pulls out a file and opens it on his desk. "I'm going to swing by her place and see if she's home. I needed her address."

"You could've got that from her account in the computer."

"Sure, but I want this drawer open anyway, so... Also, I'll be checking in with R. O. to see if they've figured out what they're going to do about a real interim manager. I'll let you know as soon as I hear. Meanwhile, where's that baseball cube you were talking about?"

"It's in the back corner of that file drawer. Behind the files."

He turns his attention to the drawer again, slides the files and says, "Yeah, I see it. Got a Kleenex?"

"In my desk. I'll get it." I go back to my office, get the Kleenex box, and return to put it on the desk in front of Jim.

He pulls a tissue out of the box and uses it to lift the plastic cube out of the file drawer and set it on the desk. "Jerry's brother reported him missing so now it's official. This will be evidence. I'm going to drop it off at the Detachment."

"It's so sad. Sounds like Jerry and his brother were very close, and no other relatives, really. I guess Ken gave up hoping he'd turn up somewhere."

"Well, he may not have given up hoping he's alive, but it's looking like it's his remains they pulled out of the lake last week."

I draw a deep breath and click my tongue. "I was afraid of that."

"No positive I.D. yet, though, just that he's the only missing person reported in this area who disappeared in the likely time frame. Not easy making a positive I.D. with the body the way it is. Still, it's surprisingly well preserved, if it is him, considering how long he's been missing. They figure it must have been down deep where the water's really cold. Did you know the lake is four hundred feet deep in places? Anyway, it's cold enough to preserve a body, or at least slow the decomp. The things you learn in the field," he says, then draws and exhales a deep breath. "They're going to get his clothes laid out and photographed to see if anyone can I.D. him from what he was wearing. Oh, and there's a tattoo. New York Yankees logo on his chest, apparently. I guess none of our staff would know about that, since he likely never had his shirt off at work, but the brother should be able to confirm if he had it. They're trying to contact him now but his team is on the road. But if having this baseball is an indication he was a Yankees fan, I, well..."

"Yeah. But if it comes down to identifying him from his tattoo, there's someone else who might be able to tell us, and we don't have to wait until they contact his brother," I tell him.

"Who?"

"Kristy. It's time we had the talk, anyway."

"You want me to go with you?"

"Um, no, not necessary," I tell him. In fact, it might be better if he wasn't with me because I'm not sure either of them would even hear me.

"Okay. I assume you can't give me directions to Corrine's place."

"Nope, can't help you there."

"Is there a street map around here?"

"There's one in the back of the phone book."

"There is? Okay, thanks."

"Nice suit, by the way."

"Thanks." He shakes his head and says, "I wasn't prepared for this. No one could be, I guess. I brought nothing but jeans. Let's just say I'm glad

Gold's has a mark-down rack and their tailor agreed to hem the pants while I waited."

"So, you didn't bring a suit, but you brought your lock picking tools."

"Hey, have to keep in practice. I have a few padlocks with me too. It's something to pass the time. Like a Chinese puzzle. I'll get you a set."

"Thanks," I say, and I mean it. Even if I never actually picked a lock, it would be cool to know I could.

When I get home, Kristy is already in her low-cut Tall Trees Pub t-shirt, ready to leave for work. "You on the afternoon shift again, Kristy?" I ask.

"Yeah, but I'm back on close tomorrow. Naturally. Shitty timing, having to work close when Jim's only here for a few days. Gonna see if I can switch shifts with someone."

"Well, I have news. Jim's going to be here for longer than just this weekend."

"He is? Yay!" she exclaims. She reminds me of Tippy, the young Border Collie at Wacasko-Wâti whose whole body wiggles with delight when she greets me. "Um, how come?"

"He's going to play branch manager until R. O. comes up with someone who is actually a manager."

"That's awesome! He has, um, er, he does this... Oh, never mind! You'll just say it's too much information," she says, then giggles and wiggles some more. "Hey! What are you doing home so early?"

"I was hoping we could talk. Private. Not at the pub."

"Oh yeah? What's up?"

"Well, er, can we talk?"

"That sounds serious." She glances at her watch and says, "I guess so. Unless this is going to take, like, half an hour. I don't mind being a little late but..."

"I don't think so. But it's important."

"Okay, then. So, what's up?"

I lean back against the counter and reply, "I, um, don't know exactly how to say this, but, well, here goes: I saw your signature on the lease. It was dated before Christmas."

"Oh, you did? How?"

"When I was at the rental office."

"They let you read the lease?"

"Not intentionally."

She shrugs and says, "And so...?"

"So? Well, you told me you only moved in shortly before I did."

"Yeah, that's right. Of course, Kyle was here months before because he got this job and had to come right away."

"Oh. You didn't come with him?"

"No, I only came for a few days so we could look for a place to live. I was taking my G. E. D. and had to finish that. He wanted me to come when he did but no way was I going to give up my diploma so close to being done! I already screwed up, leaving school when I was sixteen."

"Sixteen?"

"Yeah. There was a boyfriend involved."

"Naturally."

"So anyhow, I told him we could wait to be married until I got here but I guess he was worried I might change my mind and stay in Calgary. He was right. I might have. As things've worked out I might go back there." She cocks her head and asks, "Why is that such a big balls deal?"

I shake my head slowly, digesting this. "It's a big balls deal because I, well, er, I guess I jumped to conclusions. I assumed you were hiding it from me and I couldn't figure out why. And then I found out the guy who had my job before I did and who is now missing, presumed dead, lived in the very suite I moved into. I thought you must have known that. And you must have known him. I wondered why you didn't tell me."

"Really? That's the Jerry guy you're talking about?"

"Yeah."

"You never told me he lived downstairs."

"I didn't?" I dig through my brain, trying to remember the conversations we've had since I found out. She's right. I didn't tell her. "Oh, my God!"

"So, that's the guy?"

196

"That's the guy. But Kristy, you might have mentioned his name was Jerry, too."

"I guess I might have, and I visited Kyle once before I moved here, saw him coming and going but I never met him. He was gone when I got here to stay."

"And Kyle never met him either?"

"He probably did, but he never said nothing. Hey, is that it? Is there something else you wanted to talk to me about? Because I gotta get going."

"I should get back to work, too. Sorry I, er, was suspicious of you."

"It's okay," she says, and gets to her feet. "Oh, hey! If we're looking for clues, those boxes in the basement? That's his stuff."

"You mean they're Jerry's? Not yours?"

"Nope, not ours. I didn't see them until I moved in. Who else would put their stuff in our basement? I asked Kyle whose they were and how they got there but he said they were there from day one. I told him they weren't there when we looked at the place but he said I was wrong, they were there and I just didn't remember. I'm the airhead, after all. No use arguing with him. You must've figured that out by now. So anyhow, I looked in a few and wondered why anyone would leave their clothes and stuff behind. Photos too. Do you think there might be something useful in there?"

"Yeah, maybe. A definite maybe."

"Why don't you and Jim check it out? If you get home before I do, you can start without me. Just don't hit on him." She giggles.

"It can wait. I still have an actual job."

"Me too. Speaking of which, I'm tail lights."

I get up to follow her through the house and out the front door.

I can't deny the quiver of excitement in my gut at the thought of what might be found in Jerry's belongings, but I really do have to get back to work, even though it's been mostly non-productive work fielding phone calls from everyone in town, it seems. Everyone wants assurances Western Savings and Loan will go on without Fleet so their loans will continue and their deposits are safe. I remind them Western Savings and Loan is a big company and besides, deposits are covered by government insurance. I'm getting quite good at quoting The Bank Act.

I turn into the lot to find it's full, even my assigned stall is occupied. It's surprising, because there were plenty of open stalls when I left. I back out, drive up the street, and find an open metered spot at the curb a block away, lock up and walk back to the branch. As I'm walking through the lot on my way to the employee entrance door I notice a young couple getting into a bright yellow Camaro. "Sure, now that I parked a block away you're leaving," I mutter.

I'm back at my desk struggling to push thoughts of Jerry and Fleet and Corrine out of my head so I can focus my attention on the file in front of me, when it occurs to me Hal's Jeep wasn't in its usual place. He always parks right beside the slot marked 'Reserved—Manager' close to the door so he doesn't have to take even three steps more than necessary. I've gotten accustomed to seeing the Cherokee there, second from the building, right where that Camaro was when I came in. I look out the window and spot it by the entrance at the far end of the lot. He would never have parked that far from the door when he arrived this morning and the lot was empty. Why is it there now? He must have gone out for something.

Why does that seem sneaky? There could be any number of reasons for him to leave. Maybe he had a doctor's appointment. Maybe he forgot his lunch and went home to eat.

"Spiders, Lindy," I tell myself.

My phone rings interrupting my thoughts. But the spiders have been awakened.

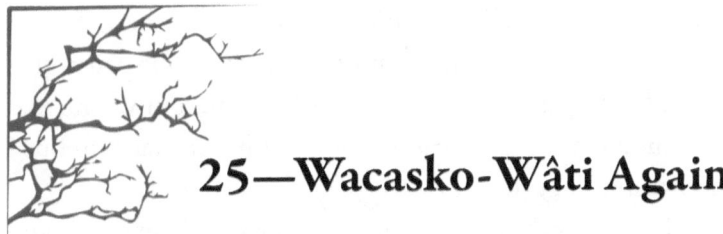

25—Wacasko-Wâti Again

If I was giddy at the prospect of searching those boxes and finding incriminating evidence, my hopes are dashed as soon as I tell Jim about them.

"Lindy, we can't go snooping through that stuff! He's a missing person, so if those boxes belonged to Jerry the cops will want them. If they suspect foul play, there may be important evidence."

"Well, that's what we thought. So..."

"So leave it for the forensics team before you destroy crucial clues."

"Like what?"

"I don't know... Fingerprints? Hair? Blood droplets, either his or someone else's? If he was still living in that suite or anywhere else for that matter when he went missing, they'd have forensics all over it. Just like they're going over Corrine's apartment as we speak."

"She's missing too? So it's her body on the boat?"

"Looks that way. They're hoping to find something to use to identify the remains. Likely it'll come down to dental records," he says, and scratches the back of his neck. "I'm glad to see you're not upset."

"Why would I be upset over Corrine being dead? Either of them, for that matter? I mean, it's awful they lost their lives and I hope they didn't suffer, but honestly, they're a big part of the reason this branch is a toxic workplace. I wouldn't wish them harm but I've often wished they would go away. I'm more worried about Jerry. We really can't look inside those boxes? They're in my basement, after all. It could be we had to check..."

"Forget it, Katawasis Girl. You know I'm right."

He is right. The Evidence Recovery Team comes. They photograph. They pack everything through our suite and out the front door into their van.

If that's all Jerry owned in the world, it's depressing to see how few boxes it took to contain his life. There's also the Yogi Berra baseball and his furniture, of course, and likely a vehicle, although that hasn't been found. But even adding those things, it's pathetic and sad. A nice young man just starting his life, gone; his hopes and dreams dashed. I hope I'm wrong and Fleet didn't do it so someone still alive can pay for it. I never met him but I feel connected, and I think I'm grieving.

Jim has rented a by-the-week motel suite just steps from the beach and Kristy has barely been home since. If I didn't go to Tall Trees for supper I'd never see her. As it is, she sweet-talked her boss into shuffling her shifts so she's off work when Jim is home, meaning she's seldom on the dinner shift, so visiting her at work is hit and miss. They divide their time between hiking some of the many wilderness trails in the area and lazing around on the beach, two activities I am welcome to join in on, and in bed, where I'm not. Not that I would go along with it anyway, but it's a measure of how smitten she is with Jim that she's never even jokingly suggested a threesome. That, and the fact she has become interested in hiking because he likes it. She bragged about making the trek up to Wapiti Falls, three hours each way. Yeah. Kristy is getting tanned *and* fit and I haven't had a hand-me-down romance novel in weeks.

Deena lives on the Rez, about an hour's commute, and we're sticking to our story about not being friends, so no spending breaks together at work. In the personnel reshuffle resulting from Corrine being gone, she was promoted and we hired a new girl for her old position. She's been spending more time with a distant cousin, too, emphasis on *distant*. I take that to mean he's a kissing cousin. It seems every time I get near her, she has something to say starting with "Well, Vic says," or, "Well, Vic thinks". K.C., Kristy, Jim and I had lunch with the two of them at Tall Trees one Saturday. He's good looking, is pretty high up in the tribe hierarchy, has a job at the mill and seems proud of Deena and her promotion. I'm happy for her, even though it seems Katawasis Girls is bust.

K.C.'s cabin isn't waterfront and it's definitely in the bush, but the area between it and the road is cleared, so there's enough direct sunlight it's not dark and gloomy. There's one bedroom, the "fireplace" is a free-standing woodstove, and a realtor would call it cozy. I'm spending a lot of nights there. When we want to see the lake, we hike down the lane through the trees down to the Kat. Sometimes we have a ridiculously expensive beer or glass of wine on their deck, but more often we bring our own and drink it dangling our feet in the water as we watch the sunset from their wharf. At least until they realize what we're doing and chase us off. It's okay to drink on their wharf as long as what you're drinking is purchased from them, it seems.

Jim won't be in Katawasis much longer, as the new manager is due to arrive right after Labour Day. Kristy was in a funk, but her mood improved when they made together plans for the long weekend. Jim is flying home to get his car and pick up his kids. He'll meet up with us in Maple Creek. I've offered to let them stay with me. I understand from Jim that his boys are stoked about spending time at a real ranch. I'm not so excited about it, because he wants his kids to meet his new girlfriend already? That's an indication of how serious things are between them even after even such a short time. I should be happy for her and I guess I am, but if she moves away there will be a void in my life, that's for sure.

Speaking of a short time, I like K.C. so much that I've pushed my suspicions about him deep into the back of my mind. I've seen enough of his interaction with the younger riders at Windsong and heard enough gossip from all the boarders that I'm sure he's not doing anything inappropriate. And I've concluded that although Easton might have been leaning on him on behalf of Fleet, K.C. handled it without killing him.

I'm not reining in my growing feelings for him and I wish he could come with me to meet everyone, but I've known for weeks that can't happen. There's a four-judge Quarter Horse show in Regina that Windsong people are entered in. K.C. is taking one of his horses, too, so visiting Wacasko-Wâti isn't on his itinerary. I wish it could be different, but I get it. As he said, there will be other weekends. He doesn't seem as disappointed as I am, so I have niggling doubts that he's as into me as deeply as I'm into him. We haven't said outright that our relationship is exclusive even if it seems to be and I wonder about the women he'll be interacting with at the show. Wonder is an understatement. Worry would be more accurate.

I'm happy to be going to the ranch even without him, though, because those long weekends I was promised have failed to materialize, shelved until the new manager gets settled in and can get Saturday openings organized. Even though the pull isn't as strong as it was before Chica was in Katawasis, Wacasko-Wâti has been calling me.

As expected on a Friday night before a long weekend, traffic is heavy and it's well after midnight when we pull into my garage. I don't get up until seven-thirty, which is considered sleeping in at Wacasko-Wâti. I leave Kristy snoozing and head down to the Bistro.

Preparations are well underway by the time I get there. Greetings are brief, since we're having a Labour Day Weekend Grand Opening and there's more work than usual to get ready. The Bistro has been in operation for a couple of years, but this is the first time the expansion that includes the wine-tasting bar has been open to the public. We're excited, and apprehensive.

To her credit, Kristy puts in an appearance early on and once introductions are made, dons a Wacasko-Wâti bib apron and pitches in to help, putting her Tall Trees experience to work. If Stu and Red wondered whether she was going to be a hindrance or a help, they soon find she is a definite asset. Family, staff, and customers, everyone loves Kristy. Just like at Tall Trees, although today she's wearing a t-shirt with a regular neckline so even the wives like her.

She takes a coffee break with Red and Stu, but otherwise doesn't even slow down until Jim arrives with his two boys. She takes them to my house to show them where they'll be sleeping, then they have lunch together in the Bistro, and she's back to work until I chase her out to spend time with them. She joins them on a trail ride. The kids love it and can't wait to go again. Kristy says now that she's ridden a horse, she never has to ride one again.

Although we hoped for more wine-buying customers, the grand opening of the tasting room and expanded bistro is a success. The weekend passes in a blur. Almost before I know it, I'm getting ready to head back to Katawasis. To no one's surprise, Kristy is going with Jim and the kids. She says she isn't staying in Calgary and promises to fly back to Katawasis 'real soon'. She waves from the passenger seat as they drive away and I wonder if that's a promise she can keep.

I've got half a dozen Red's Pies, which we now call Red's Famous Pies (three rhubarb and three saskatoon) along with a couple months' supply of Wacasko-Wâti wine loaded in my truck and I'm ready to take off almost right behind Jim and Kristy, when a familiar black dually with a logo on the door towing the Windsong four-horse trailer pulls into the lot. A wave of emotion floods through me. I try to slow my steps as I go to greet K.C. but get to his truck practically before it stops moving. He slides out, pulls me into his arms and gives me the best kiss we've shared so far.

"It's only been a couple days, but damn! I missed you," he whispers as he nuzzles my ear. And we kiss until we can't ignore the throat clearings coming from his passenger, and break apart.

"Lindy, you know Denise," he says, indicating the woman who has come around the front of the truck and now stands nearby.

She says, "Hi, Lindy."

"Of course! Hi, Denise! How'd you do at the show?"

"Good. K.C. did good, too."

"I'll tell you all about it later," K.C. says, and explains, "Denise is taking the truck and horses from here. I'll ride back with you. If that's okay?"

Okay? Is he kidding? "Of course it's okay."

"Great," he says, and gives my shoulder an affectionate rub. "Wow, this place looks terrific. Can we unload the horses and let them have a rest while you give us a tour? We'll still get home by midnight."

"Makes sense," I agree. "I'll see if we have an empty corral. If not, I'm sure there's empty stalls in the barn. You guys might as well grab something to eat and check out the tasting room while you're at it."

"Suits me," Denise agrees. "I wanted to get something to eat before we left Regina but your man, here, didn't want to take the time."

"Hey, you had a Coke and a bag of chips," K.C. points out. Then he turns to me and says, "I didn't know what time you'd be taking off, Lindy, and didn't want to miss you, so..."

Did Denise just call him my man?

I feel a warm glow.

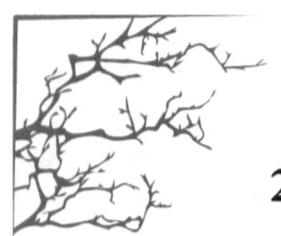

26—Hal A Palooza

The new manager couldn't be more different than the old manager if it was deliberate. Maybe it was.

He's been working at Western Savings and Loan for over thirty years and is older than I expected, late fifties, paunchy, and I'd doubt Gold's Menswear will have a new customer. I wonder what sin he committed to be transferred out to the boonies at this stage of his career. Because he's a smoker and smokes at his desk he allows everyone to do the same, so now neither Hal nor anyone else has to go outside for their nicotine fix and I can open my window without cigarette smoke funneling into my office. He hasn't shown an inclination to give anyone a neck rub, I don't have to run my work by him and he delegates more manager-type stuff to me so I'm gaining useful experience. It's all good so far.

A couple of loans were already in arrears before Jim left. He rooted out bogus loans that had been set up to make payments on other bogus loans but there was no paper trail for applications that I suspected were diverted into Fleet's side hustle. He looked into the cost overruns on the branch renovations and found Fleet got kickbacks from the trades: flooring, plumbing, electrical, everything but the counterfittings, which were manufactured in Calgary and installed by the factory's team. "That must've pissed him off, big time," Jim said when he was telling me about it. When he ran out of leads to follow he called the job done and R. O. agreed, satisfied the branch's problems died with Fleet.

There's still no arrest in connection with Easton's murder. Neither the Fleetship explosion nor the body pulled from the lake, now confirmed to be Jerry's, have been classed as suspicious deaths and public interest has faded. I get that it's hard to determine the cause of explosions because the evidence is destroyed, but it's beyond my understanding how they could think Jerry's death was anything other than murder. How did he get in the lake? Where's his car? If he swam fully clothed too far out to return in a bid to drown himself, his car should have been found. Besides, no one is stupid enough to try and commit suicide that way.

Jim is in Calgary and Kristy is still there with him. I don't know how she keeps herself busy, but I'm sure he's got lots to do both at work and at home, so I'm surprised when a package appears with the other mail on my desk one afternoon. Inside is a little leather case. The lock picking set Jim promised. His note reads: "See? I didn't forget". There's a second slip of paper reading, "Hi! Miss you! Kristy" with a heart over each letter *i*. No mention of when she's coming back.

K.C. is obsessing about the future of Windsong now that Katawasis Lake Lodge bought out the last lease and their expansion plans are gearing up. He's been trying to convince the planners to leave enough land out of their development so Windsong isn't destroyed, while at the same time scouting facilities to move the operation to. It'll be next to impossible to find something suitable close enough to keep his existing clientele, and I try not to think about the implication: that he'll have to relocate much farther away. Can we survive a long distance relationship? It's on my mind a lot so I can't blame him for being distracted, but I wish I could talk to him about my suspicions. I try. He lets me talk, then says something that proves he wasn't really listening. He'd probably nod and agree if I told him I dyed my hair green.

Deena's no help either, because she's consumed with her new job as well as with Vic.

The vibes I get from Detective Allard make me think he's about done with me.

I'm on my own.

Sure, Fleet's gone, but there's still Hal. Jim and Regional Office may have decided Hal is just what he appears to be: a socially inept low I.Q. peon promoted to his level of incompetence, but he's been on my radar ever since I noticed him sneaking out during working hours. I thought it might have been a one-time thing, but I need to be sure. With his office downstairs and mine up, I wouldn't know about his comings and goings if not for my window overlooking the parking lot. I rearranged my office and now instead of sitting with my back to the window so I have to swivel around to look out, it's on my right and I can look out when I'm on the phone or even when I'm dictating.

When my office was the alcove on the main level and he had a desk in the common area, I not only saw him every time I poked my head around the corner, but heard his ongoing grunting and throat-clearing and farting, even the squeaking of his chair every time he resettled his ample rump. I would've known if he left for an hour mid-afternoon, and I'm sure he didn't. What has changed? I'm not aware of any reason for a consumer loans officer to leave the office as much as he does.

I see his Cherokee leaving the lot and go down to his office, pretending surprise when I find he's not there. I ask the nearest teller, "Where's Hal?"

She shrugs and replies, "Out to lunch."

Well, he's always figuratively out to lunch, but I take it the way she meant it and say, "A little late for that, isn't it?"

She turns to check the schoolhouse clock on the wall behind the counter and says, "This is when he always goes."

Hal, the unqualified miser, has suddenly stopped eating lunch at his desk and is going out for lunch instead? Totally out of character. Suspicions aroused, I decide to follow him and see what he's up to. But how? By the time I see his Cherokee heading out of the lot, get down to my truck and out on the street, I'll be blocks behind him and if he turns off before I spot him I'll never catch up. So I start keeping a record of the times he leaves.

By the end of the week, I've established his schedule: he always leaves between 2:00 and 2:15 and returns in under an hour. Problem is, he doesn't go every day and while the time is always the same, it's not every day.

It's day three of me parking my truck on the street instead of in the lot, and going out to sit in it and watch. At least I only have to wait a few minutes because by 2:15 I can go back to work knowing he's not going anywhere. I'm about to give up for the third time when the red Cherokee noses out onto Main Street and turns left. I pull out onto the street three cars behind him and have no trouble keeping him in view.

I'm prepared for disappointment. He's not heading for his house but maybe he has to pick his kids up from school on the days his wife has her macrame class or something. But he makes a right turn onto Juniper. The route he follows is the one I drive every day to and from work. If there's a school in the area, I'm not aware of it.

He doesn't go as far as Katawasis Lake Road, though, instead he makes a left turn off Juniper at Robertson's Equipment Rentals. I have to wait for oncoming traffic before I can follow. I worry he might have gotten too far ahead, when I see the Cherokee turning into a fenced storage yard. I pull to the curb hoping the pyramid cedars lining the perimeter fence are enough that he won't notice me.

He drives past the trailers, campers and boats without stopping. When he continues through between the rows of storage buildings, I lose sight of him. I'm deciding whether to pull farther ahead or stay put when another car comes and turns into the lot. It doesn't go as far as the storage buildings, but pulls up on the far side of a boat on a trailer. I don't think much of it until I notice Hal walking out from between the storage buildings and hear him call a greeting to the new arrival.

I can't see the car's driver because they're on the far side of the boat, but the car! It looks like Fleet's Cadillac. It can't be. Maybe Meredith sold it. Or maybe it's just another one that looks the same.

Hal climbs up on the fender of the trailer and into the boat. He seems to be looking for something, all the while talking to the person on the other side. At one point, he turns to face the other person and the conversation becomes loud and angry, with much hand waving from Hal. It's too far away for me to catch more than a word or two so I have no clue what the argument is about. He turns away again and after a moment, straightens and hands something to the other person before clambering out. The conversation seems to continue. They must have reached an agreement because soon, the Cadillac backs away from the boat, turns, and heads back out the gate. As it passes me heading toward downtown, I duck so as not to be seen, but not before I get a good look at the driver.

It's not only someone Hal knows, but someone I know, too.

Now what do I do? I'm still mulling it over half an hour after I've returned to my desk.

No use calling Detective Allard to tell him who I think is responsible for Jerry's disappearance and the Fleetship explosion. I can hear the conversation now: Based on what, Lindy? Well, they had a clandestine meeting near a boat in a storage yard. Oh, I see. Don't you want to blame them for Easton's death too? So, um, yeah I do, actually.

Even if I don't say it out loud it sounds insane and he's already treating my requests for updates on the panty stealer and their findings in Jerry's boxes as nuisance calls. He would really think I was off my meds.

Is it logical to make the jump from seeing Hal and Meredith together for a few minutes to suspecting them of murder? Even though they never gave any sign they were friendly when Meredith came into the branch to do her banking, it makes sense they would know each other. But conspiring to kill people? That's crazy.

Or is it? There must have been something to set off a series of clicks in my brain. I think it was the boat that did it. An aluminum boat like that could run ashore anywhere. It's small enough Hal could park it in the weedy area next to the utility trailer at his house but instead he keeps it where he has to pay to park. Why would someone who turns every nickel over before spending it do that? Only one reason I can think of: he doesn't want anyone to know about it.

With that boat, Hal could be the smoker who frequented the beach where we found Easton's body. But who was he meeting there, and why not find a more convenient meeting spot?

When Kyle explained Easton's water taxi idea, he said there were resorts and remote cabin sites only accessible from the water. The boat was necessary for Easton to make deliveries at all those spots around the lake. And the little beach down the bank from my yard is so private he could meet Hal, or anyone, there with no chance of being seen.

But Hal. Was he one of Easton's customers? Surely just buying pot wouldn't motivate anyone to go to the trouble of driving to the boat launch to put their boat in the water and then crossing the lake to get to that beach every time they wanted a dime bag. Besides, I try to visualize Hal smoking pot, but can't. It had to be more than that. Or maybe the boat means nothing at all.

He would have met Easton when he came to the bank looking for a loan to buy his boat. As I told Jim, Easton could have been collecting the tribute money, possibly as a condition of getting the loan. If Hal wasn't Easton's customer, maybe he was Fleet's bag man, the guy Easton handed his collections over to. As long as no one believes my suspicions about the Fleetship explosion and Jerry's disappearance, might as well blame Hal for Easton's murder, too.

And Jerry. Did Fleet want Jerry gone because he uncovered his scam and threatened to expose it? What if Hal made like he was all buddy-buddy and took him out fishing, then hit him over the head and dumped him overboard in a remote section of the lake? That would mean Hal was in on the fraud and agreed to kill someone to protect the secret. If he was prepared to go that far, would he stop at killing Fleet? What if he was tired of being Fleet's errand boy and decided to get him out of the way so he could take over? Or maybe he was just pissed because despite all he did for him, Fleet continued to give him poor performance appraisals, preventing him from getting promotions.

I can almost hear Detective Allard's voice rise a couple of decibels when he explains how unlikely it is that these things are connected or that a bank loans officer would know how to blow up a boat, just before he tells the secretary not to put any more of my calls through. I need something more—some hard evidence—before I can expect Detective Allard to listen.

If I'm right, as impossible as it seems, benign, dim-witted Hal is a threat. I have to find out what's happening at the storage compound and to do that, I need to watch Hal closely. I'll have to be out of the office more than even a very easy-going manager would approve. I decide to explain my need to him, sort of. I go to his door and tap on the frame. When he looks up, I say, "Got a minute, John?"

"Sure, come on in, Lindy."

I go in, close the door behind me and sit in the chair across from him.

He asks, "What's up?"

"I just wanted to let you know I've run into some problems with the cat rescue I volunteer for. They need someone at odd times, um, to check traps, and sometimes to take cats back and forth from vet appointments. There are so few volunteers and I, er, kind of went ahead and said I'd do it and so now I need to be away from the office a lot more than I expected."

"Cat rescue?"

"Yeah, er, we catch feral cats, like strays, and take them to be spayed and neutered and of course vaccinated and then we release them back where we found them."

"Why spend the money? Why not just kill them?"

I hope he didn't hear my gasp. I know a lot of people think the same way. I try to keep my tone mild and reply, "Er, well, they have a right to live their lives just like any other creature. It's not their fault they're homeless. And they're not breeding anymore so..."

"Oh, I see. So it's population control."

"That's right. And just to be clear, I don't expect the bank... I mean, I don't think the bank should pay me for the time I'm away. I'll make up the time."

"So, where are these cats?"

"Oh, there are colonies all over the place. Right now we're working on a colony at Robinson's Rentals. That's out on Juniper."

He frowns as if puzzling it out and I'm starting to worry he hasn't swallowed my lie. In case that's what's happening, I hasten to add, "All those poor kitties... They suffer so much. I'll get you a brochure that explains everything." I hope my voice sounds like I'm sad. I don't like to think about the wretched lives of feral cats and I think I will volunteer sometime, I just haven't done it yet. I hope there's no way he can check up on me.

He shrugs and says, "No, it's okay, Lindy. Don't bother with the brochure. If it's important to you we can give it a try. But if your work suffers..."

"If it gets to be too much, I'll have to resign. From the cat rescue, I mean. Thank you!" I get up and leave his office, feeling only a small twinge of guilt over the blatant lie and already planning my next move.

Before I spend time surveilling the storage yard, I can check Hal's ashtray to see what brand he smokes. Thanks for allowing smoking in the branch, Mr. Reader! When I see Hal in the parking lot heading for his Cherokee, I go downstairs and cruise through behind the tellers and fool around on the communal computer there, for no good reason since I now have one on my desk. No one asks what I'm doing. The terminal is just feet from Hal's door. When everyone's attention is elsewhere, I head into his office, expecting butts in an ashtray in plain view. Well, the ashtray's there, but it's empty. I go around behind his desk and pull out his wastepaper basket. The dim bulb has dumped his butts in it. Does he want to start a fire? I pick a butt and as I'm straightening to have a good look at it, I'm startled by the man himself appearing in the doorway.

"What are you doing?" he asks.

"I, er," I stammer. I can't think of a single valid reason to be standing behind his desk holding a cigarette butt. Only now do I notice the pack of cigarettes half hidden by R. O. memos. I have to say something but my mind is blank.

"Well?" he demands.

I give myself a mental kick for being so impatient that I couldn't wait until everyone was gone for the day to check his ashtray, remind myself the best defence is a good offence, match his tone and say, "So, Hal, what's this? You dump your ashtray in your waste basket?"

"You checking up on me?" he asks with a snort. "Gonna give me a demerit because I don't like an overflowing ashtray?"

"No. But this causes fires."

"I always make sure they're all out. Haven't started a fire yet."

"There's a first time for everything. Get yourself a bigger ashtray and leave it for the janitor to empty. If the Fire Department does a surprise inspection and cites us for this…"

He snorts and says, "The Fire Department doesn't do inspections."

"You bet your ass they do," I assure him, hoping for outward calm even though I can feel the adrenalin pumping. "When I was at Maple Creek Branch, they cited us for not having a current inspection date on our fire extinguisher and for propping the fireproof door to the basement open. You mean to say they haven't inspected this place since you've been here?"

"No."

"Well, then, we're overdue!" I toss the butt back into the waste basket and come out from behind his desk. You'd think he'd be suitably chastened, but the scowl on his face says otherwise.

He goes to his desk, fishes the pack of cigarettes out from under the papers and slips it into his shirt pocket, giving me a black look as he does so. Green. Export A. Apparently I chose the one time he forgot his smokes and had to come back for them to snoop in his office.

I hurry back through the teller area to the stairwell and go up, taking the steps two at a time. I sit in my chair, eyes closed and rocking while I digest what just happened.

First, I really am concerned about the butts in the wastebasket being a fire hazard. I call Mae on the intercom and ask her to put a metal bucket for cigarette butts on her next stationery order. And to bolster my excuse for checking Hal's wastebasket, I call the Katawasis Fire Department and have a nice conversation with the chief. I explain who I am and request an inspection to make sure everything's up to snuff now that the renovations are complete.

Second, I now know Hal isn't the beach smoker. But as any detective worth his booze in any true crime novel would point out, it's not exculpatory. I still need to I find out what he's hiding at the storage yard. I'll have to spend some time there to do that. I'll park nearby and watch. It will be a bonus if I can watch both the boat and the buildings, but at the very least in order to find out what he's hiding in that storage unit I need to know which unit is his.

Thanks to Jim I have lock picking tools. I've opened the practice padlock that came with the set as well as the lock on my horse trailer, the padlock on my Windsong tack locker, and my own front door. I'm not what you'd call proficient yet and can't unlock my desk as fast as Jim unlocked Fleet's, but I'm confident I can get in.

I've been to Johnson's Hardware and bought a cat-size live animal trap, which I'll have with me in case I have to justify being somewhere I shouldn't be. The next time he leaves the office mid-afternoon, I'll be ready and waiting.

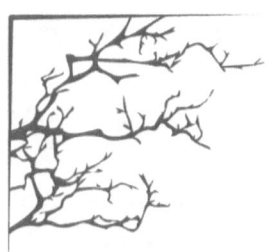

27—Stake Out

With my truck parked at the curb a couple of blocks over, I find my way through the scrub brush in the yard of what looks to be an abandoned repair garage behind the storage lot. I hold up by an aspen that has branches through and over the fence. That tree should've been taken out before it got that big because it's damaging the fence but I'm grateful for it as it's a good surveillance blind.

Before I hunker down I clear out McDonald's wrappers, discarded underwear and beer cans and make sure there are no syringes to accidentally poke me. With all this human activity making the yard a virtual garbage dump, it would be surprising if there were no feral cats here so it's a logical place for a trap. No need to worry about my cover story being blown if someone challenges me.

I'm concealed by tree branches, brush and weeds, but have a view of the open area between the two rows of storage units right to the gate. It's 2:30 and if Hal is going to show, he should be turning up soon.

I'm in luck. The red Cherokee enters the lot and drives in, parking in front of the second unit from the end. I watch him hunch over the lock and lift the overhead door, but I can only see a sliver of the interior. I move to the other side of the tree but the Cherokee is in the way, so I still can't see inside. No worries. I'll find out what's in there when I come back later.

I don't want to leave now, though, because I'm hoping Meredith will show up again. Although I wait until Hal leaves, she's a no show. I head back to my truck.

I'd like to get back to the office before Hal does in case he's keeping tabs on me, too. Fleet was suspicious of me, I'm sure of that, and he would've shared his thoughts with Hal. If Hal is the killer, catching me snooping in his wastebasket might make me next on his hit list and finding me out of the office at the same time he was might raise a red flag. I'll swing by Tim

Horton's and pick up a box of TimBits, just in time for the afternoon coffee break. It'll make it really obvious I was out of the office, definitely not sneaky. Now I know which locker I have to break into so I can go anytime and won't need to be out of the office again.

Break into? That sounds bad. In fact it *is* bad. If some security company patrols the place and catches me, I'll have a hard time talking my way out of it. That's bad enough, but if it's the cops that patrol the place I could end up being arrested.

Then I realize a security guard or cops might be the best I can hope for.

When K.C. called earlier, I begged off going to his place even though we've spent most nights and every Friday night together for the past few months. I told him I thought I was coming down with something and just wanted to get to bed early. In fact, I'm in my brand new black jeans, purchased even though they weren't on sale just because they're black, and my black parka. I'm even wearing black boots. I have my flashlight and my lock pick set. My camera has fresh batteries and I have an extra film. I'm ready to go.

Problem is, I feel guilty about the flimsy excuse I gave K.C. I owe him more than a that, but should I tell him the truth? What if he thinks I'm totally nuts and decides he can't be with me? Or what if he wants to go with me? Or what if he tries to stop me?

In the end, I decide to tell him. It's a sort of fail safe, in case Hal or some other bad guy catches me, so he can contact the authorities if I don't return within a certain amount of time. Maybe if I don't get back by 2:00 a.m. I pick up the phone and dial his number. It rings half a dozen times and I'm about to hang up, thinking he must still be at Windsong or asleep, when he answers.

"Hello?" There's music and voices in the background. Loud music and loud voices. It sounds like a party.

"Hi, K.C. It's me," I say.

"Oh, hi, Lindy. What's up? Feeling better?"

"Um, no, I, uh..." I'm rattled at the noise in the background and what I was planning to say has escaped me. "What's going on? Sounds like you're having a party."

"Um, yeah, not really. Just a couple of friends."

Right then, there's an eruption of laughter, and a feminine voice calls out, "Oh!"

"Change your mind about coming over?" he asks.

"I, um, it's... Never mind, K.C. I'll let you get back to your friends."

"No, Lindy. You must've called for something other than to check up on me," he says. "I know you. What is it?"

"I didn't call to check up on you, K.C., it's just... Okay. Fact is, I feel fine and I'm not going to bed right now. I'm not even staying in. I didn't want to go to your place tonight because I'm on my way to break into Hal's storage locker."

"What? Say again?" I hear the sound of his hand covering the mouthpiece and his muffled voice saying, "Hey, guys, keep it down, would you? I'm on the phone!"

Then he says, "Lindy, did you just say you're going to break into something?"

"Yeah. Hal's storage locker. I told you I followed him there and even that I went back and watched so I know what unit it is. I'm sure he's hiding something, and that's the logical place for it."

"Oh, sure. I remember you saying something."

He remembers me saying something? I know he's been distracted but I can't believe he was really paying so little attention. "So, I just wanted you to know I wasn't really brushing you off. It's just that I have to do this, and I thought maybe if I said I'd come to your place after, and something happened that I was, um, delayed, like maybe arrested, so I didn't show up by two, that you could er..."

"Lindy, don't be crazy!"

"I'm not crazy."

"No, I don't mean you're crazy, I just mean, well, breaking into someone's storage locker? That's crazy."

"I have to."

"Okay. Say you have to. How are you planning to do it? Both the gate and the door to his unit will be locked, right?"

"Gate?" Okay, I hadn't thought about a gate. It's logical. No use fencing the yard and not putting a gate on it. Duh. Well, it just means two locks to pick. I say, "Right. I'll pick the locks."

"Pick the locks?"

"Yeah."

It's quiet at his end except for the voices in the background, and his breathing. I can only imagine what's going through his head. Probably something like *what am I doing, dating a lock picker?* What possible reason does anyone other than a criminal have for knowing how to pick locks, after all? Well, he wanted to know about my adventures with the rustlers and I told him every detail. He thought what I did then was gutsy. Did he think I had changed? Granted, I've haven't been forthcoming about the lock picking because I wanted to be sure I could prove it if he challenged me.

I give him another moment or two to come up with something, then say, "Okay, K.C., I'll let you get back to your party. Bye." I hang up, grab my flashlight, and hurry out the door.

I'm surprised at the squeezing in my chest. I expected K.C. to have a quiet night at home just because that's what I told him I was doing and instead he has a party. Obviously with mixed company. I wonder if he does that often on the nights I'm not with him. I promised myself no new relationships until I was thirty because I expected to be smarter about men by then, and instead of waiting that extra year I let K.C. into my life. Let him in? Practically shanghaied him. If I needed proof that I'm still not smart when it comes to men, he's it. Damn it! Why are men in cowboy hats so irresistible? I choke back a sob.

Lindy! Get a hold of yourself. Focus on the job at hand.

I drive to the storage lot, turn onto the side street, and park next to the abandoned repair garage. It's dark. The nearest streetlight gives out only the occasional flicker. This isn't great for anyone out walking on a moonless night, but it suits my purposes. I just have to be careful not to trip on the broken concrete and stay clear of whatever is rustling around in the bushes.

At the gate, I discover not the padlock I expected but a combination lock built into the gate itself. There's probably a way to cheat this lock, but there is no way to pick it. Now what? The fence is six feet high chain-link topped with barbed wire. I don't see how I can climb it. I'm defeated. Unless...

I go back around the corner, then into the abandoned lot. No stray flickers of light here; it's as dark as the inside of a cow. I push through the tall weeds and low bushes to the aspen that's grown over the fence. Holding my flashlight in my mouth, I climb the chain-link to the top, then with my left hand, grab the branch that's grown through the wire. I take my right hand off the fence to grasp the branch with both hands and pull myself up so the top half of my body is over the branch. Then, I carefully pull my right foot out of the chain-link and swing it out and over the barbed wire.

Two things happen simultaneously: my left foot slips out of the chain-link and I utter a squawk. The flashlight falls out of my mouth. I'm suspended by one leg on the barbed wire. One of the nasty barbs is digging into my thigh. "Ow! Ow! Ow! Gahhh..." I try to ignore the pain of that barb drilling into my flesh as I squirm my left foot around until it gains purchase again. I wish my feet were narrower or that the makers of chain link made the openings bigger so more than just the tip of my boot would fit in, but then I suppose the point is not to make the fence easier to climb. Dammit. I should've gone farther up the tree. My leg still won't move off the barbed wire. My jeans are hooked and won't come free.

Making sure my left hand has a secure hold on the branch, I slide my right hand along the wire under my thigh and tug at the pantleg, but it doesn't budge. I put both hands on the branch again and struggle to move my left foot farther up so at least the barb isn't stuck in my flesh. It's a little better but the barb jabs me every time I move and still won't let go of my jeans. I have a mental image of me still hanging on the fence when morning comes, trying to explain what's obviously inexcusable to the first storage locker patron. If the barb in my leg didn't hurt so much and if I wasn't so frustrated, maybe I could see the humour in it. As it is, I'm not even sure how much longer I can hold on, so my predicament is growing worse by the minute. All I need now is a pack of stray dogs to come along. Or the security guard.

I dangle there, watch a car go by on the street, and make the decision to cut my brand new, first-time-worn jeans to free myself. I use my right hand to dig my Swiss Army knife out of my pocket before realizing I need two hands to open it. I'll have to take off my gloves besides. I slip the knife into my jacket pocket, pull my glove off with my teeth and stuff it in my pocket with the knife. Then I grasp the branch with my right hand, pull the glove off my left hand and stuff it into my other pocket. With my left hand holding the branch again, I dig my knife out of my pocket. The glove comes out with it and falls to the ground. I curse under my breath. But I have the knife. I'm trying to find the little slot in the blade with my left thumbnail when I hear something pushing through the bushes, and freeze.

It's so dark all I can make out is a shadowy figure coming out of the bushes beside me. My guts clench. Then he hisses, "Lindy! What the hell?!?"

"K.C.? What are you doing here?" Before he can respond, the branch I'm clinging to gets free of whatever was holding it in place, and jerks toward me. I lose my grip and fall. The barb rakes down my leg and now I'm hanging upside down on the fence. "Owwww!" I cry.

K.C. grabs me and hoists me up just as there's the sound of ripping cloth and my leg comes free. A hundred and forty pounds landing on him is too much for K.C.; he crumbles to the ground with me on top of him.

"You okay?" he asks.

"I, er, yeah, I'm okay," I say, and roll off him. "You?"

"I'm okay," he replies. He gets to his feet and pulls me up.

"What are you doing here?" I repeat my earlier question. "How did you find me?"

"As luck would have it, this is the first storage lot you come to heading into town from Windsong," he explains. "I saw your truck, but couldn't make out any activity around the buildings. I was walking back to wait by your truck when I heard your screams."

"I didn't scream."

"Okay, squeals then."

"I didn't squeal either!"

He chuckles and says, "Okay I picked up on your mental message, then." He pulls me into a hug and kisses my ear. "Lindy, why did you hang up on me? I thought you were asleep or I would've called you when Denise and John dropped in."

"I, um..."

"Never mind. Are you sure you're okay?"

"Well, yeah, thanks to you." I break out of his embrace and say, "I dropped my glove. And my flashlight." I look around but can't see anything in the dark except the flashlight, its beam along the ground disappearing into the weeds. On the other side of the fence. "Damn! My flashlight! Help me over the fence, would you?"

"No I won't help you over the fence, Lindy! What the hell? I thought you said you were going to pick the locks."

"Well, that was the plan, but the gate has a combination lock. I can't pick it."

"So you decided to climb over a six-foot chain link and barbed wire fence?"

"I, er, um, yeah, basically. The situation was, um, fluid so..." I shrug, deflated. I bend over to brush my hands across the ground in an unsuccessful attempt to find my glove.

"Now what are you doing?"

"Looking for my glove. It's so dark..."

He takes my hand to lead me out of the scrub brush. "You can look for it when we come back."

"When we come back? You mean me and you? That we?"

"That we."

I have a mental image of coming back with a ladder, maybe at first light. "You're going to help me get over the fence? Or maybe a better idea would be to cut a hole in it—"

"Don't be nuts! If you hadn't gone full speed ahead and damn the torpedoes tonight, you would've realized there's an easier way."

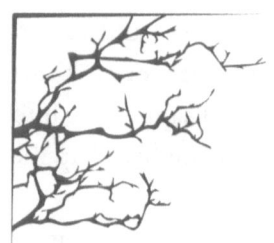

28—Moving Prep

Windsong is not yet in its death throes, but the writing is definitely on the wall. K.C. has given up finding something near enough to retain his present clients and although Windsong was busy all year long with coaching, training, boarding, and clinics, it was barely profitable, so prospects at a facility with no indoor arena are grim. I'll stay until the end because I don't need to worry about finding a place for Chica, but boarders who have to pay for stalls elsewhere or lose them have already told K.C. they're leaving. He talks of giving up the boarding, training and coaching side of the business and leasing a property in town for his horse trailer dealership but he worries that without the draw of Windsong clinics and shows, the trailer dealership won't have enough sales to make it viable as a stand-alone business.

"I'd have to branch out into utility trailers. Work trailers. Maybe boat trailers. This isn't exactly horse country," he grumbles. "Nothing but forest. Pasture almost non-existent. And the weather? Eight months of winter and four months of poor sledding."

"Your heart might not be in it but you could do that, expand your product line. If you didn't have too much overhead it could be a decent business." As I say it, I have to acknowledge to myself that I'm grasping at straws. Anything to keep him in Katawasis.

"I guess," he says as he nods and shrugs. "But with no indoor arena I'll only be able to train a few months a year. Can't stay competitive that way." He picks up my hand and gives it a squeeze. "I might have to move to Alberta, babe."

"I know," I agree, and sigh. I try not to think about what that means for me. For us.

We're on our way to SafeGuard Storage, where we've rented a storage unit. K.C. arranged the rental by phone this morning and we stopped by the business office on our way to give them a cheque and agree to the list of rules. No drinking on site. No fires. No barbeques. No storage of flammable liquids, illegal drugs or alcohol. And of course, the hours you're allowed to come on site.

It turns out it's a good thing I wasn't able to cheat the gate lock last night, because the lot is closed between 10:00 p.m. and 6:00 a.m. and there's an alarm system. I would have been nabbed by the security guard within minutes. We were barely out of the office before K.C. started laughing like it was the funniest thing he'd ever heard.

"So if you had managed to get the gate open you would have met the security guard pretty damn quick! Maybe I would've had to go to the cop shop and bail you out! Ha! Ha!" He really has a weird sense of humor. I don't know why I like him so much.

We get to the lot, drive in, find the right unit, and back the truck to its door. He raises the door, and we begin unloading plastic totes full of bridles and other small bits of tack along with his trophy saddles and other saddles he seldom uses, at least a dozen summer rain and fly sheets that won't be needed until next year and cardboard banker's boxes of business records. It's only partly for our cover story, because K.C. is packing up, getting ready to move.

The unit is the size of a single car garage and is in the building across from Hal's. Being Saturday, unless he sneaks away from work because he doesn't want his wife to know he has it, it's possible Hal will show up. I keep a watchful eye to make sure he won't see me if he does come along. He might remember K.C. applying for a loan, but he doesn't know we're together, and I'd like to keep it that way.

I leave K.C. to set up saddle racks and organize his things and stroll to the back fence, where I locate my flashlight. Of course the battery is dead. I spot my glove on the other side of the fence and make a mental note to get that when we leave. I continue casually wandering through the weedy area next to the fence until I reach the end of the building. With no one in sight, I go to the boat where I saw Hal and Meredith that day and climb up on the boat trailer's fender.

The boat is open except for a bench at the back next to the tiller and a cabinet in the bow with a padded top. It has a padlock on it. As much as I itch to check that out, there's too great a chance someone will see me and know I shouldn't be there. I jump down and rejoin K.C.

When K.C. has everything organized, we lock up and head back to Windsong. I would've liked to hang around longer but K.C. has a busy afternoon teaching.

"Hal not showing up doesn't prove he's keeping his unit a secret from his wife, you know," K.C. says as we drive away. "It would be dumb luck if he came while we were there anyway. We could hang around all day and have him show up ten minutes after we left." He lets out an exasperated snuffle. "I wish I could talk you out of it, but I doubt anything's going to stop you from breaking in because you're sure he's hiding something in there. Like I'm hiding stuff in my unit."

"Well, you are."

"Not really hiding. Just getting ready to move."

"Sure, and you aren't sneaking around to do it. But you actually did want those business records out of Windsong, right? Out of reach of the owners, right? And your tack, especially those saddles. You wanted that all out before anything had a chance to walk away."

He shrugs. "You're right. Call me paranoid and maybe you're rubbing off on me, but I don't trust people like I used to."

"You think me having my locks changed and nailing that two by four across the laundry room door makes me paranoid? I call it careful. And sensible. Plus, you know, if you think you're paranoid then you're probably just worried because paranoid people don't think they're paranoid."

"Which may be why you don't think you're paranoid."

"K.C.!"

"I know. You've got every right to be thinking about security. So I'm just being careful and sensible, moving my stuff. Just in case the owners try to screw me when it comes time for them to buy out my contract. If they lock me out of my office, there's thousands of dollars worth of silver halters and bridles without even talking about the show saddles. My horses and that stuff is all my ex left me with. But worrying the contract buy-out won't go smoothly and I need to have the business records, maybe that's being suspicious."

"Nothing wrong with being suspicious. Keeping the records makes sense to me, and moving your tack is sensible, too. Too many people have access to it. I don't mean boarders, but lots of people wander through, especially when there's a clinic. You don't always lock the door. Plus it's a real simple lock to pick."

"Trust you to come up with that."

"Want to try it? I'll let you borrow my tool set. It has a neat see-through plastic padlock to practice on."

"No," he says, and snorts. "Maybe."

"Anyway, as far as the business records, from what you've told me the owners haven't been forthcoming. You don't even know who they are, do you? I mean the owners of the holding company? They've always had lawyers acting on their behalf. I doubt they ever planned to renew your contract like they promised when you signed on. You said you found out about their development plans the same way everyone in Katawasis did, in their big public announcement. I think they would've reneged and dumped you the minute they bought out that last lease no matter when that happened."

"Well, that's basically what they did."

"I meant, even if it happened when you first got here," I clarify. We're approaching Tall Trees and it's close to lunch time, so I ask, "Got time to stop at the pub for lunch? My treat."

He glances at his watch, frowns for a second, then makes the turn into the shopping center. "You're my first student after lunch. If you don't mind missing your lesson today, we have lots of time."

"I'm okay with that."

"Okay. And this will be your treat? I think I'll order steak and lobster."

I laugh and say, "Nice try, but the most expensive thing on the menu is a steak sandwich."

He's well into his steak sandwich and I'm halfway into my Caesar salad when I'm struck with an odd thought. "Hey, K.C., do you know who the last holdout was? On the waterfront leases, I mean."

"No. Why?'

"I'm just curious. I wonder how they sweetened the deal to get him to cave after he refused to sell for so long."

"What does it matter?"

"Well, if he got an especially sweet deal, knowing what it was might help in your own negotiations."

He shrugs as if considering it. "You could be right. Wouldn't hurt to know, would it? But how can we find out?"

"Well, since we don't know who the lease holders are and I'm sure the developers won't tell us, we talk to people who live down there. That Larry guy who talks your ear off any time he can catch us as we're going by—I bet he'd know."

"Maybe. He does seem to know everyone." K.C. shakes his head, then takes a swig of his beer. The waitress comes by and he orders a second glass, and when she moves on, continues, "Well, months ago he told me there was one guy who was never going to sell out so Larry figured he could take the money and invest it, rent the house and come out on top. At least until the leases all expired in a couple decades, and he'd be dead by then anyhow."

"Dollars to donuts Larry knows who the lone holdout was, then. Let's ask him. Not tonight, though."

"Why not tonight?"

"Well, I suppose we could. I won't go to SafeGuard until maybe about midnight."

"Okay Lindy, let's get this straight. You're not going alone, so its *we* who aren't going until, um late. And remember, even though we have a unit in there, no one's supposed to be in there after 10:00. There's an alarm, remember?"

I bite my lip and puzzle out how I can eliminate any risk of Hal coming along while I'm trying to break into his unit. I can't think of a time other than when the lot is closed. "How about if we take ladders and go over the fence?"

"Lindy, for chrissakes, no! We'll get arrested."

"Only if we get caught," I argue. "I'll understand if you change your mind about going with me."

"If you get caught, you'll lose your job. It's too risky."

"Well then..."

"Well, then, you'll just have to find out what he does on weekends. Do the kids play sports? Does he take them to soccer practice or something? Maybe they're going away for Thanksgiving?"

"You think we're friendly enough he shares with me? All I know is that he has three daughters and his wife doesn't work. We barely speak to each other. And Thanksgiving? That's weeks away!"

"Someone in the branch must know something about him. Deena, maybe? And whatever you think is in that unit will still be there, won't it? It's been there, um, how long?"

"I don't know."

"You don't know because you don't know what you're looking for."

"Exactly. I won't know what I'm looking for until I find it." Since I'm not having a lesson this afternoon, I wave my glass at Bonita when she cruises by. When she brings my fresh glass of wine and asks if there's anything else, we request coffee and the bill.

"Okay," I say when Bonita walks away, "that's a good idea, asking Deena to see what she can find out about Hal's plans."

"Good," K.C. says, and punctuates it with a sharp nod. "And I think we could walk down and talk to Larry right after my last lesson this afternoon."

I see. Now that it might affect his contract negotiations, he's paying attention. I mentally scold myself for having such a mean-spirited thought. He's got every right to be consumed with worry about his business just as I was when Wacasko-Wâti was in serious trouble. I reach across to take his hand. "It'll work out, sweetie," I tell him. "You'll come out of this all right. Maybe better than before."

He squeezes my hand and gives me a little grin. I'm sure he wants to believe me, but he just isn't there yet.

29—Explosive Information

Our plans for Saturday tanked when one of K.C.'s horses colicked and we spent most of the night with the vet and sitting up with the horse. Thankfully by noon Sunday, the horse pooped and was interested in his hay again. With a huge sigh of relief we got back to normal. K.C. had a full slate of lessons in the afternoon so we don't walk down to Larry's until nearly supper time.

We come to the T-intersection at Beach Drive. Calling it a drive is grandiose. It might have been something like a driveway when built but with no maintenance, Beach Goat Trail would be more accurate. It's nothing more than a gravel path leading to the row of leased houses so narrow that if two cars meet, one has to pull over into the weeds to let the other go by. The road is littered with fallen leaves. It's chilly because the sun is nearing the horizon and the light has the brittle edge of fall.

We make a right turn onto the road that serves all the waterfront properties. Larry's yard is next to the public access and his Ford is parked in its usual place, although the Toyota usually parked next to it is gone. We follow the cracked and broken concrete walk, climb the three steps up onto the verandah, and ring the bell. Barking erupts inside; a man's voice curses the dog and in a moment Larry comes to the door, an odd-looking dog with him. When he recognizes us, he steps outside, pushes the dog back with his foot and closes the door.

"Hey," he says. "How ya doin'?"

"Good. We're good. Getting ready to move, are you?" K.C. asks, waving a hand to indicate the stack of moving boxes on the verandah.

"Yeah. But that's just what's left of the wife's stuff. She took off weeks ago."

"Oh, she's already gone to your new place?"

"No, she's gone to *her* new place."

"I'm sorry," I tell him.

"Thanks," he says, and shrugs. "On the upside, she didn't leave much so moving won't be a big job. Didn't take the mutt, though. Can't have a dog in her new apartment, she says. You guys want him?"

"I, um... No thanks," K.C. says. "I'm moving too."

"I could take him," I reply. A dog would be good company on the nights K.C. doesn't stay. And there will be a lot of those if he moves to Alberta. "Is he okay with cats?"

"Don't know. Hates the neighbor's cat, but he's good at yapping when someone rings the doorbell. That's all he's good for, near as I've been able to figure."

"Oh. Sorry, I have a cat so..." I apologize.

"It'll be the SPCA for him, I guess. So. What's up?"

"Well, I guess I'm like you, Larry," K.C. says, "I never figured to move so soon either, but I'm going to have to, and that means not just out of my cabin. Windsong is going to be wiped off the map."

"Yeah. I heard that's where the casino's going in. 'Parently there's a model of the whole shitteroo over in the lobby at the Kat. The wife said they figure the resort will be a destination, and folks will come from all over for the beach and the casino and fishing. Water skiing in summer, cross country skiing and snowmobiling in winter. Ice fishing too, I guess." He utters a snort, then continues, "I halfway hope the whole thing flops. But that's just me not being forward-thinking, according to the wife. That Friends of Katawasis bunch has poisoned her mind."

"She's one of the members?" I ask.

"Yeah, they had a vote and allowed her to join. You'd of thought she won the lottery, getting a chance to rub elbows with all those snotty—" He looks at me, snorts and stops mid-sentence, apparently thinking better of what he was going to say. He barks a laugh and says, "I wouldn't join that bunch if they got down on their knees and begged."

"Well, I'm with you, but it could be sour grapes on my part. They turned me down," I tell him.

"You should count yourself lucky you got away. Always got their hands in your pocket. What they call fund raisers is skinning the members," he says. "Well, you guys didn't stop by to hear me whine. What can I do you for?"

"We were wondering about everyone losing their homes. I heard most moved away as soon as they sold, but you stayed. How come?"

"I guess the other folks all bought houses. A few of us made it a condition of selling to stay here as tenants. The rent was cheap. I put my payout in a retirement plan earning interest, and stayed. I figured I'd live here till I tottered off to the old folks home. 'Course the wife waltzed off with half of that and now I've been evicted. Bastards!" He snorts, then continues "There was one holdout. Said they didn't need the money and the property was an investment. Going to be worth a lot more in time, they figgered. Never going to sell and they could build their damn resort all around their place if they wanted to. I figured they wouldn't be able to go ahead with the development until their lease ran out. Wouldn't be no hurry because where are they gonna get customers from anyhow? Only so many fishermen in the world and there's lakes with beaches everywhere. Not enough to draw folks this far north, I thought."

"No casino, though."

"I guess that's what they're banking on."

"You know who that last people were?"

"Course I do. The McQuinns. The missus and me, we were here first. They were second. Surprised they took the lot they did when they had their pick of all of 'em. 'Course it wasn't her, it was her folks. She got it when they moved off and it was just her and her spoiled brat livin' there until she remarried. Their place is way down at the other end, last house. Not a great beach, but the site planners figured it's the best place for the boat launch. So they kinda had 'em over a barrel. Even after they moved to their new place over on the other side of the lake, I seen their boat tied up there off and on. Still seems odd they kept it. Never even rented it, just used it like a vacation cabin. Big place like that, just to spend a couple hours there once in a while? I s'pose they enjoyed putting the screws to the developer. Go figure. But the McQuinns have been in Katawasis for generations. Own half of it. I guess when you're a big shot..." His thoughts seem to drift off, then he shrugs and says, "Wish to hell I never sold when I did. I'd of made a bundle if I hung on and never cashed out until they did. They came out of it smelling like a rose. Or I should say *she* came out smelling like a rose. He cooperated by blowing himself up."

"Oh!" I exclaim. "You mean the *Fleetwoods* were the last holdouts?"

"Yeah. Well, I guess you'd call 'em Fleetwoods. To me they were always McQuinns. It was no secret she would've sold years ago. Couldn't dump it fast enough once he was gone. Must be laughing all the way to the bank. Already driving around in his Caddy with her new boy toy."

My face must register my shock, because Larry says, "Me and my big mouth. Anyhow. I guess you won't be seeing me around here again."

"Where are you moving to?" K.C. asks.

"Back to Ontario. Got family there."

"Well, good luck," K.C. says, "and I'll take the dog. Just drop him off at Windsong when the time comes."

"Oh yeah? How about you take him now?"

"Er..."

Before K.C. can complete his thought, Larry disappears inside and in seconds is back with the dog on a leash in one hand and a dog dish in the other. "Here you go," he says. He hands K.C. the leash and pokes the dish at me. "His name's Henry. He's about seven or eight, I guess. Supposed to be part wiener dog. All I know for sure is he hates raccoons and wasps. Take care, now." He retreats into the house and closes the door hastily, as if to make sure K.C. doesn't have time to change his mind. We're left standing looking at each other, wondering what just happened. Henry seems as confused as we are. He sniffs K.C.'s boots and tentatively wags his tail.

"Well. Moving soon or not, I guess you have a dog."

"I couldn't let him go to the SPCA, Lindy. He's too big for a Dachshund. I'd say more shepherd or retriever. Going by his rough coat, some kind of terrier maybe, but so short-legged? Maybe there's Daxie in there somewhere. Looks like he's made out of spare parts. And at his age? There's gotta be a dozen dogs at the SPCA younger and, er, nicer to look at than him. He doesn't deserve to die just because he's old and ugly. That's a kill shelter, you know."

"I know."

"Look at him, he doesn't understand why he's out here with these strangers. Doesn't know what just happened," K.C. says, and scratches behind the dog's ear. "He never barked at the horses. All the times we went by, I didn't even know they had a dog."

"I guess he's quiet unless someone rings the doorbell."

K.C. is focused on the dog. I watch his face soften as he quietly tells Henry everything will be okay. *He's a kind man,* I think. My feelings for him swell.

"Wow," I say as we walk away, "Meredith has a kid from a previous marriage. Funny Fleet never mentioned it when he told me about their daughter."

"Could it be he called her their daughter?"

"No. They were married fifteen years and Larry talked about a spoiled brat. I imagine that kid would have to be at least twenty now. Meredith must've been very young when she had him. Or her. Fleet's daughter was six or so. Grade two, he told me."

"So he took on a woman with a spoiled brat. That must be hard on a relationship."

"Hmm. I guess it would be. She is attractive but quite a bit older, and came with a difficult kid. But she also came with a waterfront property and who knows what else? From the sounds of it, the McQuinn family is a big deal in Katawasis. Maybe that was part of the appeal." K.C. makes a non-committal hmpff sound but says nothing. I flick a chunk of something off the dog dish and say, "Larry seems to know everything about everybody."

"Seems to," K.C. agrees. "Probably knew we were sleeping together before we did."

That's worth a smile, but right now my mind is on Larry's information. The news that Fleet was holding up the new development is astonishing and is another motive for his murder.

We walk on in silence for a couple of minutes, and we're nearing K.C.'s cabin when I say, "Holding up a big development—that would make a few people unhappy. Wonder who might be unhappy enough to kill him."

"You mean Fleet? If you wanted to kill someone, there are easier ways. Everyone out here has a rifle."

"Sure, but then it's obvious it's a murder. Better if it looks like an accident. Think about it." I'm hoping for him to remain my partner in crime so maybe that was a little sharp. I soften it by asking, "Can we at least discuss it?"

He shrugs and says, "Okay. So you think the explosion was a bomb and not a leaky propane tank like they said on the news. Timed? Or remotely detonated?"

"Remotely, I think. A time bomb would be too unreliable. He might not be on the boat at the time, or it might go off when he's at the fuel dock or in the marina. If you can set it off by a radio signal, you can chose a time when you know he's on it and there's nothing else nearby."

"That would take knowledge. And skills."

"Someone who was in the military might have skills like that. Or anyone could hire someone with the skills, like a, um, a gangster."

"A gangster?"

"You know what I mean. Then all you need is someone manning the radio. So the question is, who would benefit from Fleet's death?"

"That might be a long list. And that's not the only question. How would the person who was supposed to send the radio signal to detonate the bomb know when the boat was out on the water?"

"Hmm. I guess it would have to be someone who saw it leave the dock."

"And that person would have to have access to the boat to plant the bomb in the first place."

"All he would have to know is where Fleet lives. Lived. I haven't been there, but even if there's no access to his dock from the road, it has to be accessible from the water. Just thinking out loud here. It's complicated. But not impossible."

"Not impossible." He breathes out a long breath and says, "Just not a run-of-the-mill small town operation. And it would have to be really worthwhile, because gangsters don't come cheap."

I say, "You're not taking this seriously."

"I just think it's too far-fetched."

"Not when you consider the other two murders."

"Two? Have they changed the status of that drowned guy?"

"Jerry? No. Not officially."

"Not officially," he says. His flat tone speaks volumes. I feel like I've fallen short somehow. We've reached his yard and I climb the steps to the porch. When he doesn't follow I turn to face him. He says, "You go on in, Lindy. It's chilly tonight. Maybe you could start a fire. Larry gave us a dish but nothing to go in it. I need to go get some dog food. I'll take Henry with me."

He turns away and goes to his truck. Henry needs only a little encouragement before he jumps in. I go into the cabin and give Henry's dish a scrub before getting the bottle of Wacasko-Wâti rhubarb wine I opened yesterday out of the fridge and filling a glass. I take it with me and hunch down by the woodstove. When I have paper, kindling and the smaller stove lengths organized in the fire box, I set a match to it. Sitting on the floor ready to add kindling to the fire if need be, I sip my wine and mull over what Larry told us.

The developers wouldn't shed a tear for someone who was holding up a multi-million dollar project, but would they go farther than just wishing and hoping? And what about Fleet and Meredith? Were there problems in the marriage that no amount of quality time could make up for? She said she didn't like going out on the boat. Too much together time in a marriage already rocky because of problems with the child from her previous marriage? And they were at odds over selling that lease. I wonder how much money was involved. Did she get tired of waiting? Was she resentful at having to share what was hers to begin with and then not being able to sell it when she wanted to? What other property or businesses did they own? Did Fleet's death solve more than just the argument over the lease?

Detective Allard probably knows Fleet was holding up the development and maybe he even knows Meredith was pissed about it, but dimes to donuts he doesn't know about the Meredith/Hal connection. I doubt Hal is the new boyfriend because unless I'm missing some irresistible trait, Meredith would never be desperate enough to hook up with him. Besides, that one exchange I witnessed between those two seemed to be an argument and not of the lover's quarrel variety.

I need to talk to Detective Allard, but if he's not in and I have to leave a message, how long will it take him to get back to me? One way to find out. I use K.C.'s phone to call the detachment. Detective Allard isn't back on days until next week. I leave a message.

But before I talk to Detective Allard, there's Hal's storage locker to be broken into, and a new address of interest: Fleet and Meredith's house. The one they kept just so he could tie his boat up to the dock for a couple of hours once in a while. How will K.C. take that? I figure I can talk him into it. There's less chance of being caught breaking into that house than the storage locker, after all.

In for a penny, in for a pound, mister.

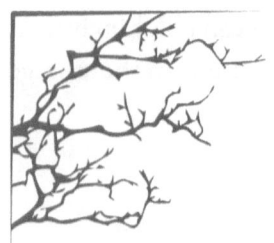

30—Dirty Hours

Unfortunately I have a real job I have to attend to. Monday morning I'm at my desk. My thoughts keep returning to what no one even thinks are crimes when I should be focusing on the proposal for a new account, Katawasis Lake Resort. If we can get it, it'll be our second biggest account. We're not financing the build, we just want the operating credit and payroll accounts. We will be at the bottom of the list of charges if they default. We've never been invited to bid on their account before. Now that I know Fleet was the fly in their ointment so to speak, I suspect he was the reason. I wish they hadn't invited us to bid because I have serious doubts about the terms Mr. Reader is offering. It won't be lucrative and I suspect he hopes merely landing the account will earn him a transfer back to civilization.

He leaves it to me to draft the letter to Regional Office because I took a semester of creative writing in university and he can barely put two paragraphs together. Somehow I have to make it sound attractive. As usual, he will take credit for it. Not so different than the old boss after all, but in light of my misgivings I'm glad it won't have my signature on it.

I'm still dithering over my choice of words in the Katawasis Lake Resort app at lunch time when Deena taps on my door. We've dropped the pretense that we're not friends, and have plans to do some shopping on our lunch break today.

"Ready to go?" she asks.

I draw a quick breath and say, "Am I ever!" I grab my purse and follow her.

We're in my truck heading for The Hitchin' Post, the one and only tack shop Katawasis has to offer. I don't need tack and since Deena doesn't have a horse she doesn't either, but we both have boyfriends and we're thinking of Christmas. I should say Deena is. Christmas is still months away, Thanksgiving isn't even behind us and there's plenty of time to shop, in my opinion. But Christmas usually sneaks up on me, so she's doing me a favour, really.

"So Kristy isn't coming back?" she asks.

"No. Not even to get her car. She sent Kyle the transfer papers and he's selling it for her."

"I bet he's happy about that."

"He is, actually. He's been tinkering on it, getting it running better. She's letting him have all the furniture too. I packed up the rest of her clothes and took them to the Goodwill like she asked. It's like she's erasing her life before Jim. Kyle is going to sell everything and give up the suite. That's one reason I had to move back downstairs."

"Why would he sell his furniture? Won't he need it, even if he moves?"

"He just said he doesn't want reminders of Kristy. Which is odd because it doesn't seem like he cares that much."

"Maybe he's putting on a brave front."

"Maybe," I agree, "but he's certainly not moping around. He's hardly ever home. I don't think I see him more than a couple times a week. Might not see him at all but he still goes out on the deck to watch the boats."

"You'd think if he likes boats so much he'd find better places to hang out," Deena muses. "Although I guess that's why I've seen that hot rod of his turning into the parking lot at the Kat. Their deck, right on the water like that, would be a good place to watch boats from."

"Yeah, it would." I shoulder check for traffic then change lanes. "You know, I never told Kristy this, but remember that day we were walking back to the office after eating lunch at the beach and I saw someone I thought I knew? It was Kyle. And he was coming out of the Toronto-Dominion Bank. I asked Kristy if they had a bank account other than the one at our branch, and she said no, so I thought I must have been mistaken or he was there for some other reason, and I didn't tell her why I asked. Now they've split so it doesn't matter, I guess, but it still puzzles me and I wonder if I should've told her. Maybe I still should. What do you think?"

Deena shrugs and replies, "I guess you should, in case he tries to hide it from the lawyers."

"Oh, yeah. There's that. I'll drop her a line." I turn into the parking area in front of The Hitchin' Post, pull into a parking spot, and turn off the engine.

Christmas shopping in the first week of October means there's plenty of selection, but having dozens of styles and colours of shirts to choose from complicates decision-making. I find one I like for myself, but for K.C. I don't know what size, so for him I get a belt. It's my go-to gift choice for a boyfriend gift anyway. Red's not here to tell me adding a buckle makes it too expensive for a boyfriend of only two or three months, so I select a nice rope-edged Montana Silversmith number featuring a gold horse head, telling myself that by Christmas we'll have been together six months. A reasonable cut-off between "new boyfriend" and "boyfriend". I also grab a couple pairs of fancy spurs for my nephews. As we head out of the shop, I have to admit I'm glad to have such a good start on my Christmas shopping.

Back in the truck, I broach the subject of Hal. "So, Deena, you talk to Hal once in a while, right?"

"Once in a while, mostly when he needs me to do something," she agrees. "Never any personal stuff. Why?"

"Well, I told you he has a secret storage locker, right?"

"I remember."

"Remember I told you I'm going to break into it?"

"Yeah, but I thought you gave up on that idea."

"No, I just put it on a back burner temporarily. Now it's back on the front burner. I need to know when there'll be a window of at least a few hours when he's busy elsewhere, no chance of him sneaking away, so I can be sure he's not going to show up and catch me in the act."

"So you want me to just casually ask him—what? When he's not going to go to his storage locker?"

"No, of course not."

"I know. It's just that, what sort of lead in is there to finding out when someone's going to be busy for a few hours, and when?"

"Well, Thanksgiving is next weekend. You could ask if he's got plans."

"I guess so," she agrees. She's so unenthusiastic I have to face the fact *Katawasis Girls* may soon be just *Katawasis Girl*.

I'm cold. I roll over to snuggle K.C., who's the best bed warmer ever, but encounter nothing but cooling sheets. I hear him moving about in the kitchen, smell coffee and hear a fire crackling in the woodstove. He must have been up for a while. Nice of him to let me sleep.

Goosebumps rise and a shiver courses through me the second I slide out from under the quilts. I get K.C.'s robe from the back of the door and wrap myself in it, then join him in the kitchen.

He sees me and says, "Good morning, sleepyhead."

"Mornin'," I mutter.

He fills a mug with coffee, hands it to me and says, "Go sit by the fire."

I'm happy to comply. I slide into one of the armchairs and put my feet up on the hassock near the stove. With a fragrant mug of the elixir of life warming my hands, the warm glow from the stove warming my feet, and that handsome man whistling under his breath as he pokes around the kitchen, life is good.

He joins me in the chair on the opposite side of the stove. "Thought you'd be raring to go," he says. "You slept till practically noon."

"Nowhere near noon," I point out. It might have come out a little growly. I check my watch, surprised to find it's nearly nine. I don't remember the last time I slept this late.

"Snowed overnight," K.C. says. "If we go today, we'll have to cover our tracks. Maybe we should postpone it until tomorrow."

"The snow will still be there tomorrow. You just don't want to do it. Forget it. I'll go without you."

"That's pretty much what I figured you'd say," he says, and sighs. "Well, how be I make you a bacon and egg sandwich and we get on with it. I've got lessons to teach, even if you decide you don't want to ride."

"Can I finish my coffee?"

I guess my tone was sharp, because he gives me a wink and says, "I know better than to expect you to do anything, even eat, until at least your second cup. But don't worry. I think you're beautiful even when you scowl."

Ordinarily someone accusing me of scowling even coupled with a compliment would be annoying. Funny, but this morning, the rush of emotion I feel isn't annoyance.

I think I'm in love.

I t's cold enough Henry ventures only a few feet off the porch into the snow, does his business and scurries back inside. He's happy to stay on the rug by the woodstove instead of coming with us. What dog doesn't want to go for a walk? He's proving to be so lazy I wonder if he's older than Larry claimed.

We hike along the lane heading for the lakefront houses. Except in shady areas the snow is already turning to slush so I'm not worried about anyone seeing our tracks. The vacant houses are marked with yellow signs declaring they are condemned, private property, and that there's no trespassing allowed by order of Katawasis Lake Development Inc.

At the very end of the lane almost in the bush we come to our destination. There's a small garage. The perimeter fence joins it and there's the yellow warning sign on the gate, but it isn't locked, so after checking for the tenth time to make sure no one is watching, I push it open and we go in.

This yard is almost completely in the shade and the snow here hasn't started to melt. It's not clear where or even if there's a walkway, so I take the shortest route from the gate to the porch. K.C. is right behind me. I head for the door. While I attack the lock, K.C. goes to the only window accessible from the stoop and peers in. "Must be the dining room. Living room in front. I can see right through to the lake," he says.

Weeks ago, I bought a couple of padlocks and the cylinder part of a deadbolt lock to practice picking, and I've had some success. Even so I'm not what you'd call proficient, so I'm still fiddling around when K.C. says, "Hey, Lindy. This window just slides open."

He proves his point by opening it all the way, climbing over the sill and in. In a moment, he comes to the door and unlocks it from the inside.

"I can't believe no one locked that window," I say. As great as it is to get in so easily, I'm annoyed, because I really wanted the satisfaction of defeating the lock rather than just sneaking in because someone left a damn window unlocked.

"Whoever's supposed to be looking after these places should be fired. They'll get squatters in here," K.C. says.

"It's colder than a witch's titty in here. Who would want to squat here?"

"See that fireplace insert? It's an airtight. You could have this place warmed up pretty quick."

"Yeah, well, someone would notice smoke from the chimney just as quick."

"Not after dark."

"Okay then, they'd notice a light inside when there shouldn't be one." I go to look out the living room window. The house is almost on top of the dock. "How were they allowed to build so close to the lake?" I wonder.

"No building code back then I guess. But it sure makes it handy to your boat. I see why they chose this lot for the boat launch," K.C. says as he comes up beside me.

We go room to room and open all the doors and drawers in the kitchen and bathroom, all empty and smelling of unuse, until we get to the last room. A rush of warm air greets us on opening the door thanks to an electric space heater humming quietly in the corner. This room is fully furnished.

"Wow," K.C. says, "looks like someone is still using this room."

It's obviously the master bedroom, with a king-sized bed complete with bedding. It's messy, like someone made a half-hearted effort to straighten it. I go into the ensuite bathroom. There are rumpled towels on the bar and a couple robes on the back of the door. A blow dryer with a tangled cord is stuck behind a towel rack. There's a bar of soap along with shampoo and cream rinse on a ledge in the shower, and on the vanity, deodorants, aftershave and even a bottle of Chanel No. 5.

"I've heard of this, but this is the first time I've ever seen it," I say from the doorway to the bathroom, and hold up the pretty cut-glass bottle of expensive perfume. "Looks like you can get cleaned up nice after a romp in that bed." I put the perfume back and return to the bedroom.

I spot a gold-coloured set of handcuffs attached to the headboard. "Look at this," I say, and lift the one nearest me so K.C. can see what I'm talking about.

"Kinky," he says. "Should we try it out?"

"I have two words for you and it's not happy birthday," I reply.

"You're right. No time. But we can set up something like that on my bed. Maybe with hobbles too."

"You first."

"I'm going to hold you to that."

I wonder why his leer looks so cute.

On the far side of the room a dozen candles of various sizes clutter the top of the dresser. I open drawers, expecting them to be empty except for sex toys or S and M gadgets, but only get as far as the second one. Its contents stop me cold and I feel an almost electric jolt in my gut. "Oh my god," I gasp.

"What is it?" K.C. asks, and comes to my side.

I hold up a pair of lacy black bikini panties.

"So Fleet was the panty stealer. I just can't believe it!" It's about the tenth time I've said it. K.C. nods indulgently. "What should we do? Should we notify Detective Allard, like right away?"

"I don't know about you, but I'd rather not draw his attention to the fact I broke into the place," K.C. reminds me, also for about the tenth time. He gets up and goes to the fridge for another beer, bringing the wine bottle to top up my glass while he's at it.

"They left the window unlocked. So it's not really breaking in."

"Semantics, Lindy. If nothing else, definitely trespassing. No one could miss those signs."

"If you came up the dock from the lake, you could," I point out.

"But we didn't."

And, lacking a boat, we couldn't say we had.

Earlier this afternoon I rode Chica but jammed out of my lesson. K.C. had four students to coach, which of course took his mind off our early morning escapade, so he hasn't thought it through like I have. Granted, while he was occupied at Windsong I was busy in the kitchen doing the total domestic thing: put a chicken in the oven and peeled potatoes, the whole time congratulating myself on becoming a real Suzie Q. Housewife. But my little spurt of domesticity left me plenty of time to ruminate on our bizarre discovery.

"You know Fleet's dead, right? He won't be sneaking in to steal any more of your fancy panties. Which, by the way, you could wear more often."

"They put the pick on me and the lace is itchy," I grumble. My thoughts drift off. I take a long drink of Wacasko-Wâti saskatoon wine.

"So I say, that little love nest will be our secret," K.C. continues. "Someone's still using it and has no idea where those panties came from."

"But there's women's stuff in the bathroom, too. What if one of them takes them? The evidence could disappear."

"Doesn't matter. Fleet's dead. Don't need evidence."

"I guess," I agree. I don't like it, but K.C. is right. "Let's eat."

We go to the kitchen. K.C. pulls the tin foil tent off the resting chicken and carves it while I mash the potatoes and stir the gravy. I taste the gravy, add salt, and pronounce it edible. We fill plates and take them to the table, where we sit across from each other.

"Mmm. Good job, Lindy. And you said you couldn't cook," K.C. says. He loads a fork with chicken, potatoes, Niblets corn and gravy and stuffs it in his mouth.

"This is barely cooking," I tell him. "I've helped Uncle Stu with his barbequed chicken many times. The gravy's hit and miss but anyone can peel potatoes and open a can of corn."

Since his mouth is full he can't speak to argue, so I choose this time to say, "So, we can still keep an eye on the place to see who's using it. You never know. They might know about the panty stealing. In fact, what if it wasn't Fleet at all, but some other slimy bastard that's been using that hideaway?"

He shakes his head, but I don't take it as a no. Rather, it's his opinion of my suspicious mind. Once he's swallowed his mouthful, he says, "You don't think it was Fleet who was using that place? Why do you think his boat was tied up there for a couple hours at a time?"

"Yeah, it was likely Fleet. And someone else. Someone has been using it since he was killed."

"Why do you think that? Maybe it's just as he left it."

"Well, for one thing, someone has to pay the electricity bill. It would have to be Meredith. She knows about it or she would have the electricity cut off, right?"

"So maybe she uses it. Maybe so she can keep her boy toy a secret from her young daughter, considering she just lost her father. Can't you be satisfied knowing it's a place for a dirty couple of hours, nothing more?"

"No. Because it could be more than that. The cars going in there have to go right past this place. You can easily keep an eye on things. Okay?"

"For chrissakes, Lindy!"

"Okay?"

"Okay," he agrees.

But later in the week he takes way too much pleasure in telling me the developers have placed large concrete blocks across the lane just past his driveway, preventing all vehicle traffic.

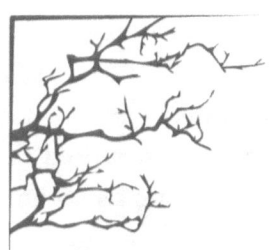

31—Storage

Deena's information proves correct: Hal and family have gone to Regina for the long weekend. Saturday and Sunday, we take more of K.C.'s things to storage. We're hoping the lot will be quiet enough for me to open Hal's unit, but the steady flow of renters prevents me from fooling around with the lock on a unit not our own. You'd think people would be with family, but it seems a popular time for putting boats and campers and vacation trailers away for the season and getting snow tires out of storage. We decide the best time will be just before the gate is closed on Thanksgiving Monday because then anyone who was going to their locker for legitimate reasons would've done so earlier in the day.

K.C. parks the truck so that unless someone comes right up to where we are, I can't be seen. He dinks around in his unit with the overhead door open. The pond of light that spills out only slightly illuminates where I am, there's a pretty good snowstorm happening and it's dark, so I'm holding the flashlight in my mouth while I work on the padlock. Once you have the tools in the lock you can't really see anything anyway so you go by feel, but it's stiff and I'm almost afraid I'm not going to get it, when it springs open.

I remove the lock and release the hasp, then lift the door. Inside, there's a cardboard box and a few life jackets along with oars and a gas can along the side wall, but I'm only dimly aware of those things because front and center is a red Honda Civic. "What the hell?" I exclaim.

"What is it?" K.C. asks. I turn my head for a moment and see him in the door of his unit. "A car?"

"Yeah."

"So?"

"Well, why stash it here? He's got room in his driveway at home, same as for the boat, and I would've thought he was too cheap to pay to rent." I try the driver's side door handle, but it's locked. The door on the passenger side is locked as well. "I don't know if I can pick this," I say.

K.C. comes across and stands at the driver's side, needlessly checking to see if he can open the door seconds after I tried it. He seems surprised to discover he can't. "You don't pick the lock, I don't think. You use a slim jim and slide it down from the window."

"You know how to do that?"

"No. But I locked my keys in my truck once. Called CAA and that's what their guy did."

"Well, we obviously can't call CAA to come here. Wonder where I can get a slim jim."

"Nowhere tonight, Lindy," K.C. says. "Might as well go home." He heads back out into the blizzard but stops halfway to his unit and hisses, "Lindy! The security guard's here! Get the hell outta there!"

A rush of adrenalin courses through me. I hurry out, haul the overhead door down, but haven't got time to set the padlock before the lime green SecureCo sedan pulls up beside the truck. As the driver gets out, K.C. calls, "Hey! Hi, Kyle."

The thumping in my chest subsides. Kyle responds, "Hi, K.C. Lindy."

"Hi, Kyle! So this is where you work," I reply, put my hand holding the padlock behind me and crowd back against the door so my body blocks his view of the hasp.

"Sometimes. Not all the time," he replies. "You know how it is with us rent-a-cops, we're just glorified prostitutes, working for anyone who'll pay us."

"Yeah," I say, and force a chuckle. "But it's shitty, having to be out here this late on Thanksgiving, in this weather. No one with any sense is out in this."

"For sure. That's why I thought it would be okay to lock up early. Then what do I see but K.C.'s truck," he explains. "Looks like I ain't the only one with no sense. Least I'm pulling double pay. What's your excuse for being here?"

I indicate K.C. with a casual wave and reply, "Oh, maybe you didn't know. K.C. is moving. Not sure where to yet. We're putting his stuff in storage for the time being. And he, um, we, er, had chores, you know, had to feed the horses and stuff, so this was the soonest we could get here."

"Oh." It's dark, but even the dim glow from K.C.'s unit is enough I can see Kyle's forehead is creased in a frown and his eyes are narrowed. My guts clench. If he asks why I'm up against the door of someone else's unit or what I have behind my back, it's game over. I release the breath I didn't realize I was holding when he continues, "Well, I'm quitting this shit show anyhow. You know I'm moving? Sold all my stuff and I'll be outta that place tomorrow."

"That's stressful," I say, gushing with fake empathy. "So many life changes in such a short time."

"Good changes, Lindy," he assures me. For the first time since he came, he smiles. "Next time you talk to your little friend, you can tell her I'm moving in with my girlfriend."

"Well, good luck."

"Thanks! You guys about done? Let's get this place buttoned down so we can all get outta the cold."

"Just a couple more minutes, Kyle," K.C. says.

"Okay. Take care," Kyle says. He gets back in the SecureCo sedan, backs to the open area, then turns and drives out to wait by the gate.

I breathe a sigh of relief, set the padlock, and scurry into the truck with K.C. closing the door to his unit and sliding into the driver's seat a moment later. As we drive out the gate, I give Kyle a big smile and a wave.

"The asshole had to pick tonight to close up early," I grumble. "I know you said I need a slim jim to unlock the car door but I wanted to at least try picking the lock. I have to get inside."

"Because...?"

"Because there was a pack of cigarettes on the passenger seat. I couldn't make out the brand, but the pack is yellow and Hal smokes Export A."

"Green pack," K.C. contributes.

"Green pack. And besides, Hal is cheap. If he doesn't want it parked at his house, why not park it out beside his boat? Open parking still costs money but it's a fraction of renting one of the enclosed units. I can't imagine him owning a third vehicle much less paying so much to store it. The only reason I can think of is that he's hiding it. I have a sick feeling that car is Jerry's."

"He wouldn't be stupid enough to keep a dead guy's car."

"Fleet kept the dead guy's baseball."

"Small, no record of owner, different altogether. A lot harder to pass off a car. He'd never be able to insure it or sell it."

"He could, if he could fake, um, something. The serial number or something. Like car thieves do. Or maybe he just had to have a place to stash it quick and now he's stuck with it because if he drives it anywhere and a cop spots it, he's done."

K.C. utters a non-committal sound like a throat clearing before saying, "How likely is it a cop would even notice? There's little red Hondas everywhere."

"Expired plates might be noticed."

"Easy enough to steal current ones and swap them out."

"Well, one way to find out. The registration is probably in the glove box."

K.C. is quiet until we reach the turnoff to Katawasis Lake Road. "I think it's time to talk to Detective Allard. Maybe he got a description of Jerry's car from his brother."

"Yes! Good idea!" I exclaim. Then I blow out a long breath and say, "You'll have to call him, though. He doesn't return my calls anymore."

"Sure," he says, and shakes his head. "But how are we going to explain knowing the car is in Hal's storage unit?"

"Well, if he got a description of the car and it doesn't match, it's an 'oh I was just wondering...thought I might have seen it' sort of thing," I suggest. "But if it does match, then I guess we can claim we saw it when Hal had the door open."

"Which would be a lie."

"You'd rather fess up?"

"I'd rather tell the truth, yeah. Hal might say he never saw us there. No way he ever had his door open when we were there. We have to be careful. We don't want to do anything that makes evidence inadmissible in court."

"Oh, yeah. I don't know...would the fact I broke in make it inadmissible? It's not like the cops did it and it would still give them probable cause for a search warrant, right?"

"I don't know. Maybe we could talk to Jim first."

Even though I call him at home after hours, it's me, not we, who ends up talking to Jim. He's not there the first night and I end up chatting with Kristy for half an hour. She's happy with Jim, likes the house, and she even enjoys the small doses of step mothering. She got a job as a hostess at the Ranchmen's Club and makes astonishing tips. She's giggly and silly and talking to her is a real lift to my spirits. I realize how much I miss her.

Now it's Tuesday morning and I'm in my office. We're short-staffed, possibly due to snowy road conditions, but that also means fewer customers, so it's quiet. My phone rings. It's Jim.

I explain our dilemma and after thinking about it for a minute or two, he says, "The first thing a defence lawyer would do would be to question the validity of the search warrant. If you're right and that car ties him to Jerry's murder, you have to make goddamn sure it can't be thrown out for any reason. I'm not a hundred percent sure if discovering it in the course of committing a felony would make it inadmissible. I don't think so, but let's make sure." I hear him breathe out a long sigh. "Lindy, I think I made a mistake sending you that lock pick set. Didn't you realize break and enter is an indictable offence?"

"Well, yeah, I guess I did. But it's a storage locker and I didn't steal anything."

"Doesn't matter. B and E into a non-dwelling property can still get you ten years in jail. Thank Christ it wasn't a house. You can get life for that."

Maybe he hears me gasp.

"Lindy? Is there something else? Oh, you know what? Forget it! Better if I don't know."

"Well, I'd just like to mention that I located my missing panties at a house Fleet used to own, but like I said, I didn't steal anything."

Silence at his end of the line. Finally I add, "That's another story. And the house is vacant. Mostly. So it's really unlikely I'd get a sentenced to life in prison for that."

"You're right. Doubt whether there would even be charges, in the circumstances. But if they did charge you, even if all you got was a suspended sentence, you'd have a criminal record. Bye-bye banking career. Don't you need that job? Aren't you still subsidizing Wacasko-Wâti? Are you willing to take a chance? Pfft!" He blows out a sharp breath and then clicks his tongue. "I could kick myself for giving you those lock picks. I thought it was a little thank you for introducing me to Kristy. Kind of a joke, a little puzzle you'd fool around with and forget about. How did I ever think you'd limit your lock picking to the practice lock?"

"Well, yes, I need the job. Wacasko-Wâti won't stand alone for a while yet. As for lock picking, I'm pretty sure you expected I'd, um, find a practical application. In fact, you're the one who said all of us Katawasis Girls should..."

"Yeah," he interjects, "I remember. Anyhow. As a starting point, why don't I get in touch with Allard and see if he got a description of Jerry's car from his brother? I know you don't have a phone number for his brother because he always called you, but maybe Allard does and maybe he'll give me that, too. As for the panties, let me think about that some more."

"I'd like to mention that how I know where the panties are, well, it wasn't actually a *break* and enter. There was an unlocked window..."

"I think the fact there's no forced entry is just splitting hairs. Don't do anything else until I get back to you. Okay?"

"Okay."

"I really mean it, Lindy. And Lindy? You know the legal term for your panty stealer? Stalker. Predatory stalker. The worst kind because it often escalates and they become murderers. Do not, I repeat, *do not* brush this off."

"But Fleet's dead."

"And that's a good thing. But you already know Hal is involved."

"I don't see blubbery, waddling Hal as capable of doing much beyond..."

"For chrissake, Lindy, anyone is capable! Just because you could outrun him doesn't mean he couldn't grab you when you're not expecting it. And don't forget, he knows where you live. Just because he's never gone in when you're home doesn't mean he never will. It could be his next move."

"I've changed the locks."

"You can pick locks. Maybe he can, too."

"I don't think he has the balls to confront me. I think at most, all he did was meet with the Beach Smoker to exchange the money. I think Easton was collecting the, er, tribute, and Hal was the go-between. Like a bag man. Maybe he was the guy who went to Gold's Menswear to pay Fleet's bill there. And maybe he was supposed to get rid of the car and decided to keep it instead. Maybe Fleet didn't even know he still had it."

"What if he did more than that? Too many maybes. Please don't do anything else until I get back to you."

"Okay," I agree, and I really mean it this time. Hal as something other than Fleet's stooge? Sobering thought. I may have to reconsider the whole thing.

I've barely hung up the phone when K.C. calls to say he heard back from one of the properties he was interested in, and he's heading for Alberta to check it out this very afternoon. He adds, "It's only a four hour drive from Wacasko-Wâti." As if that somehow makes it better.

Bad news all around.

I come home after work to find a For Sale sign on the lawn. Kyle's car is nowhere to be seen and the house is dark. I head to the back of the carport to go downstairs and discover Henry, tied to one of the supporting columns under the deck, shivering. He looks up at me and wags his tail. The saddle pad formerly in front of the woodstove in K.C.'s cabin is there for him to lay on and he's sheltered and out of the snow, but he can't stay out here.

"Great," I mutter under my breath. Henry responds with another tentative tail wag. Damn K.C.! He didn't mention he'd be leaving Henry with me when he called, likely because he knew I'd tell him to leave the dog at the barn. Devon already has two Jack Russells. Surely she could take Henry, too.

I fume for a second and then remind myself it's not the dog's fault. I go down the stairs, give Henry's ears a scratch, and untie him. "It's okay, buddy. You're not going to spend the night out here. Just don't chase Kitty."

He wags his tail more vigorously, as if understanding me.

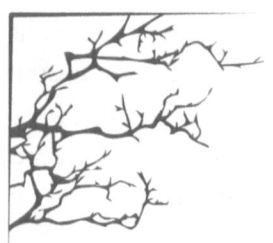

32—Whodunnit

With no wood to make a fire in the fireplace and the floor being a concrete slab that's cold even with carpet and a saddle pad on it, Henry chooses the loveseat. He's not a big dog but he manages to stretch out and take up the whole seat. After rumpling up the bedspread that hides the hideous plaid upholstery, of course. At Wacasko-Wâti dogs aren't allowed on the furniture, so I make a half-hearted effort to get that rule across to Henry. He gives me a look that makes me think he's suddenly gone brain dead. I decide he can have the loveseat. I prefer the couch anyway.

As apprehensive as I was about it, Henry meeting Kitty was almost a non-event. He approached her, quietly wagging his tail. She let him close enough to give his nose a swat. They repaired to their respective corners and now we're all relaxing to the drone of MTV videos as I read. I haven't done a lot of reading since hooking up with K.C. so I still have a couple of Cowgirl Loves Banker or City Girl and the Rancher books Kristy gave me that I haven't read. It passes the time.

At bedtime, I take Henry out to do his business, then lock up and climb between the covers. Kitty sleeps on the extra pillow. Henry apparently thinks the rest of the bed is up for grabs. The bed is cold, I miss K.C., and I'm surprised how nice it is to have the dog curled up next to my legs, warming my feet.

"Not a three dog night, so one dog will do," I mutter, and reach down to give his ears a scratch. "Hope you don't fart."

It's quiet in the house; at first it's peaceful, then it becomes unsettling. Being in the basement at the end of a cul-de-sac, there's never been any street noise, but I've come to expect sounds of someone upstairs. With Kristy and Kyle both gone, it's as silent as a morgue but for the occasional creaking of the structure, the rattle of the refrigerator as the compressor cycles on and off, and the furnace intermittently blowing warm air. The fact I'm here alone has me a little spooked and I'm having trouble falling asleep. Henry doesn't have that problem and is soon snoring. At last I fall asleep to his rhythmic snuffling.

There's a sudden loud crash and I'm instantly awake. Kitty isn't on the pillow. Did she push something off the counter? Henry's head is up and he's fixated on the door.

"What is it, boy?" I whisper.

Henry responds with a tiny whine that becomes a low growl. Whatever it is, Henry doesn't like it. It takes a second to compute, but I realize he wouldn't react with a growl if it was simply the cat knocking something down. I snap to attention. Then with speed and athleticism I never would've believed him capable of, Henry launches himself off the bed and out into the hall.

I leap out of bed, wrench open the drawer on the bedside table and grab the can of bear spray. Before I even get to the door, there's more growling and snarling and a deep male voice yelling obscenities. I hurry out. There's enough moonlight streaming through the open doorway for me to see Henry clinging to the arm of a figure in dark clothes.

"*GAARRGH*!" I shriek like a banshee as I charge.

The man shakes Henry off his arm, sending him in a barrel roll across the floor. Henry is instantly back on his feet and lunges again, this time latching onto his calf. The man howls and twists around. There's a flash of silver. Henry yelps. He loosens his grip on the man's leg just as I utter another rebel yell that would impress Billy Idol and come close enough to send a solid stream of bear spray at the man's face.

"Aarghh!" he shrieks, and rubs a hand over his eyes. He stumbles for a second then turns and runs out the door. I go after him. Despite hobbling he manages to take the stairs two at a time. He's at the top and through the hedge while I'm still wondering if I should follow, barefoot, in a nightgown and armed only with bear spray. He could be waiting just on the other side of the hedge, knife at the ready. I tell myself I'm not really all that cold and I'll be ready with the bear spray, and climb the stairs. A car engine roars to life. There's no sign of the intruder at the hedge. I go through it into the carport in time to see tail lights heading down the cul-de-sac at speed. I can't make out what kind of car it is.

Suddenly very cold, I hurry back to my suite, find Henry in a heap on the floor and kneel beside him. "Are you okay, boy?" I ask. His tail thumps on the floor so whatever happened hasn't killed him; still, when he tries to get up, he struggles and collapses. Only when I turn on the lights do I notice the warm wetness I felt on my hand is blood. I check Henry over and find the source: a wound on his side very near his neck. Another on his shoulder. Both have blood flowing from them. They seem deep, like stabbing slashes. Something is damaged enough that he can't put weight on his foreleg.

I call 911. They promise to send someone. I tell them I can't stay on the line because my dog is injured. The operator wants to argue that point so I hang up, but with no vets open for hours all I can do for Henry is staunch the bleeding with towels. I pull him close to the loveseat so I can lean back against it and hold him. I don't want to release him long enough to get my housecoat or slippers so I pull the bedspread down off the loveseat and wrap it around us.

The trees on the other side of the lake are lacy silhouettes against the rising sun when help finally arrives.

Henry is stitched up, has been given pain meds and every other expensive thing the vet could think of and is now asleep on the loveseat, his homely little face framed by the plastic cone that prevents him from worrying his stitches. The cops came and went before I took Henry to the vet, and now hours later, Detective Allard is sitting across from me at the table in the dining room.

"It was all over before I even had time to think," I tell him. "Seemed like slow motion, but I doubt it was more than a couple of minutes start to finish. Henry wasted no time going for the guy. He was already growling before he even got off the bed."

"Well, he gave as good as he got," Detective Allard says. "Blood trail in the snow up the stairs and out into the driveway."

"Must be from the asshole's leg because I doubt Henry bit his arm badly enough it would bleed like that. I think it hurt him, because he was favouring a leg. I hope the wounds get infected," I gripe.

"You weren't able to provide much of a description. Average height and build. Dark clothes. Wearing a ski mask."

"Right. I think it was the mask that saved him from the worst of the bear spray although I think I managed to get some in his eyes. He had on a heavy winter jacket, otherwise Henry might've been able to do more damage to his arm and maybe wouldn't have been stabbed." I heave a sigh.

"So. When you and your upstairs neighbor, what's his name? Patterson?"

"Right. Kyle Patterson."

"So after you traded places and he was living down here, Patterson never said anything about anyone coming into his place?"

"No. Although maybe he didn't know about it. But maybe it's not the same guy. He's never come in when I was home."

"Not that you know of, anyway," Detective Allard says. "He may have come in and just watched you sleeping."

"Eww!" A shiver courses through me.

"Yeah. You never had a dog before. And it seems to me it's too much of a coincidence that there would be two perps."

"I suppose," I agree.

"So, it's the same guy, and it's escalated. Changing the locks didn't deter him. You need to realize that if he came armed with a knife and was willing to kick the door in, stealing panties wasn't his objective."

I draw a deep breath and shiver as a chill passes through me.

Detective Allard notices, and says, "Yeah. Is there somewhere else you can stay, at least for a while? At least until we make an arrest?"

"I, er, I can stay at my boyfriend's place."

"Good. Get out of here, and I'd suggest not telling anyone where you're going. I'm leaning toward thinking it's someone who knew you moved back into this suite, but not that you have a dog."

"Well, I didn't until this afternoon."

"Oh yeah?"

"He's my boyfriend's dog. I'm just babysitting him."

"Lucky for you."

Suddenly, the truth of that hits me. I grab my quivering lower lip in my teeth. How badly would things have gone if I had been alone and I had to rely on the bear spray? Would I even have gotten it out before he was on me? That's the last time I keep it in the drawer.

"It's someone you know, or at least knows someone who knows you," Detective Allard continues, interrupting my 'what if' imagining. "Question is not only who, but why. It could be related to that bank fraud investigation you were involved in with Spears. You know the guy you were investigating had a lot more going on than just scamming loans."

"Yeah, but I never knew the whole story."

"I guess I can tell you. The stuff that's public records anyway. He was on our radar."

"Oh? Why?"

"Drugs. Never sold them himself, you understand, but we think he ran the operation. Above reproach as a bank manager. Pillar of the community and loved by everyone. Besides drugs, there were, er, stories of him procuring girls for sex with upper crust businessmen in Katawasis and for tourists. I thought those investigations might be shelved after the boat explosion but Major Crimes sent us some members and they're still working it."

"Sex trafficking," I conclude. When he nods, I add: "I guess that explains the room in that house... And how my panties got there. That explosion—it was a bomb, right?"

"Right," he confirms. "Hold on. What room in what house? And what's this about panties?"

I walked into that one. The moment of truth. "Okay. I have a confession to make. It's a long story. Coffee?"

"Yeah, please. Cream if you have it, two sugars."

"Cream, no. Milk okay?"

"Milk's fine," he says, and breathes out a long sigh. "Will this confession of yours explain why Spears is suddenly calling me again, asking about the make and model of Jerry Kristjanson's car?"

"I guess that's part of it." So, it's going to have to be full disclosure. A longer confession than I expected. I get up and fill two mugs from the two-hours-old carafe on the warmer, take them to the table and settle in to tell him everything.

33—Goodbye, Katawasis Lake!

"**R**egional Office doesn't think Katawasis Branch can survive this," Jim says.

We're at K.C.'s cabin, which until the end of the year is K.C.'s and my cabin. It's farther for me to go to work, but no use paying rent when I'm too spooked to stay at my place alone. Besides, since Devon left, all the barn chores fall to K.C., including morning feed and night check. Now the only horses that haven't moved out are his five and Chica. We've already moved all the hay except for the few bales we need until we relocate and yes, I help with the chores.

K.C. quit paying rent two months ago but even living rent free he's barely scraping by, coaching students who haul their horses in. He did a clinic in Medicine Hat one weekend but that was barely enough to keep the lights on. Thankfully, it's not for much longer.

Jim and Kristy are here for an early Christmas and we're at the kitchen table picking at the remains of the roasted chicken, my go-to fancy meal.

"What do you think?" I ask.

"I'm not sure. With the news full of the bank fraud scandal not to mention murders, loan sharking, drug and sex trafficking—well, you can understand why people have lost trust. Doesn't help that the media keeps showing the street view when they talk about the "headquarters of the criminal operation". Lindy, I'm sure you've noticed that accounts are closing and loan applications have tanked. Losing the KFP account was a killing stroke. There's a stink on the place that'll take years to overcome. But they'll keep it open for at least another year, and re-assess."

"But there were only two bank employees involved," I remind them.

"I bet if you were a fly on the wall at the Legion or any other meeting of old timers, you'd hear them blame everyone, even the janitor."

I nod and click my tongue. "I still can't believe it. Kyle! I liked Kyle, I thought he liked me, and he would've..."

"Don't think about that, babe," K.C. cuts off the rest of my sentence. "He might've only wanted to scare you off after he saw you at Hal's locker. He didn't know you actually got inside."

K.C. has already given me his theory and as much as I'd like to go along with it, I just can't get the image of Kyle's knife slashing at Henry out of my head. Who hurts a dog like that? Even before we found out the rest, I knew anyone evil enough to do that could do worse. It could have been me.

"Maybe he did know. Maybe he saw the door was open. I barely got it closed in time, remember? He's charged with murdering Easton, Fleet and Corrine. Why would he stop at that pain-in-the-ass Lindy Larsen who goes around sticking her nose in everything?"

"He did like you, Lindy," Kristy assures me, "and he thought you were hot. We fought about it once."

"Oh, really? Yet he was going to kill me?" I choke back a sob and feel the familiar tightening in my chest. K.C. doesn't contradict me this time, just picks up my hand and gives it a squeeze. The attack was back in October. You'd think I'd be over it. PTSD, Jim says. It can creep up on a person when they least expect it. As if sensing my misery, Henry, who's sitting on the floor next to me with his head in my lap, nudges my arm. If anyone should be depressed, it's him. He'll be lurching along, dragging that leg for the rest of his life, yet he acts as if it's nothing. He's never been a really active dog so I guess that's in his favor now. I give his ears a scratch and his whole body wiggles as his tail thumps the floor.

"You know it wasn't his idea. He had a legitimate job working for SecureCo at the beginning," Jim tells us, "but he was Meredith's lapdog once they started sleeping together."

"I bet Fleet knew Kyle was knocking boots with his wife. It explains his hostility when we went on that boat trip. Kyle's charade of not knowing the name of Fleet's boat threw me off. And the two of them pretending not to know each other! Didn't know your ex was such a gifted actor, eh Kristy?"

"No, I sure didn't. And sleeping with that ugly old broad while he was married to me? What an asshole! I am *so* glad I dumped him when I did," Kristy says. She's not giggling now.

It's on the tip of my tongue to point out that Meredith is actually quite beautiful, but now is not the time. Instead I say, "It explains why Kyle was so interested in the boat. I bet he was scoping it out for the best place to put the bomb. And why he watched boats from up on the deck. But Jerry... How did his baseball cube get in Fleet's desk?"

"Hal put it there."

"His prints were on it?"

"No, the cube was wiped clean. The only prints on it were yours."

"What about Jerry's car? Was Hal storing it for Fleet?"

"No, Hal was storing it for Hal. Fleet wasn't a killer, just a slimy creep Meredith called a useful idiot. All she had to do was to keep arranging for hookers to pose as horny housewives and meet him in motel rooms during bank hours, out of the way so Hal could take care of the McQuinn family business. Fleet may have suspected something but turned a blind eye and did as he was told because Meredith held the purse strings. Did you know they got married within weeks of him coming to Katawasis? Whether or not he bought into the story that Jerry just up and left, he sold it. It was Hal who wanted Jerry gone. They found a hair and traces of blood belonging to Jerry on Hal's boat. He used the fish bonker to cave his skull in and then couldn't bring himself to toss that ten dollar item overboard. Of course he thought he'd never be caught. Our mistake was assuming someone who wasn't very bright couldn't be ambitious. He wanted Jerry's job at the bank as well as his position as bag man for Meredith."

I gasp. "Jerry was Meredith's bag man?"

"Yeah. He was the Sportsman cigarette smoker. Not the innocent everyone thought he was."

"You know what? That actually makes me feel better," I say.

"Me, too," Kristy agrees. "I was thinking how awful for a nice young man to be cut down before he's even lived a life. He didn't deserve to be killed, though."

"No. He might have paid his dues, got back on the straight and narrow and become a sports writer," Jim says.

"You never know," I agree. "I guess Meredith had two useful idiots," I comment.

"More than two," Jim says. "There's a network of pushers, not just all over the lake but Elkhorn and Pensel... Every little burg in the territory. Hal only had first names and a lot of them are nicknames. The cops are still working on it.

"Well, at least for the lake customers, it explains why they used the beach," I conclude. "It finally makes sense! Jerry didn't have a boat, and a bunch of guys in boats congregating at the public wharf would be awkward and would attract attention. When Jerry was out of the picture, Hal manned the beach until Kyle, who also didn't have a boat, took over and then Hal just collected from him. Probably at the storage locker."

"Right. Of course there were other meeting places. It's a big job even for Kyle, who doesn't have other employment. It must've kept Jerry real busy. And as for Fleet and Hal, there was no love lost between those two. Hal planted that baseball cube in Fleet's desk in case they ever needed to blame Jerry's death on him. But Fleet was getting expensive, running up his account at Gold's. Not only running up the hooker's bill by meeting her more and more often, but giving her expensive gifts. Believe it or not, they had his and hers Cadillacs! He never realized she was a pro. Then he made the mistake of bragging to Meredith about his young lover. Meredith was already pissed because he wouldn't sign the sale agreement or give Hal the glowing performance appraisals he needed, so that was the last straw."

"In light of what you've told us, it's a wonder Fleet found the balls," K.C. opines.

"It must've been the one thing he could do to stick it to the two of them," Jim says with a shrug. "So anyway, they decided to take him out. Enter Kyle, willing to get into Meredith's good books by killing Easton for his crime of skimming. Easton knew him so he might have been surprised, but he wouldn't have been alarmed when he got to the beach expecting to connect with Hal and Kyle was there instead. A single bullet to the head execution style."

"So Kyle had a gun after all. A .22 by any chance?" I ask.

"Yeah. How'd you know?"

"He mentioned it once. Said he sold it so he wouldn't have to register it."

"Well, he didn't register it. That part's true," Jim says. "They haven't found it yet. Probably never will. I'd bet Kyle put it in the lake along with Easton.

Hal took his boat to meet him so they could sink Easton's boat and body at the same time. Perfect crime, except for the bad luck of the freak storm and the body washing ashore where it did. If you hadn't gone down to the beach, or if it washed ashore anywhere else, it might have taken years to be found. Still not a problem, no way to connect Easton to them. Fast forward to the Fleet problem. Thanks to his training as an ammunition tech in the military, Kyle had the skills to blow up the boat. Cops knew it was a bomb but had no leads and likely never would've solved it. Finding Jerry's car in Hal's storage locker was key. Still, if Hal had been willing to take the fall, Meredith and Kyle would've have gotten away with it."

"All because Hal was so greedy he thought he'd be able to sell that car someday. I don't think it's even worth much. What an idiot," I say.

"A useful one," Jim reminds us.

"I hope none of them ever has another good night's sleep," I say.

"Hal only worries about Hal and Meredith isn't capable of remorse," Jim opines. "Hal took over as bag man when Jerry disappeared, and was probably skimming too, although he won't admit it. I'll bet Hal's wife was surprised to learn about the bags full of cash in that storage locker while she had to drive around in a fifteen-year old beater."

"As surprised as I was to find out about Kyle's secret bank account," Kristy grumbles. "Talk about Hal's wife driving a piece of shit vehicle! You seen mine, right? And I bet Hal didn't make his wife pay half the rent!"

"Kyle is a user. Hal is a miser. He got his rocks off sitting in that storage locker counting his money."

"Like a dragon in his cave, living on top of his gold and jewels. Somehow I have trouble imagining Hal as a dragon, though," I say.

"You're right. A dragon would be feared and respected. Hal was neither. He was more a Scrooge McDuck in his money bin. Everyone saw him the way we did: unattractive, unpleasant, barely enough brains to dress himself—someone of no consequence. He could've continued his operation for years piling up tons of money until he could disappear with it, but he wanted to be noticed and respected. He saw how everyone in town sucked up to Fleet and thought being the manager would do it for him, too."

"I can't even imagine him as manager," I say.

"Yeah, might have been a really toxic workplace if he was manager," Jim agrees, "unless Corrine went away when Fleet did. Looks like she was the reason for the clerical turnover. Anyway, when the branch was under-performing and R. O. decided to eliminate the A.M. position, they figured all Meredith had to do was convince Fleet to give Hal a glowing recommendation, resign, and Hal would be a shoo-in to replace him as manager."

"But R.O. likely wouldn't bump a consumer lending officer up to branch manager," I say. "They'd send him to another branch as an A.M. first."

"Meredith didn't know that and if Hal realized it, he didn't bother to explain it to her. Then you came along, Lindy. Parachuted into a position that was supposed to be eliminated, poking around Hal's house. Snooping in his waste basket. He couldn't even toss stuff in the dumpster without you noticing. But it was the storage locker that connected Hal to Jerry's murder and put a target on your back. They brought it on themselves by making the storage yard their hand off location once Fleet wasn't around to park his car next to Hal's."

"So before that, Hal just put the money in Fleet's car?"

"Yeah. Easy. Risk free," Jim confirms. "Problem once Fleet was gone, though. They scheduled the hand off to coincide with the time of day Meredith always left whatever Friends of Katawasis work she was doing in order to pick her daughter up from school so there was no change in her usual routine. At first it was a dead drop on his boat but she didn't like having to climb in and out of it in her panty hose and five hundred dollar suits. He refused to give her the key to his locker because he didn't want her to know he still had that car, and besides—those bags of cash! Funny thing, if they hadn't done that, or if they'd thought to rent a second locker for a dead drop, you would likely never have learned about that place. Or if Meredith had cut Hal out of the picture altogether."

"Why didn't she?" I ask. "Kyle was with her a lot. They were lovers, after all. He could easily have given her the money without Hal ever touching it."

"Kyle was just a fling. He likely would've joined Jerry in the lake courtesy of the next sucker in her bed when she got tired of him. Besides, Hal was still coordinating the loan shark and extortion businesses so she needed to keep him close. Neither of them trusted the other. Otherwise, we wouldn't all be sitting here talking about this today," Jim explains. "Sending Kyle after you was a fatal mistake but it was something Hal insisted on because he worried you had figured out how busy his side business was. If you got tight with Meredith and the two of you put your heads together, you might realize what he reported didn't jibe with what he actually took in. On top of that he really didn't like you, Lindy."

"Well that much I knew from day one. I just didn't realize he hated me enough to want me dead. And it was stupid."

"No one ever said Hal was smart. Think about it. Even if there was only the one locker and it was a dead drop, Meredith would see the car but think nothing of it. She never saw Jerry or his car. Would she go digging through dirty boxes full of boat stuff and find his cash? Unlikely. But he couldn't take the chance. When he realized you were poking around, Hal could've gotten rid of the car and anything else that was incriminating, so that even if Allard believed you there would be nothing to find. They didn't know you'd been in the house across the lake but finding your panties there wouldn't have been a big deal either. Allard wasn't exactly determined to find the panty stealer, was he?"

"No. I guess he thought I was a nuisance."

"Yeah. He's busy. Like every Detachment, they're understaffed. But with the home invasion he had to pay attention. He put uniforms on the boat, the locker, all Fleet's properties including the house on Beach Drive, and got warrants the same day. Facing multiple charges and at least one life sentence, Hal sang like a bird. He gave up Meredith, Kyle—even Darius Bright Bird, who wasn't so much as a blip on their radar up to that point. Allard thanked me, for chrissakes. It should be you he thanked."

"He said he was sorry he hadn't taken me more seriously and muttered something about being so busy, what with the murders, you know."

"Well, that's something, coming from a member of the old boys' club," Jim says. He clicks his tongue and blows out a breath. "The whole thing would be neatly wrapped up except there are still the soldiers. Meredith's son is in it up to his eyeballs, but they haven't got enough to charge him, at least not yet. The most the cops can do is keep an eye on him going forward. As for the street level pushers, they'll get them one at a time even if nobody names them. You know how pointless it is anyway. All they ever get is a slap on the wrist."

We all mumble agreement. I've already got a serious wine buzz but I finish my glass anyway, and refill it from the bottle in the ice bucket before passing it to Kristy. K.C. gets up and goes to the fridge, coming back with two cold bottles of the beer he and Jim are drinking.

"So," Kristy says, "I been meaning to ask. Who was the panty stealer?"

"Now, that they don't know," Jim replies. "Someone who used that room, of course. And yours weren't the only panties there. But the traffic in and out of that place? Hundreds of fingerprints. They found prints on your dresser too, Lindy, but you know how useless that is until they have a suspect. They only know it wasn't Fleet, Hal or Kyle."

"Just great," I grumble, "could be someone I see every day. How long before he finds me again? Katawasis isn't that big." There's throat clearing and shifting of butts in chairs but no one responds.

After a bit Jim says, "No one blames you for wanting to leave Katawasis, Lindy. Personnel is working to find you an A.M. position at another branch."

"That's nice, and I'll thank them for that," I say, "but right now, Wacasko-Wâti is calling me home."

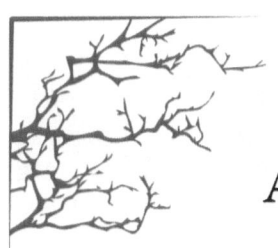

Acknowledgements

Three people have contributed greatly to make this story what it is: Lorna Beecroft, Patricia Maher and Brian Proskurniak. These generous souls suffered through early drafts of the manuscript to provide ongoing support, suggestions, and insightful recommendations. I can't thank them enough.

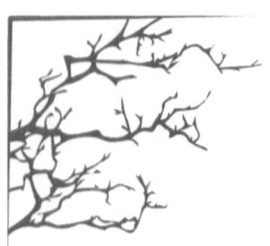

Author's Notes

I hope you enjoyed reading about Lindy's adventures in Katawasis Lake as much as I enjoyed writing about them. When this story ends, it finds her on her way back to Wacasko-Wâti with the hope of settling into a boring routine. But there's more to her story. The fourth Lindy Larsen book is as yet untitled, but the first few pages follow.

If you have a minute, a review of Katawasis Girls on Amazon, Goodreads, or your favourite social media platform would be much appreciated.

Lindy Larsen Book 4

I hear shouts and I look up from my desk to see a flurry of activity in the construction site across the yard. The excavator swings its bucket away and a couple of workers as well as the foreman hop down into the shallow trench. I can't see much beyond that so I pick up my coffee and head outside.

All seems quiet now so whatever it was must not be anything too serious. Maybe a power or waterline where we didn't think there was one? But no, we didn't cross that area when we put those lines to the corrals underground. I sigh and feel myself deflate. It must be another old Indian burial like the one we ran into when we built the wine tasting room. This will mean another lengthy delay while the archaeologists mark out an area ten times bigger than they need and begin their agonizingly slow excavation.

The area they're working in was the manure pile, in use from the time my great grandfather built the first barn in the Twenties until we started using the manure spreader. There would be no sign of even a shallow burial when they started piling manure there eighty years ago. My mind races off to the worst possible scenario, that our houses, barn, corrals, bistro and farm store are on an ancient burial site, a real possibility if this is another grave. We could end up being prevented from using any of it.

Can they move all the ancient bones? Would the Nekaneet elders allow it? They weren't happy about the last burial even though the bones were repatriated in a very respectful ceremony, so if there are a lot more, it's doubtful.

Maybe we could make a deal to go ahead with ranching and winemaking and running our farm store as usual if we set aside a little park. We could put up a marker like the monument for nearby Fort Walsh. We're already an established stopping off point for tour buses on their way there. But aside from the delay it would mean more money just to go ahead on a project that's already behind schedule and overbudget.

Now K.C. steps out from behind the excavator and looks my way. I lift my coffee mug and he nods. He's coming up to the house for coffee, but the look on his face tells me it's not a welcome break. I expect the worst.

"What's wrong? Do I need to phone the government guys?" I call out as soon as he's within range.

He shakes his head but says nothing until he's beside me on the porch. He opens the door to usher me back inside, and says, "Yeah. If you call the RCMP government guys."

Don't miss out!

Visit the website below and you can sign up to receive emails whenever Gayle Siebert publishes a new book. There's no charge and no obligation.

https://books2read.com/r/B-A-EAZM-QLIQB

BOOKS 2 READ

Connecting independent readers to independent writers.

www.ingramcontent.com/pod-product-compliance
Lightning Source LLC
Chambersburg PA
CBHW031116030726
47496CB00002BA/561